REAPER: AFTERMATH

JONATHAN PONGRATZ

Copyright Page

Reaper: Aftermath by Jonathan Pongratz

© 2021 Jonathan Pongratz

Cover by Mario Lampic.

❀ Created with Vellum

To my family and friends who have continued to amaze me with their never ending support.
Also, to Priscilla, Tammie, Iseult, Randy, and Bryan for their untiring patience and their part in making this book something I'm extremely proud of.

I crouched behind a row of old dusty cars beside my mom and two other sharpshooters, my body trembling. *Don't freak out. Be brave. Remember your training.*

I took a deep breath and dared a peek ahead between two cars. Across the street was a deserted grocery store covered in grime and soot. It was a small shop, maybe two or three times the size of an average gas station. A bunch of old, rotted wooden planks covered the windows, but the front entrance was untouched. Whoever had been here was either dead inside or long gone. No one in their right mind would leave their home unfortified, not anymore.

All was quiet except for the wind, but I knew better. We all did. Any second and the Reapers could be right on us. Though they never came out during the day, we couldn't leave anything to chance.

Mom pulled out her walkie. "Proceeding with root-out of potential Reapers." She retrieved an oddly-shaped ball constructed from cans, tins, and several small bells we called chatter boxes from her supply bag and hurled it over her head.

The chatter box clunked loudly on the ground, bouncing before stopping in front of the seemingly-empty store. For a couple moments we all sat there, waiting for any sign of Reapers.

Mom's walkie crackled to life. "Patricia, I think we should--"

"Quiet!" Mom hissed. "I think I hear something."

I couldn't hear anything, but there was definitely a difference in the air, like it was charged somehow. *Just like the basement five years ago.* Images of the past filled my mind: My little sister Imogen, the electrified feeling down in the basement, the Reaper's sudden appearance. I shook off my thoughts and edged close to my mother.

"You're right, something's coming."

Mom nodded, her gaze fixed on the grocery store. "Be brave, Gregory. If you have to, fall back."

I shook my head. There was no way I was gonna miss out on this.

Her eyes widened, and she gripped her walkie once more. "Reapers, incoming!"

I drew my Glock from my holster, turned the safety off, and tried to look through the abandoned store's smudged entrance. It was dark inside, but I could see two hulking figures scrambling to the front of the store at breakneck speed.

Oh shi--

Two Reapers crashed through the entrance in an explosion of glass that blasted shards in a thousand directions. As the projectiles clinked on the ground I stared at the monsters before us, a chill running down my spine.

Large, festering boils covered their reddish, emaciated bodies. They stood tall on two clawed feet, but could easily switch to all fours for speed, doubling the danger of their razor sharp appendages. The Reapers opened their mouths, revealing multiple layers of jagged, pointy teeth as they gave ear-piercing shrieks of rage.

A grin spread across my face. *Time to die, assholes.*

I aimed, then pulled my trigger as deafening gunshots came from my left and right. We'd hit the one on the right several times. A thick, black liquid oozed from its wounds, but it was still in fighting shape and pretty freakin' pissed based on the hideous snarl on its face.

The aggravated Reaper leaped forward on all fours, bounding over the car we were hiding behind and landing in front of the sharpshooter furthest from me. It gave a mighty roar, snatching him up and throwing him like a rag doll. He went flying, landing on a nearby car's windshield with a loud crack. The monster eyed the other sharpshooter with furious, predatory yellow eyes.

Shit, shit, shit! I lunged towards the Reaper as I targeted it, then yanked on my trigger. It gave a high-pitched cry of pain and staggered back a step. *Damn it!* I'd only hit its shoulder. Its hateful gaze was now focused on me.

A sudden gunblast boomed from my comrade, and the Reaper fell to the ground, unmoving. A large pool of black sludge gathered underneath its head where the bullet had exited.

Before I could rejoice in the kill, Mom shouted nearby. I spun around. She was battling the other Reaper in front of the grocery store with a long knife in hand. She had deep cuts on her arms and legs, while the monster sported several nonfatal gunshot wounds. I tried to aim for the Reaper but they were moving too fast, desperately circling one another for an advantage. One wrong move and I'd shoot my own mother.

The Reaper took a wide-arching swipe at her, but she dodged to the side, cutting its leg as she went. The monster screeched and turned to attack, but mom slid between its legs and was now behind it. Point blank, Mom whipped out her revolver and fired three shots into the back of the Reaper's head. It fell to the ground, twitching in its final death throes.

Mom lifted her combat boot and stomped on its head with a sickening crunch. The Reaper didn't move anymore. She spat on it, then pulled out her walkie as I approached. "All clear. Torch the bodies."

I glanced back. Twenty yards away behind another row of dead cars, our small group of noncombatants emerged. Mom strolled towards the grocery store and I jogged to catch up to her, eager to see what was inside. Whatever it was, it had better be worth it.

INSIDE THE GROCERY store was just as run-down as it was outside. The late afternoon sun did little to illuminate the space, but our flashlights revealed uneven aisles with busted shelves, dirt and litter-caked tile floors, and thick layers of dust everywhere.

There was a foul stench like rotting flesh that I attributed to the Reapers that had been hiding here. They'd most likely come charging out because we'd unearthed their nesting spot, but their bravery to reveal themselves in daylight was still unnerving. I'd never seen that happen before.

Mom had me stay with the noncombatants while she and the other sharpshooters scoped out the store for signs of Reaper offspring. Female Reapers laid large basketball-sized eggs in nasty gray-veined sacs. The slightest sound could awaken them, and they were formidable due to their size and speed.

Luckily, Mom and the sharpshooters came back momentarily and gave us the all clear. She had us split up in pairs of two, and we each took an aisle to stash supplies. I got paired with a mousy girl named Meredith who pretty much lived at the library back home. We rounded the corner of aisle four, canned goods, and I groaned when I saw its meager contents.

Cans sparsely populated the slanting shelves in tiny rows, a few dozen or so on each side. This was it? After risking our lives to get in here? I wondered how much of the food would still be good. Preservatives or not, it had been five hellish years. Nothing was exempt from that.

"I'll take the right side," I told Meredith. I walked ahead of her to my side of lopsided racks as I unzipped my large supply bag. I shone my light on the first can I saw. Sliced Beets. I recoiled. *Grandma food.* I begrudgingly threw the can and a few identical ones behind it into my bag, then moved on to the next row.

Dinty Moore beef stew. I chuckled to myself. *More like dog food.* After a couple minutes of scrounging I was done with my side, and boy was it depressing. Turnip greens, diced rutabaga, menudo. What the hell happened to carrots and green beans, peaches and pineapple? I didn't even want to think of what monstrosities the cooks would make out of this stuff back home.

I glanced back at Meredith. She was looking over the cans meticulously, taking her time before placing each one in her bag. Geez, what was her damage? Our job was simple; put the goods in the bag and go. At her speed, we wouldn't get out of here until nightfall when the Reapers came out in droves.

I tried waiting for her, but my patience wore out. In my frustration, I noticed the back aisle of the store. Several rows of knickknacks laid virtually untouched, and I weighed my options.

What was the harm? The others weren't that far away, and with Mom's birthday just weeks from now I had to find a present for her. I walked ahead in slow cautious steps, entering the back aisle. No one else was here. In front of me and panning to my left were the racks of trinkets I'd seen. This side of the aisle ended in a back room separated by tall, thin sheets of plastic. To my right was a freezer section. Whatever was in there had long since spoiled without electricity.

I rummaged through rows of untouched doodads, clouds of dust rising as I went. Most of it turned out to be junk: small stuffed teddy bears, fake jewelry, pinwheels, and other cheap crap. When I unearthed a small globe-shaped object, I didn't want to get my hopes up, but as I brushed it off I couldn't help a small squeal of excitement.

Mom always had a fascination with snow globes. I guess she just thought they were beautiful. This one said Billings, Montana and had a small, insignificant skyline. When I shook it, little flurries inside stirred to life. I smiled. She was going to love it.

I set my supply bag down on the ground, shuffling cans around to make room for the trinket down below so no one would see it. As I sorted through my supplies, one of the cans fell out and rolled down the dirty tiled floor to the entrance of the back room before settling. I groaned to myself and walked over before picking up the can. Sliced beets. I shook my head and chuckled. *Fucking beets, man.*

Suddenly, all the hairs on my body stood on end. I jerked my head up just in time to see a tall dark silhouette lurking behind the thick lines of plastic. *Fuck, fuck, fuck!*

As I backed away, the Reaper emerged from the back room into the aisle. This one was just like the other two we'd killed, boils, teeth, foul odor, and all. But unlike before, there was nothing between it and me.

"Reaper!" I spun around and bolted, only to catch my feet

on my own supply bag. I went plummeting to the ground, cushioned by trash and dirt.

The monster gave a horrendous howl of rage just feet away, and I scrambled forward futilely. It was all over. At this range, there was no way I could esca--

Several thunderous gunshots sounded ahead of me, followed by a wail of pain from the Reaper. I looked up. It was Carlos, one of the only noncombatants with a gun.

"Get behind me!" he shouted.

I double-timed my crawl to him as he fired several more shots at the Reaper, the last one ending in a click from his gun. Carlos's face went white. Oh shit, he was out of bullets! I closed my eyes in defeat, expecting the Reaper's long claws to rake into my back and through my body at any moment. Instead, all I felt was a rush of air as the Reaper leaped over me and charged Carlos.

He punched and kicked fruitlessly as the Reaper grabbed him and lifted him into the air. It gave a hideous screech as it shoved Carlos headfirst into the glass door of the refrigerated section, keeping its grip on him. As it removed Carlos, I fought the vomit that lurched up my throat.

Large glass shards embedded in his face jutted out in all directions, blood flowing freely from each wound. He gave a gurgled cry before the Reaper threw him down to the floor.

Loud footsteps echoed closer to us.

"Over here!" I called out.

As Mom and several others entered the aisle, the Reaper lifted its razor-sharp claws, bringing them down on Carlos.

A deafening hail of bullets pounded all around me. I sank to the ground, covering my ears and closing my eyes until the carnage quieted. When I opened them again, the Reaper was in front of me, lying on the floor in a pool of its own black blood. As I set my eyes on Carlos, I gaped in horror. We were too late. Carlos was dead.

CHAPTER TWO

y group and I left the abandoned grocery store and walked down the charred, crumbling street back home in silence. I staggered behind, my head bowed in shame. No one had offered me any reassuring words after what happened, and I didn't expect any. I screwed up, plain and simple.

Carlos was dead thanks to me, and nothing would bring him back. We didn't bother burying the body. We stopped doing that years ago because it left us exposed to Reaper attacks for too long. Instead, we rearranged his body into a peaceful position and covered him with a thin white sheet we found.

The image of his mutilated body flashed in my mind: his face had been a mess of glass and exposed muscle, and his chest and throat were torn to shreds where the Reaper had slashed him before being gunned down. Another wave of guilt washed over me like a tidal wave.

Damn it, why couldn't I have just followed protocol? I sighed, wiping sweaty brown strands out of my eyes. I shouldn't have wandered off, and there was no telling what repercussions I would face at home. While I was new to supply runs and the specific rules to follow, I wasn't completely clueless. We'd been scavenging for five years.

To top it off, our group didn't let minors out on expeditions anymore unless absolutely necessary, and I only turned eighteen just a few weeks ago. Mom vouched for me, and her standing as second-in-command was why I was out here in the first place. Now I'd be lucky if they ever let me out again. I'd gotten Carlos killed, and that meant the group was smaller now, more vulnerable.

When we'd first escaped from the Reapers and my hometown, we had a hundred fifty, maybe two hundred people in our group. But back then we were stupid, uncoordinated, hopeful ... We lost a lot of people in those first few months to the Reapers. Right now we were at fifty warm bodies. Sorry, make that forty-nine.

Our small scavenging unit walked across a shattered sidewalk into the potholed street. I followed after them, avoiding several large craters from where someone must've made a big final stand. *Look how well that turned out.*

We journeyed on mindlessly for several minutes, and I did my best to keep my gaze on the ground. I was well aware of the destruction that had come from the Reapers, but taking it in now would just make me more depressed than I already was for another reason entirely.

You see, I started the end of the world. Yep, that's right. Every ash-covered street, every decaying lifeless body, every screeching Reaper out for blood was my fault. That burden had haunted me for five years, and the others let me know what a screw up I was on a daily basis.

Five years ago, my sister Imogen had been taken by one of the Reapers. I'd been right there but failed to save her. I couldn't let her disappearance go, and my search for answers led me to my only remaining friend Trent. His brother had been taken, just like Imogen. It turned out we were right about the monsters, only we didn't know that killing one would set off a wave of chaos that would destroy our world. How were we *supposed* to know?

Our group rounded an intersection with a downhill view of the city's remains, a sight I couldn't avoid.

"Home ahead, one mile," one of the others announced.

My shoulders slumped as the horrific war zone around me registered through my brain. From here I could see all of Billings, or what was left of it anyways.

Several tall buildings surrounded us, most covered up with broken wooden boards, graffiti, or charred to a crisp with large chunks taken out of them. The street was a cemetery of shrapnel and debris, lifeless bodies, and huge pits the size of small swimming pools. Ahead of us was what used to be a park, now just a field of dirt and dust with a number of corpses scattered on the ground.

Despite the carnage around me, I tried to envision what the park used to look like, to see the former beauty of my broken world. It must have been wonderful at some point. A vast green field lush with life. Kids playing tag and throwing water balloons in the summer. Parents cheering their children on. I tried to remember what it felt like, to play, to be carefree like I used to. But it all seemed so far away now. The Reapers took that from us. No, *I* took that from us.

As my group moved on without me I scurried downhill after them, eyeing our destination in the distance unexcitedly. For the past six months, we'd been living at an abandoned elementary school. It was the longest we'd ever stayed in one place since the end of the world, and we'd done a pretty good job of fortifying the single-story brick building.

From here, I could make out the reflective metal sheets protecting the windows in the dying sunlight. Large spikes protruded from the gated, barb-wired entrance and other guarded access points.

My group's posture visibly relaxed as we got closer. I grimaced. *Must be nice.* What was home to them was a prison to me, a constant reminder that I had put everyone in this situation. God, why did I have to be so stupid? Every time I thought I was making amends for what happened, things turned sour and I mucked it up. But it had never been this bad.

We reached the ruined parking lot of the school and walked across to the tall, barbed chain link fence separating us from the entrance. Mom stepped forward and unlocked a series of giant padlocks before opening a small door in the gate. We gathered in, and I made sure to close the door behind me, relocking each padlock and double checking when I was done.

Ahead of us was a rough patchworked wall of steel, reinforced in several places in case the Reapers got through the gates, though they never had. Mom walked up to the door and tapped on it in a special sequence.

Knock, knock, knock. Pause. Knock, knock. Pause. Knock, knock, knock.

A tiny screen opened in the wall, and Mom stood at attention. "Patricia Martin, all secure."

A loud clunk sounded behind the wall. The enormous steel column slowly opened with a metallic screech. We filed in, coming to a stop just inside the foyer and spreading ourselves out. The narrow hall was dimly lit by several hand crank lanterns sitting atop small end tables. There was an office to my immediate left with a glass window, but the view was blocked by torn, threadbare curtains. *Samuel's office.*

A short and stout woman with fiery frazzled hair stood in front of our group by the lanterns, looking over a clipboard.

She glanced up at us as if she hadn't noticed our arrival and made a loud whistle.

Several people entered the room and approached those of our supply group nearest them, taking their supply bags and leaving before returning moments later. As nonchalantly as I could, I placed a hand on top of my bag, then dug inside when no one was looking. I had to find that damned snowglobe. I dug around desperately, doing my best to maintain a chill composure as the bag collectors came closer and closer. Just as I located the trinket and stuffed it into the pocket of my tattered jeans, a tall woman with broad shoulders took my bag with a muttered thanks.

Once all the bags were accounted for, the woman with the clipboard studied our group, counting us with her pointer finger. Her eyes narrowed. "Where's Carlos?"

Mom bowed her head. "I'm sorry, Georgia. He … he didn't make it. One of the Reapers got him while we were on our supply run."

Georgia cocked an eyebrow. "In the daytime, are you sure? That's very odd for them."

"Now wait just a minute!" A greasy, obnoxious guy from our group named Tommy stomped forward. His dirty, smudged face was red with anger, and I glared at the back of his ball capped head. He was one of the people that constantly bullied me within the walls of the school, and now his sights were set on Mom.

"That's bullshit and you know it! Why don't you tell her what really happened?"

Mom glowered back at him, but he didn't give her a chance to speak.

"Patricia's shit son wasn't following protocol, and when Carlos had to save his ass, he got torn to pieces." Tommy turned back to me and grinned smugly. "Ain't that right, world ender?"

I dropped my gaze to the ground in shame. As much as I despised him, he was right. I was responsible for Carlos's death. It was my fault that it had happened, just like the apocalypse.

"Don't talk to my son that way," Mom snarled.

"Oh yeah? What are you gonna do about it?" Tommy taunted.

Mom's hand hovered over the gun in her holster when a tall, muscular black man rushed in from the other room. He placed himself between Mom and Tommy and held up his hands.

I groaned inwardly. *Samuel.*

"Whoa now, why don't we calm down for a minute here?" Samuel urged.

Mom turned to Samuel and wrapped her arms around him. "Oh, thank god you're here. Something terrible has happened."

Samuel gave her a quick kiss, and I fought the urge to vomit. Samuel is our leader and the only remaining FBI agent from my hometown. Since the beginning he took charge of our group, and he and my mom have been dating for the past year and a half or so. Everyone worships the ground he walks on, including my mom. They think he's the perfect model citizen, but I know better.

Just like everyone else, Samuel thought I was to blame for everything. Sure, around Mom he put on the concerned, caring boyfriend face, but anytime I passed him by in the halls I received furrowed eyebrows, sneers, and a cold look in his eyes that said *Don't mess this up for me.* He wasn't fooling me for a second.

Samuel broke off from Mom, assuming a formal, neutral posture. "Alright, someone please tell me what happened out there."

Tommy instantly opened his mouth to speak, but Samuel lifted a finger to silence him.

"Calmly."

Tommy grimaced and took a deep breath. "Carlos is dead. Gregory didn't follow protocol, and Carlos died protecting him."

"That's not fair," Mom chimed in. "We all know Gregory is still new to--"

"Patricia, please," Samuel interjected. He eyed me disapprovingly like an owner whose dog shat on the floor. "Gregory, is what Tommy said true?"

Anger boiled up inside me, but I swallowed my emotions and nodded.

"And what is the protocol for our supply runs?"

"Stay with the group, don't wander off," I muttered.

"See, it's not all that hard to remember, now is it?"

Samuel frowned at me like a disapproving father, but there was anger in his brown eyes.

I clenched my fists. I didn't need his two-faced bullshit, I didn't need someone to reprimand me and make me feel like a 'bad boy', and I sure as hell didn't need everyone picking on me every chance they got. I struggled to keep my feelings at bay, waiting for his verdict.

Samuel stepped towards me, brows furrowed. "Until further notice, you are not to leave the premises. We will evaluate your position in the group in a week's time. Until then, you're on cleaning duty. Hand in your gun and equipment to the storeroom."

A furious wave of heat enveloped me, and I yanked my holster off. I stomped up to Samuel and tossed it at him. "Do it yourself."

"Gregory!" Mom shouted.

I ignored her, tearing off to the right and marching down the lantern-lit hall as my blood boiled. No one came after me, and I'm glad they didn't. I was ready to punch someone in the throat. This whole situation was so damned stupid!

Yes, Carlos died because of me, and in time I would have to make amends for that. But I was sick and tired of everyone pointing the finger of blame at me every time something went wrong. I scoffed. Like they were all so fucking perfect themselves.

Ever since the Reapers came, everything had changed. My peaceful world of the nineties had vanished and been replaced with something darker, more cruel and heartless. The more that people lost, the more they took it out on others. I'd been a victim of it myself more and more, and I couldn't take it anymore.

Kindness was no longer an endearing trait. Though we told ourselves we were a group, peoples' greed and self-interest were really what mattered to them. I'd seen it time and time again. This wasn't a real community anymore, and every time Samuel allowed people to blame me for things, the worse it got. God, I hated it here!

I rounded a corner into another hall, my rage quickly morphing into depression as tears filled my eyes. I'd been trying so hard these past five years to make something of myself. To become a man, to lead like my mom. But all anyone here ever saw was the little kid who ended the world. I was more than that, but they'd never see it. Maybe I should just run away and get it over with. Maybe I should just let the Reapers finish me off.

I took a left down an adjoining hall and stormed inside the second room on the right, switching on the battery-powered lantern as I entered. The room I shared with Trent wasn't anything special, just two twin beds on opposing sides with no windows. Even if we had them, they'd be boarded up with steel sheets like all the others.

I plopped on my bed and sighed, staring at the ceiling.

"Bad day?"

I shot up. Trent stood in the doorway, his light brown hair sticking up in all directions and his battered welding mask in hand. His wifebeater was burnt in several places and I could see his lean, muscular torso through it.

"Christ, you scared the crap outta me!"

Trent smiled weakly and shrugged. "I saw you stomping down the hall. What happened out there today?"

I sat up, then stared down at my feet. "Someone died on the supply run today ... they died because of me." I dared a glance at Trent. He frowned, his eyebrows lifted in concern. I fixed my gaze back on my bed, my cheeks burning. I couldn't face him, not now. Not like this.

Ever since the world ended, Trent was the only person I could truly count on, the only person who cared about me other than my mother. I couldn't afford to alienate him because if I really told him what was on my mind, he'd freak. The truth is, I have feelings for Trent, and I've been hiding my attraction to him for the better part of a year.

When this whole thing started, my group avoided Trent like they did me because of his involvement in the coming of the Reapers. We were social pariahs, so we spent a lot of time together. At first I thought I just really admired him, but in time it turned into so much more than that. We had a real connection: we finished each other's sentences, ate together, shared every bit of our lives with each other. I wanted to spend every waking moment with him, to make him happy.

But I couldn't tell him the truth, not without risking our friendship. And really, can you blame me for hiding it? I mean, how do you tell someone that you're gay for them? I don't even know how to be gay.

Trent leaned against the doorway, waiting for me to elaborate.

"I just ... I don't want to talk about it, okay? Not now."

Trent walked up to me and touched my forearm, sending tingles through my body and creating butterflies in my stomach. "Hey, it's okay, I get it. Whenever you want to talk, I'm here."

He took his hand off my arm, and the fluttery sensation dissipated, leaving an empty feeling behind. *This is torture.*

"Are you sure there's nothing else on your mind?" Trent asked.

I looked up at him. "What do you mean?"

"I dunno, you seem a little off lately. Like maybe there's something that's bugging you besides the supply run."

Trent frowned, and I had a crazy urge to hug him, to spill my guts about everything. *I have feelings for you. I want to kiss you. Hold you. Be with you.* Instead I said, "Um no, nothing in particular." *I am such an idiot.*

Trent raised an eyebrow, but didn't push any further. And why would he? I was a coward. Weak. Pathetic. Trent left to get dinner. He offered to bring me back some food, but I declined. I just wanted to be alone for a while.

As soon as Trent left, I pulled my covers around me like a taco and faced the wall so no one passing by could see my face in the dim lamplight. Why couldn't I just say how I felt? Would that really be the end of the world? That had already happened and I'd survived that. Doubt washed over me. If I told him and he didn't feel the same way, he might move to a different room. He may decide he doesn't want to talk to me anymore. Then I'd really be alone in this world.

My heart sunk. This whole situation was hopeless. Imogen, Carlos, the whole world had died because of me. My group hated me and was better off without me. Trent didn't have feelings for me. Who could ever care for such a failure? I stared at the wall, warm tears running down my face as I willed sleep to come.

~

A SUDDEN NOISE woke me from my fitful sleep. I groaned and rolled over, squinting in the dark as I eyed Trent's bed. He was fast asleep, snoring lightly. I sat up slowly, removing my covers.

I glanced at the doorway, flinching when I saw the outline of a dark figure standing there. I couldn't make out much in the dim light from the hall, except that the person was short and had a feminine form.

I snatched my flashlight off the small end table next to my bed and shined it forward. My jaw dropped. My little sister stood before me. Her curly brown hair fell down in little ringlets, and she had an impish grin on her face.

"I-Imogen?"

She giggled, then ran off into the hall to the right.

"Imogen!" I cried. I couldn't believe it. My little sister was back! I had to tell Mom, but first I had to get Imogen to stop running and tell me what happened, where she'd been all these years.

I scrambled out of bed and left my room, aiming my light down the hall. I caught a brief glimpse of Imogen before she turned a familiar corner to the right.

Why would she head to the library? We didn't have time for games like this. I barrelled down the hall, my bare feet loud as they slapped against the tiled floor. Seconds later, I arrived at the small double doors of the school library. One of them was slightly ajar.

I entered the library with slow, cautious steps. The entrance was the only way out, but I didn't want to spook my little sister. She must be so scared, confused to be back with everything so different.

A tall aisle of bookshelves stood before me, another opposing set on the other side of the room.

"Imogen?" I called.

I heard movement up ahead and crept closer.

When I reached the open center of the room I spotted Imogen several yards ahead, her back facing me. She stood before a large, rickety door that wasn't supposed to be there. My stomach dropped. A Reaper door. She reached for the doorknob.

"Imogen, don't!"

She ignored me, and as she opened the door a brilliant white light beamed through. I shielded my eyes with my arm. "Imogen!"

My little sister walked through the door. Without thinking I chased after her. I couldn't lose her again. As I ran through the doorway, the blinding light suddenly snuffed out, replaced by darkness. I scanned my surroundings with my flashlight, a cold tingle shooting through me like icicles.

To my right a set of stairs led upwards. On my left, numerous items of furniture were draped in white sheets. Dozens of boxes stood in tidy columns behind them. This was … no, it couldn't be. The basement from my old house in my hometown. But how was this even possible? We knew that the doors the Reapers used had to be some kind of portal, but this didn't make any sense.

I shook my head. *Find Immy first, ask questions later.* I glanced at the stairs and ruled them out immediately. I'd been right behind her. If she'd climbed the stairs I would've seen her. I turned left. The covered furniture and other sheeted items created odd, threatening shapes in the dark. When I ran my light over them, a wave of dread shot through my core.

I needed to get out of here and fast. I frantically checked around each blanketed surface, calling for my sister as I progressed further into the basement. I made my way to the back where Immy had been taken five years ago, my anxiety soaring. *Don't think about it, don't think about it,* I thought to myself as I searched high and low.

Regardless, faded gritty images from the past flashed inside my head: the sudden appearance of the door in the wall, me scrambling to find a weapon to fight whatever would come out, Imogen being taken by the Reaper. Her cries ...

No. No, no, no! I wasn't going to let the past get the better of me. I shined my light around again. "Immy, where are you? Say something, please!"

I headed down the aisle of boxes along the back wall of the basement, searching every nook and cranny. I was nearly through with my search when a familiar sofa with golf clubs sticking out from under it caught my eye. The white sheet draping the couch was discolored, misshapen. I inched closer until I could snag the sheet away.

As the white cloth fell to the floor, I cried out in horror. Imogen's dead eyes stared straight up at the ceiling. Her chest and face were covered in blood, and her expression was frozen in shock and terror. I felt around desperately for a pulse, but couldn't find one.

Oh god, oh god, oh god. This couldn't be happening! I had just gotten her back. Warm tears rolled down my face, and I held my little sister in my arms as tightly as I could. "Please don't leave me," I squeaked.

A series of guttural warbles sounded nearby, making me jump. Goosebumps raised all over my body, and the air in the basement became heavy, electric. *Reapers.*

I released Imogen for a moment, taking a cautious look around. I couldn't see them, but they could be anywhere. I reached for my gun, but grabbed at empty air. *Shit!* It was still in the storeroom back home. I mulled my situation over for a quick second. I couldn't just sit here and let them find me. I scooped up Imogen's body with a grunt and made my way back. I wouldn't leave her here. She deserved better than that.

I tottered back to the open Reaper door as best I could, stumbling several times due to the awkward load in my arms. When I was just feet away, an inhuman shriek of protest stopped me dead in my tracks. I spun around. Three Reapers approached me from the way I'd just come. A cloaked Reaper, flanked by two others on all fours. The cloaked Reaper pointed a crooked finger in my direction, and the two hunter Reapers prowled forward. Saliva oozed from their mouths and their predatory yellow eyes leered at me dangerously.

I turned back around to escape, but the door was no longer there. With one hand I struck the wall in disbelief. No, it had just been here! The Reapers on all fours closed in on me, forcing me back against the wall.

"No," I whimpered. I couldn't believe it. This was it. This was the end. I looked down at Imogen's still body, propping her up to me. I kissed her forehead, my vision watery with tears. "I love you, Immy."

I glowered at the Reapers defiantly, just in time for them to pounce upon me.

CHAPTER THREE

he Reapers screeched in rage, pinning me to the ground with Imogen's body on top of mine. They tore through Imogen's flesh with a sick, wet tearing sound, their yellow eyes fiendish, hungry.

"No, no!" I screamed. I thrashed around, desperate to get them off me, but they were too heavy.

Gregory, a faraway voice called. *Gregory ...* "GREGORY!"

The bloody nightmare around me vanished, replaced by my dark, dingy quarters. Trent hovered over me, his hand on my shoulder.

"Take some deep breaths," he said. "Everything's okay. I'm here."

I did as he instructed, and my body relaxed after several tense moments. Once I felt calm enough, I sat up in my bed.

"Imogen again?" Trent asked.

I wiped at my teary eyes and bobbed my head.

"Feel like talking about it?"

I took a deep breath and exhaled. "No, I think I'll be okay. I just need a couple minutes. What time is it?"

Trent eyed his watch. "Just after eight."

I frowned. "We'd better get going."

"Yeah, you're right. Those metal walls aren't gonna reinforce themselves." He lingered another moment. "Sure you're okay?"

"I'll be fine, promise." I gave him my best smile, and he returned it with a better one.

Trent walked over to his bed, snatching a tank top and lifting it over his head. For a moment, his bare, muscular torso was exposed. Lower, a thin trail of hair led down from his belly button to his low-riding jeans. Trent yanked his top down and caught my gaze with a puzzled look, making my cheeks burn.

He grabbed his beat-up welding mask from a peg on the wall and started to leave before turning around. "Hey, wanna get lunch together?"

"Um yeah, I'd like that," I stammered.

Trent grinned. "All right. Meet me at the cafeteria at noon. Good luck today."

As soon as Trent left I let my facade of composure go, collapsing on my bed and placing a hand on my forehead as I stared at the ceiling. Dreaming of Imogen always shook me up like this. I started having the nightmares after leaving my hometown. In some way, I always felt guilty that I didn't do more for her before she was taken from me.

Still, I hadn't had a dream about my little sister this vivid in quite a while, maybe six months or so. Something about how real the nightmare seemed bugged me, and I started thinking over the details. The Reapers we saw nowadays were more like the two that had pounced on me. Hunters, claws, simple-minded. But the cloaked Reaper seemed different somehow, more intelligent. It had pointed at me, almost like it was telling the others to attack me. Was that even a possibility?

I scoffed at myself. *Get a grip. It's all in your head, just a stupid dream.* What did it matter anyways? It's not like I was going outside anytime soon.

I checked my worn-down digital watch: 8:15 a.m. I'd better get to the job placement office to find out what I'd be doing today before they really got pissed at me. How crappy could cleaning duty be anyways?

I PULLED a bedpan from under another mattress, recoiling when I saw bits of fecal matter and urine stains on the seat. The foul, pungent smell of human waste wafted up to me and I gagged, pulling the bandanna hanging over my face closer. "Oh god, what did you *eat?*"

I left the bedpan where it was and paced around the simple two-bedded room, lowering my bandanna when I was a decent distance away. Out of all the jobs, they had to give me *this?*

My task for the day was to clean out all of the bedpans in our group's personal quarters. I guess it was my punishment for being late this morning, either that or for ending the world. The lady who assigned me the task was named Claire and made no effort to hide to her disgust of me. Shocker, I know.

I tried talking my way out of it, but she made it clear that it was either this or getting into more trouble with Samuel. As much as I wanted to fight her on it, it would only make things worse, and Mom couldn't protect me from everything.

So here I was, shoveling crap and piss into a large garbage bucket on wheels. The plumbing system didn't work at the school despite our continued efforts to repair it. We simply didn't know enough about what we were doing. I walked back to the reeking bedpan, scooped it up, and dumped its contents into the trash can.

Sixth room done. That leaves … My shoulders slumped. *More than half left.* I groaned as I placed the bedpan back underneath the bed. What happened to the person doing this job before? Maybe they couldn't stand the smell and jumped off a cliff. Whoever they were, I envied them.

I was just about to haul the disgusting garbage can out the door when the hairs on my arms shot straight up. There was a sudden static charge to the air, just like when we'd been out on the supply run. Reapers, out here?

I walked back into the room, eyeing the metal-sheeted window. White rays of sunlight filtered out of the edges. I didn't want to believe what I was thinking, but I had to know for sure. As I approached the static sensation increased, almost to a dull hum. I sat on the corner of the bed nearest the window, repositioning myself until I had a clear view outside.

The unremarkable dirt lawn spread before me, dotted with small patches of yellowed grass and litter. Out further, the ground ascended into a small, dried-out hill with a sad, wilted tree at the top. I tilted my view a bit to the right, but still couldn't see anything. I continued my search further, further, further.

I jumped, my heart thundering in my chest. Facing me ten yards away was a cloaked Reaper, standing tall on two clawed feet in the shade that the school provided. A sudden wind rattled the monster's robe, and its yellow eyes gleamed at me from underneath its hood.

An icy chill spread throughout my body. *Oh god, oh god, oh god.* Could it see me right now? Why wasn't it attacking me?

The hooded Reapers were much more dangerous than their naked hunting counterparts. They had the ability to move things with their mind, and this was my first sighting in years. But still, why was it--

My watch's alarm suddenly blared, making me flinch and breaking my concentration. "Shit," I hissed as I turned the blasted thing off. I gazed cautiously out the window once more. The Reaper was gone.

I broke away from the window and paced to the other side of the room, trying to calm my pounding pulse and collect my thoughts. Yesterday, Reapers attacked us in broad daylight. Today, I saw one of the cloaked Reapers I hadn't encountered in ages. Why were they suddenly more brave, and what was a hooded one doing watching the school?

They could be running out of prey, needing to migrate somewhere else. But if that were true, it didn't explain the hooded Reaper's appearance. What if things were more serious than that? Were they planning an attack? I shook my head. Reapers didn't think like that, not on that level. Did they? I shook off my conflicting thoughts. I couldn't just ignore this. Something was horribly wrong with this picture and I had to tell someone.

I mulled it over. Telling Claire would be pointless. She'd never let me skip out on my assigned duties, and there was no way to prove the Reaper had been there anyway. I was on thin ice with Samuel, and since Mom was dating him, telling her would get back to him. That left Trent. I glanced at my watch: 11:30 a.m.

Perfect timing. I'd empty this awful shit bucket out back and tell Trent everything at lunch. He'd know what to do.

I wheeled the stinking cart back over to Claire's office, keeping it at arm's length. When I appeared in the doorway her nose crinkled and she ran off in a hurry, telling me to wait for her while she found a guard to escort me outside.

I watched with amusement as she scampered off. *Yeah, doesn't smell great, does it?* While I waited for her, I pushed the foul waste bin into her office with a smirk, letting the stench seep into the room.

Several minutes later, I heard loud footsteps approaching. I pulled the waste bucket out of Claire's office just as she came into view. Claire bolted down the hall with an armed guard, a short, stocky guy who didn't think much of me based on the scowl on his face.

Claire's face was a light shade of red when she finally reached me. "What are you waiting for?" she shrieked. "Get that crap out of here!"

"Yes, ma'am." I gave her a sarcastic salute as I headed down the hallway.

I followed after the guard slowly, counting the seconds. Behind me, Claire cried in disgust as she re-entered her office. I grinned. *Serves you right.* I may not be the best person for doing what I did, but I was done being her and everyone else's punching bag.

The guard led the way down the dimly-lit hall, ending at a padlocked set of double doors with small, metal-sheeted windows. He unlocked them then thrust the doors open, unleashing a gust of stifling August air.

The back side of the school was a lot like the front. A chain link barbed wire fence closed around us on all sides. Large metal spikes protruded at odd angles to deter Reapers, and the gate had several additional locks on it. Twenty feet ahead was a large sewer grate that we used for dumping our waste and trash. Beyond that, a small alley intersected the back of the school, several dilapidated two-story buildings towering behind it.

The guard let me through the gate and I pushed the cart forward. When I didn't hear him behind me, I glanced back. He was just outside of the fence, lighting up a cigarette. His gun was in its holster.

"Aren't you going to follow me just in case?" I asked.

"I'm fine here," he said with a puff of smoke. "If I see one, I'll shoot it."

He looked away as if I didn't exist, and I returned to the nasty job at hand, brimming with anger. *Gee thanks, I feel so safe right now. Asshole.*

I brought the garbage bin up close to the sewer grate, then slowly tilted it. The contents of the bucket splashed against the ground, spritzing my worn shoes in shit and piss. I groaned in disgust before aiming more carefully into the grate. *Great, just great.*

When the crap bucket was empty a minute later I looked back to the guard. He had already lit up another cigarette and was turned away from me. I was about to shout at him again when the hairs on my body stood on end.

I spun around, surprised, but didn't see anything out of the norm. I concentrated on the hair-raising sensation thrumming through my veins. A Reaper was close for sure. My concerns about the cloaked Reaper I saw just minutes ago flooded back to the surface, and I froze in place, panicked.

I eyed the small alley ahead of me. Small heaps of trash and waste littered the ground, but there were no Reapers anywhere.

This didn't make any--

In the blink of an eye the electric presence of the Reaper vanished, like it had never been there. I ran my hand through my wavy brown hair as I gave the alley one last look. Had I really sensed a Reaper, or was I losing my mind? Puzzled, I grabbed the empty garbage can and rolled it inside.

Regardless of my strange, terrible day so far, I was looking forward to my lunch with Trent. He'd know what to do, and everything would make more sense when I was with him. At least, I hoped so.

CHAPTER FOUR

I eyed the green pile of slop on my plate skeptically, forcing my spoon into the concocted mess with a wet squishing sound. I leveled the edge of the utensil into my mouth for a taste test. The food was sickeningly sweet with a strange pungent tartness. The consistency was crunchy, but it seemed to melt in my mouth and left an odd, earthy aftertaste.

I grimaced, pushing aside my plate and reaching over for my fruit cup. "So much for the chef's surprise," I said to Trent across the table from me. "You want mine?"

Trent shrugged and took my plate, eagerly digging in. I always envied his iron stomach and ability to eat whatever crap they created in this dinky cafeteria.

"How's your day going?" Trent asked between giant bites.

"Awful. They've got me on bedpan duty, can you believe it?"

"Damn, that's rough. At least it's just a week, right?"

I smiled as best I could, trying to stay positive. "Yeah, I hope so. How's your day so far? It's gotta be better than mine."

Trent was a decent shot like me, but at the first locations we'd stayed at after the Reapers came, our defenses were abysmal. Trent stepped up, and although he had no idea what he was doing at first, he ended up being a natural at welding and the key to us keeping the Reapers at bay.

He chuckled. "Define better. I've been begging the scouting parties to bring me back more metal for weeks, but all they ever bring me is scrap. I keep telling them I need quality metal to reinforce the walls, but they have to go further and further to come back with anything usable every time. I've been twiddling my thumbs most of the morning."

I frowned. "Really?"

"Yeah. It's impossible to repair or make improvements to our walls without any new materials. With the way things are going, the Reapers won't have any trouble breaking through our weakened defenses. I mean, our walls are sturdy, but they can only take so much."

"Yeah." I stared blankly at my food. I had no idea things were that dire. At the same time, Trent mentioning the Reapers brought up my concerns from earlier. I glanced up at him after swallowing a mouthful of fruit. "Can I ask you something?"

"Shoot."

"Do you think the Reapers are capable of intelligence? I mean, could they coordinate an attack on us here?"

Trent looked at me, wide eyed. "Seriously?"

"Yeah, they come here sometimes after sundown, scraping and banging against the walls. On some level, they've got to be aware that they are coming to the same place, right?"

Trent's shoulders lowered. "I guess so? They do talk to each other in that weird growly language they have. But none of us have seen anything other than them hunting aimlessly in small packs for prey, and it's been years. Why do you ask?"

Images flashed in my mind: the terrifying dream I had last night, the cloaked Reaper I saw outside earlier today, the strange sensation I had out back."You're gonna think I'm crazy."

"Not any crazier than me." Trent stuck his tongue out at me. "No, seriously though, tell me what's on your mind. You know I won't judge you."

I mulled it over for a moment. "I think something is happening."

"What do you mean?"

"That dream I had this morning? It was terrible like it always is, but something about it was different this time, something that got me thinking." I told him everything that had happened in my nightmare, emphasizing the cloaked Reaper's presence. "Tell me, when was the last time you saw a cloaked Reaper?"

Trent shrugged. "I don't know, since we left our hometown? What are you getting at?"

"I saw a hooded Reaper today."

Trent's spoon clattered to the wooden table with a clang. "*What*? A hooded Reaper in the daytime *and* on camp grounds? Are you sure?"

"Of course I'm sure!" I said louder than I meant to. Several people shot steely glares in our direction and I stared down at the table, making a mental note to lower my voice. I didn't want anyone thinking I was crazier than they already did, not until I could prove my claim.

I leaned in closer. "I saw it when I was cleaning out the bedpans earlier. I felt that weird static charge I told you about when the Reapers are near and crept to the nearest window. There was a cloaked Reaper staring back at me."

"And it didn't attack you?"

"That's what's bugging me. It could've easily attacked me with that weird telekinesis it has that the others don't, but it didn't. That could only mean it's up to something else. It has to be planning something."

Trent's expression was severe as he thought over my words. "We need to talk to someone about this, someone in charge. Hooded Reapers are way too powerful, and if you're right, we're in a lot more danger than we thought."

"But I can't talk to Samuel about this, not after what happened out there yesterday!"

"Then why don't you talk to your mom about it?"

I groaned. "Do I have to?"

Trent reached over and grabbed my hand, sending warm tingles through my body. "Listen, I know that things have been weird with your mom ever since she started dating Sam, but who else is going to listen to you and take you seriously? I mean, have you *seen* how people look at us?"

As much as I loathed the idea, Trent was right. If what I suspected was true, we had to find a way to send the Reapers running for the hills before something horrific happened. I couldn't put this off.

"Yeah, you're right." I scraped up the last spoonful of my fruit cup and swallowed it, then tossed the empty cup into a nearby trash can. "Well, I guess I better go talk to my mom. Claire's gonna be up my ass if I don't get back soon."

Trent had a weird, unreadable look on his face for a second, then his expression returned to normal. "Sure, sure. Say, you wanna hang out after work? I wanted to show you something."

Butterflies flew around in my stomach. "Um, yeah. Sounds great. See ya later." I got up and walked out of the cafeteria into the main hall.

What did Trent want to show me? I'd pretty much seen everything there was within the school, even the small hiding spots and closets that people snuck into to screw around. Whatever it was, it would definitely be better than my next few hours.

Despite my anticipation, my chest tightened at the thought of informing Mom on what I'd seen. There was no telling what would happen when I told her the truth. If she took it to heart, she'd obviously have to tell Samuel. Would he believe me, and if he did, would we end up relocating?

This was the first place that our group had felt remotely safe from the Reapers. If I took that away, how long would it be before they started blaming me for that too?

A wave of doubt washed over me, and I stopped halfway to Mom's quarters, worried what would happen if Samuel was present. I shook my head, remembering Trent's advice. *Do the right thing for the group.* Besides, Samuel wouldn't berate me, not when Mom was around.

I sped the rest of the way before I could change my mind and stopped when I came to her closed door. I was about to knock when I heard escalating voices inside.

"Nine bags full," Mom was saying, tension in her voice. "How long do you think that's going to last us when a third of the food we find is rotten?"

"Patricia, we just have to--"

"No, listen to me, Sam. Every day we journey further just to find enough food for all of us. I've been logging the distance."

"We've got to try harder."

"Try *harder*? We're utilizing all the local maps we have and sending out scouts in between supply runs. And that's dangerous enough as it is."

Samuel huffed. "Not this again. The Reapers you saw during the day were a fluke, a one-time exception. Maybe they got separated from their pack somehow."

"Sam, everyone on the supply run saw them, you can't

deny that. And who's to say they aren't getting smarter, or at least more desperate? When was the last time you saw another group of humans around?"

Samuel was silent.

"The world is changing, and if we're not smarter than the Reapers, we won't survive."

I breathed a sigh of relief. Mom thought something was up too.

Samuel laughed. "Nothing is happening. When has anything changed since this all started? I'm in command, Patricia, and I won't hear any more about this. To be honest, I came here to talk to you about your son."

"What about him?"

"Do you even have to ask? He got someone killed today! He's a blight on our community. Discipline him, or I will. God knows he needs it."

I clenched my fists. Discipline? That bastard had some nerve. I waited a few moments, expecting Mom to say something, but she remained silent. Why wasn't she saying anything? She always stuck up for me.

Suddenly, a firm hand gripped my arm, and I spun around to see Claire's pale face contorted in rage.

"I've been looking for you *everywhere*," she hissed, pulling me away.

"Wait, I--"

Claire's hold on me grew tighter as she dragged me back towards her office. "I don't care what you do with your time outside of your duties, but until five o' clock, you're on my watch. Got it?"

I snagged myself free of her vice grip. "You don't have to pull me around like a little kid."

Claire scoffed. "Apparently I do, or you'd still be sitting outside your mommy's door listening to her and Sam getting it on. You seriously have some mommy issues, *freak*."

I glared at her, longing to smack the smug look off her face, but my anger quickly deflated. The one person I counted on to stick up for me had been silent. What did it mean? Did Mom really believe I was the little pissant that everyone thought I was?

I followed Claire back to her office, dragging my feet. I didn't know what to believe, but Trent and I were on our own until I got a chance to speak to Mom. I just hoped that would be soon enough.

I STOMPED INTO MY ROOM, yanking off my dirty shirt and throwing it against the wall. I couldn't believe how shitty my day ended up. After Claire dragged me back to my disgusting assignment, I finished with the bedpans only for her to put me on trash duty. Eventually she let me go, but it was at least two hours later than I should've stayed.

Now I smelled like shit, I was exhausted, and to top it all off I still didn't know what to do about my suspicions with the Reapers.

I'd passed by Mom's quarters on the way to mine to talk, but she hadn't been there. A small part of me was grateful for her absence regardless of my concerns. I couldn't talk to her without bringing up what I'd heard earlier, and her silence scared me.

Already it seemed like no one wanted me here. If Mom couldn't bring herself to speak up for me anymore, how long would it be before Samuel and the others ousted me from the group altogether? I groaned. All I wanted was to crawl into bed and forget this day ever happened.

I took a deep breath, then sank to my knees on the side of my bed. I reached underneath and pulled out a small cardboard box of personal belongings. I fished through the contents, mainly stuff from my life before the Reapers, and pulled out my favorite X-Men t-shirt and comic book. I tossed the comic onto my bed and slipped on the shirt. It was a little tight now, but still fit well enough. A ghost of a smile tugged at the corners of my mouth.

Being reminded of the happy times of the past always put me at ease when I was stressed out. I hopped onto my bed and let out a heavy breath. Everything would be okay. I just needed time to calm down. Besides, Trent and I were hanging out tonight. What better way to forget my shit-tastic day?

I studied the cover of my comic book for the millionth time. *Uncanny X-Men #141, Days of Future Past*. This was my second favorite X-Men story of all time. My beloved mutant heroes were stuck in a dark future where they are hunted down and placed in internment camps, and Kitty Pryde goes back to her past self to prevent the present from happening.

I'd imagined myself doing the same thing so many times I lost count. I'd stop the Reapers from ending the world, graduate high school, have a life worth living. I frowned.

Fantasizing about a better life for myself usually made me feel better, but today the thought just made me feel helpless, defeated. I wanted to believe that there was a way to make things better, but it had been five years. If there was something we could do, we would have figured it out by now. I tossed the comic book to the side and stared at the ceiling tiles.

After a few minutes of replaying today's events in my head, Trent appeared and stood in the doorway with a big grin on his face.

"Hey there."

He was wearing his nice clothes: a raggedy casual button-down shirt and his worn pair of jeans instead of his usual tank top and holey pants with burn marks all over them. I smiled, trying to suppress my excitement to an acceptable level. He looked good.

"How was your day?" I asked.

"Eh, can't complain. You ready to go?"

"Sure. Go where?"

Trent gave a lopsided smirk. "That's for me to know and you to find out." He pulled out a frayed red bandanna from his back pocket and presented it to me.

I cocked an eyebrow. "Seriously?"

"Yup, now put it on. We've gotta move. You'll like it, I swear."

"Alright." I took the bandanna, tying it around my head in a way that let me see out the bottom. I feigned blindness, thrusting my hands in front of me. "All good?"

"Oh, no you don't. Pull it down all the way."

I laughed and lowered the bandanna over my eyes. I heard Trent grab some things around his bed, then he took hold of my arm. I couldn't help but grin as he guided me out into the hallway. We made a right, and I tried to mentally picture our route.

Where could we be going? Down this hall was more quarters, the library, and a couple classrooms, but nothing of real significance. After walking down the hall a bit, we took a left.

Now I was really confused. Down this hall, all I could remember was a small supply closet, nothing more. What were we doing down he--

"Here we are," Trent announced.

My stomach lurched, and I started to remove my bandanna, but Trent's hand clamped down on mine.

"Not yet."

There was a jingle of keys, then a door groaned open in front of us. Trent pulled me in and shut the door after us before lifting up my blindfold. We were in a tiny, unfamiliar room, illuminated by a single small lightbulb. In front of me was a set of metal bars leading upwards.

"We're going up on the roof?" I asked. I'd never been up there because I didn't have the keys to get in. I guess I didn't know every nook and cranny of the school as well as I thought I did.

"Yep. I thought we could use a little fresh air after being cooped up all day."

He started climbing the ladder one rung at a time and I hesitated for a moment, enjoying the view.

Trent turned his head back when he was halfway up, catching me in mid-stare. "You coming up or what?"

My cheeks burned as I jumped to action. I ran up to the ladder, following after him eagerly. Whatever he was going to show me, I couldn't wait.

CHAPTER FIVE

The night air was crisp and cool. A light wind formed goosebumps on my arms and legs and I shivered, crossing my arms for warmth as I surveyed the rooftop area. It was a simple concrete patio with a short chain link fence around the edge. A small wooden table and several lawn chairs were scattered about, but nothing else. It wasn't much, but I was already feeling more relaxed.

"This is cool," I said. "I've never been out here before."

"Oh yeah? I come out here sometimes when I can't stand it inside."

Trent set his knapsack down on the table and pulled out a couple of thin, worn blankets. He laid one down on the ground, then motioned me over. Once I sat down on the blanket, he squatted next to me then wrapped the second blanket around us both, our shoulders touching.

I looked up at the night sky. Thousands of stars dotted the black expanse, twinkling with a life of their own. I hated to admit it, but since the Reapers came the sky was breathtaking at night with no city lights to cloud it. I lowered my gaze to the damaged, broken buildings in the near distance.

Trent grabbed his bag off the table and pulled out a small bottle halfway filled with amber liquid. He spun the top off and took a swig, then offered it to me.

I shrugged and grabbed the bottle, gulping some down. I tried not to make a face as the overwhelming taste of cinnamon liquor burned in my mouth and down my throat.

Trent laughed. "Noob."

I pushed him playfully. "Hey, not all of us are alcoholics."

"You don't know what you're missing." He stuck his tongue out. He fidgeted a bit before looking at me. "So uh, I know I didn't get you a birthday present a couple weeks ago, but I wanted to make up for it now."

"Oh, you don't have to--"

"Too late. Hold on a sec." Trent rustled through his pack again and handed me a thin rectangular item wrapped in brown paper. "Happy birthday, Gregory."

I unwrapped the item and gasped in shock. *"Uncanny X-Men #235, Genosha Island?* This is my--"

"Favorite X-Men story of all time. I know, you nerd."

I gaped at the comic, still in awe. "How did you get your hands on this?"

Trent smirked devilishly. "I put in a special request to my scout friend a few months back. The other day his friend on the supply route found a copy."

I held the comic book out in front of me. I couldn't think of a more perfect gift, but ever-pressing guilt and shame settled on my shoulders. After everything I'd done, everything I'd screwed up, did I really deserve this? "I can't accept this," I muttered.

"Don't be silly, of course you can. It was your birthday."

"No, it's not that, I…" I turned my head away from him as tears came to my eyes.

Damn it, why was I so weak? Trent just wanted to give me a birthday gift and here I was, crying like a baby.

It was no wonder why everyone treated me the way they did. I couldn't do anything right. Couldn't go on a supply run without killing somebody, couldn't save Imogen, Carlos, the world ... I was a failure. I didn't deserve Trent's kindness or anyone else's for that matter.

"What is it?" Trent turned me gently to face him.

I shook my head. "I'm sorry, I shouldn't have come up here with you." I started to rise, but Trent pulled me back down. I averted his gaze.

"Greg, stop it. Tell me what's wrong. I know something's been bugging you lately."

I breathed shakily, my emotions overpowering my urge to leave. "All of this." I gestured to the surrounding buildings. "It's because of me. Imogen and Carlos, they died because of me. It's my fault that we're all in this situation. Why are you so nice to me? I don't deserve it. I don't deserve anything." I stared at the ground as tears ran down my face, too ashamed to look him in the face.

"How can you say any of that? Greg, you know you weren't the only person involved in the Reapers coming. I was there, so was your mom. The Order was too. We did what we had to, and you can't keep beating yourself up for something that you aren't responsible for. Christ, why can't you see how amazing you are?"

I glanced up at him through my blurry vision, puzzled.

"You're the bravest person I've ever met. Unlike those soulless shitheads in there, you've got heart. You've never lost who you are. You still care about people. Don't let them make you doubt yourself. You're ten times better than any one of them." Trent fixated on me with an intensity in his beautiful blue eyes, as if he was resisting something. "Oh, fuck it."

Trent pulled me to him, and his lips met mine. A jolt of electricity ran through my body, and all my hairs stood up on end. I couldn't believe it. This was really happening. Trent felt the same way about me!

I kissed him back, closing my eyes. I'd wanted this for so long. His soft lips tasted like cinnamon. A sudden excitement lurched in my lower half, and I broke off the kiss, nervous.

From the surprised look on Trent's face, he was anxious too.

"Sorry. I got a little, um, excited. I've never done this before."

Trent smirked. "It's okay, neither have I. Not with a guy at least." He edged closer and held my hand. "I meant what I said, every word. I care about you, Greg. I've been thinking about this for a long time."

Heat rose in my cheeks. "Me too."

I leaned in for another kiss when a terrible, rending screech of metal made me jump. A series of heavy clanks and clangs echoed up to Trent and me. We looked at each other in shock, then scrambled over to the edge of the patio for a look.

Below, six Reapers lurked around the reinforced metal sheets protecting the windows on this side of the school. They clawed and scraped together in small groups, and I could see bits and pieces of the metal barrier fling off in several directions. Behind them, a tall shrouded figure stood, watching the attack. As I gazed upon the cloaked Reaper, its yellow eyes turned toward mine, sending tingling pinpricks down my back.

"Impossible," Trent muttered.

I grabbed Trent's hand in a vice grip, my heart thundering in my chest as I watched the scene below. The Reapers were here, and they wanted blood.

I stared downward, frozen in terror as the Reapers attacked the side of the school. They had never attacked with this many before, and not nearly as focused as they were now. How long would the walls hold? Faint screams from inside cut through the shrieks of tearing metal.

"Greg!" Trent shook my shoulders.

I snapped out of my trance and examined his face. He looked just as terrified as I felt.

"We've got to get inside before they cut through the windows. Come on!"

We grabbed our things in a hurry and rushed down the ladder back inside. When we entered the hallway we'd come from, I was assaulted by a cacophony of sights and sounds. Battery-powered floodlights illuminated the passage, projecting dark and threatening shadows on the walls as people ran to and fro in panic. Orders were shouted out over screams of terror and loud, hurried footsteps and squeaks. High-pitched grating screeches pierced the air as the Reapers tore at the windows' metal coverings outside.

I looked at Trent. "What do we do?"

He shook his head. "Those window barriers are built to withstand one Reaper, two at best. We've got to get back to our room for weapons before they break through, then we'll head to the rendezvous point."

I nodded along. Right, the storeroom. We ran down the short hall, turning the corner into the corridor housing our quarters. I tried to keep calm, but my body was tensing up. At any second the Reapers could shatter our defenses and begin their massacre. Did everyone remember the emergency plan? And what about Mom? I had to know she was safe.

We bolted down the hall, passing confused, panicked people and glimpsing several occupied rooms on the way. In the first, a mother and child threw random items into a big luggage bag. In the next, several men hammered wooden boards across the inside window. I prayed they would all get to safety before it was too late.

Gasping for breath, we finally made it back to our room near the end of the hallway. Trent darted over to his bed and yanked his knapsack off. He snatched the cardboard box from under his bed and started throwing things into his bag.

I followed suit, rustling through my things for anything useful. As I shuffled through my stuff and hurled it into my pack, I unearthed an odd gray chunk of candle with black bits embedded within. The candle from five years ago that attracted Reapers … Wait, where was the white one that repelled them? It was just here the other day. *No time.* I threw the candle into my bag, unsure when we'd be back here or if I'd need it somehow. I glanced over my other belongings. "What do I--"

"Just leave it!" Trent shouted. "Grab your knife. We've got to go *now!*"

I strapped on my knapsack and grabbed my hunting knife. We had only made it to our doorway when a loud rending crash and feminine scream sounded to our right. A shiver shot down my spine. The Reapers had gotten through, and the mother and her child were being attacked.

"What are you waiting for?" Trent demanded. "We have to go!"

"We can't just let them die!" I sprinted down the hall, Trent's delayed footsteps right behind me.

I passed the first room. Trent stopped and yelled at the people inside to head to the storeroom. As I neared the second one, a small boy stumbled out, covered in blood and holding a knife coated in a thick, black substance. He gawked at me in horror, freezing in place.

"Get to the storeroom!" I shouted as I sprinted past him.

I picked up speed, readying myself to charge inside the room when sharp, spindly fingers thrust out at me from within. I ducked out of reach and countered, severing multiple fingers from the Reaper's hand. They rolled onto the floor, wriggling and writhing as a dense, ebony ooze flowed from them.

The Reaper screeched in rage, charging into the hall and nearly crashing into the nearest wall. I froze in fear.

What should I do now? I only had my knife to protect me, and close-quarters combat only ended badly with Reapers. But if I ran, it would mow me down.

The monster poised to strike, and I cursed my weakness. There was no escape now.

Suddenly, a woman with deep bloody gashes on her arms, legs, and face emerged from the room. She held a long knife in her hand, and she flung herself forward with a primitive cry of fury, stabbing the Reaper in its side.

The Reaper wailed in pain, but another appeared from the same room and yanked the woman back inside, followed by a scream of agony. The Reaper in the hallway turned and joined the other one.

As much as I wanted to help, there was nothing more I could do. I bolted back down the hall as fast as I could, the last excruciating cries of the woman assaulting my ears. *Fuck, fuck, fuck!* Two Reapers were inside the school, and we were already losing people.

Trent lingered impatiently at the end of the hall, ushering me to run faster. As soon as I caught up with him, we ran together through the small network of hallways towards the storeroom. With any luck, that mother's kid had gotten there safe and sound. There was nothing else I could've done for him, but what about my mom?

"Hey, keep up," Trent ordered in a huff.

I tried to keep up with him, but my worries about Mom's safety demanded my attention. I stopped, catching my breath.

Trent circled back, brows furrowed. "What are you doing? We have to move!"

I shook my head. "I can't. What if Mom's still in her quarters?"

"Your mom is safe with Samuel in the storeroom. We don't have time to stop by her room. It's too dangerous, too big of a detour."

"But I have to know for sure!"

Trent pinned me against the nearest wall, his face close to mine. "Listen to me, okay? We don't have time for this shit. We have to protect ourselves, and the only way we can do that is to join the others. Your mom will be in that storeroom, trust me."

I opened my mouth to protest, but a series of shrieks from multiple Reapers interrupted me. They sounded far enough away, but knowing their speed, they'd be on us in no time. Trent was right. We couldn't risk going by Mom's quarters. We just had to trust she was okay and save ourselves.

I glanced at the intersecting hall behind us that led to Mom's quarters. *Please be safe, Mom.*

"Alright, let's go."

I chased after Trent down the west wing. Within a couple minutes, we were just one hall down from the storeroom. We'd be safe there, at least for now. Its doors were heavily fortified, and I hoped they would hold long enough to buy us some time.

We blasted around the corner onto the last hallway, right into a lone Reaper in front of us. It screeched with a deafening wail, claws outstretched to attack. I tried to slow down, but I had way too much momentum. Trent and I slammed into the monster, sending it to the ground with us.

As we tumbled, I lifted my hunting knife and started stabbing the evil creature. The Reaper roared in pain and swiped at me, but I dodged and it hit Trent instead. Trent flew off of the Reaper with a cry, sliding a few feet on the tiled floor.

A burning anger enveloped me, and I hardly recognized the scream that tore out of my mouth as I brought my knife up and down into the Reaper's body. I stabbed at it in a blind fury with increasing velocity until I felt hands on me. I spun around, arm raised to attack.

"Greg, it's me." Trent raised his hands, palms facing towards me in surrender. "Come on, we've got to move! The storeroom is just ahead."

I wiped my wet face clean of black ooze and tears of rage, then struggled to my feet. Trent and I shot down the passageway. At the end of the hall, the storeroom's heavy metal doors were propped open, and one of the sharpshooters from my supply run yesterday waved frantically at us, an AR-15 rifle in his other hand.

That's when another Reaper shrieked behind us, *very* close.

"Run!" Trent screamed.

We bolted at the doors in a full-on sprint. My lungs burned in my chest, begging me to slow down. *Thirty feet, twenty-five.* The sharpshooter knelt down on the right side of the hall and aimed his rifle. He nodded his head sharply to our left, and Trent and I careened out of the way.

Bullets whizzed past, just inches away from us. I couldn't tell if he'd hit the Reaper or not, but based on the inhuman cries behind us, he definitely hadn't killed it.

Ten feet, five. The sharpshooter stood up, spraying the air behind us with bullets and edging back to the storeroom.

With a final surge of exertion, Trent and I lunged through the doorway, falling to the ground as the doors slammed behind us.

I rolled onto my back, breath ragged as I stared up at the ceiling. We had made it.

CHAPTER SIX

I watched the huge metal doors, holding my breath as I waited for the Reaper to come slashing and banging. After several seconds of silence, my spirits lifted a bit. I guess the guard was successful in taking out the Reaper chasing us, but it wouldn't be long before the rest of them came, including the cloaked one. We had to get moving.

Hushed chatter filled the area as Trent and I helped each other up and looked around. I'd always thought of the storeroom as one of the biggest rooms in the school, but with our entire group in here it seemed a lot smaller.

The simple space was packed with people; men, women, and children huddled in groups, inspecting their backpacks and supply bags or keeping their little ones close to them and quiet. At a nearby long wooden table, another crowd rifled through a mound of supplies, gearing up with guns, ammunition, and whatever items we had stored in case of emergency.

I edged towards the equipment table with Trent, scanning every face I could see. I was relieved that so many of our people had survived the initial Reaper attack, but a twinge of fear still shook me. I hadn't found Mom yet. What if she wasn't here? If she was still out there with the Reapers ...

No. She was here, damn it. I just hadn't found her yet. I left Trent, pushing my way through groups of people and ignoring their pushbacks and grunts of irritation as I called out for my mom. When I completed a full rotation of the room empty handed, my legs felt like they were gonna give out. She wasn't here, I couldn't believe it.

God, why had I let Trent convince me to come here? Mom was out there, and thanks to me she was probably already dead, just another victim of those fucking monsters that killed my little sister and the rest of the world.

"Gregory?" a muffled voice called.

I spun on one foot and peered through the masses. I couldn't see anyone friendly, and with the blanket of noise hampering other sounds I couldn't tell where it came from. Just when I was about to head back to Trent, I saw my mother in a sudden shift of movement in the crowd.

"Mom!" I cried.

"Gregory!"

We ran to each other. As my mom's arms enveloped me, I buried my head into her shoulder.

"I thought I'd lost you," I croaked.

"Shh, shh, it's alright. Everything's okay," Mom said, her voice shaky. "I'm just glad you're safe. I was so worried about you."

I reveled in her embrace for a long moment, inhaling her sweet, pleasant scent I could never give a name to. I thanked whatever God or fate that had protected her.

Mom released me and took my hand, her expression grave. "Come on, let's get you ready to go. We have to head out before the other Reapers get here."

"But Mom, where can we go? The Reapers are in the halls."

"I'll explain when we join Trent. I saw him when I heard you calling me."

She led me back towards the supply table. Trent was on the outer edge of the horde I'd forced myself through, and Mom brought him in for a hug and a warm pat on the back. "Good to see you're safe, Trent. There's not much time. You and Gregory need to stock up on supplies and be prepared to leave."

Trent tilted his head. "Where, Ms. M? We're stuck in here with no way out."

"Not quite. We have an escape route we'll be using from this room. Now, do as I instructed. I have to attend to some things before we depart."

Mom left us, and Trent and I went over to the supply table. I cleaned my dirty face, then plopped my mostly-empty knapsack on the table next to Trent's before loading it with a flashlight, food, and ammunition. I found a holster in my preferred style and started slipping it through the belt loops of my jeans when a murmur went through the core of the crowd nearby.

People shuffled around, clearing a small, circular space. Samuel walked into its center. He didn't have a bit of wear on him from the Reaper attack, and he stood proudly with his big muscled shoulders and million-dollar smile. I rolled my eyes. No wonder no one could say no to him. He was their white knight in shining armor.

Samuel held his hands up, and everyone quieted down. Trent and I continued stuffing our knapsacks with necessities as we listened in.

"As you all probably know by now, we are evacuating the building," Samuel said.

A few people groaned and cursed in response.

"Believe me, I understand how you feel. I don't want to leave either, but we don't have any other choice if we want to survive. In a moment we'll evacuate through a sewer grate, and together we'll find a new base from there. Remember, the Reapers hunt by sight and sound, so we'll have to be as quiet as possible in the sewers until we reach safety. Sharpshooters will bring up the front and rear. All right, let's move it out, people!"

Samuel left the small circle, and I digested the information he'd given as everyone shuffled around in a panic.

A sewer, *seriously*? What kind of lame-assed plan B was this? I cringed at the thought of wading through even more piss and shit than I already had today, but there was nothing I could do about it.

I kept my focus on Samuel. Several armed men followed him to an enormous supply chest. Together they hoisted the gargantuan thing up and over, then peered downwards. A couple of the guys hunkered down and disappeared, probably checking to make sure the sewer was safe.

I rifled through my pack one last time, then grabbed my loaded Glock and hunting knife before placing them in my holster. I was strapping the knapsack on my back when I noticed the single-file line forming where Samuel was standing.

With everyone shifted, I could now make out the large sewer grate. We'd have no problem fitting through it, but with several sharpshooters already up front, Trent and I would be backing up the rear.

Oh the fucking irony.

Right now the line wasn't moving. We were still waiting on the men who'd gone down to give the okay. Samuel stared down into the darkness with a frown, and despite my enmity for him, I couldn't blame him for worrying.

We were running out of options and time. If this didn't pan out, we'd be facing the Reapers head on, and the last thing we needed was another bloodbath. Grisly images from past battles flashed through my head, and I winced. *Come on, come on.*

Finally, a gloved hand reached out from the sewer grate. It gave a thumbs up, and people cheered, eagerly moving forward to start the climb down.

I nudged Trent. "You ready for this?"

He looked back at me with an adorable smirk. "Yep, all gravy."

I restrained the overpowering urge to kiss him.

With Trent and me bringing up the back end of our group, there wasn't much else to do except wait, and it wasn't long before things started to go south. Only a few people had climbed down so far, but the energy in the room had already gone frantic. As each person started their way down, others shifted irritably, rolling their eyes and pushing forward when there wasn't room to move.

I wiped my sweaty palms against my jeans. This situation could easily spiral out of control. I watched for another tense moment when a loud clang erupted against the storeroom doors. There was a communal gasp of shock, then everyone froze like time had stood still.

One of the sharpshooters from our supply runs approached the door quietly, creeping forward with his rifle trained on the door. When he was just feet away another metallic bang sounded, a small dent appearing in the door. An inhuman screech of rage pierced the air.

The guard jumped back, and several people cried out in terror. The Reapers knew where we were, and they had us cornered.

"Everyone keep moving," Samuel instructed with a wave. "The doors will hold."

Everyone picked up the pace, and six or seven more people had hurried down into the sewer grate when another Reaper joined in on attacking the door. Now the hollow clanks were starting to form larger, deeper dents in the door. The heavy bangs continued, increasing in intensity before abruptly ceasing moments later. Everything went silent.

Why did they stop attacking? That wasn't like them. The Reapers were ruthless, would stop at nothing until they got their next kill, even if it meant hurting themselves in the process. My stomach lurched. Something was wrong.

All of a sudden, the ground beneath me seemed to vibrate. At first I thought I was just imagining it, but when I looked back at Trent, his widened blue eyes were fixed on the floor too.

The vibration escalated fast, and in just a few short seconds the whole room was shaking violently. The storeroom doors rumbled, items fell off counters and shelves, and dust fell down on us from new cracks that were forming in the ceiling. The space filled with screams of horror, and Samuel tried to soothe people's worries while hurrying them through the sewer grate.

I clutched the supply table like my life depended on it. What the hell was going on? This was no earthquake. Could it be the cloaked Reaper? The one that Trent and I hunted down five years ago never had this kind of power. Then again, we'd killed it before it had the chance to show us.

The guard near the storeroom doors edged closer as an enormous wave of static seeped into the room. The hairs on the back of my neck prickled up, triggering my gut instinct.

"Wait! Get away from the--"

With a horrendous, wrenching shriek, a huge metal beam shot through one of the doors. I cried out, falling to the ground and thrusting my arms in front of me protectively. Not that that would've done anything.

I dared a glance at the damage and gagged in disgust. The guard hadn't had enough time to react. The pole had run straight through his midsection and into the ceiling, coated in blood and bits of skin, bone, and organ. He dropped his gun with a clatter, gurgling and clutching at the pipe.

In that moment, everyone lost it. People screamed and pushed past each other, trying to force their way down below the grate. Others shoved back against them. Samuel yelled at all of them to calm down.

"Fuck!" Trent lunged forward, grabbing the dead guard's rifle and bending down into a crouch.

I drew my Glock, stepping forward with shaky hesitance.

Just as fast as it had come, the metal pole was yanked back through the hole in the doors, narrowly missing Trent. The guard impaled by the beam smacked into the doors with a deafening clang, then fell to the ground, lifeless.

"Trent, get away from the doors!" I shouted.

But he didn't move. He just stared blankly forward at the hole in the wall like he was in some kind of daze.

I followed his gaze, my blood freezing like icicles in my veins.

Staring back at me were the intelligent yellow eyes of the cloaked Reaper.

Another surge of static energy erupted, and the hole in the door began to widen and stretch with a screech of tearing metal. The terrible noise snapped me out of my trance, bringing me back to reality.

I aimed my Glock at the expanding hole and fired several times. The Reaper gave a monstrous cry of pain before leaving my vantage point, and Trent snapped out of his temporary hypnosis, looking around in confusion.

I ran over to him, but by then the banging of the Reapers had returned. Now the sound was overbearing, the new dents forming fast and deep. *Shit.* There had to be at least three or four of them out there, and now they had enough room to reach a hand or two through the hole in the door.

Long, spindly fingers clawed out at Trent and I, and we scrambled back to avoid contact.

"Hey, we need some fucking help over here!" Trent cried.

I glanced back at Samuel and the others. There were maybe ten of us left in the room: Mom, several sharpshooters, and the rest of the civilians. One of the last sharpshooters darted over and hacked away at the Reapers' grasping fingers, but in mere moments a new hole opened up in the door. Several Reapers reached out for him, missing by centimeters.

A lump formed in my throat as I witnessed the chaos unraveling before me. The Reapers were going to get through, and there was no way out but down. There wasn't anything else we could do.

"We've got to go," Samuel called. "Come on!"

I ran over to the grate with Trent. The last of the civilians climbed down the ladder, and Mom was next. I followed after her, taking one last look. The storeroom doors had gaping holes in them, and the sharpshooter was slashing wildly at the Reapers without much effect.

Defeated, I continued my climb down into the sewer. As I descended, I recoiled at the god-awful stench that radiated up to me. I guess that was what five years of hopeless shit smelled like. Trent followed after me, then Samuel. I heard the sharpshooter above shout something, and as Samuel came down, he lowered the sewer grate over himself.

"Hey, what are you doing?" I objected. "He's still up there!"

Samuel's expression was grim as he finished his descent, jumping off the ladder onto the concrete. "Riley decided to stay back and hold them off as long as he could. We have to respect his decision and move out." Through the dim communal light from the flashlights down here, he eyed my mom with a weak smile. "Come on, Patricia. Let's go up front."

I watched the sewer grate from below. Something lowered over it slowly, sealing us in. My thoughts raced as the depressing reality of our situation washed over me. We were stuck down here, playing our luck with no real promise of safety.

Were there Reapers down here? If so, would we be able to fight them off, or would we all just die in this shithole? God, this was all so fucking hopeless.

Trent's hand closed around mine. "Everything's gonna be alright."

I smiled at him and gave his hand a squeeze, trying to suppress my doubts. I hoped he was right, for all our sakes.

CHAPTER SEVEN

I pulled my red, ragged bandanna up over my nose to lessen the awful funk that permeated everything around me. *Note to self, never enter another shitty sewer again.*

Trent, myself, and two other sharpshooters brought up the rear of our group. As we followed, we didn't have much of an idea of where we were going, but it didn't really matter. Our job was to protect our backs, plain and simple. It was best to leave the navigating to those in front.

We moved at a snail's pace, unsure of our surroundings. A number of people shone their flashlights this way and that as we moved forward, and I joined them with my own. The sewer wasn't huge. Maybe twenty feet from bottom to top. Filthy like you would expect it, and quiet too.

We progressed along a five-foot wide dirty concrete walkway with a lake of stagnant green water on our right that stank to high hell. I scanned the water with my light, recoiling at the sight of a halfway submerged dog corpse and averting my gaze. *Don't look at the water, got it.*

In the distance behind us, gunfire echoed faintly. On

some level, it was reassuring to know Riley was still up there, fighting so all of us could live. About a minute had passed when the shots abruptly stopped, and my shoulders slumped. Another one of our people, gone. He had been so brave … Did the cloaked Reaper get him?

Its intelligent yellow eyes flashed in my mind with a screeching growl, and I flinched. The sudden thought helped me remember that Trent had seen it too, and all my worries came rushing back to the surface. I lowered my makeshift face mask and leaned in close.

"You saw it too, didn't you?" I whispered.

"What?" Trent asked.

"The cloaked Reaper. You know, on the balcony, in the storeroom."

"Yeah, I think so. Why?"

"I've seen the same one several times now. I think …" I angled in even closer. "I think somehow it's controlling the others."

"Wait, what? How is that even possible?"

"I don't know how, but think about it. That Reaper stayed behind the others when they attacked the metal-plated windows. Have you ever seen them that coordinated before?"

Trent frowned. "No. Where are you going with this?"

"I don't think we're safe, here or anywhere else. The cloaked Reaper is way more powerful than I thought, and if it really is controlling the others it doesn't matter where we go. It'll keep hunting us down, and next time we won't have fortified walls to protect us."

One of the other sharpshooters shushed us, and several others turned back, staring at us angrily.

Trent and I lingered back a few paces. His brows were furrowed when he looked at me in the light of his flashlight. "Listen, let's just talk about this later when we've gotten ourselves out of this mess, yeah?"

"But you don't under--"

"*Greg*. Later, okay? We need to focus on getting out of this hellhole. We can talk it over when we get to safety."

I nodded hesitantly, swallowing my concerns. *If there is such a thing as safety anymore.*

We continued to slog our way through the sewers. To distract my dark thoughts of plotting Reapers and the hopelessness of our situation, I focused on our surroundings for the next stretch of our journey.

The path we walked on was slippery with sludge in places and thin, making it hard to cover our backs when we hit an unexpected patch. The concrete walls on our left were covered in grime and a wet, gel-like substance I didn't recognize, so I stayed as far away as I could.

The deeper we went, the worse the stench of the sewer got. It was like rotten eggs mixed with spoiled cottage cheese, only if they'd been festering for five years. I'd never been in a sewer before now, but the longer we walked, the more I couldn't wait to get out of this nightmare.

We were at a disadvantage here. Down in the dark our sight was diminished, even with the aid of our lights. If we were attacked, who could say we'd hit our target at all? Most of our group were crap shots besides the sharpshooters, and even though we hadn't seen any Reapers yet that didn't mean they weren't lurking down the next corner waiting for us. We were playing with fire, and it was just a matter of time before our luck ran out.

About ten minutes after we started walking, we hit the first intersecting pathway. Samuel walkied us, telling us to stop while those in front peered around the corner and made sure no Reapers were present. Once they verified we were safe, they ushered us forward. We went on this way, passing four pathways before Samuel's voice crackled to life on my walkie.

"Stop where you are, please," his voice instructed calmly. "We are inspecting our first access point. Set time for examination is five minutes. Please stay calm and quiet."

Murmurs echoed around our group, and I stood on my tiptoes for a better look at what was happening. Up ahead, two of our sharpshooters ascended from the floor, climbing a metal ladder to a sewer grate. They hesitated a moment before lifting the cover above them and disappearing into darkness.

For what seemed like an eternity we all sat there and waited. I wanted to keep calm like Samuel suggested, but my mind was racing. A lot rode on this. What if the sharpshooters didn't come back? If they did, how would we protect our new home? The school didn't work out, and it was built like a fort.

I felt Trent's hand on my shoulder. His hot breath warmed my left ear. "Hey, it's gonna be okay. Don't stress yourself out."

I touched his hand on my shoulder and tried to smile. "Sorry, I'm just nervous about all of this."

"Me too."

Trent and I stood there, waiting out the moments until my walkie suddenly screeched with a static whine. "Abort, abort! Unsafe. I repeat, unsafe!"

Gunblasts erupted above us, and my breathing became unstable as they echoed closer and closer. I clutched Trent's hand tighter. Several gasps and muffled cries sounded from our group, and Samuel's voice came through my walkie. "Remain calm, everyone. There are other access points we can try."

The sewer grate above lifted, and the two sharpshooters hurried down, followed by a distant wail of fury from a Reaper. One of them seemed injured based on the odd way he was moving, but I couldn't tell at this distance. At least we hadn't lost anyone, and for now there weren't any Reapers down here with us. I just hoped that would last until we could escape to safety.

My walkie sparked to life once more. "As you heard, this access point is unsafe," Samuel stated. "We will move out and keep trying until we find safety. Remember, we're all in this together. Stay strong."

We continued onward through the sewer passage, but it was obvious that morale had dropped. People's shoulders were slumped, their heads tilted downwards. I even glimpsed several others rubbing at their eyes between my scans backwards and forwards.

We stopped at two more access points to the ground above and found nothing but Reapers. Then on the third inspection, something terrible happened. One of our sharpshooters didn't come back. Our group had to scurry away as fast as we could to quiet the Reaper that screeched through the sewer grate at us. Thank god it was too big to fit through the cover.

Samuel reassured us that we would find safety and that everything would be okay, but now his words seemed to have little effect on the group. People dragged their feet, scratched at their arms and faces, and puffed little sighs of frustration. I couldn't blame them one bit. We were tired, flustered, restless.

It wasn't long before we were notified of another access point further ahead. We soldiered onward, approaching another intersecting pathway when Samuel suddenly hissed into his walkie talkie. "Everyone, stop! Back up slowly, and don't make any noise."

We did as we were told, my stomach lurching as I realized the only thing it could be.

A tense moment passed before he spoke again. "A Reaper family is nesting in the pathway crossing ours to the left."

A few people in our group murmured, and the walkie crackled back to life. "I said be quiet. If we're going to get through this alive, listen to me closely. We must cross the passageway."

No one said anything after Samuel's statement, but I'm sure they were just as baffled as I was. What the hell was he thinking? Crossing exposed was suicide! Our group had only encountered a nesting Reaper family in a few instances, and each time our casualties were high. The mothers were extremely protective of their young and more vicious than the standard Reaper. And that wasn't counting their tiny murderous offspring.

"Look, I understand how nerve-racking the situation is," Samuel said in a calming tone. "But there's no other way to get across. We can't sit here and wait, and we can't go back. The mother Reaper appears to be sleeping at the moment, so as long as we stay quiet we should be fine. We'll go one small group at a time, three or four people, no more. I'll signal when the coast is clear after each group, then the next will cross. Keep your lights fixed on the ground, and do *not* make a sound. I'll cross first to make sure it's safe."

I couldn't see Samuel from where we were, but each second we waited felt like a small eternity, one with infinitely dark possibilities. If the mother woke up, we'd be forced to kill her, but then we'd have to deal with her babies and other nearby Reapers. How many of them were even down here? We were so screwed.

Finally, Samuel's voice sounded over my walkie. "I made it safely across. No sign of Reapers beyond this passageway. First row, approach. *Take your time.*"

Trent, the two other sharpshooters, and I inched forward as each small group went. Beads of sweat gathered on my forehead as my nerves flared, and I continually slicked back my wet brown hair. Everyone followed Sam's instructions to a tee, and the Reapers hadn't seemed to notice our crossing. Finally, the last row of civilians before us went forward and cut across the passageway without issue.

I wiped my sweaty palms on my jeans. This was it.

Samuel had us approach until we were right at the corner of the intersecting passage. He told us to stop for a moment, then spoke once more. "All right, the coast is clear. Remember what I said. Keep your lights down. Don't make any sound. Once you cross, we'll continue on. Got it?"

"Gotcha," Trent replied, then we were off.

The two sharpshooters with us took the lead. They walked in calm, measured steps, and Trent and I trailed behind, mimicking them. We passed into the exposed area, a fluttery feeling in my stomach.

Keep your eyes on the ground. Don't fall, don't fall, don't fall.

I heard a strange rustling sound off to my left and turned on impulse. My stomach flipped, and I froze at the sight before me. Under pale slivers of moonlight filtering from above, a large female Reaper was in the far left corner of the passageway, her pink boil-infested body curled into a fetal position. Her bony chest heaved up and down with breath, and I was almost relieved until I spotted what was behind her.

A gray mass was plastered against the wall, maybe two to three feet in diameter. Large globules of a strange, wrinkled substance comprised most of the mass, but it was held together with stringy matter that looked and pulsated like veins. The vein-like material clung to the sewer wall and stretched out in all directions.

I gagged in disgust. I'd seen the Reaper sacs before, but never in this much sickening detail.

I was just about to run off when one of the blobs shifted, making the sound I'd heard seconds ago. The mother instantly awoke and crawled over to the gray mass. I inched away, keeping my eyes on the nightmare before me.

The mother began licking the wrinkled gray globules with a long, thin tongue. Some of the globules seemed to shift in response. She made a growling sort of cooing noise, and vomit lurched up my throat.

Hold it in, hold it--

Suddenly, something grabbed my arm. I spun around, relaxing when I realized it was Trent. He pulled me along, and we crept forward until we were halfway through the exposed area.

The other two sharpshooters had already made it safely across and were accompanied by Samuel. Everyone else had already moved on. From what I could see in the communal light beyond Samuel looked pissed, but you know what? He could kiss my ass. If he'd seen what I had, he'd be shitting his pants.

Trent and I were three quarters of the way across when I lost my footing. I was able to right myself, but a loud scuffle sounded from my shoes. Trent and I froze for an instant, then scurried forward as fast as we could. Just as we made it around the corner, a horrendous, inhuman shriek boomed through the passageway.

Fuck, it had heard us! Had it seen us too?

Trent and I kept moving, nearly plowing into Samuel.

"Stay where you are and be quiet," he hissed. "Not a peep. Don't even breathe."

The mother Reaper's loud, pounding footsteps and low guttural growls came closer and closer. I squished my body against the concrete wall behind me, freezing myself in place. As the monster neared, its foul, acrid stench washed over me, and I plugged my nose, breathing through my mouth as faintly as possible.

The footsteps stopped. I could feel it just around the

corner. It sniffed the air heavily, but didn't move any closer. It waited there for a long moment, probably hoping one of us would make some kind of noise.

Come on. Go away, go away, go away. Sweat trickled down my face and my hands went clammy.

Finally, the mother Reaper screeched in defeat, its cry blasting through my core as its heavy clawed footsteps echoed away. When I could hardly hear her anymore, I took a deep, grateful breath. That was close, too close.

We followed Samuel without a word, joining our group around the next corner and assuming our former positions.

The next access point wasn't far, and as much as I wanted to talk to Trent about what just happened, I kept my mouth shut. If anyone else was aware of what happened, they were most likely furious with me, and they had every right to be.

If I hadn't looked back, I probably wouldn't have lost my balance. I'd put the entire group in danger, and we'd barely escaped. I sighed, tired of beating myself up. It had been a terribly long day, and I was exhausted and irritable. If this next location was safe we would all be able to rest, then I could worry which asshole would call me out later.

The access point loomed ahead of us now. I watched two sharpshooters from the front climb up the metal ladder, warring concerns crowding my head.

If this location wasn't safe we were still stuck down here in the sewers. We'd have to rest soon, and with the acoustics down here, I seriously doubted we could stop ourselves from snoring and waking up every Reaper around.

But on the other hand, how did we really know we were safe above ground? We'd thought the school was secure, and look what happened there. My shoulders slumped, and I pinched the bridge of my nose. *I'm so done with this shitty day.*

In an odd stroke of luck, the sharpshooters came back down in a few minutes, visibly relieved when they told us the location seemed safe. I was even more relieved when they told us it was a library. As I waited my turn to climb the ladder, my mind flurried with excitement.

Everyone had their thing after the Reaper invasion. Some knitted, some painted. Hell, some had sex with anything on two legs. But for me, reading was my only escape from the shitty world I'd played my part in creating. Besides comics, I had a fondness for anything fantasy. Tolkien, King, Eddings, I loved it all. I just hoped there would be something left up there.

When it was my turn, I ascended the ladder with renewed vigor and hope.Though we'd lost the school, maybe things would be different this time. The books within could have priceless practical knowledge that could make life better for all of us. I gave the sewer one last glance, giving it the finger before entering the treasure trove I would now call home.

CHAPTER EIGHT

*E*merging from the rusty sewer grate, I was instantly surrounded by sights and sounds that eased the weighted tension I'd been carrying all day.

In the dim light of the basement we'd entered, people huddled in small groups, hugging each other with cries of relief or holding hands in circles. The sharpshooters lingered yards away at a door at the top of a small set of stairs, visibly relaxed. Some of them were even smiling.

I couldn't see Trent anywhere, so I wedged through the crowd to take in the rest of the area. As I broke free, I gasped in awe.

The small storage space we'd entered was filled to the brim with row upon row of tall bookshelves. I ran up to the nearest one, letting my fingers graze the aged spines as I inhaled the sweet, musky smell of old books. Some of them had been roughed up or torn apart, but the majority of them were still in one piece. I was nearly salivating with excitement. If our stay here panned out, I would have time to read them all if I wanted.

Suddenly, someone grabbed my arm in an iron vice,

pulling me away from the books. I turned my head and sneered. *Samuel.* His face was filled with rage as he led me back to a corner of the room.

I snatched my arm back, rubbing at it to soothe the slight aching pain. "What's your problem?"

"Do you have *any* idea how much danger you put us in?"

"What are you talking about? We made it here in one piece."

Samuel pointed a finger right in my face. "You know exactly what I'm talking about. The nesting Reapers. How could you have been so careless, so stupid?"

I glared back at him, clenching my fists. I didn't know if it was the fatigue or just his stupid face, but I was done with Samuel's shit.

Several people had gathered around us, one of them Trent. He moved to join me, but I held up a hand to stop him. This was my fight.

I crossed my arms. "I wasn't being careless *or* stupid. I lost my footing, and it's not my fault. I'm done trying to live up to your ridiculous expectations."

Samuel's face contorted in fury, then he laughed. "We've been far too lenient on you, you little shit. But that's going to stop right here. You're going to pull your weight, and if you don't--"

"Stop!"

The small circle of people that had amassed broke, and Mom stormed through, her dark brown eyes dangerous. "Samuel, what do you think you're doing?"

"What should have been done a long time ago. Disciplining your spoiled son."

Mom stepped between Samuel and me, getting right in his face. "Who the hell do you think you are? Gregory is *my* son, and he doesn't need discipline. What he needs is understanding."

She gave a brief glance to the crowd surrounding us. "Look around, Sam. Can't you see how tired everyone is? We barely escaped the Reapers, and instead of ensuring our safety you're blaming my son for something that isn't his fault. Is this what you call leadership?"

Samuel glowered at my mom. I'd never seen him look at her like that, but she didn't back down. After several tense moments Samuel grunted, giving me a hateful scowl before he walked off to the sharpshooters. "What are you waiting for? Secure the perimeter!"

The sharpshooters and Samuel left through the door at the top of the stairs, shutting it with a bang. My eyes lingered on it, anger and bitterness coursing through my veins. I wanted to run after him, beat him senseless in front of the other sharpshooters. But what good would that do? Everyone already hated me, and you know what? I hated them too.

The onlookers around us dispersed, leaving Mom, Trent, and me alone.

Mom turned to Trent. "Could you give us a moment please?"

"Sure thing, Ms. M." Trent wandered off with a lingering look in my direction.

Once he was gone, Mom frowned as she scanned my face. "Gregory, are you all right?"

"Do I *look* all right?"

"I'm sorry that Sam got out of control. I promise--"

I scoffed. "What could you promise me that would mean anything, Mom? Samuel's been throwing me under the bus for as long as I can remember, and you just sit there while he trash talks me. I heard him today when you were talking in your quarters. He was telling you what a little shit I am and you said nothing!"

"That's not what happened."

"Save it." I turned on a heel and stomped over to a dense cluster of bookshelves where I could be alone.

I picked up a book and scanned through the first few pages to try and calm myself, but I was too pissed off. We'd only just gotten here, and already Samuel was shaming me in front of everyone like some stupid little kid. I don't know why I thought things would be any different away from the school. No matter where I went, this weight on my shoulders just followed me. When would it lift, when would it all stop?

I closed the book with a thump and sat down in the secluded corner of the room, letting my rampant thoughts run amok. It didn't make me feel any better, but at least it passed the time.

Some time later, the door to the basement opened. One of the sharpshooters announced that the main area of the library was secured and we could settle in for the night, but not to wander off.

Mom told everyone to go upstairs and find a place to rest in groups. Those who weren't completely beat were to meet with her once they settled in so they could find extra supplies.

I listened intently as our group filtered out of the basement. Once everyone was gone, I'd follow them and find my own place to sleep for the night. I didn't care if the entire library wasn't secure. I wanted to be alone, and I needed time to think things through.

The basement grew quieter and quieter, and finally I decided to emerge from my hiding spot. I switched my flashlight on and fast-walked towards the door, but before I could reach it, Mom slid out in front of me, arms crossed.

I rolled my eyes. *Great.*

"Gregory, we're not done talking."

"Jesus, you waited here in the dark? Why can't you just leave me alone?"

"Because I'm your mother, and I love you."

I grunted. "You've got a funny way of showing it." Mom's eyes looked watery, but I wasn't going to apologize. She'd been a factor in the escalation of my bullying whether she wanted to admit it or not.

"You know, it's not easy being second-in-command. I didn't want this responsibility, but it was the only way to protect all of our livelihoods."

"Oh, like how Samuel *screwing you* is protecting our livelihood?"

A sudden, hard slap from my mom sent painful tingles through my face. I stared at her in disbelief, holding my throbbing face with a hand.

"Don't you dare talk to me like that! I have given up *everything* for our life in this community."

Tears filled my eyes as I glared at my mom. I dodged around her and ran up the stairs to the library before she could say anything else.

On the ground level, I hardly acknowledged my surroundings as I raced past groups of fatigued people that gathered in wide aisles between bookshelves. Just looking at them made me more enraged. I was tired of running, tired of being treated like some freak of nature, tired of this freaking trainwreck of a world.

Once I was a good distance away from everyone, I turned to an empty, dark aisle of my own. I sat down in the darkness, struggling to keep my eyes open. My whole body ached with a dull throb, and while I was still furious I knew I needed to rest, if only for a little while. I would figure it all out soon. A strategy to deal with the Reapers, a plan to keep us protected, a way to free myself from my personal hell. I rested my eyes, just for a moment ...

∽

I JOLTED AWAKE, drawing my knife from my holster on reflex. I held it out to the enveloping darkness around me, waving it left to right and daring whatever Reaper lurked to come at me. After several long moments, I sheathed my short blade. *God damn Reaper nightmares.*

I grabbed my flashlight and shined it around me. Trent slept nearby, curled up in a fetal position and lightly snoring. I smiled to myself, glad he found me after the drama from last night. I wasn't in any mood at the time, and I couldn't afford to alienate him.

I glanced at my watch in the secondary light: 3 a.m. I considered going back to sleep, but I was wide awake. Dreaming of flesh-eating monsters tends to do that to you. I did a quick stretch, then got up on my feet. This was the perfect time to seek out some of those books I craved so desperately, and I could learn the layout of the library in the process. I strapped my knapsack on and left my aisle of bookcases.

I headed back towards the entry of the library where everyone had settled for the night. I hadn't taken the time to see what kind of barricade we'd managed to scrounge up, and I needed to know just how safe we really were here.

I didn't want to wake anyone, so I crept forward on my toes. Small groups of our people slept close together, heads resting on their supply bags or small stacks of books.

As I passed by, I flashed my light on the ends of the aisles nearest me and grimaced. Nonfiction. Blech! Who needs that when you can have magic and mystery?

I left the populated area and approached the entrance beyond the checkout area, keeping my flashlight aimed at the ground. The sharpshooters would be standing guard, and I didn't want to alert them to my presence.

Nearing the last row of bookcases before the entryway, I crept behind it for cover. In the partial moonlight that seeped through, four sharpshooters stood behind two large glass doors, talking to one another in hushed tones. Several more human-shaped forms laid down on the ground nearby, more gunmen I assumed. Barricading the entry were a series of overturned tables and desks, and nearby windows were covered with wooden boards.

That was our defense? This was nothing compared to our setup at the school. I guessed we could count ourselves lucky that no Reapers had come by the entrance from outside, but the rinky dink fortification wouldn't last against a Reaper or two, let alone a cloaked one.

Disappointed, I went back the way I came, eager to scope out the rest of the library before all hell broke loose again.

The carpeted path narrowed before opening back up again into a space that seemed untouched by the past five years.

A number of short bookcases coated in thick layers of dust rounded the perimeter of the large, vaulted room. In its center was an open reading area with old, comfy-looking sofa chairs. Further out were more rows of tall, neglected bookcases. I grinned from ear to ear. This was breathtaking compared to the crappy library we'd had back at the school.

I waved my flashlight around enthusiastically, squealing when I saw the grimy sign hanging overhead titled *Fiction*.

My chest warmed at the thought of reading some of the great books of the past. I'd have to be really selective for now, at least until we got a *real* barricade up. I approached the bookcase before me and started rifling through its contents.

"Quite the selection, huh?" someone said behind me.

I jumped, spinning around and flashing my light on the intruder. I sighed in relief. "Jesus, Trent, you've gotta stop doing that."

Trent shrugged with a frown. "Sorry, guess I just have bad timing. How are you feeling?"

"What do you mean? I'm fine, I just needed some sleep. We all did after yesterday's shitstorm."

Trent meandered up to the far end of the bookshelf I was sorting through and inspected a book spine with his flashlight. "I meant from earlier. You know, the thing with Samuel and your mom."

I rolled my eyes. *Not this again.* I set the book I was glancing at down and placed my hands on top of the bookcase "Listen, can we not?"

The same anger from yesterday bubbled up inside me, but I couldn't bear to expose Trent to it. I broke off, walked into the open reading area, and started pacing.

Trent's scuffled footsteps followed behind me. "Why are you pushing me away? I just want to know what's going on with you."

The errant emotions inside me reached a sudden fever pitch, and I spun on one heel to face Trent. "You wanna know what's going on with me? Fine. Everyone still hates me, we have no plan for the future, and this whole situation is totally fucked!"

My vision went blurry as warm tears spilled down my cheeks. "Do you seriously think we'll last long here? How many times have we moved in the past five years? We hardly know more about the Reapers than we did from day one. How are we going to get back to the way things were if all we ever do is survive? God *damn it!*" My voice cracked.

"We're going to figure it out, Gregory. We can fortify the walls, grow crops, come up with a real plan this time. Let's talk to the others, make them hear us out." Trent laced his fingers through mine and pulled me close.

Looking into his beautiful green eyes, my worries started to drift away. Trent had such faith in me, in our group. But was he right? Could we really make a home here? If he truly believed, then I had to at least try.

"You really think we have a chance?"

"Yeah, what more do we have to lose? We're in this together, and if they won't listen, we can make it on our own. Where you go, I go."

Trent closed the distance between us. His soft lips caressed mine, and a jolt shot through my body like electricity. I kissed him back, lightly grazing his lips with my tongue. The next thing I knew, our arms were wrapped around each other. I kissed him deeply, fiercely, and he returned the favor. My hands groped around his body blindly. I had no idea what I was doing, but it felt freaking fantastic. I wanted to explore every part of him.

After what felt like a brief moment in an endless sea of affection, Trent broke off from me, adjusting his jeans and patting down his messy brown hair.

"Sorry, you *really* got me excited. I didn't want to do anything we'd regret later by moving too fast."

Heat rushed to my cheeks, and I chuckled nervously. "Yeah, we're kind of exposed here too. We would definitely need some privacy … You know, uh, if we ever did something."

Trent grinned. "Yeah. Hey, would you hate me if I headed back? I'm still pretty tired, but we can talk more in the morning."

"Sure."

"Thanks for understanding. I'll head back first, then you can follow a minute or so later if you're done looking at books. Don't want to give everyone another reason to hate us, right?"

"Yeah, that's probably best." I had enough issues on my plate that I didn't need to add any more.

Trent started walking away, then stopped and turned around. "Hey, Greg?"

I took a step forward. "Yeah?"

Trent opened his mouth to say something, then his gaze flickered behind me, his expression morphing into sheer terror. A sudden burst of static energy boomed behind me.

"Reaper door!" Trent shouted at the top of his lungs.

I spun around, my blood turning cold. Right in front of me was a Reaper door. Instead of the rickety door from my nightmares in my old basement, this door was burgundy and panelled like others I'd seen in the library. Smoke filtered out from underneath it at an alarming rate.

I started to back away. Any moment and--

The Reaper door swung open. A cloaked Reaper emerged, ducking its head to fit through.

My hands went clammy as I quaked in terror. *Fuck, fuck, fuck!* What should I do? Run, fight?

The Reaper stood erect at its full height, towering over me and eyeing me with dangerous, intelligent yellow eyes.

I whimpered.

"Take cover, Gregory!" someone shouted from my far right.

The familiar voice snapped me out of my fear, and I bolted to my left where the taller bookshelves would help cover me. As I ran, a series of deafening gunshots fired, followed by a shriek of pain from the Reaper.

I glanced over my shoulder, then stopped in my tracks. Two guards stood a dozen feet away from the Reaper, armed with rifles. The Reaper was hunched over, but in a quick moment it stood back up. Its long, spindly fingers pointed at the guards, then it flicked its wrist.

An insane surge of static energy burst in the air, and both of the guards went flying, smashing into the far wall with a crash and falling to the ground. They didn't move.

My stomach churned. Where were the other sharpshooters? If no one slowed down the Reaper, it would go after the rest of our group, especially the women and children.

I drew my Glock from my holster and aimed at the Reaper. Before I could shoot, Trent darted into my line of fire, brandishing a long knife in his hand. The Reaper turned to attack, but not fast enough.

Trent lunged forward, impaling the monster in its side with a fierce battle cry.

The Reaper bellowed, and with another burst of energy Trent soared into the air, crashing into a large bookcase that toppled on top of him.

Trent! God damn it, where *was* everybody? We'd all be dead in no time. The Reaper hadn't found my hiding spot, and it didn't seem to care. The creature approached the two sharpshooters against the far wall.

I leered at the back of the cloaked Reaper's head, rage coursing through my veins. I had to stop it.

In quiet, swift steps I left my hiding spot, scampering forward. All I needed was one good shot and this fucker would be six feet under. I passed the open Reaper door, sinking down on one knee and taking aim at the Reaper's head.

"Burn in hell, asshole." I pressed my finger down on the trigger. A deafening gunblast assaulted my ears as the gun recoiled.

I gasped in shock when I saw the bullet I'd shot spinning in midair, inches from the back of the Reaper's head. It turned to face me, eyeing me menacingly with its gleaming eyes. A small surge of intangible power emitted, and the bullet fell to the ground.

I tried to get up from my position, but another burst of energy radiated and an invisible rigid force enveloped me. I struggled against it, but I could hardly move.

The Reaper raised one of its long hands, and I felt myself lift off the ground. I kicked around like a helpless vegetable, shouting every curse I knew at the beast. It just stood there, staring at me with those predatory eyes.

"What the fuck do you want? You'll never get out of here alive, you bastard!"

The Reaper clenched its hand, and the energy holding me tightened on my neck. I gasped for air as the pressure built, struggling to maintain some kind of controlled breathing.

Slowly, the Reaper walked forward. With each step it took, my body floated backwards a step.

Cold dread filled my core as I realized what was behind me. *The Reaper door.*

As if it heard my thoughts, the skin around the Reaper's eyes squinched, almost as if it were smiling. It flicked its wrist, and in one cruel motion I flew backwards. I hit the ground hard, tumbling as clouds of black smoke smothered around me.

I desperately clawed at my clouded surroundings, coughing as I clutched to a wall and dragged myself up above the black fog. I was on the other side of the Reaper door. I had to get outta here!

Beyond the door frame, the Reaper lurked a dozen feet away. It watched me with an odd expression on its ugly face. Amusement. *No!* I lunged at the door to escape when the Reaper flicked its wrist once more. The door slammed in my face, disappearing before my eyes as if it had never been there.

I stared at the wall in horror. I was alone, trapped wherever the Reapers came from. And I had no way back home.

CHAPTER NINE

hick, black smoke rose up, burning my nostrils and filtering into my lungs. I coughed violently as I pounded at the wall where the Reaper Door no longer was. After several long futile moments I collapsed against it, hot tears streaming down my face.

Trent, Mom, the group. They were all gone. How would I get back to them again? They were still in great danger. The cloaked Reaper ...

A white furious heat spread through my chest and arms, and I banged my fist against the wall again with a cry of desperation. Damn it, this wasn't fair! I didn't deserve to be here. I beat at the wall a few more times before my anger fizzled out.

Nothing good would happen if I kept freaking out like this. I had to face the facts. I had no idea where I was, and unless I figured this out, I would probably never make it back alive.

I covered my nose and mouth with my bandanna, taking a couple breaths to calm myself. The black smoke around me was dissipating, but I still couldn't see anything. I grasped at the wall, pulling myself forward until I broke through the thickest layer. I gaped at the scene before me.

Hanging from the ceiling ahead was an enormous hulking mass of metal bathed in the cold blue light of the room. A bramble of cables and coils wrapped around in an intricate braidwork, ending in three huge, smoking metal heads. Behind the behemoth was an elevated platform with stairs on the right-hand side.

What the hell *was* that thing, and how was there power in here? Better yet, how had the cloaked Reaper operated this monstrosity? I knew they were capable of some form of higher intelligence, but this was insane. There was no way they could've pulled off something like this.

I shook my head. I had to focus on getting out of here. I looked behind me to the small recess I'd come from. The smoke was almost gone, and the faint outline of a door was etched into the wall I'd assaulted moments ago.

Okay, so somehow this high-tech thingamajig did something to create a door capable of transporting me here. And if it brought me here, there had to be a way to send myself back. All I had to do was find it.

I shuffled forward a few steps and nearly lost my balance on something slippery. I gazed at the floor. In the dim icy light, a thick, dark substance was smeared on the ground, leading to the stairs of the platform.

Blood.

I drew my Glock without hesitation, fixing my aim on the stairs as I inched ahead. I wasn't going to be taken by surprise again. Creeping onward, I began my ascent, avoiding the trail of blood. Atop the platform was a kiosk of sorts. I also noticed something sticking out at the top of the platform, but couldn't tell what it was in this crappy light.

When I was halfway up, I realized what it was and jumped back. A person in strange, tailored clothes lay face down on the floor, a lake of deep red, almost purple around them. They had to be dead, but I needed to know for sure.

I inched closer. "H-hello?"

No answer.

Keeping my gun trained on the person, I bent down and pushed their body over, recoiling with a yelp.

The person's face had been completely ripped off. It was little more than a mound of torn flesh and muscle. Flayed bits of skin hung around the edges like they'd been through a paper shredder.

I took a couple deep breaths to steady myself, focusing on what I knew. There were no Reapers present at the moment, and the distinct odor of decay wasn't coming off of this person's body yet. What happened here had to have occurred recently, and the Reaper responsible was probably the cloaked one that had attacked us in the library. Though my group on the other side was still in danger, I was safe for the moment.

A tiny glimmer of hope sparked in me. Maybe I could get the machine operational somehow or find a survivor who could help me.

Edging around the corpse, I approached the kiosk, which turned out to be a bulky computer terminal. There was a large blank central screen with half a dozen smaller ones hovering around it, most of them cracked and broken. I waved a hand between the littler ones; no strings or physical connections. How were they floating on their own? Magnets?

Whatever. I had to get this thing working. In front of the central screen was a keyboard with dozens of oddly shaped buttons and levers, all with strange symbols on them. I hesitantly touched one of the buttons. No response. I touched another, then another and another until I was pounding on all of the keys.

In a sudden blaze of orange, the main screen and several of the smaller ones jolted to life. I winced at the brightness, glancing sideways to allow my vision to adjust before focusing back on the center monitor.

Across the bright orange background, oddly-shaped crimson characters in a foreign language scrolled in a row, pulsing with urgency. In the right-hand corner, a red blinking light flared angrily next to an icon that resembled an empty gauge. Whatever the computer was trying to tell me, it wasn't good.

I slammed my hands on the terminal. *Damn it!* I had to get back to Trent, Mom, and the others before things spiraled out of control with the cloaked Reaper. If they hadn't already …

My options were extremely limited now. If I wanted to get back home, I'd have to find someone to help me fix this machine, and that meant leaving this room.

My stomach lurched. Nothing about this felt right. I had no idea where I was, who the people here were, or how they managed to maintain electricity for this long. And that wasn't even considering the possibility of other Reapers lurking around.

You don't have a choice anymore. Just look for an exit and be brave like Mom always said.

I climbed down the steps of the platform and glanced about the blue-lit smoky room. I didn't see a door anywhere, and in my confusion I did a quick double take. What kind of room doesn't have any doors?

I walked over to the nearest wall and began grasping around. There had to be something here; a switch, a lever, hell, another magic door. I had almost done a complete rotation of the room when a soft glow on the wall ahead of me drew my attention.

Scampering up to the light, I discovered a small computer

screen attached to the wall, lit up in a light blue background. The same unknown characters from the other monitor scrolled across it, pulsating. I inspected the device. Just like before, no connections. We had never invented technology like this.

Unlike the kiosk computer, this screen had no keyboard, but there were half a dozen buttons displayed on the monitor. Was I supposed to touch it? I tapped a red oval-shaped button. Instantly, the room's temperature soared. Sweat beaded on my forehead and my neck, rolling down my back.

"Ah!"

I quickly pressed a similarly-shaped blue button. The heat subsided, replaced with an icy chill that made my teeth chatter. Frantic, I smacked the next button, a purple rectangular. A weird sucking sound emitted nearby. Ten feet away, the indentation of a door appeared where there wasn't one before.

For a moment I stood there, perplexed. The huge hulking machine that brought me here, the strange language on the monitors, the other advanced technology I'd never seen before. Something wasn't right here, something I couldn't quite put my finger on.

With no other options, I approached the door, noting with dread that there was no knob to it. But as I got closer, the door slid open sideways. I gagged as an overwhelming stench of death flooded in, my heart stopping when my eyes fixed on the destruction and chaos.

"Oh my god."

CLUSTERS of broken bodies lay scattered across the long, vaulted area before me. Some were slumped over lab tables and strange equipment I couldn't name, while others were sprawled out on the floor in lakes of crimson. None of them moved.

The laboratory was lit by blinking red lights that made the carnage seem worse, like something I'd seen in the scary movies I used to watch as a kid.

I shuddered involuntarily as I stepped into the hall, redrawing my gun from its holster. With a bloodbath like this, Reapers couldn't be far away. At the same time, I had to help these people if I could. They could tell me what this place was and who they were, but most of all they could help me get back home.

As I inched into the space, a dozen towering tubes stood on either side of me, each ten feet tall with a wide girth. All of them were broken from the inside, and shards of glass littered the floor in every direction. I looked inside the nearest tube, finding smears of thick, black ooze. Reapers must've been contained in these pods, but why?

I suppressed my curious wanderings. *Focus on your surroundings. You have to get home.*

I neared the first still forms on the ground several feet away, my shoes crunching on broken glass. All of them had been ripped to shreds, faces, arms, and legs just large mounds of eviscerated flesh and bone. The stench of death and decay was ungodly, and a sudden rush of nausea overtook me.

I scurried away from the gore and dry heaved, hands on my knees. After several gut-wrenching moments, I regained my composure and tied my bandanna over my nose and mouth. I couldn't afford to get sick now. I'd have to keep a distance and focus on the chest of each body. If it didn't rise and fall with life, I'd keep moving.

I broke past the tubes, entering the main laboratory area with tables lining both sides of the room. More bodies were strewn on the floor, tables, and against the walls, which were lit up in a sea of colored blinking lights.

Once again I noted the odd, tailored clothes these people wore. Where the blood hadn't reached, they seemed clean, unlike my scuffed, torn jeans and raggedy shirt. I glanced over them, but everything was still. They couldn't all be dead, could they?

On several of the tables sat small cylinders about a foot wide in a variety of vivid colors. A few had been cracked open, but most of them were still intact and had bizarre-shaped forms within them. My curiosity peaked, and I approached the one closest to me. I peered inside, shrinking back when the contents of the tube drifted to face me.

Within the containment pipe was a monstrosity that made my stomach lurch. It looked like a jellyfish, if you stuck one in nuclear waste and allowed it to mutate for a century or two.

The weird jellyfish creature had a fleshy, ribbed head that oozed a thick, black liquid. Three beady lifeless eyes gazed back at me, and a short, curved beak protruded below them. The long, thin tentacles that dangled from its lower half had little spikes every few inches that glowed green in the amber liquid it was submerged in.

I broke off from the table, trying to keep myself calm when sudden movement flashed in my peripheral. I spun to my left. In the corner of the room, a large bundle of dirty, bloody sheets laid in a pile. The topmost sheet rose and fell gently, as if with breath.

I hurried over to the heap, gun aimed on the sheets. I was scared shitless, but tried to sound brave. "Hello? Who's there? Show yourself, or I swear to God I'll shoot!"

Underneath the sheets I saw movement, followed by a muffled groan.

"I'm not playing with you. I *will* shoot."

All movement and sound under the pile stopped.

Fuck. This had my death certificate written all over it, but there wasn't much else I could do. If there was someone alive under all this crap, they could be my ticket out of here.

Cursing my rotten luck, I inched over and sifted through layers of soiled sheets with one hand while keeping my Glock fixed on the center of the mass. As I pulled back the third thin layer of cloth, the inhabitant beneath was revealed.

"Ah!" I jumped back in shock, slipping on something wet and falling on my butt. My pulse beat in my eardrums as I stared forward in total disbelief.

Before me was a ... what *was* it? It had a human-like face and seemed male, but with stark differences. Large dark freckles framed the being's high cheekbones and ran up the sides of his forehead where two small horns made of skin peaked out. His tan face was scrunched in pain, eyes closed, and his dark brown hair hung limply around his shoulders.

Whatever I was looking at, it couldn't be human. Damn it, where the hell was I?

The alien opened its eyes, and I gasped. What should've been the whites of his eyes was black, and his irises were an eerily vivid green color. He said something to me in a foreign language that varied in pitch and sounded almost musical. I gaped at him and he repeated the bizarre phrase in his baritone voice, the intonation rising at the end.

Okay, it was asking me something. I lowered my bandanna off my face and shook my head. Not knowing what else to do, I trained my gun back on him. "Who. Are. You?" I enunciated clearly.

The alien yelped and grimaced, clutching his side. He repeated the undecipherable words he'd said to me a second time, pointing to the wall near me that was lit up like a christmas tree.

I glanced at the blinking blanket of lights, then back to the alien. I think he wanted me to help him, but I wasn't sure if I could really trust him. I mulled it over for a moment, deciding to go along with the alien's wishes. Though I had no idea who he was, he wasn't a threat, at least not yet. Besides, I had a freaking gun. He couldn't do much of anything to me when he was clearly injured.

I got up on my feet, facing him as I inched over to the flashing wall. "What now?" I gestured around me and shrugged.

The alien pointed at the red blinking light in front of me and motioned for me to press the button.

I did as he instructed, and a drawer emerged with a strange sucking sound. I looked inside at its contents, grabbing the first thing I saw. I displayed the strange baton-shaped mechanism to the alien. "This?"

He nodded, then gestured again to the bin, making a circle motion with a finger.

Okay, something circular. I rifled around the drawer's weird objects, settling on a small, stretchy band that formed a circle, kind of like the resistance bands my mom used to work out with once upon a time. The only difference was that this device had a small mechanical section in the middle. Teeny characters in an unknown language flashed on a tiny screen with several buttons.

I showed the alien the object and he bobbed his head, signaling me to come to him. Once I was within arm's reach, he gestured for me to put the circular device around my neck.

I froze. Should I give this alien the benefit of the doubt and put the doohickey on? What if it choked me to death?

So far he'd done nothing to harm me, though he didn't really have a chance to yet. He seemed gentle, maybe even kind. Despite the past five years' experience of interactions with others screaming at me to not trust him blindly, something in my gut told me I wasn't in danger.

Before I could overthink the situation any more, I slipped

the circular mechanism over my neck. Automatically the device constricted, pulling closer to my skin. At first I freaked out and pulled at it, but relaxed when it stopped a comfortable distance from my skin.

The device's screen blinked green, and a sudden wave of dizziness washed over me. I grabbed onto the table nearest me. It felt like my head had been tickled from the inside somehow.

"Please, help me," a familiar voice said.

I turned my head and stared at the alien. Was that him?

"Please, help me," he repeated. Though the words didn't match the shapes his lips made, the pitch of his voice matched perfectly.

"Holy shit, I can understand you! How is this even possible?"

The alien shook his head. "There is no time. The other device you found. You have to use it on my wound before it gets infected."

I knelt down in front of him, unsure what to do next. "How is this thing supposed to help you?"

"Press it against my skin near the wound."

The alien lifted the bottom of his well-tailored shirt, exposing an injury I'd seen time and time again. A Reaper slash, three bloody claw marks. The wound was deep, but my eyes were fixated on the color of his blood. It was abnormally dark, almost purple.

"When the device makes contact with my skin, press the button on the side," the alien instructed.

I pressed the small wand against his skin and pushed the button. A strange hissing sound came from it, and several small black globules emerged from the tip of the device, delving into the alien's open lacerations with a life of their own.

The alien cried out in agony.

I sat there dumbfounded until my thoughts finally caught up with me. "Are you okay? What is that stuff?"

The alien winced as he propped himself up into a sitting position. "Yes, I will be alright. The nanites will heal me from the inside out. It will take a while for my pain to lessen." He spared a quick glance at me, narrowing his gaze. "Ungh, you are … human."

"Of course I'm human. What else would I be?"

The alien gave me a puzzled look, but didn't answer my question. "How did you get here?"

I paused, unsure how to respond. It was probably best to keep my explanation simple in case he ended up being dangerous. "A door appeared in the library and a Reaper tossed me inside."

The alien's green eyes widened. *"Ree-purr? Lie-buh-rare-y?"*

An inhuman shriek of rage sounded nearby, and I froze as adrenaline surged through my veins.

"Quick, hide with me under the sheets before it sees us!"

I looked hesitantly at the alien. While I had my gun, I didn't have unlimited ammo. If more Reapers came, I'd need to conserve my supply. The Reaper's loud, pounding footsteps approached dangerously fast. Spiting this never-ending shitstorm, I dove under the bloody sheets with the alien next to me.

He pulled several layers of cloth over us. "Breathe softly."

I rolled my eyes. "I know that."

The whole room went quiet except for the Reaper's movement. Its thunderous, quaking footsteps came closer, closer, until its dark shadow engulfed the light filtering through the layers of sheets on top of us.

The beast lingered, and it took all of my willpower to stay still. *Go away, go away. Please, just go away.* The seconds dragged on until the Reaper screeched in anger, rushing off with heavy, earth-shaking steps.

After its noisy departure, I cautiously removed the soiled sheets on top of the alien and me. The coast was clear, for now. "Looks like we got lucky. Are you feeling better yet?"

He put a six-fingered hand near his diminishing wound before wincing and shaking his head. "I will … require your assistance, if you are able."

I got up to my feet, then offered him a hand and hoisted him up with a grunt. "What's your name?"

"I am Ja'tare."

Juh-tar-eh, I sounded out in my head. Man, they had strange ways of naming people here.

"Gregory." I held out my hand.

Ja'tare eyeballed my hand suspiciously, then poked it with a finger. "*Grey-gor-ie.*"

"No, no. *Greh-gor-ie*, and you're supposed to shake my hand."

He shook my hand with two fingers. "*Greh-gor-ie*," he said long and slow.

Acceptable enough. "Right."

Introductions aside, Ja'tare staggered off, tying his stringy shoulder-length brown hair into a knot atop his head. He opened several drawers set in the blinking wall of lights and sorted through them.

Now that I could observe Ja'tare without scrutiny, I was more perplexed than before. Everything about him was so foreign. He was extremely tall and lanky, towering over me by half a foot and wearing what resembled black military boots and baggy pants that tapered at the legs. His tailored short-sleeved shirt had an elevated neck and was textured on the top half with a cracked neon green column in the middle, six inches in length.

Just who was Ja'tare and his people, and where were we?

Ja'tare came back towards me, stuffing a small cylinder into his pants before adjusting a strange set of mechanical cuffs around his wrists.

"What are those for?"

Ja'tare grimaced. "Protection, should we need it." He touched the damaged column of his shirt, which gave a high-pitched beep in response. "Ja'tare to Kro'da, can you hear me?" He paused for a moment with no response. "I repeat, Ja'tare to Kro'da, can you hear me?"

After another brief silence, Ja'tare gave up. "We have to go now. My communications are down and it is not safe here."

"Wait, leave? But I can't go! I have to return through the door that brought me here. I have to get back to my family. They're going to die without me!"

I spun around and took a step towards the strange room I'd come from, but Ja'tare grabbed my arm.

"Let go of me."

Ja'tare released me. "I apologize, I should not have done that. But we can not go back. I do not know how to operate the portal generator."

I turned back around. "Portal ... *generator?*"

"Yes."

"Who *can* work the machine?"

Ja'tare gestured to the shredded bodies strewn across the laboratory. "They would, if they were still alive."

I planted a hand on my forehead. *Shit.* What was I supposed to do now? I couldn't just leave without trying to go back, but according to Ja'tare there was no way back, at least not here.

"Are there other portal generators around?" I asked.

"Yes, but not nearby. We can travel to them, but we must reach safety first."

At Ja'tare's words, my gaze fixated on the door to the portal generator room, Trent and Mom's faces flashing in my mind. There really was no easy way back to them right now. They'd have to fend for themselves, but I had faith that they would be alright. Mom was a badass in battle, and Trent was smart. Surely they'd find a way to escape the cloaked Reaper or incapacitate it somehow.

I hesitated another moment. *Hold on, just a little longer.*

I focused back on Ja'tare, propping my hands on my hips. "All right, fine. I'll go with you. Where are we heading?"

"To my people. They'll protect us." Ja'tare pointed towards a small opening on the right edge of the room. "We can leave that way. There is a side exit we can use to get outside without detection."

Together we entered the tiny hallway, just wide enough for us to walk through. I followed Ja'tare down the passage, then we stopped at a small side panel with an image of a palm displayed on it.

Ja'tare pressed his hand against it, and the outline of a door appeared and opened for us. A gust of cool fetid air blasted me and I stumbled outside, overcome by my surroundings.

The ground beneath me was black and brittle with strange, gray petalless flowers scattered sparsely. Up above, the sky was dark, threatening green and gray clouds looming. To the west, two suns rose from opposing sides of the atmosphere towards each other.

My body went ice cold. Where was I? Was I even on ... No, no, no! This couldn't be happening!

I spotted a small elevated hill ahead of me and bolted for it.

"Gregory, stop!" Ja'tare called after me.

But I couldn't. I had to know what lay beyond, I had to know the truth. I reached the top of the hill in several desperate lunges, and my body trembled at the sight of the bizarre landscape before me.

An enormous city of broken black spires sat in the distance, crumbling and smoking in a gray haze. Further beyond, blue, holey mountains stood, a bright violet glow emanating from within that reminded me of lava. The sky above erupted in daisy chains of purple lightning, and as reality sunk in, I fell to my knees.

I was no longer on Earth.

Blinding purple spears of light crackled across the dark sky, illuminating the vast, foreign terrain as my stomach flip flopped. I was no longer on Earth, I couldn't believe it. Trent and Mom were millions, maybe billions of miles away, and the only salvation I had was following some alien deeper into this unknown planet.

Movement from my vantage point atop the hill caught my attention. In the gray valley below, a horde of Reapers scurried about in groups on four legs. Thick veins spread from enormous sacs of Reaper spawn, stretching out on the ground in a hundred directions.

A wave of dizziness hit me, and for a second I thought I was going to pass out. I'd never seen this many Reapers in one place. Getting anywhere was going to be nearly impossible if the rest of the planet was overrun like this. How would we even survive?

I backed away and plopped on the ground, wrapping my arms around my knees as hot tears ran down my face. This was all so hopeless. "Why is this happening to me? How am I ever going to get back home to Mom and Trent? Where *am* I?"

I sobbed, resting my head on my knees.

A hand rested on my shoulder. *Ja'tare.* I turned my head, his distorted lanky form like something out of a funhouse mirror through my teary vision.

"Are you alright?" Ja'tare leaned in closer to me. "There is water coming out of your eyes."

My face heated up. "I'm crying, okay? Humans do it when they're sad. Geez."

Ja'tare's face scrunched up. "I see. I am … sorry for what has happened to you. You are correct, we are not on your home world. This is the planet Velerius, home to my people, the Veloxans. You wish to go back to Earth, correct?"

"V-Velerius?" I sniffled. "Yes, I have to get back to my family. Wait, how do you know about Earth and us humans?"

Ja'tare shuffled on his feet. "It is a long tale, but I can tell you on the way. We really should get moving. It is not safe here."

Despair wracked my body in a frigid, numbing vice, and I kicked the dirt at my feet. "Just leave me. I'm sure the Reapers would love a snack."

"Why do you keep saying that? *Ree-purr?* Do you mean the Dak'kar?"

I flicked a wrist dismissively. "Sure, whatever. I'll tell them you said hi. See ya."

I fixed my blurred gaze back on the ominous, hellish world before me.

"Gregory, getting back to Earth will be difficult, but it is not impossible. If you stay here, you will most certainly perish. You must make a decision before it is too late. You can come with me now, or stay and die." He hesitated a moment before speaking up again. "What would this Mom, this Trent do without you?"

Ja'tare's rational words struck a chord in me. If I stayed around here, the Reapers would find me and I'd never see Mom or Trent again. But they needed me, and Ja'tare's people had the technology to send me back to them. Even if I only had a shot in hell, following Ja'tare to the other Veloxans was better than waiting to be ripped apart by Reapers. If we made it, we could find the nearest portal generator and they could work their high-tech magic to get me home.

I wiped my eyes, dusted off my ragged jeans, and got up on my feet. "All right, I'll go with you. Which way are we headed?"

"Follow me." Ja'tare walked down the worn dirt trail away from the valley of Reapers.

I stalked after him, trying to keep up with his long strides, but my exotic surroundings were a huge distraction. Beyond the black dirt path and sprinkling of petalless gray flowers, large and curved leafless trees were scattered around the area. They resembled a mix between question marks and tentacles, and while I watched them I could've sworn I saw some of them curl the slightest bit.

Beyond the trees, bizarre, towering rock formations loomed in semi-translucent shades of blue, gray, and green. Their angular jutting shapes reminded me of crystals and rock candy.

Man, this was a weird planet.

After a couple minutes of shadowing Ja'tare, the path dead-ended at an enormous mountain of rock that dwarfed all the others I'd seen. It had to be at least fifty feet tall.

What did he want us to do? We couldn't climb the damn thing.

"Um, this is a dead end," I pointed out.

Ja'tare picked up a nearby purple stone and tossed it at the crystalline height.

It vanished as it made contact.

I gaped in disbelief. "What the hell just happened?"

"This is a hologram. My people created this one and others to misdirect the Dak'kar so we could travel freely without being hunted."

"Whoa, seriously? The level of detail is amazing, just like in the fiction novels I read."

"*Fik-shun?* What's that?"

Really? I thought about how to explain it for a sec. "They're um, entertaining stories that humans like to tell each other even though they're not true."

Ja'tare tilted his head at me.

"Never mind, forget it."

"All right. Shall we?" Ja'tare approached the rock formation and plunged a six-fingered hand through it. He withdrew his hand, showing it to me. "See? It is safe, nothing to worry about."

I walked up beside Ja'tare and tested it out for myself. "Son of a bitch, this is really happening. Yeah, let's do this."

Ja'tare walked directly into the hologram, and I followed. As I made contact with the false image, a kaleidoscope of bright vivid colors assaulted my eyes in swirling, merging patterns. I stepped forward in awe, and the dazzling array gave way to dull, diminished light.

Before me was a winding, narrow path, not much wider than Ja'tare and I. Surrounding us on both sides were the same curled trees I'd seen before, clustered tightly together and extending overhead, partially blocking what little illumination there was from the dim-lit sky.

I squinted. "It's dark here."

"My apologies. Veloxan eyes have developed to see in almost complete darkness due to our dark atmosphere." Ja'tare searched through his pockets, pulling out a small transparent sphere and handing it to me.

He motioned for me to hold it on top of my palm, and I mimicked him, giving it a quick tap at his request. The ball came to life, glowing a soft blue color and levitating from my hand. I stared into the comforting light. *Whoa, cool.*

"Is the light sufficient?" Ja'tare asked.

"Um yeah, thanks," I muttered. I took a step forward, and the floating sphere trailed me. A step back, and it adjusted to stick with me.

We continued along the passage, Ja'tare always a couple long strides ahead of me. We walked in silence, but the further we went more and more questions popped into my head about who his people were, where we were headed, and how he knew about my race until I couldn't take it anymore.

"Hey, wait up."

Ja'tare slowed down, allowing me to catch up. He watched me with curiosity. "Is there something on your mind? Your face is having strange spasms."

"Yeah, sorry. I'm still kind of overwhelmed by all of this. Do you mind if I ask you some questions? I think it'll help me make some sense out of things."

"Of course."

"Alright." I fidgeted, trying to gather my thoughts. "So uh, where exactly are we going again? You said your people are this way, right?"

"Yes. We will head down this path and through the *Valen.* After that, it is a short distance to where my tribe has taken shelter."

"The Valen? What's that?"

"Believe me, you will know when you see it. I will point it out to you."

I shrugged. "Okay." I had no idea what to expect, but it couldn't be any worse than the hundreds of hungry Reapers just itching to tear us apart and fight over the scraps.

Focus, I reminded myself.

"Why were you at the laboratory? Were you working there?"

"No. The Dak'kar around that area are increasing in number exponentially. Our leaders had no choice but to call for an evacuation. They sent me along with a scouting party to make sure everyone left safely, but we were intercepted by Dak'kar on the way and got separated. When I arrived at the laboratory, we were attacked. I was too late …" Ja'tare grimaced.

Though I didn't know him very well, witnessing Ja'tare's guilt made me pity him. I'd seen my own people butchered time and time again, and it never got any easier.

"I'm sorry for your loss," I said. "I've seen some things too, things I'd like to forget. So many humans died, we don't really know how many of us are left anymore. Speaking of my race, how did you know I was human? I've never heard of the Veloxans before now."

Ja'tare smiled weakly, his emerald eyes almost glowing in the dim light. "You're not the first human we've encountered. Far from it, actually. Decades ago, we invented the portal technology that transported you here. The humans were one of the first races we met in our travels."

"I see." I tried to put the puzzle pieces together in my head. The Veloxans had interacted with my people before, but if they already met my race, why weren't they common knowledge? And what about the Reapers? Were they from here?

"We're almost at the Valen," Ja'tare said, his words dashing through my thoughts. "At the top of this hill."

I bit my lip as we climbed up the slope. Whatever this Valen thing was, I was sure it was just as bizarre as everything else on this planet. We came to the crest of the incline, and the narrow path we'd been following opened up into a wide valley. I gasped in awe and astonishment at the other-worldly sight displayed before me.

"Ho-ly shit."

CHAPTER ELEVEN

I soaked in the dazzling alien utopia of the valley below. Massive magnificent trees dotted the expansive area, a mesmerizing canopy of shimmering purple leaves atop them. The leaves reflected the golden light of the planet's two suns, and the grass below was a pink hue, starkly contrasting the black dirt underneath. A faint, sweet aroma drifted through my nose upon a light breeze, and I relished it. Finally, something beautiful in this dismal, gritty world.

I couldn't hold back a smile. "It's amazing."

Ja'tare frowned. "I must warn you. Regardless of how inviting the Valen may seem, this is not a safe place."

I looked again to the forest of glistening white-trunked trees before us. The leaves shifted in the wind, sending a wave of calm over me. "What are you talking about? This place is paradise."

"No, you are wrong. The creatures within this place: the kri, the ipten, even the Valen themselves are predatory." Ja'tare glanced above us, his emerald eyes widening. He pointed to the sky. "Do you see the two suns?"

"Yeah, what about them?"

"When they overlap each other, our journey will become very difficult. We must get through the Valen before that happens."

I followed his gaze. The last time I looked, they *had* been further apart, but what was so threatening about the suns? "Why? What will happen?"

"Just stay close to me. We must get moving. *Now.*"

Ja'tare descended the vale towards the Valen and I trailed after, wondering just how dangerous this oasis really was. I hoped I wouldn't find out.

"Stop here," Ja'tare ordered as soon as we hit the first treeline of the Valen. He scanned left to right, his posture tensing up.

"If you'd just tell me what kind of danger--"

"I just need a few moments. Please, bear with me." Ja'tare stalked the treeline cautiously, not too far from me.

I sighed. Clearly he was being paranoid. There were no animals lurking around, and this close, everything was even more stunning and peaceful than before.

The Valen had thick, elevated roots that created spaces big enough to walk under. Their trunks were pale like ivory, but had a sparkle to them that made them shine as if they were encrusted with diamonds. In the golden, almost orange light of the two suns, they twinkled brilliantly.

With Ja'tare preoccupied, I bent down and snatched a blade of pale pink grass. It was soft to the touch, but fuzzy and thick also. If we got stuck here, I could probably sleep on a bed of it and have no complaints.

Sudden movement caught my attention. A small, furry critter scurried down from one of the nearby Valen trees, skittering within several feet of me. It reminded me of a squirrel, only a bit larger and more exotic; it had the same bushy tail and body type, but its fur was pale green and spotted, and it had big, red catlike eyes.

I froze, unsure what to do. Was this one of the creatures Ja'tare warned me about? I glanced around. He was nowhere to be found. *Well that's just great.*

The little animal scratched its tiny nose with its paws then looked up at me, tilting its head. It hopped a couple feet closer, just outside of arm's reach before sitting up on its hind legs.

I didn't care what Ja'tare said, this squirrel thing was cute. Maybe I could take it with us as a pet. "Aww," I cooed. I bent over to pet the cutie's head.

Right as I was about to touch the animal, a small arrow-shaped pin shot into its side. I jumped back as blue crackles of electric light erupted around its body in violent spurts. It squeaked and spasmed before toppling over on the ground, lifeless.

I whipped around to see Ja'tare standing a dozen feet away. His left arm was outstretched, and the odd cuff thing he'd taken from the lab gave off a thin trail of smoke.

He lowered his arm with a grimace and marched towards me. I trudged towards him just as fast, heat spreading through my chest and face. Ja'tare grabbed me by the shoulders before I could get my mitts on him.

"What were you thinking?" he demanded.

I swatted his hands off me and pushed his chest. "Wrong with *me*? What the hell is wrong with *you*? I was just going to pet the little squirrel and you fucking killed it!"

Ja'tare's expression warred between anger and confusion, and he planted a long hand on his forehead. "That is no … *ska-wuhr-uhl,* or whatever you humans have on your planet. It is an ipto, and I told you they were dangerous!"

"How was I supposed to know what an ipto looks like? That's why I asked you for more information." I crossed my arms. "There's no way that thing was dangerous."

Ja'tare shook his head and strode over to the ipto's corpse. He bent over and opened its mouth.

Rows of tiny razor sharp teeth filled the maw of the innocent-looking animal I was just about to make friends with.

Ja'tare stood erect, then glowered at me in disapproval. "There is much about my world that you do not understand. You are lucky this ipto was not travelling in a pack like they usually do. We cannot afford to be foolish. Now come, we must hurry before the two suns converge."

Ja'tare took off at a brisk pace and I stormed after him, glaring at the back of his head.

How was any of this *my* fault? Ja'tare hadn't explained anything to me. If he would just slow down for a goddamned second we could've avoided the whole stupid situation. God, I couldn't wait to get home. Mom's face flashed in my mind, and I blinked away the tears that welled up in my eyes. She wouldn't have berated me like that.

I walked swiftly to keep up with Ja'tare. Up ahead, another wide treeline loomed with small winding paths curling between the trees. As we approached, the light quality diminished around Ja'tare and me.

I stopped in my tracks and looked around in confusion. The two golden suns above shined just as brilliantly as before. "What's going on?"

"The kri," Ja'tare hissed.

"*Kree*? What's that?"

"Flight-capable creatures known for their hallucinatory abilities. It is not truly darker here, but they must be influencing our minds, trying to throw us off course."

"What do they want?" I asked.

"Most likely they are looking for a meal. They feast off of the dead but are small in stature, so they will probably try to lure us to a bigger creature within the Valen."

I pinched the bridge of my nose with my fingers. It was

just one thing after another on this shitty planet. "Can't we just find another way around?"

"I am afraid not. This is the only way through. Do not worry. As long as you follow me closely everything will be fine. Do you still have the sphere?"

I glanced behind me. "Yes, it's still following me."

"Good, then we should head out. A word of warning before we go. Despite what your senses tell you, focus on me. The kri will do anything to separate us. Ready?"

I gulped. "As ready as I can be."

Together we entered a forked, crooked path of tightly clustered Valen. Unlike the colossal trees I'd seen before, these were much shorter and packed so close that the shimmering purple leaves almost completely blocked out whatever light the two suns would've provided.

With each step I took, the lingering light within the trail faded, like someone had a dimmer switch for the Valen and was screwing with the settings.

I struggled to follow after Ja'tare, squinting as his form threatened to disappear at the edge of my sight. We rounded a sharp turn in the winding trail, and suddenly he vanished from view. I freaked, scrambling ahead, only to stumble on something hard. I fell to the ground with a loud thud.

A searing pain erupted in my left leg. I ignored it, clambering back on my feet in fear that Ja'tare would leave me behind.

Luckily, Ja'tare came back for me, his speckled tan face appearing seemingly out of thin air. "Are you all right?"

"Fine, just slow down," I grumbled. "I can't see well in the dark like you can." I inspected my wound. It hurt but was superficial.

"I will try, but we must hurry before the two suns converge."

"I know, okay? Geez!" Irritated, I snatched the glowing

blue sphere behind me and held it out in front of me as we continued.

If Ja'tare was moving slower, I sure as hell couldn't tell. He stayed at the furthest border of my vision, disappearing only to reappear seconds later. The glowing sphere helped, but only for a short while. The more we twisted and turned our way through the maze of trees, the more the darkness around us seemed to close in, as if it was an evil, living force hellbent on separating us.

I became aware of the heavy pounding in my chest and slowed my pace just a bit, taking several deep breaths. *Stay calm. Think of something pleasant.* I pictured Trent in my mind and the passionate moment we'd shared on the roof of the school, his tender lips on mine that tasted like cinnamon.

A faint flicker of hope sparked within me. I had to make it through this. For him, for Mom, for all of us.

My mind clear, I focused fully on the path only to realize I was alone. I thrust my glowing sphere around in a panic, my stomach clenching. Did Ja'tare seriously leave me behind? He wouldn't, would he? *Oh god, oh god, oh god.*

"Ja'tare?" I called. No answer. "Ja'tare!" Again nothing, but this time my voice sounded dull, as if something was dampening it, keeping it from carrying through the trees.

"Fuck, fuck, fuck!" I scanned the wooded area around me once more. There were several directions Ja'tare could've gone from here, but all the thin paths seemed so similar in the encroaching darkness.

A sudden light flashed in my peripherals, and I looked to my right. A golden orb floated towards me, about the size of my fist. I squinted my eyes. Was that … a creature in the middle creating the light? I couldn't quite discern its features with the bright illumination around it, but its silhouette reminded me of stories I'd read where fairies would lure little girls into rings of toadstools to a magical world.

I wondered if this thing was the kri that Ja'tare had warned me about. Its size and flying ability matched what he had described.

The fairy-like being hovered to me before breaking off and floating to my right on another path, lighting the way. When I didn't follow, it came back and repeated its path. I was pretty sure it wanted me to follow, but if this was a kri, I should run the other way. Even if it wasn't, it could still be dangerous in some way it hadn't shown me yet.

"Screw this." I veered to my left towards another path, but was halted by several more floating orbs that appeared right in front of me. Unlike the first , these ones swayed from left to right in a strange cadence.

They rocked to and fro, then twirled with a strange tinkling sound. A bizarre, intangible weight seemed to press on my mind; then it dissipated as fast as it had come.

A fragment of panic surfaced. What had I been doing out here? There was nothing here but me and these fairies. Of course! I must've come here to watch them.

I smiled as they continued their intricate dance. They were putting on a show for me. I clapped, urging them to continue.

The sprites formed a triangle, moving closer together, then further apart in a slow, delicate waltz. Their hypnotic rhythm had my body swaying with their movements.

"So pretty," I said in awe. I reached up to them with my fingertips.

They swung back and forth in their mesmerizing movements, slowly hovering away from me.

"Hey, where are you going?" I called. "Don't leave me!"

The fairies kept moving, and suddenly the darkness of these woods without their warm, radiating light gave me a chill I couldn't shake.

I ran after them, shadowing their beautiful spectral glow

down a trail thickly clustered with Valen until we entered a clearing about thirty feet wide.

Pale, luminous Valen trees lined the perimeter of the small space, illuminated by a dim but warm golden light. Unlike the other Valen I'd seen thus far, blood colored vines wrapped around them, some hanging from branches above. The centermost tree had tiny circular holes carved into them, lining up higher than I could see. In each cubby a radiant halo pulsated brightly.

My heart bounced in elation. This was where the fairies lived! It was so … "Beautiful," I gasped.

The fairies that led me here swarmed around me, spiraling from my head to my toes before floating off toward the arboreal giants nearby. Whatever they wanted to show me, I had to see it.

I followed after the sprites, swimming in the simple sea of beauty that surrounded me. They stopped around a cluster of vines and flew upwards. As I craned my neck, I gaped at the breathtakingly gorgeous flowers they were rising to.

Three large, bulbous plants were situated above me. Their leaves were buttermilk white with almond-shaped petals, a light shade of purple at their bases. The color cascaded into a rust-colored red at the top. None of them had blossomed, and the fairies elevated higher at a steady pace until their amber glow shone upon them. They wanted to show me the beauty of the flowers!

"Yes, show me!" I cried happily.

The flowers began to shake, then trembled more violently as the golden light of the fairies cast over them. The vines around me began to shake and convulse, and I stared upward, perplexed.

The plants above me awakened, and terror quaked through my body, eradicating whatever spell the kri had put on me. The plants' open faces revealed many rows of razor sharp points embedded into their petals. At their cores were nightmarish mounds of teeth that made up their mouths. I turned to run, but several long fuzzy vines wrapped around my core, constricting so tightly that I couldn't move.

I screamed in horror, kicking my legs as the vines lifted me towards the carnivorous plants. The kri had tricked me, and unless I figured some way out of this, I was going to be their next meal.

CHAPTER TWELVE

I thrashed against the vine's unyielding hold as I was thrust towards the three bloodthirsty plants above me. *I can't die like this! I've gotta get outta here! Think, Gregory, think!*

A cringe-inducing grating sound cleaved through my frantic internal ramblings, and I gaped at the rows of sharp teeth that lined the plants' detached open mouths. They spun in a fast scraping motion, then wheeled in the other direction like mother nature's demented blender.

I twisted and turned, trying to squirm my way free, but the vines enveloping me didn't budge an inch.

My fear intensified. I couldn't just do nothing! If I didn't act now, those evil plants would … "Help!" I cried at the top of my lungs. "Someone help me!"

In response, the vines constricted painfully tighter around me, black spots appearing in my vision.

"Fuck you and your stupid vines!" I snarled.

The kri that awakened the carnivorous plants spiraled downwards, hovering around me. They inched closer, as if inspecting their soon-to-be meal, and I thrashed violently.

"I'm gonna kill every last one of you!"

The vines propelled me past the conniving bottom feeders, and the bleak reality of my situation hit me like a brick wall. There was no one here to help me. No one could hear my cries, would stop the carnivorous plants from cutting me to pieces. It was all ov--

A primal roar blasted into the area. For a moment the vines around me loosened, probably just as surprised as I was by the interruption. In their confusion, I managed to wrench an arm free.

"Let him go!" a familiar voice boomed.

I turned my head towards the sound. Ja'tare's tall, spindly form was crouched in an offensive stance at the entrance of the clearing.

"Ja'tare, help me!"

His gaze darted between me, the nearby kri, and the hungry flesh-eating plants above me. Whatever he had planned, I had to try and free myself now that I had a chance.

I reached behind me with my free hand, desperately scrounging around in my knapsack for my knife and lighter. As I rifled around, several kri flitted towards Ja'tare.

He lifted one of his cuffs and shot three quick electrical pulses at them. The kri went down easily, their golden lights fading out. Others that had flown closer started to back away.

He was winning!

My excitement faltered as other vines hanging limply from the trees awakened. They twisted and contorted, flailing towards him. Ja'tare fired a voltaic charge into the nearest one; it squirmed for a moment, then whipped at him with the others. He lunged back just out of range.

I dug through my bag faster, sweat beading my forehead. Damn it, where was my-- My hands closed around a cylindrical object, and I pulled it out in triumph. My lighter!

I gave another quick look down at Ja'tare. He evaded the vines in quick, graceful movements and had pulled out one of the circular tubes from the lab. With the click of a button, a spear with a glowing green head extended from the cylinder. Another vine flung itself at him. He sidestepped out of the way and pierced it with his spear. The vine blackened and shriveled, convulsing before dropping lifelessly to the ground.

A sudden upward jolt from the vice around me catapulted me back to reality. The bloodthirsty, bulbous plants were just ten feet away now. Their open mouths were wide open, and they writhed about as if they couldn't wait to meet me. At this proximity, I could see that the red at the tips of their fanged petals wasn't their natural color but old, caked blood.

I flicked my lighter and set it against the tiny hairs on the vines, hoping to ignite it, but all they did was sizzle and fall off. I tried pressing the flame directly against the thickness of the vine, but other than creating minor burns, the lighter had no effect.

Shit! Why did I even think the lighter would work? I'd need a freaking flamethrower to get these things off me.

I glanced at the plants above. Six feet now. I desperately reached into the pack on my back, searching for my knife.

Come on, come on ... yes!

I yanked the knife out of my knapsack, only to realize I had to unfurl it one-handed. I picked at the metal poking out at the base with my thumb, but it wouldn't budge. I started messing with the handle again when it fumbled out of my hands and dropped to the ground below.

No! My stomach roiled. It was all over. Unless ...

I turned my neck as far as it would go with the plants wrapped around me. Ja'tare was still fighting off vines, but there were less of them than before. Whatever that green stuff was on the tip of the spear, it was working.

"Ja'tare, I can't get free!" I cried.

Ja'tare looked from me to the vines and back to the spear in his hand. After stabbing another vine he lunged forward, hurling the spear towards me in a graceful overhanded thrust that would make any Olympian green with envy. I cringed as the spear made a huge thunk in a Valen branch several feet away from me.

"Attack the plants!" Ja'tare shouted. "The vines are connected to the--ah!"

I gasped in terror. The vines Ja'tare had been fighting off had wrapped around his ankles. They pulled him to the ground and started dragging him to the same tree as me.

I eyed the nearby Valen branch Ja'tare had pierced. It had quickly turned a sickly blackish brown color. As if they knew what I was planning, the vines holding me propelled me up with a burst of speed. Right before the spear was out of reach, I gripped its handle and plucked it from the branch.

The first of the plants was right up in my face now, its many rows of teeth making their awful grinding sound. I thrust the spear into the center of its unholy mound of sharp teeth. The plant screeched in a high-pitched whine that assaulted my eardrums.

One by one, the carnivorous plant's toothed petals drooped with dull thuds, the brown sickness of the poison spreading like wildfire. The venom circulated through the vines at its base to the other interconnected plants. In seconds they wilted and withered, and with a sudden jolt, the vines holding me slackened and released me.

I screamed as I fell to the ground below, desperately clawing at anything to lessen my fall. *Shit, shit, shiiit!*

I plummeted to the ground, crashing with an impact that obliterated my senses.

I awoke to darkness and a dull throbbing pain that echoed throughout my body. Was I ... alive? What happened?

I felt underneath me. Layers of something soft and fuzzy supported my body. Whatever it was must've cushioned my fall.

Scanning around me, only the tiniest trickles of light filtered through the trees' canopy into the clearing. The kri's golden orbs were gone. They must've fled after the carnivorous plants were destroyed. *Good riddance.*

I wrenched my pack off my back with a moan of discomfort and fished through it for my flashlight, flicking it on once I found it.

Surrounding me was an enormous pile of dead vines. Well that explained why I wasn't a paraplegic right now. I checked myself for injuries. Besides the extreme soreness pulsating through me and several cuts and bruises, I was relatively unharmed.

Ja'tare!

I searched the piles of dead vines with my flashlight, stopping when I located a six-fingered hand poking through the tangles. I forced myself up with a surge of pain and crawled over, every tendon and muscle screaming at me along the way.

When I reached the mass, I ripped and wrenched at the vines, some of them falling apart like soggy paper in my hands. Scrabbling through, I unearthed Ja'tare. He was unconscious with some scrapes and ugly lacerations, but he seemed alright.

I put a hand on his shoulder and shook him. "Ja'tare, wake up! We did it. The plants are dead."

Ja'tare opened his gleaming emerald eyes, then groaned as he tried to sit up.

"Easy, easy. Not too fast. Are you okay?"

Ja'tare winced. "I am in pain, but should be alright. Can you help me up?"

"I think so, give me a sec." I hauled myself up with a grunt.

After a few exhausting tugs and pulls, Ja'tare was up on his feet. We rested against each other to get our bearings.

"So what now?" I asked.

"We must get moving before the convergence of the two suns. Have you seen the spear? We will need it if we encounter any other dangerous animals."

Though I doubted the spear would help us much in our condition, I beamed my light around the area and found it protruding from a nearby pile of dead vines. I staggered over and grabbed it before returning it to Ja'tare. He clicked a button at the base of his weapon and the spear retracted into itself with a sharp snap, once again a small cylinder.

"Can you walk?" I asked.

"Yes, I believe so. Come, let us go."

Ja'tare and I exited the clearing at a snail's pace, supporting each other's weight. Almost immediately the light quality brightened to a dim but acceptable level. We trudged our way through the maze of winding, crooked paths at Ja'tare's direction.

As we walked, guilt knotted my stomach at the way I'd treated Ja'tare. He'd saved my life a total of three times now: in the lab, from the ipto, and now from the evil kri and the flesh-eating plants. He didn't have to rescue me. He could've just gone home to his people, safe and sound.

"Thanks for coming back for me," I said. "I know you didn't have to, and I'm sorry I got upset with you earlier. This planet, it's still a lot to take in."

Ja'tare smiled. "Think nothing of it. The Veloxans have a strong sense of duty. We protect our own, and since you are a guest of ours, I am responsible for your well-being. Ah, here we are."

We broke through the tightly packed wood into a bright and immense open area filled with Valen of every shape and size.

My shoulders slumped. *"More* Valen? Jesus, when does this thing stop?"

"Not to worry. This is the last stretch." Ja'tare pointed ahead of us. "Do you see how the path narrows and the Valen and vegetation peter out? Once we get there, we should be relatively safe."

Ja'tare shielded his eyes as the sky's amber light burned into a bright orange color. When he looked back at me, his tan freckled face had paled several shades. He snatched my hand. "Gregory, we have to move. Now!"

Ja'tare dragged me along in a fast walk up a small hill, my beaten body throbbing in protest.

What was the big deal? I knew he wanted to get back to his people, but suns weren't dangerous. They lit up the world. They didn't go on murderous rampages.

As we crested the incline I gaped, finally understanding Ja'tare's concerns.

In the tangerine light of the two suns, the Valen swayed, as if to some invisible wind. Their branches twisted and gnarled like grippy little fingertips, snapping out at every movement near them. Then to my complete and utter horror their elevated roots ripped out of the ground.

"What's happening?" I cried.

"The Valen have come to life. We must hurry, before they fully awaken!"

Ja'tare tugged at me, but I resisted. As much as I wanted to believe that was possible, I knew that option was long gone. "Ja'tare, we can't. My body's too sore, and I doubt you're in any condition either. We have to find another way."

Ja'tare grimaced, but after a moment his head hung in defeat. "You are right, but we must cross somehow."

"Have you ever dealt with this situation before?"

"I have not."

I frowned. "It's too dangerous to chance it. Maybe if we

watch their activity, we'll be able to come up with something. There's gotta be a way we can outsmart the Valen."

"Agreed."

Ja'tare and I stood atop the small hill, overlooking the mayhem below. Dozens of towering magnificent Valen slithered and shifted in every direction, their branches flailing like medusa heads of snakes.

My focus settled on several small creatures nearby that resembled the ipto I'd seen earlier. They scurried along the pale pink grass near an enormous, uprooted Valen. The tree advanced on them slowly, scuttling across the earth until it was twenty feet away. Its branches flurried wildly, unfurling and stretching several times their length before lashing out with a sudden cracking snap. The ipto gave off squeals of pain as they erupted in small bursts of blood.

I flinched. Okay, so keeping away was important, but what had the ipto done that had gotten its attention? I wasn't about to be another corpse on the forest floor.

"Your face is doing odd things again," Ja'tare observed.

"I was watching those ipto below." I pointed. "They did something to agitate the trees, but I can't quite figure it out. Maybe if we watch a little longer we can--"

A scratchy rustling sound came from behind us, and I spun around. A tall Valen shadowed just thirty feet away, slithering to us as its branches uncoiled, serpentine.

"Look out!" I lunged forward, tackling Ja'tare as the first of the branches came whipping down at us. Sharp wooden daggers struck and tore at the forest floor as we rolled over the top of the hill, several of them cutting into my arm with searing pain.

Ja'tare and I barreled down the slope uncontrollably. Our velocity eventually petered out and we rolled to a stop, my head spinning with vertigo.

"Are you alri--"

I slapped a hand over Ja'tare's mouth, holding a finger to my lips.

I looked around us as my vision continued to swim. Several Valen stood nearby, just outside striking distance. Unlike the others scuttling around, they remained still, as if they were listening. We froze, the moments dragging by until the Valen finally shifted away towards the cacophony of the forest.

When they were a safe distance away, I removed my hand from Ja'tare's mouth.

"I think we're safe for the moment."

"You are injured. Your arm."

I glanced at the lacerations flowering my upper arm. "I've had worse. Getting out of here is more important. Let's get up, but be very quiet about it."

We repositioned ourselves, slow and cautious. In the near distance, Valen trees continued to shake and snap their limbs at anything nearby. They shuffled smoothly across the ground like fish in the sea, paying no attention to us.

"What now?" Ja'tare whispered to me.

"I have an idea, but until I know for sure we have to stay here."

"For how long?"

"I just need something to prove my theory. We can't go balls to the wall here."

Ja'tare's brows raised. "Balls to the wall? What kind of balls, and why are they going to this wall you speak of?"

I shook my head. "Never mind. Just hold on for a moment."

I scanned around us for any sign of activity.

Ahead and to our left a dark, block-headed creature on four legs bolted from underneath a Valen. The Valen's predatory branches thrust and scraped towards it, but the animal kept just out of range with powerful strides from its massive fists that catapulted it forward. With an impressive bound, the animal launched into the air, stopping on bare, black dirt. It turned around, facing the Valen defiantly.

The Valen approached the strange mammal, stopping just feet away. No crazy flailing limbs, no whipping strikes, it just stood there. After several tense moments, the burly creature moved quietly along the thin dirt track before disappearing out of sight.

When I glanced back at Ja'tare, his eyes were wide like saucers. "How did the animal do that? The Valen did not notice its movements."

"That's what I was trying to prove," I said. "The Valen don't seem to have eyes, so the

only other logical conclusion is that they are hunting by sound. The Reap-- er, the Dak'kar hunt in a similar way."

"So how do we avoid the Valen?"

"Easy, we just mimic that monkey-looking thing. Walking on the grass seems to make

too much sound, so if we stay on the dirt and move in cautious, measured steps, we may be able to get by unnoticed. My people have done something similar when around sleeping Dak'kar."

Ja'tare scanned the path for a moment. "I think you are right. This is our best option."

"Okay, let's do this."

Ja'tare and I crept to the black dirt path one slow, agonizing step at a time to lessen the noise we made on the pink grass. The Valen around us continued to flail and shift, but none approached.

Once we reached the thin trail, Ja'tare's posture visibly relaxed, but I was still anxious. Valen surrounded us on all sides, a sea of living claws that could rip us apart in a moment's time. Just because the monkey creature had made it out didn't mean we would. With any sudden noise it could all be over.

I kept my gaze fixed between the Valen towering ominously around us and my own two feet. After a while I began to relax, especially when I saw the final edge of the forest that Ja'tare had pointed out earlier.

The Valen petered out fifty yards ahead, the dirt path ending at a small incline of blue stone. Beyond that, the promise of safety with Ja'tare's people and a way home.

With renewed vigor, I inched forward faster and faster as the Valen sought out other, noisier prey. We were about halfway there when several green and blue-furred ipten bolted across our dirt path.

An enormous cluster of Valen branches slammed down just feet away, spraying blood, dirt, and grass everywhere.

In the chaos, I jumped back, landing awkwardly on my right foot. My equilibrium shattered, and I spun to the ground with a loud thud.

Oh god ...

I jerked my head up. The nearest Valen's limbs cracked away at the last of the ipto, but several others had heard me fall and were angling in. We had to get out of here right now!

I jumped to my feet, turned to Ja'tare, and grabbed his hand in one swift excruciating motion. "Come on, we have to make a run for it!"

Together, we rushed around the bloody scene, needles of pain piercing every cell of my body. I gritted my teeth. My soreness could fuck right off.

Numerous Valen swarmed towards us from both sides, their deadly branches thrashing and whipping violently.

"Run faster, we can outpace them!"

We bulleted forward, muscles and tendons burning with exertion. Ja'tare and I rushed past the Valen, the air cracking and snapping with murderous activity behind us.

Ja'tare looked over his shoulder. "We're not going to make it!"

I dared a quick glance back. The Valen were gaining on us fast.

Well, shit. "Keep going!" I loosened a strap on my knapsack, wheeling it to me as I ran. I rifled through the contents desperately. *Come on, come on.* My hands closed around a small, familiar box. *Yes!*

I tore the box open in seconds, grabbing the two small chatterboxes I'd taken in case of a Reaper emergency. "When I say, stop running okay? Alright, stop!"

We halted dead in our tracks, and I spun around to face the nearest Valen just outside of striking distance.

I thrust the two chatterboxes in separate directions.

The Valen halted their chase as the chatterboxes struck the ground with a rusty, tinkling sound. For a moment they stood still as if wondering where we'd gone, then swished over in the directions of the chatterboxes.

I turned back to Ja'tare and grabbed his hand. "Let's get the hell outta here!"

Ja'tare and I nearly flew to the stone incline at the end of the forest. As soon as we reached the base of the natural rock I scrambled upwards, my muscles threatening to cave under the effort. Foot by foot, I dragged myself to the top, then collapsed on the smooth, hard surface, breath ragged.

We'd done it. We'd survived the Valen.

CHAPTER THIRTEEN

"Are we there yet?" I dragged forward on feet that ached like they'd been beaten with a meat tenderizer. After barely escaping a forest of homicidal wildlife and trees that wanted to rip the flesh from my bones, I was ready to collapse on the ground and throw the towel in.

"Have patience, Gregory," Ja'tare assured me. "We are nearly there."

I folded my arms across my chest, focusing back on the depressing, bleak environment.

The vibrant yet dangerous forest landscape of the Valen had given way to a desolate canyon that stretched on as far as the eye could see. Mountains of holey stone towered above us in dull shades of gray, blue, and green, misshapen and rounded as if they'd been melted down by some strange force over the years. The sky had faded from a bright tangerine to a dull green that bathed everything in a dreary light.

The dismal area we now traversed had obviously been a war zone at some point. The remains of Veloxans and Reapers littered the ground in various states of decay, many so aged they were mummified. Where the lifeless forms ended huge fissures gaped, the ground around them charred, black, and cracked. Ja'tare had kept his gaze fixed forward since we left the Valen, but as much as I wanted to ask about what happened here, I didn't have the energy.

Ja'tare stopped walking for a moment and glanced around, recognition lighting his green eyes. "Almost there, right around this next corner."

We turned at the far edge of a series of boulders on our right, arriving at the base of another porous, towering mound of stone. The multitude of open holes in it resembled a giant pockmarked face, and its gray color cascaded into a faded blue on its right side.

I stared at the mountain. "This is where you are staying?"

"Yes, the mountain provides an excellent natural defense. Come, let us head over."

I frowned as I gave the towering peak another once over. I didn't know what to expect when Ja'tare had promised me safety with the other Veloxans. A castle, maybe even a bunker. But *this*?

Ease up, you're just tired and irritable, I told myself. As shabby as this setup seemed, it beat hanging out with Reapers and Valen. This probably wasn't the Veloxans' ideal situation either.

I took several heavy breaths as we approached the sentinel of rock, Ja'tare stopping me near a cave entrance at its base.

"With my communications down, it would probably be safest if you stay here momentarily. We have gotten used to defending ourselves against intruders, and I do not want you to get hurt." Ja'tare took off one of his wrist cuffs and handed it to me. "If a Dak'kar comes, aim and shoot, then run into the cave. Head right."

I scratched my arms as I watched Ja'tare enter the cave and disappear from sight. Why did I have the feeling I was getting tossed to the wolves being out here by myself? I focused my gaze on the mountain.

The other Veloxans were in there. Would they be kind like Ja'tare, or hesitant to trust an alien human? Did they look like him, or were they as diverse as my race was? Most of all, I wondered if they could get me home. I doubted there was a portal generator housed within their base, but the sooner I left Velerius, the better.

It had already been several hours since I'd arrived on this planet, and I needed to get back to Trent, Mom, and my group. For all I knew they were still fighting the hooded Reaper and needed my help. Whatever solution the Veloxans offered, I would take it in a heartbeat. I'd been here long enough.

Hoping to quell my flurrying thoughts, I headed over to a large patch of vegetation that was vivid in color and lush with life. I meandered around the outer edge of the space, letting my hand graze the rows of corn-like husk plants. A rich blue hue, they stood four feet tall with curved thorns at their base. Atop each stalk was an unblossomed purple flower that emitted a faint glow.

Interesting. Maybe the Veloxans ate the flower?

I continued into the center of the area, my gaze fixating on several short, plum-colored plants that resembled coral. Small brown bulbs grew out of them in random places, and when I touched one I was surprised that it had a soft, leathery feel to it.

I smiled to myself, then it hit me. Whatever crops the Veloxans grew for sustenance would probably be my meal too if they took me in. My stomach grumbled.

A sudden scuffle nearby alerted me and I crouched in a defensive position, my hand poised on my other cuffed arm.

"Hello, who's there?" I surveyed the green semi-darkness around me but didn't find anything. It couldn't be a Reaper.

I'd already be dead if that were the case. "I said, who's there?"

Movement again, this time behind me. I spun around, flinching in shock.

A stout Veloxan male about my height stood several feet away from me. Shoulder-length black hair framed his pale, dark-freckled face, and he clutched a green-tipped spear in his hands.

"Who are you?" he demanded with a scowl.

"I ... I ..."

The angry Veloxan lunged towards me with the spear and I sprang back, holding my hands up in surrender. He stepped forward until he was right in my face, then analyzed my features with apparent interest.

"I-I'm with Ja'tare. My name is Gregory, and I'm a human from planet Earth."

The Veloxan tilted his head and hesitated for a moment.

A voice shouted from a distance, "Ko'ta, stop!"

The Veloxan named Ko'ta lowered his spear but remained armed, his angry brown eyes boring into me.

In the green dimness, I could just barely make out Ja'tare approaching fast from the cave he'd entered minutes ago. He caught up to us, breathing heavily.

"Explain yourself, Ja'tare," Ko'ta demanded. "Who is this human and why is he on our planet?" He glanced around, cocking an eyebrow. "Better yet, why are you alone? What happened to the scouting party and the others you were sent to evacuate?"

"It is a long story, my friend," Ja'tare said. "One that will require the council's attention. Please, put away your weapon. He is no threat to us."

Ko'ta seemed a little less apprehensive, but didn't move. "I will decide when I sheath my weapon, but you are correct. We should head inside. The council awaits your report and will be interested to speak with this human boy."

Ja'tare and I walked towards the mountain, Ko'ta trailing behind.

Whoever this council was, they must be in charge of everything here. Would they be apprehensive like Ko'ta? Why did it suddenly feel like I was in trouble for even being here?

As we entered the cave, I hoped that things wouldn't escalate. The Veloxans held my life in their hands, and if they didn't see things my way I couldn't fight their decision. This planet could very easily become my prison, one that I might never escape from.

I LEANED against the uneven wall of rock, breath heavy as I gave myself a quick rest. The dull throb of fatigue was now a roaring fire in all my joints. "Can we stop here for a moment?"

Ko'ta grimaced. "We should not keep the council waiting."

"*Please*," I whined.

"Gregory is right, Ko'ta," Ja'tare said. "He and I have travelled an incredible distance today. I am exhausted myself."

Ko'ta leered at Ja'tare with his brown glistening eyes and crossed his arms. "Fine, but we cannot stay for long."

I sat upon the cave floor, glancing at the low ceiling then back down the tunnel. It was lined with glowing, floating blue orbs like the one Ja'tare had given me.

We'd been wandering this mountain's labyrinthine passages for what seemed like an eternity, and I was not just fatigued but paranoid too. Ko'ta had put his spear away but held a permanent scowl on his face. He glared at me every time I looked his way like I'd done something wrong. Further spurring my paranoia was the fact that we hadn't seen another Veloxan yet. If there were many I'd have seen some by now. Could this be a trap?

You're just tired, I told myself.

I relaxed, my shoulders sagging. The urge to lay down on the ground and sleep was strong despite the cold that was already nipping my butt.

Ko'ta's stern gaze focused on me. "That is long enough. It should not be much farther now."

I got up with a groan and dragged my feet forward. We continued through the winding passageway for several more minutes until the path gave way to a wide, vaulted cavern.

Dozens of Veloxans lined the perimeter. Their features varying greatly, from their skin tone and the freckled markings on their faces to the striking shades their irises nearly glowed in the dimness. An ocean of vibrant eyes focused on us as we marched forward, my stomach in knots.

I kept my eyes ahead of me despite my curiosity. The last thing I wanted to do was show an ounce of disrespect, especially if some of them had conflicting thoughts about a human being on their world. The cave ended in a chamber thirty feet ahead, where three Veloxans sat atop small boulders shaped like chairs.

The council.

Two male Veloxans with tan skin, dark long hair, and finely-tailored clothes took up the outer seats. The older one to my left watched me with hawk-like golden eyes devoid of emotion, while the other's cold blue eyes fixed on me icily. The center spot was occupied by a pale older female with braided copper-colored hair and layered, drapey clothing that sparkled like the Valen. Her lavender eyes shined as the slightest of smiles graced her face.

Unconsciously, I took a step forward and felt Ko'ta's iron grip on my arm.

"No," he growled.

The elderly female Veloxan waved her hand dismissively. "It is alright, Ko'ta. Let the human and Ja'tare approach."

Ko'ta gave me one last scathing look before allowing Ja'tare and I forward. I matched Ja'tare's steps until he stopped ten paces from the council.

The female Veloxan's gaze focused on Ja'tare, then shifted to me. "Ja'tare, we are pleased you have returned to us safely. We have many questions that need answering, the foremost being the sudden presence of this human boy."

Ja'tare bowed. "Thank you, Nehma. It is good to be back home. I understand your surprise at Gregory's arrival and can explain everything."

"Then get on with it," the irritated blue-eyed Veloxan to Nehma's left snapped. "Give us your full report, then we will interrogate this human."

Interrogate me? Okay, something was definitely up. If the Veloxans had history with other humans and were skeptical of me, there had to be some beef with my race.

Ja'tare clenched his fists, taking a step forward. "But Gregory is innocent!"

Nehma held up a hand, silencing him. "De'jartha is right, Ja'tare. Given our history, we must question the human to be certain of his motives."

Ja'tare mumbled agreement in defeat.

De'jartha straightened his composure before clearing his throat. "State your mission, Commander."

"My mission was to supervise the rescue party to the designated laboratory and vacate all Veloxans present."

"And where exactly are the refugees and your accompanying party?"

Ja'tare's head drooped. "They are all gone. I failed my mission."

A communal gasp sounded around us, and my insides

quivered. What would they do to Ja'tare for his failure to rescue his people?

De'jartha grinned maliciously, just long enough for me to notice before his features hardened again. "Explain yourself."

"Two days ago the council sent me to oversee the evacuation of the inhabitants of the laboratory after receiving reports of increased Dak'kar activity," Ja'tare explained. "Our journey began without issue, but when we encountered a large group of Dak'kar, everything fell apart."

Ja'tare's brows furrowed. "The majority of our party was killed in the assault. Several of us managed to escape, but we were separated. I still do not know if they have survived or not. I tried to relay these developments to the council, but my communications were damaged during the attacks." Ja'tare pointed to the cracked button on the elevated neckline of his shirt. The council members nodded in understanding except for De'jartha, whose features remained unchanged.

"Once I located another route to the laboratory I continued my mission, but before I could evacuate them we were attacked by a swarm of Dak'kar."

De'jartha crossed his arms. "And did you defend your brethren with your life?"

Ja'tare's face reddened a couple shades. "I did all I could for my brothers and sisters, but while I was defending them, I was injured and rendered unconscious. When I awoke they were all dead."

A heavy silence overtook the vaulted chamber, so intense I was afraid to breathe. Ja'tare was injured in the line of duty. Clearly this wasn't his fault, but I was too nervous to interrupt. I knew nothing about their customs or what repercussions would come from that kind of disrespect.

De'jartha frigid gaze remained on Ja'tare. "So you mean to tell this council you failed your primary objective because you were knocked out? Fellow members, this is clearly a lie to cover up for Ja'tare's cowardice and weakness. He abandoned our people when they needed him the most!"

The older male Veloxan held up a calloused hand, silencing De'jartha. Unlike his younger counterpart, his craggy weathered face emulated sincere compassion. "Please finish your report, Ja'tare."

"Thank you, Kro'da. After I awoke, Gregory was instrumental in our return here." Ja'tare gestured to me. "This heroic human has helped heal me, avoid the Dak'kar, and is the sole reason we escaped the Valen. I owe him my life, and I request that in return for Gregory's valor and courage we assist him in returning to Earth. With that, I conclude my report."

I looked to Ja'tare appreciatively. He'd colored me as a hero in hopes that they would be more willing to help me. Why had he done that? He hardly knew me.

"The council will come to a decision momentarily," Nehma said.

Ja'tare backed away and I mimicked his steps, keeping my eyes on the council.

They whispered amongst each other animatedly. Based on their body language, De'jartha didn't like what Nehma and Kro'da were suggesting. I hoped that was a good thing.

Several moments later they ushered us forward, Nehma addressing us. "Ja'tare, you will suffer no punishment from your actions involving the evacuation of the laboratory."

Ja'tare gave a deep bow. "I am deeply grateful."

I focused my gaze on De'jartha. He stared at the chamber wall, nostrils flared. *Whatever.*

"Now we must question *Grey-gree*," Nehma announced. "Ja'tare, you may stay for clarification if it is needed."

I held my tongue at the butchering of my name as the council's attention focused on me.

"Introduce yourself," Ja'tare whispered to me.

"Uh, right," I blurted out. "My name is Gregory Martin. I'm eighteen years old, I'm from planet Earth, and I'm trying to get back home."

"How is it that you came to Velerius?" Kro'da asked.

"Well, that's the thing. I was forced here by a Reaper through one of your portals."

The Veloxans gaped at me like I'd done a song and dance number in the nude.

Ja'tare stepped forward. "Apologies. The humans call the Dak'kar *Ree-purrs*."

"Um, yes, that's correct. One of those monsters took me away from my family and the group I was travelling with. It's extremely important I get back to them as soon as possible. I was taken in the middle of battle, and I have to know that they're okay."

The council's stone-faced gazes fixed on me. They seemed upset. Why? I was the one who was stranded here.

Kro'da leaned forward in his earthen seat. "Tell us, what do you know of the human organization known as The Order?"

My skin prickled with shock, raising goosebumps on my arms and legs. How did they know of The Order? Was this the issue they had with humans? I opened my mouth to speak, but the jumbled mess of words that came out were, "The Order, I, what?"

Kro'da's expression hardened, his golden eyes piercing through me. "Are you or have you ever been affiliated with the Order?"

"No, of course not!" I shot back, anger bubbling through my veins.

"But you recognize that name," Nehma observed calmly.

I gritted my teeth, trying to focus on the painful facts of the past while suppressing my escalating emotions. "The

Order was responsible for the Dak'kar taking my sister away five years ago, for all of the kids that disappeared from my hometown. They were sacrificing them to those monsters to keep them at bay. I tried stopping them five years ago, but none of it mattered. How do *you* know of the Order?"

"They betrayed us," Nehma said, a tightness in her eyes. "Decades ago, we discovered the coordinates to Earth and approached your race in hopes of peaceful relations. The Order was the first group of humans that was not scared of us. We showed them our world and technology, but the peace ended when they stole our entire reserve of Dak'kar pheromone candles we used for trapping and tracking."

"Wait, tracking?" I rifled through my knapsack, pulling out the remainder of my Reaper candle to the council's surprise. "These can be tracked?"

"Where did you obtain that?" Nehma demanded.

"After my sister was taken I found it in my basement. I've kept it ever since in hopes that one day it would be useful."

"I ... see," Nehma said, skepticism in her tone. "We must contain the candle. Each one has a beacon installed. In the past we used them to attract and trap Dak'kar via our portal technology, but with most of our facilities under Dak'kar dominion, this device makes us detectable, vulnerable. Ko'ta?"

Ko'ta stepped forward and I handed the candle over, feeling queasy at what their information meant. The hooded Reaper's attack on my group in the library was all my fault. If I hadn't brought that stupid candle, they never would've found us. I wouldn't even be here right now. To make matters worse, I looked questionable in the council's eyes now. It was obvious from the way they were staring me down.

"The betrayal by The Order caused innumerable casualties at a time in our war where the candles could have shifted the tide in our favor. That is why we cannot afford to blindly trust any human."

Nehma's questioning gaze lingered upon me, and I looked away anxiously as I connected the dots.

The Order knew about the Reapers, the Veloxans, everything this entire time. But instead of fighting the Reapers together they betrayed the Veloxans, using the pilfered candles to create a cult of control in our world. And now here I was, the first human they'd seen in ages who not only knew of the Order, but had a Reaper candle in tow that exposed their location. I practically had traitor tattooed on my forehead.

"I don't know what to say," I confessed. "I had no idea their greed and treachery went this far. I'm sorry for the losses my race has caused you, but I assure you, I have never aided the Order in any way. Most humans never even knew of them."

The council gazed upon me tensely before Kro'da edged forward in his seat. "I think we have heard enough of Grey-gree's story to make an assessment."

"Can we though?" De'jartha countered. "How do we know this human is not lying? They have done it before, and the presence of the Dak'kar pheromone candle implies his motives. He could have been sent here by The Order to gain our trust just to strike another blow, this time one we will not survive."

Nehma turned to De'jartha. "While your concerns are valid, we have no real way of verifying this information without other humans present, and that requires resources we do not have. Gregory should not be assumed guilty based on the sole fact that he is human. We must at least consider that he is telling the truth."

Kro'da agreed, while De'jartha glowered and looked away.

Nehma rose from her seat, hands clasped together. "Since

we are unable to verify Gregory's claims of innocence, we cannot punish or assist him. Ja'tare, you will be responsible for monitoring his activities until we can determine whether or not he is trustworthy. This meeting is officially over. Please return to your duties."

At her words, the Veloxans filling the chamber noisily hustled and bustled their way around as I stared forward in utter shock.

Ja'tare placed a hand on my shoulder, and I pulled away.

"I am sorry, Gregory. We will figure this out, I promise."

I shot Ja'tare daggers. "How? You can't promise me that. You already tried and failed."

"Nothing is set in stone. I will find a way, I prom--"

"If you make one more meaningless promise, I'm going to scream."

Ja'tare's head lowered. "Alright, I will stop. Please, follow me. I will show you around."

Ja'tare led the way out of the chamber, and I stomped after him.

How had this happened? Ja'tare had failed, and now I was a prisoner of the Veloxans, the very thing I'd feared. I was stuck here, and until my captors were convinced of my trustworthiness, I'd never make it back home.

CHAPTER FOURTEEN

I stormed down the dimly-lit tunnel after Ja'tare, my knuckles white as I clenched my fists.

Who the hell were the Veloxans to decide my fate? It wasn't my fault that they got burned by The Order. Coming here had been a huge mistake. Had trusting Ja'tare been one too?

Ja'tare stopped up ahead, and as I caught up with him I crossed my arms. *What now?*

"Gregory, you and I have been through a lot today. I know with the council's verdict the last thing you want is to be around Veloxans right now, but you need food and rest. I will show you our eating space and you can decide if you would rather be alone or not."

My stomach rumbled at the thought of food. Maybe with some sustenance I could brainstorm a way to make the Veloxans trust me. "Fine."

I followed Ja'tare down a series of winding, intersecting tunnels that ascended and descended at random. Small openings within the cave revealed tiny spaces that appeared to be sleeping quarters. This level of the labyrinth of passages must be residential.

After rounding another bend in the passageway, a strong, funky scent wafted into my nostrils, like burnt pot roast mixed with something pungent and sweet.

I must've made a face, because Ja'tare's lips curled into a grin.

"Veloxan food may take a while to get used to, but you are in luck. The cook is making *Ehk'ret ta* tonight."

I crinkled my nose. "*Ehk'ret ta*? What the hell is that?"

"Come, let us go in and see. The dining area is just ahead."

We approached an opening on the left, chitchat overflowing into the hall. When we entered the room, everything went quiet.

Several groups of Veloxans sat together upon woven blankets and exotically-colored furs, gleaming eyes glued on us.

I froze.

"It is okay, they are just curious," Ja'tare said softly to me.

He urged me forward, and we walked across the small space where a stout Veloxan with tiny horns stirred a large, cauldron-like pot. With a quick exchange, the cook retrieved two earthen bowls and poured several scoops from the kettle into them.

Steam rose from my bowl, and I looked down at my dinner. Purple and brown noodle-like things floated in a white broth of sorts. I frowned. This literally looked like shit.

Ja'tare and I meandered back to the eating area. He had a cheesy smile plastered on his face. "You are going to love this. Shall we sit, or would you rather eat alone?"

I glanced around, considering my options. As pissed as I was, I was also very alone. Isolating myself from the Veloxans could affect their opinion of me and the level of trust I was supposed to be building. Until they were willing to send me back home, I had to keep up pretenses.

I snatched one of the bowls from Ja'tare and sat down on a vacant powder blue fur. I positioned myself so that Ja'tare's back was to the other Veloxans, partially blocking their view of me. I didn't want to be gawked at the whole time I ate.

"Um, how do I eat this?" I asked Ja'tare.

"Oh, how forgetful of me!" Ja'tare jumped up and jogged to the short cook, who handed him several utensils. He returned with a couple two-pronged forks and small curved blades, handing me a set.

"Thanks," I muttered. I kept my eyes on him.

Ja'tare impaled one of the purple noodles with his fork, cutting into it with his knife. Stabbing the piece he'd severed, he submerged it in the white broth before lifting it out of the bowl, exposing several roots at its bottom. He lifted the veggie noodle to his mouth and bit down with a squishy crunch before dunking the remainder in his bowl again.

I looked at my dinner again, wondering what it would taste like. I armed myself with a fork. Anything was better than sliced beets or rutabaga. I pierced a root and took my first bite.

The outside had a texture and taste of potato, then as my teeth sunk in, a pocket of thick juice erupted into my mouth. The flavor was that of a spicy jam and had hard bits of something within it that was hard to chew.

After munching on my first mouthful, I winced as I swallowed the food down. It wasn't great, but at least I wasn't gagging or anything.

"Is something wrong?" Ja'tare asked. He slurped up the last of the roots sticking out of his mouth.

Unsure of what to do, I gave Ja'tare a thumbs up.

He tilted his head. "What are you doing?"

"It's a human symbol. It means everything is alright."

"Oh." Ja'tare set down his utensils. "Like this, right?" He curled all of his fingers but his thumb, then poked it towards me like he had a TV remote in his hand.

Jesus. If my dinner didn't kill me first, my annoyance at Ja'tare would. "Um, yeah. Great."

After poking at the odd combination of alien roots and broth for a while, Ja'tare and I gave our bowls to the cook, then departed the cavern.

"What now?" I asked.

"You must be anxious to get clean after the trek we had. I will show you to the bathing cavern."

I followed after him down the passage, happy I wouldn't have to reek the entire time I was here. We stopped in front of another nondescript opening.

"Here we are," Ja'tare announced. "Let me show you around."

It was a simple chamber, really. Stone walls, several flat surfaces for placing personal belongings, and to my left a large earthen slab with a cylindrical metal contraption hanging above.

"It is a very simple system," Ja'tare explained. "This cavern and several others are natural reservoirs for rainwater. We were able to store water in tanks and installed that lever you see to dispense water. We are limited on the resource, so please do not overuse. You may also use the adjoining room to relieve yourself."

Ja'tare gave me a once over and headed over to a shelf in the rock wall, returning with a small bundle of clothes, a towel, and a vial of amber liquid. "The clothes you are wearing will not protect you from the cold season approaching. The *sa'do* should clean you, just rub it on your body."

"Uh, yeah, I know how soap works."

Ja'tare gave a look of surprise before chuckling to himself. He made a hasty exit, promising to return soon.

I ventured into the Veloxans' version of a bathroom, swept back a step by the stench of feces and urine. It was a simple, tiny room with small holes in the ground. I wasn't expecting a toilet, but I wasn't expecting to pop a squat either.

Plugging my nose, I attended to my business. Once I finished, I re-entered the small bathing cavern, disrobed, and walked over to the shower area. I pulled the lever overhead and a thick stream of lukewarm water splashed over me, sending sharp tingles of pain over my injuries acquired from the Valen.

I poured the small vial of soap over me and lathered it on my body, closing my eyes. Though I was still pretty upset with the council's decision, I was grateful to be alive. Yes, Ja'tare had failed to convince them of my innocence, but I still owed him a lot. I never would've gotten this far without him.

The running water ebbed my frustrations, but so much about the Veloxans remained unanswered.

Now that I was stuck with them, I had no idea what they would make me do. Was I their slave or just a guest? More importantly, I needed to figure out a way to get them to trust me.

I didn't know if Trent, Mom, and the group were safe, and I couldn't just sit around waiting for the Veloxans to trust me when their lives could be in danger.

At the same time, being here gave me a chance to get the truth about the Reapers: where they came from, what had happened in the past, how all of that information could aid in the survival of the human race.

I sighed, shelving my thoughts for later. Today had been too long already, and exhaustion was sending dull aches through every inch of my body.

Maybe I could hash this all out with the council, get some answers and make them see why they should send me home.

I turned off the water and vacated the wet stone slab. I walked over to my belongings and grabbed a thin, fuzzy towel to dry off, trying on my new clothes shortly after.

The tailored shirt provided was much like Ja'tare's. A thick and dark ribbed material embellished the upper half, ending in an elevated neck that lacked the communication device embedded in Ja'tare's shirt.

My pants were nice and roomy. I slipped on my new plain-looking shoes, giving a gasp when a strange suction tugged at the bottom of my feet. I stepped around a bit on the soft, pillowy soles; they didn't budge unless I put some force into it. I smiled to myself. Who needs shoelaces anyways?

Clean and content, I left the humid cavern with my old clothes bundled under an arm.

"Was everything to your liking?" A familiar voice sounded right next to me, making me jump.

I turned with a grimace. First Trent constantly spooked the shit outta me, now Ja'tare?

Despite my annoyance, he looked a lot better now. He had on a fresh outfit, identical to the one he wore before minus the metal cuffs. His dark brown hair was wet and slicked back, emphasizing his emerald eyes and speckled horns.

"Um, yeah. I'm just really tired," I said. "Do you mind if we--"

"Of course. Follow me, my quarters are not far from here."

"*Your* quarters?"

"Yes. Since I am responsible for you, we will sleep in the same quarters."

I followed after Ja'tare, dumbstruck. I didn't know how I

felt about sleeping in the same room with him. I hardly knew him or anything about how Veloxans slept. For all I knew they slept against the wall like the Coneheads. I shook out of my hesitant thoughts. Everything would be fine. It's not like I had to crawl into bed with him.

We arrived at another small cave inlet. Ja'tare stepped in and clapped his hands. A blue globe of light sparked to life, and he came back out, waving me inside.

The dim-lit room was tiny, hardly bigger than a closet. Exotic, striped furs covered the floor, and in the far corner a thin mattress of sorts sat upon the ground with small stuffed triangles I assumed were pillows. I scratched at my arms. It was going to be a snug fit between the two of us.

"We were not able to take much with us when we evacuated our homes, but it is what we have," Ja'tare explained.

"Don't worry about it. My group and I have had to deal with much worse conditions. Um, where should I sleep?"

"You can have the mattress, and I can rest on the furs. I have a couple of blankets that should keep us warm."

Ja'tare handed me a blanket, and I settled down onto the slender mattress. Surprisingly, it was pretty comfortable and hardly caved under my weight. I pressed my fingers against the material, surprised by its elasticity.

I focused my gaze on the natural rock ceiling, willing sleep to come. Ja'tare stretched himself out on the furs, just feet away. I could feel his eyes on me.

"Is there something on my face?" I asked.

"I know you may not want to hear it, but I really am sorry, Gregory. I feel terrible about the council's decision, especially after I promised you would be able to go home quickly. I will do whatever I can to expedite your travel back to Earth. I mean it."

I smiled weakly. As unhappy as I was with my present situation, my gut told me to continue to trust Ja'tare. I knew he wouldn't let any harm come to me, and I felt he was the only real ally I had in this strange world. "Thank you. I'm just worried about my group back on Earth. Thinking about them has been eating away at me."

"I understand. When we left our homes for safety, we were forced to leave many behind as the Dak'kar overtook the city. I still do not know what became of my friends and family."

I frowned. The Veloxans and my race had both suffered massive losses and widespread destruction from the Reapers. Maybe our species weren't so different after all. "So uh, what's tomorrow going to be like? Am I supposed to help you out or something? What do you do as commander?"

"It is not really all that complicated honestly. On a typical day I implement training for our warriors and supervise expeditions. This base has not seen battle in weeks, but we must be prepared for it at any time. As for tomorrow, we will check in with the council on any developing expeditions. I will try to urge them to reconsider their decision regarding you, but I cannot guarantee anything."

"I get it. Thanks for trying. Well, I'm gonna try to sleep now. Rest well."

"You as well, Gregory."

Ja'tare deactivated the cold blue light, bathing us in darkness. I stared blankly into the pitch black around me.

In spite of how chaotic this day had been, I'd made it out in one piece. Tomorrow I could figure out a way to build the Veloxans' trust, and with Ja'tare by my side, I knew he'd help make that happen. Everything would be alright in time, and I would get back home. I just hoped it would be soon enough.

CHAPTER FIFTEEN

I sat upon the furred floor of the empty dining area, yanking at a tough, navy-colored stick of *artarta* with my teeth.

I'd woken up to find Ja'tare's blanket neatly folded on the furs he'd slept on. Sore, grumpy, and ravenous, I meandered down the stone passageway, letting the smell of food lead me here.

The cook let me know I'd missed the morning rush for sustenance, and I grunted in approval, not in any mood to bother with social interaction. I asked him for coffee or anything with caffeine to help wake me up, but he had no idea what I was talking about.

Drowsy and insanely decaffeinated, I tried to pull myself together for my meeting with the council. Ja'tare would be trying to convince them to change their mind about helping me get home. Whatever he planned on saying, I hoped they would believe him.

Ja'tare entered the room looking a bit tense. His rigid posture relaxed when he spotted me, and after a brief visit with the cook, he sat next to me with his own artarta stick. "Good morning. How are you feeling?"

I chomped at the strange beef jerky with my canines, pulling until I got a good bite of the sweet yet spicy hardened jam inside. Hmm, this stuff wasn't half bad. "Peachy."

Ja'tare shot me a puzzled look, then shrugged it off. "I just spoke with Ko'ta. Before I could request an audience, he said the council wanted to speak with us."

"Oh really, what about? Do you think it's about yesterday's decision? Maybe they reconsidered their verdict on me."

"I am not sure. Ko'ta did not elaborate any further. The council does not change stances on issues often, but have done so in the past. I guess we will just have to see, but if they do not bring it up, I will."

Ja'tare and I made quick work of our food, then we headed out.

Minutes later, Ko'ta led Ja'tare and I to the entry of the council's chamber. We stood there, waiting for our turn to speak with them. As my patience whittled away to nothing, my nerves flared up again. Had the council changed their minds overnight? Maybe I was in trouble now. What if they refused to help me get back home at all?

Jesus, calm down.

A tall female Veloxan with thin brown hair and small pointed horns approached Ko'ta. She whispered several words into his ear before stalking off.

Ko'ta eyed Ja'tare and I blankly. "The council will see you now."

He made a move to grab my arm, but I evaded him. "I'm fine," I grumbled.

Ko'ta walked past me into the vaulted chamber, and Ja'tare and I followed. Unlike yesterday, the space was devoid of Veloxan spectators with only the council present. We marched forward until we were ten paces away.

"The human, *Grey-gory* and Commander Ja'tare," Ko'ta announced.

"Um, actually, it's *Greh-gor-ee*," I corrected.

Ko'ta snorted and settled against a nearby wall, crossing his arms and keeping his gaze focused on me.

I smiled back at him sarcastically before turning my gaze back to the council. *Whatever, doofus.*

Kro'da, Nehma, and De'jartha sat a little more comfortably today, and their clothes were less ceremonious. Kro'da and De'jartha wore a slightly more elaborate version of the Veloxan form-fitting uniform, while Nehma wore a loose yet structured toga in a dark shade of blue.

"Good morning Nehma, Kro'da, De'jartha," Ja'tare said, then eyed me expectantly.

"Uh, yes, good morning. It's nice to see you again," I said, trying to sound cordial.

Nehma smiled, her lavender eyes sparkling. "You as well. Ja'tare, we called you here today to advise of a new expedition you will be overseeing. Although there is sensitive information in this meeting, we have decided to share with Gregory present due to his supposed honesty, your responsibility to watch over him, and the fact that he will be staying with us for a while. Kro'da, please tell them the news."

Nehma's somewhat optimistic words lifted a tiny weight off my shoulders. So I wasn't a slave after all, but not exactly an 'honored guest' either.

Kro'da leaned forward in his earthen seat. "Last night we received communication from Verus."

Ja'tare took a step forward, eyes wide. "Verus, you are sure? Are there survivors?"

"Yes. We tracked the origin of the communication to the city, but cannot pinpoint the location further. The message was simple in nature. Veloxans have taken shelter and are requesting aid. Beyond that, we have no additional details."

"What's Verus?" I asked. "Is it a base like the one here?"

Nehma shook her head. "Verus is one of our larger cities and a Veloxan hub that was evacuated two years ago due to a massive Dak'kar migration."

"I see." I glanced over at Ja'tare's troubled face. Based on his reaction, that must be where he came from. I could only imagine the emotional whiplash he was going through right now.

Nehma continued. "Ja'tare, we must track the origin of the communication and rendezvous with the Veloxan survivors. You will take a squadron of warriors to assist you. Once you have located our brethren and assessed the situation, you will communicate with us for further instruction."

"What about Gregory?" Ja'tare asked.

"We can watch over him while you are gone," De'jartha suggested. His response was devoid of his snarky attitude from yesterday.

Ja'tare frowned. "Can Gregory not accompany me? He has proven himself to be a formidable warrior from our travels together, and I would only need a day or two to prepare him for the journey."

The council members whispered amongst each other before coming to an agreement. Nehma addressed us."This is an acceptable request, but the choice will be Gregory's. We do not want to put him in unnecessary danger if he is not willing."

All eyes went to me, and I looked down at my feet as I weighed my options. If I stayed here, I'd be a sitting duck. That wouldn't exactly inspire trust with the Veloxans. But if I assisted Ja'tare and we were successful, the council would almost certainly be more trustful of me. This mission could be crucial in getting me home sooner.

On the other hand, it sounded dangerous. There was no guarantee we wouldn't die out there, and I had no idea how capable the other Veloxan warriors were or how we would even go about tracking the communication. I let out the breath I'd been holding as I made the impossible decision. "I'll go with Ja'tare, but I have a question. If we are successful, will we be bringing the other Veloxans back here?"

Kro'da looked expectantly to Nehma, who gave a terse nod.

"No," Kro'da said. "We did not want to speak of this just yet, but I think it cannot be helped. The shelter we have constructed here will not be safe for much longer. Given the migration patterns of the Dak'kar, we expect this region to be overrun within a few months. Also, our power sources of solar and storm energy are insufficient here. Joining our fellow Veloxans in Verus is our best chance at survival. Please note this change in objective but tell no one else. We will advise when we see fit and do not want to cause a panic."

Ja'tare looked just as shocked as I felt. The Veloxans were betting a lot on this chance to reconnect with their own and bolster their numbers.

"We will not let you down," Ja'tare promised.

"Thank you both," Nehma said. "If there is nothing further--"

I stepped forward. "Actually, I had another question if I may."

"Go ahead."

I hesitated a moment as I mulled over what to say. As much as I wanted to press the council on their reluctance to assist me in getting home, I was afraid challenging them would make things worse. I would have to trust that going on this mission would be enough to convince them of my honesty. Regardless of that, this was a golden opportunity to get answers about the Reapers only they could provide.

I cleared my throat. "Yesterday you mentioned your portal technology and how you found my race decades ago, but you didn't mention the Dak'kar. For the past five years, my race has debated back and forth on what caused them to enter our world at such a catastrophic level. Please, can you tell me where the Dak'kar came from? Are they from here?"

The council's features soured a bit, and De'jartha sneered at me. "What good will telling this human do?"

Nehma turned to face him. "De'jartha, we already decided to trust that Gregory was telling the truth. If everything he has told us is genuine, then it makes sense that he would want answers. He deserves to know the truth. Kro'da?"

Kro'da's head sunk. "It is unavoidable now."

Nehma's focus went back to me. "Nearly fifty years ago when we first developed our portal-generating technology, we began our search for intelligent life in the universe. We wanted to extend our goodwill across the universe, to forge lasting connections with other races. From those efforts we encountered two separate species, the humans ... and the Dak'kar. The humans intrigued us, and we began to explore possibilities. But the Dak'kar were another story. Any Veloxans we sent to the Dak'kar homeworld never returned. Instead, they came into ours."

She shook her head. "We were foolish then. The Dak'kar were violent, dangerous, but we wanted to understand them to see if we might change them somehow. We were able to trap some of the Dak'kar. We tried rehabilitating them for years, but our attempts ended in failure or worse ..."

An image of the broken tubes I'd seen in the laboratory flashed in my mind. That must be how they were containing the Reapers.

Kro'da took hold of Nehma's hand and spoke up. "After our failure we tried to eradicate the Dak'kar, but they were too evasive, too strong. We battled them for decades, their increasing dominion of our laboratories allowing them to figure out how we traveled across worlds under the direction of a strange breed capable of higher intelligence. Their population rose exponentially while our people died. Things have only been worse since the event."

"The event?" I asked. "What's that?"

"Five years ago was a turning point in our war against the Dak'kar. They attacked a vast number of our laboratories with portal-generating capabilities under the command of the smarter Dak'kar. We tried fighting them off, but there were too many of them. We were forced to retreat. With control of most of our portal generators, they were able to attack Earth in full force."

I took a step back, my hands like small icebergs as I fully digested what they had just told me. The Reapers had almost fully taken over their portal generators five years ago, around the same time Trent and I killed our first Reaper. But that would mean ... "Are you telling me you are responsible for the attack on my planet five years ago?"

Nehma seemed to withdraw into herself, and as I saw the shame in her eyes, I knew I was right.

I clenched my fists.

All this time I thought I'd caused the end of the world, had carried that weight on my shoulders, had suffered endless neglect and abuse. And for what? None of this was my fault! The Veloxans were to blame for Earth's destruction. They had let the Reapers into their world, they had royally fucked up, and Earth paid the price for it.

"Do you have any idea of the level of devastation your people have caused my planet? Nearly everyone on Earth died because of the Dak'kar invasion! My world, my *life* ended the day they came. God *damn it!*"

I threw my hands up and stormed off. Ja'tare called after

me, but I ignored him, leaving the chamber and stomping down the endless stone halls.

Everything I'd known had been a lie. The Reapers, how they came to Earth, my supposed part in all of it. Fury surged through my veins like electricity, ready to strike at the slightest provocation.

What was I supposed to do, help the very people who'd ended my world? Yeah, fat chance. I had to get out of here, had to find my own way back home even if it was impossible.

"Gregory, wait!" Ja'tare called again, this time much closer.

I kept walking until he jumped in front of me, barring my way. "Gregory, please stop."

I crossed my arms. "What could you possibly have to say?"

"Listen, I am sorry. There was no easy way to tell you."

I scoffed. "It's a little late to start apologizing now, don't you think? How could you let them hold me here and distrust me knowing what your people have done? You know what? Don't bother explaining. I'm not going to be a part of this bullshit any longer. I'm leaving."

I tried to slip past Ja'tare, but he blocked me.

"You cannot. It is not safe out there."

"I think I can handle myself, thank you very much." I made another fruitless attempt at getting past him. "You know, this is getting very annoying, *very* quickly."

"Please, hear me out. We are not proud of our past with the Dak'kar, but we cannot change that. Do you not think I wish I could? Our mistakes have haunted us for decades. There is not a day that goes by that I do not think of all the lives we could have saved by being more prudent and disabling all of our portal generators."

"Great, you feel like shit. Welcome to the club. How does that fix anything?"

"Let me speak with the council, get them to see things from your perspective."

I laughed. "Yeah, because that worked so well last time."

"I mean it, really I do. If I can get them to agree on helping get you home, will you consider staying? I do not want you to give up your life for nothing, and if you leave now, that is exactly what you will be doing."

I turned away from Ja'tare, my face still flush with rage. Damn it, this situation was completely fucked. If I left now, I had no plan, no way of locating the labs or going back home. How long would I last before I was ambushed by Reapers? Days? Hours? Minutes? It was a death sentence.

But if I trusted Ja'tare again, I had no way of knowing he'd follow through on his promise. Why did this feel like yet another lose-lose situation?

"Do it," I spat. I walked away from Ja'tare into the depths of the labyrinthine halls.

Whatever happened next, I was more determined than ever to get off this god-forsaken planet, and once I was back home I could forget all about this chaotic nightmare.

CHAPTER SIXTEEN

J focused on the triangular target before me, my Glock aimed and ready. *Stupid. Click. Fucking. Click. Planet. Click.*

Due to my limited ammunition I was forced to dry fire until there was something to actually shoot at.

I repositioned myself for another round, my stomach twisting in knots when I spotted Ja'tare heading my way.

I'd been avoiding him and all other Veloxans for the past two days. Knowing they were responsible for the destruction of Earth was an impossible pill to swallow. How was I supposed to act like nothing happened, to give them an ounce of trust?

Shortly after the council revealed the truth behind the Reaper invasion of Earth, Ja'tare fulfilled his promise to me, negotiating with the council on my behalf and coming to a quick agreement. If I accompanied Ja'tare to Verus and our mission was a success, they would help me get home once they were united with the tribe in Verus.

I didn't know what Ja'tare said to convince them and I honestly didn't care. All I had to do was go along with this expedition, then I could be free of this Reaper-ridden hell-hole. Sure, I felt a little guilty for being so cold to the Veloxans after they'd shown me hospitality, but it wasn't just my life they had affected. Billions of humans died when the Reapers came. There was no way to justify that.

Ja'tare caught up to me, looking a little deflated despite the smile on his face. "Hello Gregory, how is your training going?"

I shrugged. "Uh, fine I guess. Just honing my aim and blade skills."

"That is good to hear. We are fortunate you have had former training and appreciate what you are doing to assist us." Ja'tare's gleaming emerald eyes lingered on me.

Ugh, this was awkward. "Was there something you wanted to talk to me about?"

Ja'tare broke out of his trance. "Yes. The council has moved up our voyage to Verus. We leave in a couple hours."

"Why? Wasn't that scheduled for tomorrow?"

"It was, but there is a major storm system approaching that will negatively affect our journey unless we leave soon. I thought you might want to gather your personal items and get more time with your *bretaren* before we depart."

I scratched the back of my neck. "Yeah, I guess I don't have much of a choice, do I?"

I grabbed the weapons I'd need for the trip before Ja'tare and I left the training cavern for his quarters. He tried to make small talk along the way, and I gave the briefest of answers in hopes of discouraging him. I didn't want to open up to him, and I doubted I ever would again.

To my relief, he finally got the hint and stopped talking. I had plenty else to be nervous about, especially the bretaren he mentioned. Bretaren were a strange breed of animal that was basically a four-legged bird covered in scales. The Veloxans rode them like humans did with horses, using them to travel long distances. I'd been told they could outrun Reapers, which was reassuring, but learning to steer and control them had been a struggle for me. If I couldn't manage to stay on one's back, I wouldn't be going anywhere.

We arrived at Ja'tare's quarters and I gathered my things, sprawling them out over Ja'tare's thin mattress.

Flashlight, check. Hunting knives and blade, check check. Gun and ammo, check check check.

I started packing my knapsack, hustle and bustle picking up from the stone hall outside the room. The Veloxans had been extremely busy since the council publicly announced their intentions with this mission.

The news was a shock to many of the other Veloxans, and they voiced the same worries that had been swirling in my head. They were concerned about leaving relative safety here and trading it for the unknown dangers of Verus. There was no promise that we would find the other Veloxan tribe or that we'd even make it to the abandoned city. Even if we did, what then? We'd be stuck there at the mercy of migrating Reaper hordes.

The council stuck to their decision, and I understood why. Obviously the Veloxans needed to change their fortune in the war against the Reapers, but I doubted this was the smartest move or that it would be enough.

Not my problem, I reminded myself as I shoved the last of my things into my bag.

"Are you all packed up?" Ja'tare asked.

"Yeah, I'm ready." I slung my knapsack across my back and stopped when I reached the entry to the hall. "I need to stop by the eating area before we head to the stables. Artarta is about all I can stomach of your food so far."

Ja'tare led the way through the maze of tunnels to the dining quarters. There was no food being cooked at the moment, but plenty of sticks of artarta were left out. I crammed as many of them into my pack as possible and we left for the stables.

As we walked, it dawned on me how little I knew about the details of our plan once we reached Verus. I guess I'd done that to myself by avoiding the Veloxans, and I'd need answers from Ja'tare.

I wiped my clammy palms on my pants. "So uh, what's the game plan once we get to the city?"

Ja'tare kept his gaze forward. "When we near the city border, we will need to pinpoint the location of the distress beacon to find our Veloxan brethren. Although Verus was evacuated, the self-sustaining power sources left behind should still be operational, enough to help our devices locate them."

"And after that?"

"Assuming the refuge the other tribe located is adequately protected against the Dak'kar, we will take shelter and advise the council it is safe to join us. The biggest unknown variable in this mission is the Dak'kar. At any stage they could delay or destroy our chances of success. We must remain vigilant."

"Understood." I swallowed the concern that followed his words. Getting me home banked on a lot of assumptions.

We turned a sharp corner, ducking our heads as the ceiling suddenly dropped a few feet. Soon after we arrived at a crude stone door, warbling cries of the bretaren echoing from inside.

Ja'tare turned to face me. "Are you ready?"

My stomach fluttered thinking about my previous inter-actions with the strange animals. "As ready as I can be."

Ja'tare wedged open the door and I entered the large vaulted cave.

Scattered throughout the expansive area in little divided stalls were a dozen bretaren, most being attended to by Veloxans. The creatures stood on four scaly legs, each with the same number of claws. Most were a bizarre greenish blue color, and they had large protruding beaks below orange birdlike eyes. The Veloxans fed them red and purple grass that lay around the room in large bundles.

I grabbed some spare grass before walking over to my designated bretaren and entering the stall. His name was Skri'to, and he was more of a blue color than his brothers and sisters around him. I offered him a small handful of grass, and he slurped it up with a long tongue. He munched on the grass with the teeth hidden behind his beak.

I put my hands on Skri'to's side, petting him. He raised his head and gave a loud warble before turning to me and licking my face.

I cringed, wiping at my saturated face as Ja'tare gave a chuckle behind me.

"See? He likes you," Ja'tare said.

"Uh huh, a little too much if you ask me."

"Nonsense." Ja'tare waved off my comment. "Ready to give riding him another go?"

I looked upon my steed with hesitance. "Yeah, I guess so."

If you think riding a bretaren is anything like riding a horse, you're terribly wrong. Unlike a horse, they don't have a body type that supports saddles, not to mention that the Veloxans hadn't created anything like that anyways.

Instead, they have these weird knobules protruding from their backs in certain spots. You have to grab those knobules to hoist yourself up and guide them directionally.

It may sound easy, but Skri'to was relatively young, which made him as excitable as a dog in a room littered with table scraps.

Ja'tare came beside me. "I will do it with you if that makes you feel better."

I glared at Ja'tare. *Not really.* Instead I grumbled, "Fine."

Ja'tare hopped over to the stall next to me with his

bretaren, Ar'toth. He jogged towards it, grabbed onto its center knobule, and hoisted himself onto its back in one graceful motion. Ar'toth straightened its spine out as Ja'tare settled. "It is quite simple. Now you try."

"Yeah, yeah," I fussed. I glanced over at Skri'to.

You can do this, Gregory.

I scampered towards Skri'to, grabbing his knobule when within reach and pulling myself up. There was too much strength in my pull and I nearly catapulted over the other side, but I was able to yank myself back with my hand on the knob. I rested lightly against the knobules behind me and straightened my posture, Skri'to's positioning adjusting with my own.

"Great job," Ja'tare said. "Can you do a rotation for me?"

There were three knobs in front of me; one to my left, the center one for balance, and another to the right. I grabbed the knob to my left and twisted it in a quick rotation.

Skri'to jolted to life, spinning around so fast I had to cling on for dear life.

"Shit!" I cried.

"Remember, when you do a rotation on your bretaren, you must do it as fast as you intend. When you twisted Skri'to's knobule, you did it too quickly. Try it again, this time slower."

I did as he instructed. This time, Skri'to rotated slowly. I smiled despite my uneasy feelings. "All right, what's next?"

SKRI'TO LED me around the cavern in a wide circle, my hands steady on the two knobs I used to guide him.

The past hour hadn't been too bad. I'd fallen off Skri'to several times, but afterwards I'd been able to instruct him more precisely. Now I could steer, spin, stop, and enter a trot around the room. This particular roundabout felt effortless, and I pulled back slightly on the right knobule as I neared Ja'tare, no longer atop his bretaren. Skri'to slowed to a stop.

"Good, very good," Ja'tare said with a smile. "You are a natural."

I scoffed. "Hardly. Did you see those falls?"

"Every Veloxan struggles just as much as they train. Do you feel ready?"

"Nervous is more like it."

"Do not be. Bretaren naturally stay in packs, so Skri'to should be able to follow his brothers and sisters without much input on your end. I just wanted to be sure you would be alright on your own in case anything happens."

I shrugged. "I guess so--"

A metallic pinging drone sounded, permeating the air like a tuning fork.

"That is our cue. It is time to head out." Ja'tare mounted his bretaren in a graceful leap and approached the exit leading outside before turning to face the inhabitants of the room. "Brothers and sisters, it is time to journey to Verus. Let us find our brethren and take back what is rightfully ours!"

The other Veloxans cheered, quickly mounting their warbling bretaren and hurtling to the exit.

My stomach clenched. This was it.

I grabbed Skri'to's knobules, tilting them forward, and we shot ahead with an insane burst of speed. "Whoooahhh!"

CHAPTER SEVENTEEN

Skri'to's heavy clawed feet thundered on the bleak gray landscape as I held on for dear life. It felt like we'd been riding forever, and my butt was seriously aching despite the thick knobules behind me to keep me balanced.

We'd left the Veloxan mountain base heading east, the terrain quickly changing to dried out ridges and valleys. Reapers dotted our route, stalking the countryside for prey, but by the time they noticed us we'd already bolted far out of reach.

Racing forward like the wind we continued on, the dead scenery blurring into a desolate portrait of the Veloxan world.

We began a steep gallop up another ridge when something flicked into one of my eyes. I didn't dare lose my grip, so I hard blinked until whatever it was dislodged itself. When my vision cleared, I saw the other Veloxans had halted right in front of me. Freaked, I steered Skri'to on a hard right and came to a sudden stop, nearly catapulting off him.

Damn, that was a close one. I inched back towards the others, settling next to Ja'tare and his bretaren. He broke off his conversation with another Veloxan, a tightness in his eyes as he glanced at me.

"What is it?" I asked.

"We have arrived. Verus is at the top of this ridge."

"I'm going to take a look."

"That is fine, just stay where I can see you."

I guided Skri'to to the apex, trying not to let Ja'tare's anxiety and concern get to me.

As I reached the top and looked upon the fallen city of Verus, a chill rocked my core. A sea of towering, thin black spires stretched out before me. Most of the buildings had huge chunks taken out of them, and some of them had toppled over, leaning dangerously on others. Another fleck of something hit near my eye, and when I wiped it away this time my finger had a dark gray smudge on it.

Ash ...

My stomach roiled. I had a bad feeling about this.

I glanced back at my companions. Several had small tablets drawn out and were punching commands into them. A couple others had joined me in my viewpoint, and I noticed Ko'ta next to me, his jaw clenched as he laid eyes on the ruinous city. What had he lost in all of this?

I shook the thought away, directing Skri'to back to the bulk of our Veloxan force. A Veloxan with brown hair tied in a tight bun and strange goggles atop his forehead hopped off his bretaren, tablet in hand as he approached Ja'tare.

"I am detecting Veloxan and Dak'kar life forms nearby," he said. He showed his screen to Ja'tare. "What do you advise?"

Ko'ta and his bretaren tromped past me and rode up to Ja'tare, his posture rigid as a statue. "We cannot just sit here while our brothers are attacked. They must be the ones that sent the distress beacon."

The Veloxan with the tablet grimaced. "This is a rescue

mission, not a battle. We didn't come here to die at the hands of the Dak'kar."

Both of them looked to Ja'tare, and his eyes narrowed in concentration.

"Our primary goal is to find the other Veloxans, even if it means a battle with the Dak'kar," Ja'tare said. "We must protect them at all costs. Get ready to head out, and arm yourselves. Gregory, stay behind the front line until we have gauged the situation more fully."

I rolled my eyes as I steered Skri'to back in Verus's direction. I'd been fighting Reapers for five years. I wasn't going to stay in the background if shit hit the fan.

We charged over the top of the hill leading into the destroyed city, wind roaring in my ears as velocity shot us forward. We hit the bottom like an anvil dropping on a nail's head, the collective bretaren claws making a deafening clumping sound on the black dirt. The dark earth gave way to broken, tiled pavement that cracked and splintered as we trampled along.

Our boosted speed petered out, and as we approached the first dilapidated buildings a chaos encircled us that I was all too familiar with: mummified bodies, the awful lingering stench of death, shattered streets and crumbling structures. Hope had long since left this place.

About a block into the destroyed city, the Veloxans in front slowed to a trot, then to a crawl. I caught up to them as they gathered in a tight cluster.

The Veloxan with goggles on his head analyzed his device, glancing up a time or two at our surroundings with red, gleaming eyes. He turned to Ja'tare. "The life forms have relocated. It appears that the Veloxans are evading the Dak'kar, but they cannot seem to shake them off."

Ja'tare frowned. "Thanks, P'taro. It looks like we have a

battle on our hands, then. Which way would be the most efficient to intercept our brothers and cut off the Dak'kar?"

P'taro mulled over his tablet for a moment, then pointed to a broad square on the map. "The Veloxans are heading to this spot here. This location would give them multiple escape routes from the Dak'kar chasing them. Our quickest route there is down a small avenue on our right."

"Well, what are we waiting for?" Ko'ta growled, a murderous look on his face.

"Let us bathe in the blood of the Dak'kar!"

Ja'tare gave me a wary glance, and I suppressed my annoyance at his incessant doting over me. "Don't worry about me. This isn't my first rodeo with the Dak'kar. Let's annihilate this filth and save your people."

Ja'tare issued the go ahead, and our group stampeded forward, turning down a long, thin path with ash smoldering down on us. As we galloped on, swift movement from above caught my attention. I could've sworn I saw someone atop one of the battered, broken buildings, but when I looked up nothing was there.

I shuddered involuntarily. *Come on, focus.*

We reached the end of the alley, which opened into a small square market area littered with debris and rotting carcasses. The perimeter was made up of the skeletal remains of numerous oblong buildings, several of them tipping against each other like fallen dominoes. We came to a halt.

"P'taro, how close are they?" Ja'tare asked.

"They should be here within the next minute, maybe sooner."

"Alright everyone, dismount your bretaren. We cannot risk losing them to the Dak'kar. Ko'ta?"

Ko'ta stepped ahead and turned to face us. "Once the Dak'kar arrive, follow me and stay close together. We will separate them from our brothers. Show no mercy." He drew and activated his spear, lifting it up in the air. "For our brethren!"

The other warriors cheered, following suit with a sharp communal click.

I equipped my weapons, keeping my Glock in hand. We'd make quick work of these assholes.

"Any second now!" P'taro warned.

A dozen bedraggled Veloxans burst into the square from another alley directly across from us. They hadn't seen us and sprinted diagonally through the area, several others lagging behind as they carried an injured teammate of theirs.

Half a dozen Reapers swarmed out of the path the Veloxans had come from, gaining on them quickly.

"Now!" Ko'ta roared.

I sprung forward after Ko'ta and the warriors into the rubble-filled square, adrenaline coursing through me. The escaping group of Veloxans passed us to the left, and we spread out to block the hulking, bloodthirsty Reapers.

The ten of us formed a line of defense, cutting off the Reapers with a wide berth. They stopped in their tracks, giving earsplitting shrieks of rage as they eyed us ravenously.

"Gregory, De'roh, get back and protect the others!" Ko'ta shouted.

De'roh and I broke off from the group, running towards the fleeing party. Most of them had huddled behind a large fallen remnant from a nearby structure, but the injured Veloxan and the two lugging him along were still out in the open, vulnerable.

Sudden shouts from behind made me turn my head. A Dak'kar had charged one of our warriors, breaking through formation. Instead of slicing into him, it shot straight past him towards the exposed Veloxans.

Shit! It was faster than De'roh and I were. If it got to them first it would rip them apart.

"Get to the others, I've got this!" I told De'roh.

I bolted, trying to close the distance between the Reaper and I as fast as I could as my calves burned. Damn it, it was closing in on them too quickly. I'd have to distract it. "Hey, asshole!"

The Reaper spun around with an otherworldly screech, showing off its many rows of jagged teeth.

I aimed my Glock and fired two shots, hitting it in the shoulder and stomach. The Reaper gave a ghastly roar that reverberated in my chest.

Fuck!

I shoved my gun in its holster and drew my blade as I dashed forward. The Reaper did the same, rocketing towards me with an explosion of speed.

In a second the Reaper was right in front of me, its razor-sharp claws slashing down in a wide arc. Panicked, I rolled out of range then lunged to its side, stabbing it in the chest with an upward thrust. The beast bellowed in furious pain, and I redrew my gun, firing several shots into its head, point blank.

The Reaper dropped to the ground with a spray of black ooze, and I spun around to check on the injured Veloxan and company. They had rejoined their group safely, De'roh hovering protectively a few feet away.

"Are you guys o--"

"Behind you!" De'roh cried.

I flung myself forward, hitting the ground with a hard jolt. My gun skittered several feet away as heavy claws clanked on the gray pavement inches away from me.

I rolled on my back, the Reaper's claws already delving towards me. I thrust my blade in front of me defensively. The monster swung at it with such force it went flying out of my hands.

Defenseless, I tried to crab walk away, the Reaper unrelenting as it towered over me. It raised its deadly fingers once more. This time it wouldn't miss.

Oh god, no!

A high-pitched whistling sound cut through the air as a Veloxan spear shot straight into the Reaper's forehead with a spritz of blackened blood.

It twitched violently, then fell towards me. I scrambled away, aghast.

Ko'ta ran up to the Reaper and put a booted foot to its deflating leaking head, withdrawing the spear with a sickening crunch. "Be careful, Gregory."

He lacked the harsh tone or scowl he normally used when speaking to me, but I didn't have time to think about it. I got up to my feet and scrambled around for my weapons as I kept an eye on the battle.

Three more Reapers were still fighting the five remaining Veloxans in our line of defense. Two of our crew were down, one not moving. Ko'ta and I moved to join them when activity in my peripheral drew my attention.

Atop a nearby burnt-out building the silhouette of a cloaked Reaper stood, its cape flowing in the wind. As I locked eyes with it, an icy dread ran through me. That was what I'd seen in the alley. But if it knew about our arrival in Verus, why was it lingering around? Unless ...

"Trap, it's a trap!" I shouted.

Ko'ta spun back to face me, his gleaming brown eyes wide with shock.

With an explosive communal shriek, seven additional Reapers burst from a tiny alley dangerously close to the Veloxans we'd rescued.

"Run, run!" I yelled. I windmilled an arm, motioning them to me.

The fatigued Veloxans rushed towards me as best they could, but several hesitated a moment, a moment they didn't have. The Reapers descended on them with predatory zeal, tearing them apart with sprays of purple-blue blood.

My pulse raged as those fortunate enough to have their lives clustered around Ko'ta and I. There was no way we could fight off this many Reapers, not without significant loss of life. But what other choice did we have?

"What do we do?" I asked Ko'ta as the Reapers finished their quick kills.

His expression darkened as he looked over our ragtag group. "We fight with honor. Those of you who can still fight, please aid us. We cannot fight them alone." Several bedraggled Veloxans drew weapons of their own and gathered behind us, the rest retreating further.

The Reapers prowled forward, their yellow eyes honing in on us with bestial intention.

"On three, we strike together," Ko'ta commanded. "Three … two …"

The sudden blaring of a horn filled the square, and we all froze in confusion.

The Reapers did the same, shrieking as they swiveled their heads in search for the source of the sound.

Out of a nearby alley, half a dozen Veloxans atop bretaren stamped into the square with a savage cry. They were clad in black tattered clothes and wielded spears and wicked curved blades. The Reapers spun around as the Veloxans attacked, impaling and trampling upon them without mercy.

I shrank back at the abrupt carnage. Who the hell were these Veloxans? We didn't bring reinforcements with us. They could be associated with the group we were rescuing, but they didn't seem anything like them with their wild assault and unkempt appearance.

More robust battlecries echoed around us as additional groups of Veloxans charged into the square from multiple pathways, all riding bretaren with the same black garb as the others.

"What's going on?" I asked Ko'ta.

He frowned as he gripped his spear tight. "I do not know. Stay on your guard, but do not act, not yet."

I observed the mounted Veloxans that had saved us when a figure among them caught my eye. The individual was abnormally short in stature for a Veloxan and had a swath of curly brown hair resting atop its head. A mask covered its face from the nose down, hiding its features. As it neared the Reaper and Veloxan skirmish close by it leapt from its bretaren straight into the jumbled mass and drew two extremely sharp looking daggers.

I watched in disbelief as the small figure weaved between the Reapers, stabbing them as it burst through with great agility.

The Reapers in its path fell quickly, and the mysterious figure continued its bloody sprint towards one of the last monsters standing. It jumped on the Reaper's back, thrusting the daggers in and out of the beast so fast I could hardly see them plunge down. The Reaper crumbled to the ground, its life force oozing out on the pavement.

The individual set its sights on me, pulling down its mask to reveal its face and the same language translator I wore around my neck.

A wave of dizziness hit me as I took in her features. The three claw-marked scars above the bridge of her nose were new, but her curly brown hair, big blue eyes, and facial structure were too familiar for me to ignore.

She wasn't Veloxan at all. She was ... no, it couldn't be!

"I-Imogen?" I squeaked.

Imogen cried out in rage, lunging towards me.

"Who is that?" Ko'ta asked.

"S-sister," I croaked.

I froze, tears blurring my vision. Imogen was alive? How could this be? I saw the Reaper take her. This was impossible!

My vision spiraled out of control, cutting out as my little sister raised her daggers to strike.

CHAPTER EIGHTEEN

*D*eep, faraway voices echoed in the neverending darkness surrounding me, muffled and distorted. So far away ... No, wait, getting closer. A little more clear now.

"He is alright ... think ... still breathing."

Slowly the blackness receded and a shadowed blurry form came into focus. Ja'tare hovered over me, brows drawn together as he inspected my face.

"He is awake!" he called out with a beaming smile. "Gregory, how are you feeling?"

I groaned as my body throbbed with fatigue. Why was I so tired? In a flash it all came back to me: the battle, the cloaked Reaper, Imogen was alive!

"Imogen!" I shot up, but Ja'tare halted me with a six-fingered hand.

"Take it easy. You fainted."

"Like hell I will!" I batted him off me. "My sister is alive. I have to talk to her."

Ja'tare stared at me, wide eyed. "Your sister, the one who was taken?"

"*Yes.*"

"I am amazed that she managed to survive her capture, but Gregory, she tried to kill you. We had to pull her off of you."

"Don't you think I know that?" I snapped. "That's why I need to speak with her. There has to be some kind of misunderstanding. She's family. We don't turn our backs on each other."

Ja'tare's lips pressed into a grimace. "I do not know what results you expect from a conversation with her, but I will not stop you."

A loud scuffle and shouts of resistance rang out. I caught a glimpse of two of our Veloxans dragging Imogen away, followed by several others. She thrashed against their hold on her.

I launched up to my feet, stumbling a little. "Hey, what are you doing? Let go of her!" I turned back to Ja'tare. "Make them stop!"

"I will not until we know it is safe. She is dangerous."

"Whatever." I tromped off towards my sister and her captors through a haze of dust and debris. I didn't care what Ja'tare thought. They couldn't treat Imogen like this, and I needed to talk to her.

Imogen's actions didn't make any sense. Clearly she recognized me, but why had she tried to kill me? I hadn't ever done anything to hurt her. Maybe if I explained everything she would understand.

At the same time, I worried how her force of guerilla Veloxans would react to her being restrained. So far they hadn't noticed as they roamed the bloody, rubble-filled battlefield to ensure the Reapers were dead with stabs of their spears. A sudden scream of protest from Imogen ruined all that. Several black-garbed Veloxans looked our way, quickly steering their bretaren in our direction and breaking off in a gallop.

Shit!

I bolted, hoping to outpace them, but they reached her in no time. They jumped off their bretaren, led by a tall Veloxan with long, slicked back hair and a jagged scar running down the side of his face.

"Let our commander go," he demanded.

I gaped at Imogen, who had a vicious smug look on her face. Their *commander*?

She was only twelve years old!

Our Veloxans glared back at Imogen's just as ferociously, silent and immoveable.

"Release her now or there will be consequences!" Imogen's tall Veloxan snarled impatiently.

One of Ja'tare's guards puffed his chest. "We will not! How do we know she will not attack Gregory again?"

The tall Veloxan scowled, then gestured to his comrades. They activated their spears with a sharp click.

"Stop!" Ja'tare's voice rang behind me. He ran up to the heated conflict, wedging himself between the two groups. "Enough of this pointless fighting. I ordered the girl to be restrained. She tried to kill Gregory, her own human brother."

The black-garbed Veloxans gave varying incredulous looks of confusion. Apparently she hadn't told anyone about me, but why?

Ja'tare spun around, facing Imogen. "Explain your actions. Why did you attack him?"

Imogen scoffed, giving a dignified look that I was surprised a twelve-year-old could pull off. "It was a gut reaction. That bastard is the reason I'm here in the first place."

I gaped at my little sister. How could she say that? "Imogen, that's not true. I tried to save you five years ago. How could you not remember that?"

"I remember the Dak'kar pulling me into this hellhole and you not doing a thing to stop it."

"That's a lie!"

"Please, we do not have time for this," Ja'tare said. "What is important is that we reach safety. Imogen, if we release you, will you give your word that you will not attack him again?"

Imogen leered at me for a long moment. "Fine. He's not worth my time anyways."

I clenched my jaw but kept my mouth shut. Fighting wasn't going to fix anything between us. I'd have to smooth things over later.

Ja'tare exchanged looks with our guards. "All right then. Let her go and give her weapons back."

Our Veloxans broke away from Imogen, handing over her daggers and giving her a wide berth. Imogen had a wide grin plastered on her face as she rejoined her black garbed men.

"Despite our differences, I suggest we stay together to bolster our forces," Ja'tare said.

Imogen glowered and opened her mouth to respond, but stopped. Her features softened. "As much as I hate to admit it, there is strength in numbers. My tribe and I hunt Dak'kar, and this region is rife with them. It won't be long before more come."

"Do you have shelter nearby we may use?"

Imogen shook her head. "Not for how many people we have."

Ja'tare clicked his embedded comm device. "P'taro, please come over and bring whoever is in charge of the Verus Veloxans with you."

P'taro came running over with a lanky, disheveled Veloxan with errant chin-length hair. "Yes, Commander?"

"Run a lifeform scan and tell me what you find."

P'taro punched several commands into his tablet, his red eyes bulging with the results. "Sensors are picking up a drastic increase in Dak'kar lifeforms, at least several dozen. They are not close yet, but that could change quickly. We should move as soon as possible."

Ja'tare turned to face the lanky Veloxan beside him. "What is your name?"

"En'doh, sir."

"En'doh, we journeyed here after receiving communications from a Veloxan tribe seeking assistance. Was that you?"

En'doh smiled from ear to ear. "Yes, yes! We were worried no one would hear us. Is this all of your tribe?"

"No, just a scouting party. We can talk more details later. Tell me, do you have shelter here?"

"Yes, and you are all more than welcome to stay with us. I can lead the way. It is not far away."

Ja'tare gave a slight bow. "Thank you for your hospitality. Please ask your Veloxans to get ready and show P'taro the coordinates as best you can."

En'doh stalked off with P'taro, and everyone dispersed to ready their bretaren. I followed Ja'tare back to where we left ours. Despite my lingering reservations with the Veloxans, I was glad I came here.

I never imagined Imogen could still be alive after what happened to her. Now there was hope for the future. My family could be reunited, whole again. Who even got a chance like that anymore?

Still, there was a long way to go with my long lost sister. She blamed me for her disappearance. I had to find a way for her to forgive me and come back home with me to Earth.

I mounted Skri'to and focused on Imogen, her back to me. I'd have to keep reaching out to her and break down her walls, even if she did try to kill me again. I wasn't leaving this planet without her.

~

I TRAMPLED DOWN THE CRUMBLING, destroyed streets of Verus atop Skri'to, holding tight to the knobules that kept me secure. Ja'tare's group surrounded me with the Verus Veloxans behind us and Imogen's troup flanking them. P'taro, Ko'ta, and several of Imogen's guard stayed at the front to help lead the way and provide a first defense in case we encountered any Reapers, but the city was empty, eerily silent after the bloodbath we'd been through. I kept my eyes forward, trying to concentrate on the mission at hand.

Once we reached shelter, we'd contact Ja'tare's tribe and let them know what had happened. Hopefully they would make it here in one piece, and from there they could help get me home. Home ... with Imogen right beside me.

Her face flashed in my mind, and my focus dissolved away like salt in a storm.

What had happened to her these past five years? I tried to picture my seven-year-old sister alone in this desolate world. God, it must have been awful. Being here had changed her, hardened her. It was pretty clear she hadn't been as lucky as I'd been since I got here. What could I say to extinguish the animosity she felt for me and convince her to come home with me? And even if I succeeded, what barriers lay ahead for her? She'd spent nearly as much time on this planet as she had back home.

I shook my head. It was pointless to brood on this now. I refocused on our trek to safety.

We took a sharp left at the next intersection of streets, proceeding to climb over hills of rubble and large chunks of buildings that had been severed in some nightmarish battle of the past. Clearing the worst of the remnants, I laid eyes on our destination the Verus Veloxans described as we broke through clouds of dust that rose around us. A block ahead, a towering black spire jutted into the sky, nearly touching the dark clouds overhead. Its structure looked asymmetrical and thin, but as we approached it turned out to be much larger.

The front line came to a halt at the base of the structure, an obsidian wall carved with bizarre Veloxan symbols in intricate patterns.

A sharp crackle emitted from Ja'tare's communication receiver feet away. "Hurry, please. Nearby Dak'kar lifeforms are closing in on our location."

Our ragtag party caught up just as En'doh dismounted his bretaren and approached the wall. He tapped the surface in a complicated sequence of knocks. With a woosh of air, a large entry opened vertically in the building, a thick pit of blackness beyond.

My stomach knotted, and I looked to Ja'tare for reassurance, but he shrugged and continued onward. I followed him hesitantly.

Please let this not be another fucked up situation.

Our small army inched forward into the dark space. I lingered behind as long as I could, eyeballing the doorway as I passed. Once the last of us made it inside, the entry slammed closed, making me jump. Without the filtered light from outside, the darkness was all encompassing.

"I can't see anything," I muttered. My voice sounded small and insignificant.

"Apologies, Gregory," a familiar voice said.

A blazing blue light set within the wall burned to life. It danced across the perimeter of the area in complex and beautiful geometric patterns, a dazzling grid of luminescence. Within seconds, the entire space was lit up well enough for me to see clearly.

We had entered a lobby of sorts with oblong-shaped furniture scattered around in minimalist fashion. The tile we walked on looked like speckled marble, and the elevated ceiling was at least thirty feet high. The bright azure lights gathered in a central point above, forming an otherworldly flowery shape.

"What is this place?" I asked.

En'doh turned to face us, his blue eyes glowing excitedly. He lifted his hands

up in reverence. "Welcome to the Verus tower of communications."

Despite the boring name, I was impressed with this place. It reminded me of the fancy office building my dad worked at when I was younger.

"How long have you been here?" Ja'tare asked.

"Not very long, maybe a week or two," En'doh said. "We came from the southern cities looking for safety. Luckily, one of us knew how to get inside the building. Now come, let us rest. You can all dismount your bretaren and leave them here. We will take the lift to where the others are and send them down to tend to them."

Everyone descended from their mounts and followed after En'doh, who stopped at a blank wall with a control panel set on the right-hand side. With the press of a button, the outline of a large metal door appeared and opened.

The lift was huge, and together the several dozen of us shuffled inside easily. When the door closed, we were once again submerged in almost total darkness, the only light source a faint maroon glow from the backlighting at the top of the lift.

We came to a stop after a few seconds, and as the lift entry opened I made to leave, but En'doh barred my way. "Injured only, please. This floor houses our medical bay. It is not much and we only have a small team, but they should be able to help. Continue straight through the door at the end of the hall, and they will take good care of you."

A small group of injured Veloxans shuffled into the unadorned, dimly lit hall, supported by their comrades.

As I watched them leave, my curiosity sparked. How many people were here if they had a medical staff to tend to their wounded? Fifty? A hundred? A thousand? The more of us there were, the better chance Imogen and I stood at getting home.

The lift continued upwards, and we stopped one final time. When the doors opened I gasped in shock, taking a step back. Armed Veloxans surrounded the way out, pointing green-tipped poison spears in our faces that glowed in the dim light.

Endo raised his six-fingered hands. "It is alright."

One of the guards stepped forward from the others, placing a hand on En'doh's shoulder. "Are you alright, brother? We received your distress beacon but could not risk sending out a rescue party."

"I am fine, but we lost several of our brethren in a Dak'kar attack while scavenging. Luckily, these people saved us." En'doh spun around. "Actually, how *did* you know to come rescue us?"

"Your first transmission led us to Verus. When we arrived, we picked up on your life readings," Ja'tare explained. "It was pure luck, really."

"Can we *please* get off this god-damned lift already?" Imogen grumbled behind me.

En'doh motioned to the guards, and they let us pass.

As we piled out, a warmth spread through my chest. Dozens of Veloxans milled about the large, sparsely furnished space, at least fifty in number. Women and children laid on furs in exotic colors stretched out along the speckled marble-like floor, while others dressed in differing garb stood in groups in animated conversations. Some were clearly warriors based on the weapons sheathed at their sides and their rigid posture. Others seemed to have more of a scientific role with their tablets, studious demeanor, and casual, less structured clothing.

Though this wasn't the army I was hoping for, a glimmer of hope blossomed within me. Once Ja'tare's tribe joined us, the combined forces should be formidable enough to get me and Imogen home. But what plans did our Veloxans have from here?

Remember, not your problem, I scolded myself.

I wandered the room's outer edge for a moment. It resembled the lobby with its black obsidian walls inlaid with glowing Veloxan symbols and shapes that encircled the entire area. At both ends of this level were identical doors, each with their own control panel.

An eerie sensation of being watched made the hair raise on my neck. I looked around to find every nearby Veloxan staring at me in a rainbow of vivid colored eyes. I fixed my gaze on the floor and rubbed at my arms. I should regroup with Ja'tare and Ko'ta and see what our next steps were.

"Attention, everyone!" a voice shouted at the opposite end of the space.

Veloxans hustled and bustled towards the commotion, blocking my view. I walked over, curious to see what was going on. Breaking through a small group of Veloxans, I got a better view. A towering male Veloxan with braided copper hair stood with a wide berth around him, arms outstretched.

"We have some new arrivals joining our ranks. To those of you who just arrived, we welcome you. My name is Ral'ta, and I am the commanding officer of this base. Out of those joining us today, we have some very special guests. Please welcome the humans *Grey-gor-y* and *Ee-moh-gen*."

Whispers arose in a chorus as the Veloxans around me

sized me up. I couldn't see Imogen anywhere, but I doubted she wanted any kind of attention. She was probably in a dark corner somewhere. Why didn't I think of that? I focused my eyes on a spot on the wall.

"Please, try not to stare too much. It is considered rude in the human culture I have been told. Everyone, make room for the new arrivals on your furs and allow them to rest. Their journey has been long and arduous. In a few hours, food will be ready once they have had a chance to sleep. You may now resume normal activities."

The crowd began to disperse, and in the movement I located Ko'ta and Ja'tare not far from me. I walked briskly to them, Ko'ta seeing me first.

"Ah, there you are. Where have you been?" he asked.

I shrugged. "Um, just taking things in. What happens now?"

"I need to accompany P'taro to the communications hub so we can send the tribe our report and advise them," Ja'tare said. "You two go get some rest. Right now there is nothing else to be done."

I agreed and followed Ko'ta to a nearby purple fur with several of our group resting on it. The material was soft and warm as I sat next to him, and I exhaled deeply.

As much as I wanted to keep hating the Veloxans for humanity's plight, it got harder the longer I was around them. They weren't fully to blame for what happened, and they were stuck in the same shitty situation Earth was, just trying to make a difference. All they wanted was peace, a life without Reapers and fearing for their lives. I couldn't condemn them for that.

I glanced over at Ko'ta and nudged him. "I'm sorry for the way I've been treating you guys lately. After learning the truth about what happened five years ago, I took it out on you. But you were just doing what you could to fight them like we were on Earth."

Ko'ta's honey-colored eyes beamed at me as he gave a weak smile. "I accept your apology. For what it is worth, I am happy to welcome you into our tribe. You are not a bad warrior. A little wild perhaps, but strong, fast, brave." He gripped my shoulder softly. "Let us get some rest, yes? When you wake up, you will feel better."

"Yeah, thanks."

I layed down on the shaggy cozy fur, using my pack as a pillow. I closed my eyes, but my mind flurried with activity. So much was up in the air.

Nehma and the others needed to get here in one piece. From there, we would need to locate the nearest portal generator and do whatever was needed to get it to work.

Even if both of those things went off without a hitch, I still had to smooth things over with Imogen if I expected her to come back to Earth with me. Right now I doubted she would go anywhere with me.

I had to convince her, and fast. We couldn't stay here forever, and sooner or later, we'd have to leave.

The Reapers would be waiting.

CHAPTER NINETEEN

*J*jolted to life in a cold sweat, my heart thundering like a piston on overdrive.

Reapers everywhere! We had to run, we had to ... wait a second.

I sat up and looked around. Dozens of Veloxans slumbered, stretched out on exotically-colored furs dotting the floor. My pulse slowed a bit.

Just a dream, thank god.

On second glance, I noticed I wasn't the only one having trouble sleeping. Imogen sat on a nearby pelt with her arms around her knees, pressed against her chin. She looked pained, vulnerable. It was jarring considering her murderous, unapologetic demeanor just a few hours ago.

I felt nervous about approaching her, but I wouldn't get a better time than now, so I got up and headed over. Surprisingly, she didn't leer at me. Instead, a tired knowing look crossed her features. She must've figured I wouldn't give up so easily.

"Couldn't sleep either, huh?" I asked.

"No," she said icily. She stared at me with her piercing blue eyes. "What do you want?"

"To speak to my sister."

Imogen scoffed and looked away.

I sat down next to her, unsure of what to say.

"How's Earth?" she asked.

"Honestly? Not much better than here."

She turned back towards me with a scowl. "Then what are you doing here? Come to give me a proper send off into oblivion?"

"I didn't come here by choice. One of the Dak'kar brought me here."

Imogen grinned impishly. "How ironic."

A wave of anger flushed through me and I fought to keep it at bay. I couldn't let her get the best of me, not if I was going to get her to open up. But how could I do that?

We sat there for a few awkward moments when a realization struck me. Imogen didn't know the details behind her being taken, just that it had happened. Without that knowledge, her actions made sense. I was the last person she'd seen. Of course she would blame me for not rescuing her. I had to tell her the truth. As painful as it would be to hear, if she was going to trust me I owed it to her.

I took a deep breath. "I understand how upset you are and how you must feel about me showing up, but there are some things about your disappearance five years ago that you don't know, things I need to explain to you.

"Five years ago, you were taken by a hooded Dak'kar in our basement. I tried to fight it, but it was too strong. After you were gone, I was devastated. I didn't know what to do. Everyone moved on like nothing had happened, but I couldn't accept it. So I looked around town for answers." I paused for a moment. She wasn't going to like this, but what other choice did I have?

"My search led me to an organization called The Order. They knew about the Dak'kar and had been sacrificing children for decades to keep them at bay. Imogen, your disappearance wasn't a random occurrence ... Mom and Dad--"

"Don't," Imogen grumbled.

I shook my head. "You need to know the truth. Mom and Dad thought they were doing the right thing by giving you to the Dak'kar. All the adults thought that. They were being brainwashed by The Order. But I couldn't give you up. You are my little sister, Immy. I tried to find you, but it was too late. You were already here."

Imogen's gaze focused on the floor, her expression warring between pain, anger, then settling on fury. "Get away from me," she growled.

"Imogen, all I ever did was try to save you. Don't you see? We can go back now with the Veloxans' help. Mom's still alive. We can be a family again!"

"I said get away!" she screamed.

Several Veloxans stirred around us and I panicked, scurrying back to my own fur. I plopped down on it with my back to Imogen.

That went bad quickly, but at least Imogen knew the truth. Still, it hadn't made anything better between us. What was I supposed to do now?

I closed my eyes, falling into a fitful sleep.

THE SOUND of chatter woke me from my troubled slumber. I sat up and rubbed the sleep from my eyes. An earthy aroma filled the space, making my stomach grumble.

I was the only one on my fur, or any others for that matter. At the northern end of the space a huge crowd of Veloxans were gathered, many more than had been here before. Could Ja'tare's tribe have arrived while I was sleeping?

Getting up and speeding over, I found Ko'ta along the outer edge of the gathering.

I tapped his shoulder. "Hi Ko'ta. What's going on? Is your tribe here?"

He turned around with a large orange piece of something that resembled bread

sticking out of his mouth. "Yes, and food!" He swallowed the mouthful quickly before pointing another piece in my direction. "Are you hungry?"

"Yeah, but what about your tribe? Shouldn't we speak with them?"

Ko'ta shook his head. "No, no, no. Best to let them eat and attend to business."

I cocked an eyebrow. What did he mean 'attend to business'?

Before I could object any further, Ko'ta strong-armed me over to the left, where a cook was handing out orange bread and small bowls of purple ... chili? Once I got a fair portion and Ko'ta a robust amount for himself, he led me back to the fur we'd slept on and we sat.

I took a bite of my bread. Though I hadn't had bread since before the Dak'kar invasion, it was similar to what I remembered, only more grainy, crunchy, and spicy, like someone had put cayenne and other herbs in it. I dipped the bread into the purple chili and took another munch. At first, the chili tasted pretty bland, but as I chewed the spice increased exponentially until my eyes watered and heat flooded to my head. I set my food down and waved my hands to fan myself.

Ko'ta slapped his leg and chuckled. "Are you melting, Gregory?" Something caught his attention, and he glanced behind me. "Ja'tare! Where have you been, fearless commander?"

Ja'tare sat beside me, his angular face flush. "I have been speaking with the council in private and catching them up on events. They did not have the rocky ride that we did and suffered no casualties. Gregory, after you are done eating the council would like to speak with you."

I chomped into my bread again, avoiding the chili this time. "Sure, what for?"

Ja'tare shifted uncomfortably.

"Ja'tare, tell me. What do they want to talk to me about?"

"I am … not allowed to say."

I frowned. What couldn't Ja'tare tell me that he hadn't already spilled the beans about? Did this have to do with getting back to Earth? Suddenly my stomach felt like it was gonna drop through my butt.

I threw the rest of my bread into the bowl of chili and wiped my hands free of crumbs. "Alright, I'm done. Let's go."

We stood up, and to my shock Ja'tare walked over to Imogen and spoke with her for a brief moment. *No way.* What could the council want to speak with me about that would have to do with her?

Ja'tare approached me with Imogen in tow, a warning in his furrowed brows. *Let it be.*

Begrudgingly I kept my mouth shut, following after them to the southern end of the space opposite the hungry Veloxan crowd. We passed through a door that led us into a winding hallway lined with big control panels more complex than any I'd seen yet. At the end of the narrow passage, another door opened with a swoosh and we stepped into a tiny, stark white room.

The council faced us, sitting in high-backed white chairs behind a short table in bizarre abstract shapes I couldn't name. Three stools stood before us.

Nehma motioned to us with a smile on her pale face, her purple eyes gleaming brilliantly. "Hello Gregory, Imogen. Please, take a seat. There is much for us to discuss."

I rubbed my sweaty palms on my Veloxan garb and sat

between Imogen and Ja'tare, placing my hands in my lap. I bounced my leg nervously for a moment before stopping myself.

Just talk to them, you know them.

I cleared my throat. "Um, thank you for meeting us. I'm glad you made it here okay. May I ask why you called us here?"

Kro'da frowned, betraying his beaming golden eyes. "We will not waste any time dancing

around the subject any longer than we have, and time is precious, especially now. Gregory, we were not completely truthful to you when you first came to us, and for that we apologize. You were a stranger to us, human, and we did not know how much we should tell you or if we could even trust you. We were wrong in our actions."

I stared blankly at Kro'da. What exactly was he talking about?

Nehma broke the awkward silence that lingered. "We did not come to Verus to migrate to a safer location, at least not just for that reason. The tower of communications has some of the most powerful and wide-ranging technology available on Velerius. We do intend to rally our people together, but our situation is much graver than we originally led you to believe."

De'jartha pulled out a tablet and handed it over to Nehma, who studied it and shook her head. "According to a recent long-range scan of lifeforms on our planet, the Veloxan population has dropped to an astronomical low. We number nearly fifty thousand over several hundred colonies. Those numbers continue to drop daily, while the Dak'kar number nearly a million and are increasing exponentially. Within a year, our population could easily be half of what it is now or less."

A wave of dizziness swept over me as I processed the

disturbing information. A million Reapers? A *million*? The Veloxans didn't stand a chance, not unless they had an ace hidden up their sleeves, which I seriously doubted.

Ja'tare placed a hand on my shoulder. "Are you alright?"

"No, I'm not okay. Your people are totally screwed. What hope do you possibly have of defeating the Dak'kar?"

"That is why we called you here," Nehma said. "There is still hope, but not on Velerius. Our people must evacuate to another planet, one where life is more sustainable." Her gaze lingered on me for a long moment.

Not on Velerius … she couldn't possibly mean--

"You want to escape to Earth," Imogen stated calmly.

I slapped my hands down on the table in front of me. "Are you kidding me? You waited until now to mention something this important? How could you lie to me like that?"

Nehma looked down at her hands. "We are truly sorry Gregory, but again, we didn't know if we could trust you. You coming here proved that we could."

"Why Earth?"

"We have had contact with your race before," Kro'da said. "Our interactions were peaceful outside of the situation with The Order. We also know your planet can support life. Those factors alone make it our best chance at survival."

I shook my head. "You don't understand. If my people find out about your involvement with the Dak'kar and how they got to Earth, they may not take it well. I know you are peaceful and mean us no harm, but they don't. There could be violence, death, war. What about the other planets you've been to?"

"All the other planets we have encountered in the past were either unsupportive of life or violent, like the Dak'kar home planet. Even if we wanted to attempt travel to other viable planets, the resource we use to power our portal generators called *tarcin* is so finite that it would be a one-way trip. We cannot put our people at that level of risk for a planet that may end up not being suitable.

"You have lived on Earth your entire life in relative peace until the Dak'kar came. Though the Dak'kar presence there is increasing, they have only had five years to populate versus decades here. We could help you defeat them, reclaim your planet. We could forge an alliance between our races. Please, give it some thought."

My posture stiffened. "What you're suggesting is a huge risk."

"Indeed it is," Kro'da agreed. "But it is one we are willing to take, only if you and your sister will allow it. Evacuating to your world without your acceptance as ambassadors would be considered a disgrace to our race. We will not do it, even if it means our demise. We will give you some time to think this over. Once you have reached a decision, please let Ja'tare know."

The council rose to their feet. Kro'da led the way out, followed by Nehma and De'jartha.

Once they were gone, a deafening silence filled the room. I looked to Imogen, but she scowled and turned her back to me.

Okay, I guess I'm on my own.

I mulled over the impossible situation, the gravity of it hitting me like a bucket of ice water. Where did I start, and how could they leave me with such a major decision?

Unless ... they really did trust me and see me as an ambassador, a leader.

For the past five years, I let myself be defined by others peoples' opinions. They told me I was nothing, so I believed it. They treated me like crap, and I allowed them to. But lately something *had* sparked in me. A thirst for life, for something more than survival. I wanted to make a difference. The Veloxans saw potential in me, and looking back into that mirror now, so did I.

Even with my willingness to lead, this decision affected not just the Veloxans, but my race too. I got up and paced around the small room.

On one hand, the Veloxans had made a very valid point. They possessed weapons and knowledge that we could use to our benefit. Joining forces with them could give us a fighting chance to turn the tide in the human war against the Dak'kar.

On the other, I knew how low humans had sunk in the past five years. They could be mistrustful, greedy, and downright crazy at times. Could my race accept the Veloxans' past and rise together to challenge this threat, or would we wind up killing each other?

If I said no, the Veloxans would be stuck here, prey of the Dak'kar. Even if they had enough of this tarcin stuff to last them a lifetime, finding another suitable planet would take time, time they may not have.

I sat back on my stool, bringing my fingertips to my temples. When it came down to it the real question was, could the Veloxans and the humans survive together? I tried to envision an Earth that both humans and Veloxans shared. It was an odd picture and an even crazier concept, but we had a lot in common.

We shared this war with the Dak'kar, we wanted peace, and we would do anything to protect our own. At the end of the day, those things were what mattered most.

The Veloxans had an inherent goodness, a goodness that I think my race desperately needed to be reminded that they had within them. In time, they would see that genuine kindness and appreciate it despite the Veloxans' somewhat devilish appearance.

With our combined forces, the Dak'kar would falter

under our strength. Apart, nothing would change, and I couldn't let both of our races suffer for that.

"Ja'tare, call the council back."

Several moments later the council came in and sat down, waiting for our answer.

I wiped my clammy palms on my pants again. "I don't know how this idea of yours will play out, but I can't let the Dak'kar hunt humans and Veloxans if there's something we can do about it. I accept your offer to come to Earth with us, given the difficulties I've warned you about. Imogen?"

Imogen straightened her posture. "I agree with Gregory, but I will not be joining you on Earth."

What? I opened my mouth to object.

Imogen turned to me with a scathing glare. "Be quiet." She focused back on the council. "I have no life to go back to on Earth. All I have known is the war against the Dak'kar, and it has given me purpose. I will not give up on Velerius or my squadron of Veloxans. My troops will support you however we can, but we will not go with you."

Nehma's shoulders drooped at Imogen's choice. "We respect your decision and are grateful for the opportunity you have given us. It is our hope that we can help repair your broken world and grow stronger together in our alliance. Before I forget, Gregory, we have something for you."

Nehma gestured to De'jartha. To my shock he pulled out the gray Reaper candle they'd confiscated from me and handed it to her.

"This belongs to you," Nehma said. She placed the partially melted candle in front of me.

I almost grabbed it, then stopped myself. "Why are you giving it back? Isn't this trackable? I thought you said it was dangerous."

"We had the tracking chip removed. It has been in your

possession for so long it is rightfully yours. Let this be a gesture of our faith in you."

My hands closed around the candle. "Thank you."

The council stood as one, Kro'da speaking up this time. "We will meet with the other Veloxans and share this news as well as our next steps. The tarcin we need will not be easy to procure, but without it we cannot leave Velerius. Again, thank you for your generosity, and we look forward to forging this alliance."

The council filed out of the small white room, and we followed.

As excited as I was about the potential groundbreaking alliance between our two races, I couldn't get over Imogen's decision to stay here.

There was no point in staying on Velerius, not when we all knew death was imminent. She had to know her decision was suicidal at best.

As I walked behind Imogen, I was more determined than ever to break down her walls. Something told me she didn't truly believe in her own decision, and I wasn't going to let her throw away her chance at a better life. I had to bring my family back together again, even if it meant dragging Imogen back to Earth kicking and screaming.

CHAPTER TWENTY

 sat on the green striped exotic fur with Ko'ta and Ja'tare, grimacing as Ko'ta dabbed a heaping glob of purple chili on his orange bread and crammed it into his mouth.

"Want some before our trip?" he asked with his mouth full.

"No thanks," I said. I rummaged through my pack for what leftover artarta I had. I pulled out a long navy stick and sank my teeth into the sweet, spicy jam inside.

"You know, you do not have to do this," Ja'tare pointed out. "It is perfectly acceptable."

I shook my head. "I have to. I can't just sit back while you risk your lives. Besides, Imogen …"

Ja'tare put a six-fingered hand on my shoulder. "I understand."

Ja'tare knew how I felt about Imogen's decision to stay behind on Velerius. He saw how upset I was after the meeting and let me vent, promising he'd do everything he could to help convince her. Most of his family had died in

Verus, and he didn't want me to suffer a similar loss. His support made me feel better, but it didn't change anything.

Velerius's days were numbered, and I refused to believe anyone would choose the hell of never-ending Reaper attacks over a relatively safer Earth. No one had a future here, not even Imogen with her sharp, deadly daggers.

I ate in silence, thinking about what had just happened and the journey ahead.

The meeting with all of the Veloxans had been anything but smooth. When the council advised of their planned departure for Earth, feelings were mixed. Some were quiet, grateful for a chance at a new life, but others demanded to know what Earth was like and how it was any better than here. Most importantly, they wanted to know they could trust humans and be treated as equals in a world that didn't belong to them.

The council broke down the bleak Reaper situation on Velerius, stressing their faith in our unlikely union. We told them we couldn't guarantee how the other humans would react to their presence, but as an ambassador to Earth I gave my word I would do my best to foster peaceful relations. Our argument seemed to quell their worries, and though I was grateful, we had a long way to go before needing to worry about human-Veloxan interactions.

The tarcin resource the council mentioned was a form of refined magma they mined from their volcanoes, the same glowing, holey mountains I'd seen right after arriving on this planet. Together, Veloxan warriors and engineers were to travel to the refinery at the nearest peak and extract whatever usable tarcin was left.

Imogen volunteered to accompany the party, and I followed suit in hopes of breaking through to her. The council accepted Imogen's decision, but fought mine due to my role in helping them migrate and adjust to Earth. Ja'tare bit back, arguing that the volcanoes had long since been dormant and there shouldn't be any reason for the Dak'kar to venture there. Begrudgingly, the council accepted his response but insisted on the deployment of additional troops.

Once our party obtained the tarcin, we would rendezvous back in Verus at an underground way station. We'd traverse the tunnels to the nearest functional laboratory, using the tarcin to fuel the portal generator so we and outside tribes they'd notified of our plans could leave for Earth.

On paper our mission sounded relatively easy, but I doubted it would end up that way. The laboratory, the Valen, getting to Verus, all of my travels here had an abundant share of danger, and I was betting this volcano had inherent perils of its own.

Ja'tare, Ko'ta, and I finished our meal and geared up before heading to the lift, joining the others that had just arrived. I tallied everyone up. Two dozen plus me. Everyone was here except ...

I turned around, my stomach dropping as Imogen approached, wearing her battle gear. Her structured form-fitting Veloxan garb made her appear catlike in nature, dangerous. Wickedly sharp daggers hung at her sides in small holsters, and her curly brown hair was pinned atop her head, small ringlets cascading down the sides of her face.

She looked like a warrior princess, impenetrable. I'd have to bide my time if I wanted her to open up to me. Right now she'd probably deck me.

Imogen walked by me without so much as a glance, approaching Ja'tare directly. "Looks like we're all here. What are we waiting for?"

"Nothing at all," Ja'tare said. He pushed the lift button.

The doors opened and we filed in. Whatever dangers lay

ahead of us at the volcano, nothing was going to stop us from getting that tarcin.

∼

I GRIPPED Skri'to's knobules for dear life as we and the other mounted bretaren hurtled across the desolate, crumbling wasteland. A thick spray of dirt, rock, and dust shot in every direction, and I readjusted my face mask as I squinted through the haze.

From here I could just barely make out the towering volcano we charged towards. It looked like a misshapen blue candle that had been lit one too many times. A gathering of ominous gray-green clouds hovered around the molten mountain, summoning blinding bolts of purple lightning that formed dangerous angular shapes.

When we were several hundred yards from the volcano, I could see bursts of almost neon purple magma spraying from the many tiny openings in its face.

Shit. I thought Ja'tare said this thing wasn't active! How were we supposed to climb this bad boy when it was leaking magma?

Ja'tare motioned for us to stop, pulling his face mask down as he addressed us. "This is bizarre. The volcano was not supposed to be active based on our research. We must press on and exercise the utmost caution. The tarcin refinery lies above."

I glanced upwards. Atop the volcano sat a gray rectangular structure, but from here it looked pretty dinky.

That's it? That's the tarcin refinery?

"Once we obtain the tarcin we will descend the volcano and head back to Verus. We will have to leave our bretaren behind due to the thin uphill paths. There are some overhanging caves that we can use to shelter them not far away. Follow me!"

We left our bretaren with several Veloxan warriors, then traveled alongside the malformed holey beast of cooled molten rock. Enormous boulders were strewn everywhere, and our brief walk ended at two towering spires of stone that leaned upon each other lopsidedly.

"This is the path that will lead us up to the tarcin," Ja'tare announced. "Again, we will have to watch our step and be wary. At any second a magma burst could complicate our way upwards."

Ja'tare looked at Imogen and me. "For those of you who are not familiar with this terrain, beware of *tarcils*. They are burrowing worms that feed on what magma they can. They can be territorial and hostile when disturbed, so just keep moving forward if you see any of them. Is everyone all set?"

I rolled my eyes. *Great, another wonderful life-threatening creature of Velerius.*

The group moved forward, and I followed after them hesitantly. I had a bad feeling about this.

BEADS OF SWEAT dripped down my face as I staggered up the steep dirt path. My burning calves demanded rest, and I took a quick pause to wipe my brow and catch my breath. Everyone was further ahead except for Imogen, who waited ten feet away with her arms crossed and a pissed off look on her sweat-soaked face.

"By all means, take your time," she grumbled.

I ignored her comment. "They didn't say this hike would be a never-ending sauna."

"It's a *volcano*."

I glanced upward as my breathing returned to normal.

The tarcin refinery towered way above us, a smidgen bigger than it was when I first looked at it. I groaned. How much longer was this going to take?

The volcano answered with a deep rumbling that shook the ground violently. I fell against the wall of debris next to me, using it to steady myself. The earth trembled every minute or so since we started our climb, and while I was getting used to it, each quake made me more and more anxious.

So far the volcano's angry outbursts hadn't unearthed any of the dangerous tarcils Ja'tare had warned us about, but who knew what lay around the next corner?

Rested, I caught up to Imogen and we continued along the rock-strewn path. I scanned her from my peripherals. This journey was affecting her too. Her steps were labored, and small huffs came with each breath.

Say something comforting, you doofus!

"If I'd known it was gonna be like this, I would've brought a fan with me." I fanned myself.

Imogen stared forward, her eyes cold like steel. "Maybe you should just give up. It wouldn't be the first time."

I frowned. Imogen's dig hurt, but I wasn't going to let her get to me. "Nah, it's sort of nice actually. Kinda like a day spa."

My little sister looked my way, and I gave her my best lopsided, goofy smile. Wonder of wonders, the tiniest hint of a smile appeared on her face, right before the world shook around us.

I plowed right into Imogen, who shoved me away like a contagious disease. "Watch it."

Ja'tare came running down the path to us. "Are you okay?"

I brushed dirt off my Veloxan garb. "Yeah, I think we're alright."

"Stay closer to the group. The tremors seem to be increasing in magnitude, and I do not want anything happening to you two."

Imogen and I did as instructed, staying ten paces behind Veloxan engineers lugging huge packs on their backs. The warriors led the way ahead of them.

We hadn't been walking for more than a minute when the ground rattled beneath us again, this time so strong that everyone fell to the ground.

"Incoming!" Ja'tare shouted.

All around us, bursts of lava spat and sizzled upon the ground from above. I cringed, curling into a fetal position and throwing my arms in front of my face protectively. The serpentine hisses continued, but no harm came to me. As the chaotic noise and rumblings from below faded, I dared a glance to assess the damage.

Our party was righting themselves, helping each other up. It looked like no one had been hurt. The lava had created small fissures in our path, but it was nothing we couldn't avoid. We'd been luck--

Another quaking boom resounded through the volcano, the intensity so severe I worried this giant mound of molten rock would crumble away. Something was wrong here, terribly wrong.

After a few terrifying moments the great trembling stopped, replaced by cries of surprise. I was about to see what the commotion was when a scratchy, sizzly sound came from behind me.

Several feet away the ground shifted and cracked, a violet light emerging. I watched in horror as a foot-long worm the size of a small poodle squirmed out of the hole it made. Its body was a dull sick-looking gray with glowing purple veins that made it look radioactive. The creature turned its eyeless head this way and that, opening its magma-filled, many-toothed mouth.

I stumbled back, debris rustling under my feet.

The magma worm wheezed, turning its ugly face in my direction.

Shit! It had found me.

I scrambled away as fast as I could, Imogen's still form catching my attention.

She sat against a wall of molten rock on the opposite side of the worm, a wide-eyed look of disbelief on her face. The earth above her began to stir and fall away.

"Imogen, watch out!" I cried.

Imogen rolled to her right as the second magma worm surfaced. It plopped face first onto the space where she'd just been, the ground sizzling in little streams of steam from its bite. I drew my Glock and fired without hesitation. A small trail of magma oozed from the hole I'd shot into its head. It slumped to the ground as more hissing sounds echoed behind me.

I leaped over the first magma worm blocking my way to Imogen and bolted up to her. "Come on, we've got to go!" As I pulled her up, a scream of pain demanded my attention.

The thin path ahead was littered with at least a dozen magma worms. Most of our party had run forward to escape them, but one of the engineers had been pincered in by a couple worms against an earthen barrier too tall to climb.

He had a horrid circular wound on his leg that smoked and bubbled, and he hopped backwards on one leg. The two worms' bodies began to scrunch up, almost like how a snake coiled before striking. Oh god, they were going to pounce on him!

Before I could react, the magma worms uncoiled, launching themselves into the air. They descended on the Veloxan, forcing him to the ground. They wasted no time sinking their many teeth into him, and he cried in agony as his body steamed and burned.

My chest tightened at seeing the poor victim's plight, but it was too late to save him.

"Gregory, run!" a familiar voice shouted up ahead.

Ja'tare and Ko'ta waved their hands frantically further down the path with the rest of the group.

I looked to the worm-ridden space ahead of us. We couldn't avoid the magma and the worms at the same time, but if I blasted the worms as we ran, we might just make it past.

I gripped my Glock firmly. "Imogen, make a run for it. I'll back you up as we go. Now!"

She broke into a full sprint.

I bolted after my sister, aiming for any worms that coiled up or were close enough to strike. One magma worm, bang! Two, bang! Three, four, bang bang!

We cleared the tarcils, catching up with the group a safe distance away. I took deep ragged breaths as I bent over, hands on my knees.

"Is everyone okay?" Ja'tare asked.

The Veloxans muttered back forlornly, their severe expressions displaying their inner pain. Clearly their brother's death had impacted them, but there was no way they could've saved him without endangering themselves.

Ja'tare gave us a moment of silence, then told us to get ready to keep going.

"How much further?" I asked.

"We still have a ways to go, maybe an hour or so."

"*Great.* Will any more of our worm friends be joining us?"

Ja'tare frowned. "Let us hope not. Remember, stay close. We cannot afford to lose anyone else." With that, he returned to the front of the group and we got moving again.

The almost vertical inclination of the volcano was

unbearable now, made even more difficult by the constant quakes. With each step my muscles screamed with pain, but as we inched closer to the refinery, getting there seemed more and more feasible.

Imogen had been quiet since our encounter with the magma worms, but as we eased onto a flat stretch of path, her gaze rested on me with rapidly-changing expressions. Finally, she spurted out, "Thanks for that back there."

Wait, Imogen was *thanking me*? Hell must have frozen over. *Keep your cool, man.* I tried to hide my shock at her words and shrugged. "No biggie. If we're being honest, I almost wet myself when they showed up out of nowhere. I can't wait to get off this dumpster fire of a volcano."

Imogen smiled, then caught herself and looked down at her feet. "So … Mom is alive?"

"Uh, yeah, she helps manage our group of survivors back home. She's turned into a real Dak'kar-slaying badass. You must've gotten that from her. I sure as hell didn't."

Immy grinned. "Maybe you're not *completely* hopeless." Her expression went severe once more. "What about Dad?"

I winced at the painful memory at my father's death. It had been a long time since I'd thought of him. It was all stored away where I kept my memories of those hellish first months of the invasion. "He didn't make it through the first wave. He died protecting Mom, my friend Trent, and I."

Tears welled in Imogen's eyes. "No … Gregory, I--"

The volcano rampaged through our tender moment, the earth beneath us quaking. No, not quaking, falling apart. Oh god, it was going to cave beneath us!

Imogen yelped in terror.

"Run, run!" I yelled.

We bolted ahead, the ground churning behind us. With each step we took, the terrible crumbling sound followed faster and faster, gaining on us. Imogen started to stumble.

"No!" I pushed her forward as hard as I could, and she went sprawling outside the range of the collapse. With Imogen safe I tried to keep running, but the earth around me had already begun to drop into nothingness. In a last-ditch effort to save myself, I lunged for stable ground several feet away.

My upper half hit the edge of safety hard, knocking the wind out of my lungs. I slid back as I scrambled for purchase until I was gripping the rim of the chasm. The dirt fell away under my fingers, and I shouted in horror.

"Gregory!" Imogen cried.

Her call drifted farther and farther away as I plummeted into the ever-deepening pit, engulfed by darkness.

CHAPTER TWENTY-ONE

I screamed as the ground ate me alive. My stomach flip-flopped as I flailed fruitlessly for something, anything to stop my descent. I hit the bottom of the pit like a sack of bricks, crying out in agony as searing needles of pain scorched my body. Every inch of me throbbed, and I couldn't feel my extremities.

I sat there for several excruciating moments until the terror of my situation overrode the unbearable hurt that raged on. Somehow I'd survived my nasty fall, but that wouldn't mean much if I didn't get out of here soon.

Craning my neck in the diminished light from above, I gave myself a once over. Deep cuts and bruises covered me from head to toe, and something looked terribly wrong with my left leg. It was swollen around my shin with dark coloring underneath. I tried putting the lightest of pressure on it.

"Ah!"

It was definitely broken, but I couldn't let that distract me. I had to act fast.

I glanced around me. The volcano's rumblings had

opened a deep fissure about fifteen feet wide and thirty feet high. Walls of rock and dirt surrounded me with no distinguishable features. I scraped a finger against it, tiny clumps falling away.

My throat constricted as a flush of heat washed over me. How the hell was I supposed to get out of here with my injuries?

Imogen's voice pulled me out of my panic. "Gregory, are you okay?" Her silhouette and a couple others partially blocked the light from above.

"I-I'm alive, but I'm hurt!" I shouted. "My leg--"

"Hold on, we're going to get you out of there!"

My heartbeat thrashed in my ears as I took shallow, rapid breaths. *Hurry, please hurry.*

Seconds later she returned. "Gregory, we're going to get a rope and lower it down to you. Tie it around yourself and we'll hoist you up. We'll have to do this quick, before--"

As if on cue, the ground shook violently. Dust and debris fell all around me, a rock falling sharply on my forehead.

"Ow, fuck! Imogen, please hurry!"

Imogen disappeared from view, and my fear really started to kick in.

Would I survive another quake or would the earth just swallow me whole? I couldn't die down here!

A tiny scraping sound nearby broke through my hysteria.

No, no, no. You're just hearing things.

Was I? I pulled my pack off my back with a groan and rifled through it, grabbing my flashlight. A warm yellow glow illuminated my surroundings as I flicked it on. I waved it to and fro, checking for any signs of those bastard worms.

I couldn't see anything, but the scratchy sound had gotten louder. They were coming for me.

"Imogen, there's something down here with me! Where's that rope?"

Another silhouette joined the others shadowing me. "Here!"

A despairingly thin cord of rope hurtled down, landing several feet away. I dragged myself over, my body protesting with sharp stabs of pain. As I grabbed the rope, a magma worm began to emerge from the wall with a sharp hiss, its open mouth glowing a deadly purple.

Desperately I tried to tie the rope around me with sweaty palms. I completed the knot, but when I tested it, it fell apart.

Fuck, calm down!

The first magma worm plopped on the ground mere feet away, more raking sounds erupting all around me.

Cross, wrap around, under and over, over again, there!

"Pull me up now!" I shouted.

The magma worm launched itself as I was propelled upwards with a jolt, its jagged teeth missing me by inches. I drifted out of harm's way, giving the worm the bird as the light from above gradually increased.

Once I reached the top of the fissure Imogen and several Veloxans pulled me out and laid me aside.

Imogen hovered over me, inspecting my injuries with a grimace. "Oh my gosh, your leg! Ja'tare, get over here now!"

My vision blurred with tears and I jerked upright, hugging my little sister despite the pinpricks of pain that shot across my body. She didn't push me away or hug me back. "I thought it was all over." Warm tears ran down my face.

Imogen gently pried me off her with a weak smile. "I guess we're even now. No more sudden movements, okay?"

Ja'tare and another Veloxan approached, the other Veloxan taking a knee and inspecting my mangled leg that was now a deep, sick purple.

"It is definitely broken," he stated.

A pained expression washed over Ja'tare's face. "Do you have anything that will help him now?"

"No, but if I remember protocol correctly, there should be an emergency nanite kit in the refinery. Once we get there, we can treat him."

"Well, what are we waiting for?" Imogen said. "Let's get a move on. We've been here long enough."

Together, Ja'tare and the other Veloxan propped me up. I hopped on my good foot to regain my balance, and we hobbled to the rest of the group. Despite my near death experience, I was hopeful. The refinery was in sight, and Imogen was talking to me now. Maybe her coming back to Earth with me wasn't so far-fetched after all.

JA'TARE and another Veloxan supported my weight as I limped through the refinery's coded entry, met with a warm rush of air.

The room was small and simple in design. Several gray islands stood at one end with complex inlaid panels covered in a smooth, rounded material that resembled plastic. On the right hand side were two doorways, one of them leading to the tarcin we so desperately needed.

"Let us get him set up over there," Ja'tare said. He gestured to a vacant table at the far left corner with his free hand.

We lurched over. They helped elevate me, and I winced as my maimed leg was jostled.

The rest of our party quickly poured into the room and Ja'tare turned to face them.

"Engineers and Ko'ta, check the other rooms for the tarcin canisters. You three, take a post outside for tarcils or any other kind of danger. Imogen, you and the others check the rest of the facility for anything useful. Descending the volcano may prove more difficult than it was getting up here."

With that, everyone went their separate ways. Ja'tare and the other Veloxan started digging through the room's contents to find the nanites that would heal my leg. I glanced up at the window set above the gray islands in front of me. A strong, purple glow emitted from it.

Getting to the refinery had taken us longer than we'd hoped with my injury. We hadn't encountered any magma worms, but as the mountain of molten rock ached and quaked, I couldn't shake the feeling that we were being watched from afar. The worms weren't capable of that, but what else could be on this damned volcano that Ja'tare hadn't told us about? Reapers?

I shook my head. No way. There was nothing here for the Reapers to hunt. Besides, they had no way of knowing we were coming here.

Ja'tare and the other Veloxan rushed over with a baton-shaped device in hand, just like the one I used on Ja'tare when I first met him. The world spun as I watched them roll up my pant leg.

Ja'tare's bright emerald eyes locked onto mine. "This will be painful, Gregory, but you can do this. Ready?"

He pressed the nanite device to my skin, and I stared up at the ceiling as I forced down the bile crawling up my throat. However bad it was, it couldn't be any worse than what I'd already been--

A scream of agony tore from my lips as an overwhelming pain surged through my leg. I could feel the nanites inside me, scraping between muscle, bone, and tendon. Needling lances of heat soared, sending tremors through my body. I tried to silence myself, but as the ungodly pain flared over and over again I couldn't hold back the cries that erupted from my mouth.

My breathing grew rapid and unstable, and Ja'tare grabbed my hand as I shook in torment. "Take deep breaths. You must stabilize your breathing or you will pass out. The pain will lessen. The nanites just have to repair the worst of the damage."

I nodded my head shakily. "I under-- ah!"

I wailed as my shin bone shifted, tears forming in my eyes.

The nanites must be resetting my ... oh god! My vision grew hazy and Ja'tare clamped his hand on mine harder, bringing me back to reality.

"You have to stay awake. We are so close to getting you back home. Do not give up now. Your mother and Trent would be so proud of you for what you have accomplished here. Hold on to that."

I focused on Ja'tare's words, doing my best to suppress the escalating needles of pain. Mom, Trent. I would see them soon. God, I missed them so much. I hoped they were okay.

Ja'tare continued to speak soothing words to me, and in the next few minutes, the intolerable pain diminished. The nanites' work on my leg was still quite painful, but I wasn't trembling anymore.

I let go of Ja'tare's hand. "I think the worst is over. I can't thank you enough. I--" I winced as a lance of pain assaulted my leg.

"Shh, it will be alright," Ja'tare reassured me. "No need to thank us. Just sit back and relax. We will be right here if you need anything."

"Okay. How long until I can walk on it?"

"Maybe another thirty minutes or so. Until then, stay put and let the nanites do their job."

The ground quaked around us suddenly, and I clutched the table for support. A door on the other end of the room opened vertically with a swoosh, and a disheveled Veloxan approached Ja'tare.

"Commander Ja'tare, we have located the tarcin, but there is not much to account for. Maybe two or three canisters."

Ja'tare frowned. "Collect what we have. It may be enough to get us all to Earth."

The Veloxan lingered.

"Is something the matter?" Ja'tare asked.

The engineer scratched his dark freckled arms. "Um, yes. All of the canisters are stuck in the underground containment chamber and we cannot seem to get them out. We did not want to damage the equipment."

"I do not care about the equipment. Do whatever it takes and do it fast. It is not safe here and we need that tarcin. Was there anything else?"

The bedraggled Veloxan shifted uncomfortably. "There is another space beyond the tarcin containment chamber, a small hangar. We have located an old glider."

Ja'tare's brows raised. "Really? Tell Imogen's group to inspect it for any damage. If it is in working order, we may be able to use it to leave here. I will be over in a moment."

The engineer ran off and I sat up, a small twinge of pain echoing in my left leg. "What's a glider?"

Ja'tare grimaced. "Gregory, it is too soon for you to get up."

"What is a glider?" I insisted.

He gave a long, low sigh. "It is a transportation vehicle capable of limited flight."

I gaped at him. "Why haven't we been using those this entire time?"

"Before the Dak'kar takeover there were plans to make gliders the default method of travel, but that all fell apart when the invasion occurred. The gliders use a small amount of tarcin, little enough that we should consider using it to escape this volcano and expedite our departure to Earth."

A wicked rocking of the earth below made the refinery rattle violently, enough to make me worry that it had knocked us off center a bit.

"What the hell was that?" I asked.

"I do not know. The other quakes were not like that." He touched the communication device on his shirt. "Guards, please report. Have you seen anything outside of the refinery?" The device only crackled in response. "Damn it."

The entry to the refinery wooshed open, and two of the three guards stationed burst in. "Commander Ja'tare! There is a situation outside."

"What is it?"

"We have spotted a group of hooded Dak'kar near the rim of the volcano. We believe they are responsible for the heightened eruptions and earthquakes we have been experiencing."

Ja'tare shot over to the nearest window, his wide-eyed gaze frozen on whatever he was seeing. "No, it cannot be!"

"I am afraid so. After we saw them, we checked the path we used to get here. It is already halfway submerged in lava."

"Is there another way?"

"We are unsure. There has only ever been one known path here. We could search for another, but we do not know if we will find anything in time. What do you advise, sir?"

Ja'tare mulled it over a moment, brows furrowed. "Continue to keep watch, but stay close. Do not engage the Dak'kar under any circumstances. We cannot afford a battle right now. Go."

Ja'tare and the Veloxan that helped treat me stalked off to the far end of the room, disappearing into the tarcin containment chamber. I watched them go, still in shock from this sudden development.

The volcano was active when we got here. That meant the Dak'kar probably didn't follow us from Verus and had to have been here for some time. Did they know of the significance of the tarcin? Was that what they were after, a way to stop the Veloxans from escaping them?

I sat up and lowered myself to the ground on my good foot, then hobbled over to the large window to look at the rim. A couple hundred yards away, the volcanic lake of purple magma swirled and churned chaotically, bursting in large geysers up and over the threshold of earth. On the far side of the pool, three hooded Reapers stood, arms outstretched with their claws touching one another.

From here I could sense the tingle of Reaper activity, but that was impossible. I'd never felt so much power emanating from Reapers before. I analyzed them, focusing on their physical contact with one another. I'd never seen them do that before. Could they somehow be able to combine their power when they touched? If that was true, then we had to get out of here before they really started screwing shit up.

With the path we'd taken up here blocked, the Reapers had us cornered. Unless we found another path, our only hope was the glider Ja'tare went off to inspect. I had to help, even if I was still recovering. There wasn't any time. I limped across the room to the other end, the door ahead of me opening vertically.

Inside, the tarcin containment chamber was nothing like I expected. The walls and floor were covered in thick cords of glowing metal wire, converging in the center of the room to a large circular network of stationary gears and spokes.

A small group of Veloxans stood around the bizarre circle, surrounding Ko'ta and several others. They stretched upon the ground, reaching down into the gearwork with metal tools. Heavy clanks and clangs sounded as they worked.

"Finally!" Ko'ta cried. He lifted a thin cylindrical canister out of the machinery and set it beside him. Inside it a radiant purple liquid stirred slowly, lit by erratic bursts of electric blue light like a lava lamp on crack.

"Is that the tarcin?" I asked.

Ko'ta and the others spun around.

"Gregory, you should not be moving about," Ko'ta objected.

"I don't care. The hooded Dak'kar outside are up to something, and we don't have much time. What can I do to help?"

Ko'ta shook his head. He got up to his feet, grabbed the canister, and walked over to me. "This is the tarcin we will need to get back to Earth. Ja'tare is in the hangar working on the glider. Give this to him so he can test it out."

He handed over the canister. Surprisingly, it felt cool to the touch and was extremely light.

Ko'ta waved a hand. "Go on, get out of here. We will need as much time as possible to crank the other two canisters out of the refining machine."

I thanked him and walked to the other doorway within the room. When the door swooshed open, I shambled forward as I gaped around me. Numerous bizarrely-shaped vehicles littered the small hangar, my eyes focusing on the vision straight ahead of me.

In the middle of the plain metal hangar stood a sleek, beautiful ship that resembled a manta ray. The large gray shuttle stood about twenty feet high and had an elegant curved design, starting with its downward-curving nose and extending out in two wings that were more like fins. Several Veloxans hustled and bustled around the ship.

I went in for a closer look, circling the spaceship in awe. The back of each wing held four engines and the rear was open with a ramp descending to the ground. The whole thing was coated in a layer of grime and dust, but I was spellbound.

"Gregory, is that you?" Ja'tare's strained voice called from inside.

"Uh yeah, it's me." I edged towards the back of the spacecraft. As I made it to the ramp Imogen emerged, covered in grease.

She wiped her hands on a filthy rag and cocked an eyebrow at me. "I saw you coming. What are you doing up?"

"I can't just sit around. Ko'ta gave me this tarcin to test out with the glider." I handed Imogen the tarcin and followed after her into the spaceship.

The interior of the glider was smaller than I'd hoped, about fifteen feet from side to side. Tiny, uncomfortable looking seats lined the outer wall that were hardly bigger than bike wedges. If we got this thing flying it was going to be a tight, uncomfortable fit for our group, but we would manage.

I shadowed Imogen to the small cockpit area. Between two large chairs, a grate set in the floor had been removed. Clanks and clatters echoed from below. Imogen lowered the canister into the grate, and Ja'tare's six-fingered hand reached out to grab it.

After a few moments a steady vibration stirred from below. Ja'tare climbed out of the hole, grease smeared across his angular face and form-fitting clothes. Imogen handed him the filthy rag she'd been using and he wiped his hands off.

"That should be it," he said. He hopped up to the large seat of the cockpit and started working the complex control panel, flicking a series of odd buttons and levers.

"So we're ready to fly?" I asked.

"Almost. I have to remember how these controls work and get this thing up and running."

"How long has it been?"

"Six years, and that was only the one time."

My stomach roiled. He'd only flown one of these things *once*? What if he forgot something vital, something that would keep us from crashing into the ground to our deaths? I hoped he knew what he was doing.

"This should be it." Ja'tare flicked one last switch on the main control panel.

We waited expectantly in silence. When nothing happened, my anxiety peaked. We were fucked, so fucked.

"Oh, missed one." Ja'tare pressed another button.

With a heavy rumble the aircraft came to life, small panels powering up around us and lighting activating within the walls.

The ground beneath us suddenly quaked, the glider tilting a noticeable few degrees.

Ja'tare studied the main control panels, his features hardening. "Imogen, take the warriors and get the others, now!"

"What if they haven't retrieved all the tarcin?" Imogen asked.

"There is not any time!"

Imogen ran off and took her group of Veloxans with her, disappearing into the next room.

I glanced at the control panel, which had several red bubbles that pulsated with Veloxan characters. "What is it saying?"

"The earthquakes are damaging the refinery's foundation, more so each time. We have maybe five minutes before it falls off the face of the volcano, probably less."

"Shit." A thought hit me. "Wait, shouldn't we try to contact the others at Verus and let them know about the situation?"

"I already tried that. The glider does not have long-range communication capabilities. I was able to inform the

Veloxans on the ground to take the bretaren and head to the way station."

"Well at least there's that." I wandered away from Ja'tare, crossing my arms as I peered out the back of the glider.

The entry at the far end of the hangar shlooped open, a dozen or so Veloxans including Ko'ta charging towards the glider. Several of them were injured, dark splotches of blood on their faces and arms, and a few others were yelling something that I couldn't make out.

I edged outside of the glider, afraid to go too far with my healing leg.

"Dak'kar, the Dak'kar are coming!" the closest Veloxan shouted as he approached me. "We have to take off!"

I went back into the glider. Ja'tare had turned the large cockpit chair to face me.

"What is going on out there?" he asked.

"The Dak'kar are here! We have to leave, but they're not all here yet."

"Alright, I will get the glider ready and open the hangar's hatch for departure. Let me know when everyone is here."

I descended the glider's ramp as the first of the Veloxans stormed in. They secured their supplies to hooks on the wall and strapped themselves into their tiny seats. As Ko'ta rushed in with the tarcin canisters I grabbed his arm.

"Where's Imogen? Wasn't she with you guys?"

He frowned and shook his head. "She went outside to help the others escape the Dak'kar."

Ko'ta charged past me to set down his precious cargo, and I steered my gaze back to the door at the far end of the hangar, my chest tightening.

Damn it, Imogen, why did you have to be a hero?

"Is everyone onboard?" Ja'tare called.

"No, Imogen and the Veloxans outside still haven't made it back. We can't leave without them!"

The earth below us shook chaotically, metal screeches piercing the air as the hangar walls stretched and ripped all around us. Everything shifted downwards another few degrees.

"We cannot take another hit like that!" Ja'tare shouted over. "We leave in sixty seconds."

As much as I wanted to protest, I couldn't. Everything was falling apart around us. I watched the door at the end of the room, the hairs on my body standing on end as I willed Imogen and the others to arrive.

Come on, where are you guys?

The door to the hangar swooshed open, and several Veloxans bolted towards the glider.

My chest tingled. Where was Imogen? In a sudden shift of movement, Imogen was revealed behind one of the taller Veloxans.

Oh, thank god!

"Hurry up, we only have thirty seconds!" I shouted. Three lesser Dak'kar emerged in the open doorway, scrambling after them. "Dak'kar, behind you! Run, run, *run!*"

I drew my Glock and fired several warning shots, hoping it would delay the monsters enough precious seconds to matter.

The glider roared to life, hovering above the ravaged metal floor about a foot. The ramp began to withdraw into the ship.

"Ja'tare, wait, they're not close enough yet!" I cried.

"I cannot, there is not enough time!" he shouted back.

The first of the Veloxans was twenty feet away as we began to thrust forward. I shoved my Glock into its holster and held my hand out as they closed the distance.

Come on, come on. Just a little bit closer ... yes!

I pulled the first Veloxan in as another launched himself

inside the glider. Imogen was just ten feet away now, but we were speeding up too fast.

"Come on Imogen, you can do this!"

Imogen increased her velocity and was just outside arm's reach, but now the glider outpaced her and the Dak'kar were quickly catching up to her.

"You've got to jump!"

Imogen winced. "I can't!"

"You have to! I've got you!"

With a cry of exertion, Imogen thrust herself forward, inches short of the glider. I dove, catching her hands, but started slipping myself.

No!

Suddenly, a strong weight pulled Imogen and myself back into the glider.

"Close it!" Ko'ta shouted.

With screeches of rage, we left the bloodthirsty Dak'kar behind.

"We did it." I held Imogen close to me. This time she didn't pull back.

CHAPTER TWENTY-TWO

The glider shook and oscillated as Imogen and I held each other.

"Gregory, Imogen, what are you doing?" Ko'ta shouted. "We are about to descend over the volcano's edge. Get in your seats, *now!*"

Imogen and I nearly flew into the nearest seats, buckling ourselves in with the straps as Ja'tare's voice boomed over the comm.

"Everyone, hold on!"

The world went sideways as we barrelled down the side of the volcano. My stomach plummeted as we free-fell, and I struggled to resist the urge to puke my guts out. I'd always loved roller coasters, but this was a whole other level.

I looked across the glider at Imogen. Her eyes were closed tight, teeth clenched. I followed suit, gripping my seat belt with an iron vice. *Oh god, oh god, please don't let us die, please don't let us die.*

We catapulted down for what felt like an eternity until the glider suddenly jerked upright, jolting my body so badly that stars spotted my vision. I groaned as I fought to reclaim my senses. Once the room stopped spinning, I noticed that everyone in the cabin looked just as disheveled and pissed off as I felt.

The glider's turbulence ceased and resumed its gentle humming vibration. Ja'tare got up from his pilot seat and staggered over, not looking much better than the rest of us.

"Is everyone okay?" he asked.

Several Veloxans muttered unenthusiastic confirmations, while another simply vomited on the floor. Within seconds, the awful stench filled the space.

I covered my nose. "Hardly. Were you *trying* to kill us?"

"I am sorry, but I did tell you I have not flown one of these in quite some time. I have no intention of hovering down any more volcanoes, I promise. You can all move freely in the cabin now. I have set a course for Verus on the glider's autopilot. We should reach the way station in about thirty minutes, but I am unsure when we will be within range for contact."

Ja'tare went back to the cockpit, and the uninjured Veloxans got out of their seats and started examining their wounded brethren. Just watching them move around made me wanna barf. How could they recover so damned quickly? My insides still felt like mush.

I glanced across the cabin to Imogen. Her eyes were open now, but they had a glazed distant look to them. As persistent as my nausea was being, I couldn't stand seeing her like this.

I slowly unstrapped myself and crossed over to her, nearly falling over twice. I plopped into the empty seat next to her and put a hand on her shoulder. "Are you okay?"

She smiled weakly, removing my hand. "Yeah, I'm fine."

"I was so scared I was gonna lose you back there, I--"

"Gregory, stop. There's something I need to say."

"Okay."

Immy stared down at her lap, warring emotions battling for dominance of her features. "I'm sorry for the way I've been treating you. All this time I thought you were to blame for why I was here. Knowing that isn't true doesn't make things any better, but I never should've attacked you."

I opened my mouth to respond, but Imogen held up a hand.

"Please, I'm not finished yet. I want to go back to Earth with you. After everything I've been through in the past few days, it's clear that this world is dying. I guess I didn't want to see it for so long that I blinded myself. Keeping my Veloxans here would be a death sentence. It's not fair to them or myself. I'm ready to go home, to learn to be human again. What do you think?"

My sight blurred with tears. This was all I ever wanted. Her, Mom, and I could be a family again. I hugged Imogen tightly. "I'm so glad to hear you say that. Nothing would make me happier than for you to join us. You're my little sister, and I love you." I peeled myself off her. "Everything will be better on Earth, I promise."

"Attention everyone," Ja'tare's voice rang over the comm speakers. "I just received a recorded message from the others in Verus. Initiating playback now."

The first thing we heard were screams, followed by distant shouts. Everyone in the cabin gaped at each other until a familiar voice broke the nightmarish cacophony of sound.

"Commander Ja'tare, this is Nehma," Nehma said, her voice strained. "We were waiting for the right time to head to the way station, but we cannot--" In the background, closer this time, were more cries, followed by the inhuman shrieks of Reapers.

"It is no longer safe here. We do not know how, but the Dak'kar have infiltrated the tower. We have suffered casualties and are retreating to the way station with the transmission of this message. Meet us there, and hurry!"

No one said a word, even Ja'tare, who had joined us during the playback.

"What the hell was that?" I asked.

"You heard the recording," Ja'tare said.

"Yeah, but how could this happen? How did the Dak'kar find them?"

"When we left the tower, they must have seen us," Imogen reasoned. "That's the only logical explanation I can think of."

Her observation didn't seem to reassure Ja'tare based on his distant, glassy stare. "It is unfortunate that this happened, but this changes nothing. We will meet at the way station as planned and provide assistance."

"Why?" the sick Veloxan who'd thrown up earlier said. "How do we know that this is not another trap and the others were followed again? We have the tarcin. We can just go straight to the nearest laboratory and leave for Earth."

Ja'tare dashed over to the Veloxan and slammed him against the wall, holding him by his shirt. "You are bound by honor, Veloxan."

The Veloxan's gleaming blue eyes went wide.

"We will not betray our people like cowards when they need us the most. We will meet at the way station as planned, and we will aid our people in getting to the laboratory. Do I make myself clear?"

"Y-Yes, Commander," the Veloxan said.

Ja'tare released him and he scrambled back, averting his gaze.

"So," I interjected, hoping to redirect the tense energy in the cabin, "What's this way station you mentioned?"

"It is an underground transportation hub."

"Oh, like a subway."

Ja'tare simply tilted his head at me.

I waved a hand dismissively. "Never mind. What I mean to say is, isn't this good for us? Can we take transportation from the way station straight to the laboratory?"

"Possibly," Ko'ta mused. "If I remember correctly there is a viable route we can take, but the odds of the transportation pods being operational is extremely thin. Also, I hate to admit it, but the Dak'kar *could* have followed our tribe there. This may mean another battle, Commander."

Ja'tare paced, brows furrowed. He stopped mid-pace and addressed us. "Agreed. Upon landing, ready yourselves for battle to be safe. I will monitor the communications network for any other incoming transmissions. That is all."

Ja'tare went back to the cockpit and the others started prepping for combat, but I sat there in shock.

Could we already have another battle on the horizon? Didn't we just barely escape the volcano with our lives? I glanced over at Imogen. She had a cold, focused look on her face.

"Do you really think we'll have to fight again so soon?" I asked.

She shrugged. "I don't know, but we've been dragged around quite a bit. If there are Dak'kar at the way station, we won't last long without help."

Unsure of how to cope with the bleak reality of what Imogen said, I plopped back in my seat. I clutched my knapsack and wrapped my arms around myself.

I hoped we were wrong about the Dak'kar. We were so close to getting back home I could almost taste it.

As I rocked myself back and forth, I prayed that things would go right for once.

∿

THE GLIDER'S GENTLE hum faded to a whisper as our speed slowed to a crawl. We descended, landing so softly I hardly felt it.

Everyone unbuckled themselves and rose, cramming into two defensive columns in the small space available. Imogen and I were smushed in the middle, 'for our protection' as Ja'tare had put it.

Ja'tare lingered in the cockpit, messing with the controls until the vibration of the glider's engines died out. He rattled around noisily, then shuffled his way to the front of our group, tarcin canister in hand.

"The short-range scanners did not detect any Dak'kar or Veloxan lifeforms, but the way station has always been a blind spot for our scanners due to the elements in the natural rock. Be on your guard. Is everyone ready?"

Our party was armed with poisoned, glowing spears except for me with my blade and Imogen with her daggers. To be honest, I felt completely naked without my Glock in hand. I only had a few rounds left, so unless it was an emergency, I'd have to slice and dice every screwed up creature that came at me.

Ko'ta looked us over, a satisfactory gleam in his brown eyes before giving Ja'tare the okay.

Ja'tare hit a large red button and the back of the glider opened up, the ramp lowering with a metallic groan. A cold erratic wind greeted us, raising goosebumps all over my body.

We edged outside, and I lifted my face mask over my nose as wisps of soot pelted every which way. Clouds of thick brown dust swirled in torrents, obscuring our vision, but I could still make out our surroundings with a bit of effort. Several squat oval-shaped buildings lay ahead, deserted like every other building we'd seen in Verus. Above, dagger-like flashes of purple lightning struck, highlighting more abandoned, empty spaces.

"Gregory, come on," Imogen shouted against the shrieking wind.

"Sorry!" I called.

I picked up my pace, keeping along a thin stretch of dirt-covered pavement while trying to keep my wits about me. If the Dak'kar attacked us now, we'd be easy pickings.

As we passed the short buildings I'd seen before, I noticed several of them had small openings like kiosks, all of them damaged. Beyond that, a large dilapidated archway towered with steps leading below. The front line of Veloxans stopped at the foot of the stairs, allowing us to catch up.

Ja'tare turned and pulled down his face mask. "This is it, everyone. Be prepared for anything."

Together we descended the many crumbling stone steps in pairs of two. Faint, flickering magenta lights set in the wall guided our way down in a broken strobe, making me question my footing. It didn't help that I was skittish as a chicken at a slaughterhouse. What if the Reapers were down here? Had the others evacuated Verus fast enough?

These brooding thoughts consumed me until Imogen's hand shot in front of me, breaking my trance. "We're almost at the bottom, slow down."

The landing was ten steps below. Ko'ta and another Veloxan had just reached it. They moved out of view, right before I heard a scuffle and cry of surprise.

Throwing caution to the wind, I barreled through the Veloxans in front of me and jumped down the remaining steps, landing with my blade arched in case an attack was needed.

A tall female Veloxan with black braided hair stood several yards beyond the landing. Her orange eyes drifted from me back to Ko'ta as she poised to strike with a glowing spear. "Who are … Ko'ta, is that you? Oh, thank goodness!"

The female lowered her weapon and hugged Ko'ta tight.

"Mir'sah," he breathed. He pulled her away from him gently. "I am glad you are alright. What about the others?"

Mir'sah shook her horned head. "There is no time, we must move. I can fill you in on the way."

We followed Mir'sah and Ko'ta's hasty pace as they walked alongside each other into a long winding tunnel. The worn passageway was arched and angled at a steady decline. More magenta lights set inside the stone walls blinked and stuttered in beautiful flowery patterns.

"We were attacked," Mir'sah explained. "After you left, we were readying ourselves for the journey here when the tower shook at its base. We sent a scouting party down, and they warned that Dak'kar had broken through right before their comms cut out. The Dak'kar took the lift up and attacked us. We were lucky that a group of warriors were able to hold them off long enough for us to escape, but we have been extremely worried ever since."

"I am very grateful you survived," Ko'ta said.

Something about the emotion in his voice made me wonder if he had feelings for Mir'sah.

We continued onward in silence, but as I dwelled on the saddening loss of life something about Mir'sah's story bugged me. How *were* the Dak'kar able to get through the walls? An image flashed in my head of the three hooded Dak'kar atop the volcano with their claws touching.

"Mir'sah," I called.

She turned around, brows raised.

"Were there any hooded Dak'kar present in the assault?"

"How did you know?"

"I saw something at the volcano that worried me. The hooded Dak'kar were making physical contact with one another, and when they used their powers it was catastrophic. I think … no, I know that together their telekinesis is more powerful, maybe exponentially. That may be how they broke into the tower. If we see any more hooded Dak'kar, we have to separate them."

Mir'sah grimaced. "The council will be interested to hear this. Come on, the way station is not far."

With that, we trekked briskly down the dimly-lit tunnel. The passage wound and turned upon itself until we arrived at the shocking end of the path, a pile of rubble.

I shuffled back a step. How could the entrance have caved when Mir'sah just came from here? Other members of our group looked just as confused as I was.

"Do not worry, it is a hologram meant to throw off the Dak'kar," Mir'sah said.

Relief relaxed my tense posture, and one by one we passed through the illusion. On the other side, a vast space opened before me.

Clear, cylindrical support columns towered fifty feet tall, flickering with rainbow neon light that illuminated the area. Scattered throughout were abstractly-shaped benches, most of them broken or occupied by refugee Veloxans. Up ahead was a docking station of sorts, but all I could see from here was rubble and remnants of small pod-like vehicles that looked big enough to fit maybe two people.

There goes our hope of a comfy ride off of this planet.

Mir'sah led us past the dock and to the right, where a large congregation of Veloxans had gathered. All gleaming eyes were on us as we headed over.

As we neared the crowd shifted, revealing the three members of the council. Their shaken, bedraggled appearance surprised me. Obviously no one was exempt from a close call with the Dak'kar, but up until now I didn't think affecting them was even possible.

Kro'da stepped forward with a prideful air despite his dusty, torn clothes and minor cuts on his tan skin. "Everyone, it is good to see you safe and sound."

Ja'tare took a slight bow. "You as well, esteemed council. We have returned with the tarcin for our voyage to Earth, but not without casualties."

Nehma frowned. "We are disheartened to hear that. However, we must mourn our dead another time. Right now we must move forward, and quickly. We cannot be sure that we were not followed by the Dak'kar, or that the hologram we placed will fool them for long. P'taro?"

P'taro emerged from the crowd with his tablet, his goggles tilted and his hair bun loose and unkempt. "The laboratory nearest us is not very far, a total of seven miles."

"How are we going to get there?" I asked. "Can we use some of the vehicles here?"

"I am afraid not. We will have to travel on foot. This station used to be a hub for transportation via pod shuttles, but as you can see, all that is left here is wreckage that we will have to maneuver around and climb over. Even if we did manage to repair a pod or two, separating from the group is not wise."

My shoulders drooped. God, this was going to take forever. How were we supposed to keep the Reapers away if we were stuck in a tunnel? We would be at a strategic disadvantage the entire time. There had to be another ... "Wait, what about the glider?"

"We cannot risk using any more tarcin," Ja'tare said. "With the number of people we need to transport through the portal paired with the possibility of other tribes meeting us at the laboratory it is impossible. We must make our way through the shuttle tunnels."

"Okay, but what do we do if the Dak'kar find us down here?"

"We fight and protect the others so they can make it to the laboratory."

I tapped my fingers against my thigh, trying to remind myself to stay positive. There was no guarantee what would happen once we set out. Maybe the Dak'kar wouldn't come. "Alright, so then what? We leave for Earth once we get to the laboratory?"

"Possibly," P'taro said. "We do not know the exact state of the portal generator, only that it should be salvageable based on our scans from the tower in Verus. Once our technicians take a look they will know more."

I clenched my fists, unable to stop the angry heat from flooding to my face. "How are we settling on a maybe here? What guarantees do we have that the portal generator will be up and running in time, that the Dak'kar won't come for us before that? That--"

I felt a hand on my shoulder and looked back. Imogen smiled weakly at me, then shook her head.

My head sank. "I'm sorry for my outburst. I just don't want anyone else to get hurt."

"Your worries are understandable, Gregory," Nehma said. "But we no longer have any guarantees to give. This plan is all we have, and we have to trust that we will be able to leave for Earth without further bloodshed."

Nehma gestured to Ja'tare, and he stepped forward. "Alright everyone, get your things ready. We head out in ten minutes."

CHAPTER TWENTY-THREE

I clawed my way up the crumbling remnants of a huge shuttle crash, my body slick and dripping with sweat. Reaching the apex of the towering heap, I bent over and took ragged breaths as my muscles throbbed with exhaustion. Who's bright idea was this again?

We'd been hiking up and down this damned collision graveyard for several hours with no end in sight. It didn't help that our pace was hellishly sluggish. The Veloxan civilians moved lethargically, unaffected by Imogen and Ja'tare's groups of warriors nipping at their heels. Their refusal to speed up meant more time for me to spiral between impatience, restlessness, and ever-increasing anxiety.

Once my breathing was normal again, I glanced back down the tunnel the way we'd come. Still no Reapers, but how long would that last? An hour? A minute? Were we already too late? Ja'tare and the others scrambled up the rocks towards me, and I helped Ja'tare up to his feet once he was within arm's reach.

"How much longer do you think we have?" I asked.

Ja'tare wiped at the sweat on his brow, eyes narrowed. "I do not know, Gregory. A mile? Half a mile? Two?"

"Maybe if you stopped asking every five minutes, we'd move along faster," Imogen chastised as she joined us.

"I'm just curious, sheesh," I grumbled.

Together we descended the hill. I made a mental note to stop emulating a whiny kid asking 'are we there yet', but my concern was justified. We were stuck in this labyrinth of tunnels, vulnerable and exposed. If the Reapers came, it would be sheer chaos. Every noise, every little tumble of rubble or scuffle of movement put me on edge.

We trudged on, several warriors staying behind to ensure nothing was following us. Twenty yards ahead, scores of bedraggled Veloxans dragged forward alongside our bretaren, which had enormous supply packs loaded onto their backs.

Watching them gave me a sense of deja vu from when my human group was forced into the sewers to escape the Reapers. I hoped we would make it through to the other side safely.

Someone's comm device sparked to life nearby. "All clear," P'taro reported.

The tightness in my chest loosened a tiny bit.

P'taro was in the front with the remainder of our battle-ready Veloxans, leading us towards an emergency under-ground gate to the laboratory. Along the way, he would routinely use his tablet to scan short-range for lifeforms. So far we'd been lucky.

We continued down the shitty dilapidated remains of the tunnel, Imogen by my side. She looked how I felt, tense and exhausted.

She caught me looking at her and smiled weakly. "I'm glad this is almost over."

I looked down at my feet, kicking pebbles of rubble. "Yeah, me too."

"Would you mind telling me more about Earth? The few things I can remember seem like a dream. How have things changed? Is it like here?"

"Well I'm not gonna lie to you, things are pretty bad on Earth. Most of the world's population died out with the invasion of the Dak'kar, at least that's what we believe. We've had to scavenge in order to survive, but I'm hoping the Veloxans will help us change all that."

Imogen frowned. "I see."

Shit, was I too pessimistic just now? "It's not all bad. A lot of things are gone, but there's still plenty of great things to enjoy. Books, comics ..." *Kissing Trent.* "Um, candy. You used to love smearing Snickers and Reese's all over your face."

Imogen snickered. "I actually remember that."

Ja'tare and Ko'ta walked up to us with puzzled looks on their faces.

"What is *can-dee*, and why would you smear it on your face?" Ja'tare asked.

Imogen and I burst out laughing, and I patted Ja'tare on the shoulder.

"Snickers and Reese's are types of candy. It's a food we humans eat, very sweet and full of sugar."

Ko'ta scratched his cheek. "*Shoo-garr?*"

I smirked. "I'll add it to the list of things for you to try out once we get to Earth. Speaking of which, once we reunite with the group I've been travelling with, things should be relatively safer with our combined numbers. Immy, what's the first thing you'd like to do?"

Imogen bit at her lower lip. "I don't know, there's so much to get used to again."

"Don't worry, there's plenty of time to figure things out."

Suddenly, Ko'ta stopped dead in his tracks, his eyebrows drawing together.

"What is it?" Ja'tare asked.

"Hold on. I think I heard something."

He held up a hand and we all froze, still as statues.

After a long moment, Ko'ta shook his head. "It is gone, but I know I heard something." He clicked his shirt's comm device. "P'taro, are you experiencing anything unusual up ahead?"

P'taro's voice crackled. "It is odd you mention that. I am experiencing some inter-- My connection to the short-range scan is gone! We will have to rely on the last update on my reader to guide us to the emergency gate."

Ja'tare triggered his comm device. "P'taro, tell the civilians to pick up the pace and have the guards keep close to you and the others. Something does not seem right."

"Affirmative, Commander."

A deafening silence took over the tunnels as we scrambled ahead, and my anxiety resurfaced with a vengeance.

Was the interference from the natural rock Ja'tare had mentioned or could this be the Reapers? Whatever it was, I hoped we wouldn't be around to find out.

I CLIMBED down the debris and rubble of another shuttle crash, a thick cloud of dust rising around me. I sneezed, then rubbed my nose. Jesus, how many Veloxans had come this way? This was the umpteenth crash we'd encountered in the past thirty minutes.

Imogen, Ko'ta, and Ja'tare descended the large heap after me and approached, wiping grime off of themselves.

"Is it just me or is it getting really congested around here?" I asked.

Ja'tare's forehead wrinkled. "Yes. Whoever rode these shuttles must have had the same idea we did. It is sad that they did not make it."

"Yeah, but isn't it weird that there are so many?"

"I do not believe so. The evacuation of Verus caused a mass panic. The Veloxans driving these shuttles must have overridden the autopilot controls in an attempt to get to safety. Without proper training, that decision would have been extremely hazardous."

I glanced around me cautiously. "Do you think the Dak'kar could've roamed these tunnels?"

"It's not unlikely," Immy chimed in. "But what does it matter now? They're not here."

"That we know of," I objected. "But Ko'ta heard something earlier. What if it's them? What if all of this is a trap, an easy way to pick us off?"

Imogen sighed. "Gregory, what good is all this freaking out going to do us? Let's just stick to the plan and move on."

My head sunk. "You're right. Sorry, I just really don't like this place. It gives me the creeps and I need fresh air."

"Stop worrying so much. We're almost there, right Ja'tare?"

"Correct," Ja'tare confirmed. "Based on the markings on the walls, it should be just ahead."

We shadowed after the Veloxan citizens once more only to realize they'd come to a full stop. The entire passage ahead was blocked by an enormous mountain of wreckage.

Ja'tare was about to click his comm device when P'taro's voice transmitted through, beating him to the punch. "Commander Ja'tare, we have a situation up here. You are going to want to see this."

Ja'tare broke into a jog and we chased after him, jostling the citizens in our way. When we cleared the last of them, I gasped at the horrific sight of the catastrophe before us.

A molten mass of broken shuttles, debris, and blackened bodies loomed, stacked to the top of the thirty-foot ceiling. The overwhelming stench of death made me gag. I pulled my face mask up, several others doing the same.

Christ, what happened here? Despite the crashes we'd seen along the way, this seemed too coincidental, deliberate. Could the Reapers have been behind this?

P'taro paced the edge of the pileup, shaking his head. "We have to unblock this tunnel. The emergency gate is right ahead and there is no other way to it."

"Do you think the gate might be inoperable?" Ja'tare asked.

"It is a possibility, but right now all we can do is--"

A bone-chilling shriek of rage echoed down through the tunnel, interrupting P'taro. Terrified Veloxans cried out in panic.

"The Dak'kar are here!"

"They followed us, I knew it!"

"What are we going to do?"

"We cannot go back!"

The shouts and fearful gibbering crescendoed louder and louder, reaching a fever pitch.

Ja'tare jumped atop a nearby boulder and covered the sides of his mouth with his hands. "Quiet!"

Everyone went silent.

"We must remain calm. Yes, it appears the Dak'kar are coming, but panicking will only make things worse. We have to join together and tear down this wall of debris. If we do not do this we will never get to Earth, do you understand?"

Slowly but surely, Veloxans murmured their agreement.

"Young ones, stick together and keep your voices down please. The warriors will watch over you. Everyone else, clear the rubble and follow P'taro's instructions. I need a dozen warriors to follow me, *now*."

Ja'tare stalked off, and Immy and I went after him along with a small squadron of battle-ready Veloxans. As much as I wanted to help remove the blockage in the tunnel, I felt compelled to assist in stopping the Reapers. If they were far enough away, we might still have time to come up with a diversion or trap.

We came upon the last large mound of rubble we'd passed. Ja'tare turned around, putting a finger to his lips and we stood still, listening.

In the distance I could make out an infinitesimal scraping sound, soon followed by another Dak'kar screech that was the tiniest bit louder. The disturbing sound of their approach continued.

"Now what?" I asked.

"We have to find a way to throw them off of our trail," Ja'tare said. "That or find a way to trap or kill them in this confined space."

"But how?" one of the warriors asked.

Ja'tare grimaced. "I am not sure, but we do not have long. Think everyone, think!"

Our frustrated group formed a loose circle in an attempt to brainstorm some ideas.

"I know," one of the warriors said. "What about the poison we use for the spears? We could lace the tunnel with it."

Ja'tare shook his head. "The fumes are dangerous for all of us. If the slightest breeze brings the poison back to us, we will be weakened or worse."

"How about baiting them?" a female Veloxan suggested.

Ja'tare smiled. "That is a good idea, but with what?"

The Veloxan stared down at her feet, and Ja'tare paced as we all struggled to think of something.

When no one spoke up, I meandered over to a large flat stone and sat upon it, followed by Imogen. I plopped my knapsack down next to me. Several of the contents spilled out, and I cursed my clumsiness. I picked up my things, and as I was packing them back into my sack, my hands grazed a waxy, cylindrical object. I pulled it out. The Reaper candle!

If we placed it down the tunnel and lit it, it would draw the Reapers with its putrid scent. Not for long, but maybe enough to allow us to escape. It wasn't much, but it just might work.

I nudged Imogen. "Hey, what if we used this Dak'kar pheromone candle? If we take it down the tunnel a little further and light it, they won't be able to resist the scent."

Imogen's face lit up. "Oh my gosh, that's perfect! Let's go tell the others."

"Hold on a sec. Do we really want to do that?"

"What do you mean?"

"Well, think about it. Do you think they can take care of it? We can't afford to lose any more warriors."

"They can't afford to lose us either," Imogen reasoned.

"I understand that, but ... I feel a sense of duty to carry this out myself. Ja'tare and his people have saved my life many times. I have to do this for them."

Imogen mulled it over. "Alright, I won't tell them. But if you're doing this, I'm going with you. And don't even think about fighting me on it."

I smiled. "Nothing gets past you, does it sis?"

She grinned. "Nope. Now, what are we going to do?"

I looked over at the small gathering of Veloxan warriors. Their backs were turned to us. "We have to make a run for it, but if they see us we'll need a backup plan to explain things without being apprehended."

"Hm, what about a brief note? It may not stop them from pursuing, but there's little else we can do."

"I agree. Wait, you know how to write Veloxan?"

Imogen scoffed. "Of course I do. I've been here for five years."

I shuffled through my bag, ripping off part of the colorful cloth I'd wrapped my spare weapons in. I found a large sooty rock and handed the materials to Imogen. She carefully etched some Veloxan symbols onto it before tying the fabric around the stone and handing it back to me.

"If we leave this on the crash site nearby, they should see it."

I gave Imogen a thumbs up as I slung my knapsack back on.

We took off, edging closer to the heap with the lightest of footfalls while watching the warriors intently.

A sudden Dak'kar shriek echoed to us, jolting Ja'tare and the others. Taking advantage of their distraction, Imogen and I bolted to the mound of rubble.

"Hey, what are you doing?" Ja'tare called. "Stop them!"

Shit!

Imogen and I scrambled up the hill. We came to the apex, and I placed the weighted note on a clear space before sliding down the other side. We used our momentum to propel us forward.

A part of me felt bad for leaving Ja'tare and the others, but I had to do this. They'd just have to forgive us later.

As we sprinted away, I could hear the Veloxans chasing after us. We were losing ground against their long strides fast. *Damn it!* We had to lose them, but how? Just ahead was a small crash site. If it was the one I hoped it was, on the other side would be a tiny enclosure we could hide in to lose them. I'd nearly slipped in by accident on the way in.

"When we clear this rubble veer left, okay?" I said.

"Got it."

Our shoes crunched upon the mound, and once we cleared it we shot left. Sure enough, in the dim light of the tunnel was a small recess that looked like shadows to the naked eye.

"In here!"

Immy and I crammed into the tight little space, crouching low. Our breathing was deafening as the Veloxans' steps thundered after us. I covered my mouth as bits of rock crunched and sprayed from their footsteps.

"They could not have gone far," one of them said.

"*Far?*" another asked. "They were just here! I saw them myself."

"What do you want me to say? We should not even be here. We should be helping the others."

"Ja'tare will be extremely angry if we do not find Gregory and Imogen. They must be hiding somewhere."

A Reaper screech interrupted the Veloxans' argument, this time a little too close for comfort.

"What do we do?" Imogen whispered. "They're going to find us if they look around here."

More rubble flung from the Veloxans' movement, some of it tumbling to a rest near our tiny recess. As I watched, a plan formed in my mind. "I have an idea. If it works, be ready to move."

I crept cautiously to the recess's opening and scooped up several small chunks of stone. I observed the Veloxans, waiting until their backs were turned to me. Once the coast was clear, I stepped out just long enough to hurl the stones back down the tunnel away from us. The rocks clattered upon the ground loudly.

"What was that?" one of the Veloxans asked.

"That must be them. Come on!"

The Veloxans ran back the way they came, and I rose to my feet. "Immy, now!"

Together we crept further down the tunnel, slow at first to avoid making too much noise, then faster the more distance we put between the Veloxans and us. As we ran, we searched each side tunnel, looking for one with enough space to contain several Reapers. We stopped at a large intersecting path, both panting like dogs.

"Just ... gimme a sec," I huffed. "Gotta catch my breath."

As if in response a Reaper cry of rage sounded, shockingly close.

Imogen yanked me into the safety of the dark passage. We stumbled forward blindly, using the wall to keep us steady until I fished out my lighter to guide us. Like every other path we'd seen, remnants littered the ground everywhere. We edged forward, watching our step. If we alerted the Reapers before lighting the pheromone candle, we'd be dead meat.

"How much farther should we go?" I asked.

"I don't know. Far enough to help the others as much as possible. Let's keep going."

We continued down the tunnel another minute before we reached an impasse. The tunnel was blocked off by a huge mound of debris we wouldn't be able to pass without difficulty.

"Looks like this is it," I said.

"It's going to have to be. We don't have much time before the Dak'kar pass us. Let's light this thing up and get out of here."

I pulled the partially melted Reaper candle out of my knapsack, lit it, and set it down on the ground. Almost immediately, a thick black smoke rose from it, wafting around us.

Imogen covered her nose with her arm. "God, that's awful!"

"Come on, let's get back to the others. It's out of our hands now."

We started to walk back the way we came when a number of large hulking shapes shadowed the dim light from the main tunnel. Imogen and I pressed ourselves against the wall, shrinking into the darkness. I muttered a quick prayer to whatever god might be watching that the Reapers hadn't seen us.

At first the Reapers kept on moving, but one of them lingered and let out a short inhuman shriek, drawing them back. They skulked into the passage, communicating to each other in grating cries that could break glass.

The Reapers prowled onward, their arrival punctuated by their increasing awful odor and claws scraping loudly against the ground. They crept forward, several feet away now. I held my breath.

Come on, pass us you fuckers.

Most of them continued on towards the Reaper candle, but one of them stopped as if it was suspicious of its surroundings. It gazed in my direction and sniffed at the air, creeping closer, closer, closer…

When it was just inches away from me, one of the other Reapers bayed, a sound that resonated like rending metal. The monster in front of me snapped out of its curious wanderings and scrambled to join the others up ahead. The anxious bundle of energy stirring in my stomach loosened. I've never been so grateful for Reaper intervention.

Once the Reapers were a safe distance away, I grabbed Imogen's hand. We stalked away slowly, inching ahead until we finally rounded the corner to the main tunnel. We broke out into a full-on sprint.

We'd bought us some time, but I had no idea how much. Five minutes? Ten? I hoped it would be enough.

Within a minute or so we passed the recess we'd hidden in and charged onward. We didn't see the Veloxans that had been looking for us. I hoped that meant they were safe with Ja'tare and the others.

Imogen and I came upon the last mound of rubble and

started climbing. Ja'tare would be there and he'd be pissed but he'd have to under--

A pair of hands closed in on mine, yanking me over the apex of the heap. Another Veloxan pulled Imogen up.

Ja'tare glared at us, his gleaming green eyes piercing mine. "What were you thinking, running off like that? Not only did you endanger my warriors, but yourselves as well!"

"Ja'tare, I'm sorry," I said. "This is all my idea, but we had to do it or the Dak'kar would've already gotten here."

Ja'tare grimaced, still visibly upset. "I … we were worried about you."

I touched his upper arm gently. "I'm sorry for breaking your trust. We didn't mean to leave you in the dark, but Imogen and I felt it was our duty to do this for your people."

Ja'tare stared at me, his angular face devoid of emotion.

Damn it, we really freaked him out. I'd have to find a way to make it up to him once we got to Earth.

"Ja'tare, I'm sorry too," Imogen said. "We meant no harm in what we did, but at least now we have some extra time to work with. How is the unblocking of the tunnel going?"

"Not as well as we hoped," Ja'tare said. "See for yourself."

I looked over to the nightmarish collision site. Several long lines of Veloxans hauled large chunks of debris down one side of the heap. In the middle, adult Veloxans guided younger ones through a small hole to the other side, but our end was still filled with nearly a hundred Veloxans and all of our bretaren.

"The gate was damaged but operational. We were able to get it open, but progress is slow going."

"How much longer do you think they need to clear space to get the bretaren through?" I asked.

"Not much, but we have to keep an eye out for the Dak'kar. If the pheromone candle loses effect, we will have to stall them."

We camped out on our elevated lookout, watching the tunnel closely. There weren't any signs of the Reapers yet, but I knew the candle wouldn't last much longer. Imogen paced restlessly next to me, Ja'tare leaning against the stone wall nearby.

"I hate this," Imogen grumbled. "We can't just sit here waiting for the Dak'kar to charge us while the others break their backs trying to clear an escape." Imogen glanced back at the Veloxans, and suddenly her eyes went wide. "Wait, that's it! Why don't we block this side of the path? While the Dak'kar struggle to get through, we can attack them."

My pulse quickened in excitement. "Holy crap, I can't believe we didn't think of it before. Immy, you're a genius! Ja'tare?"

Ja'tare roused from his perch against the wall. "It is worth a shot. Come on, there is no time to lose!"

Ja'tare alerted the other warriors, and we began hauling large fragments of wreckage up the hill, stacking them to create a barrier. We'd been working at the pile for a couple minutes when a collective Reaper wail of fury thundered down the tunnel.

My stomach plummeted. "They're coming! Ja'tare, what do we do? We haven't piled enough rubble yet."

Ja'tare looked left to right, desperation in his green eyes . He pointed to the hulk of a crashed shuttle some yards away. "There! Grab the remnants of that shuttle. If we position it correctly, it might block the majority of the opening."

We assembled around the gargantuan chunk of broken machinery. At first we had issues lifting it, but when we tilted it a certain way we were able to creep it along towards the hill in a slow broken scuttle. The trek up the mound was another matter entirely. I felt like Atlas as we heaved the boulder up the mountain, but somehow we inched our way up. As we lodged the shuttle's remains into place, more cries from the Reapers rebounded down the tunnel, very close.

"Get back, and arm yourselves!" Ja'tare commanded. "Once the Dak'kar are within range, attack them through the gaps in the wall."

Imogen, the other warriors, and I edged back, readying ourselves. All of the hairs on my body stood on end, and I looked back to the escaping Veloxan civilians. They had cleared enough debris to squeeze the bretaren through, but there were still at least thirty or forty Veloxans on our side. I gripped my blade hard. I wasn't going to let anything happen to them.

Earth-quaking footsteps shook the ground as the Reapers thundered up the mound with shrieks of fury. They hit our barrier with collective force. The large remnant of the shuttle we'd placed swayed wildly, threatening to topple over. Several warriors darted forward, putting their weight against it to keep it upright.

Just as we were stabilizing our defenses, a pair of Reaper claws dove through small gaps in the wall, flailing wildly for a victim.

Ja'tare dove forward, stabbing the Reaper's claw with his spear. The creature yelped in pain, yanking back its maimed appendage.

Seconds later, more sets of Reaper claws jutted from openings in the wall, reaching out for Ja'tare and missing him by inches. I lunged forward, striking at the clawed fingers. "Come on, don't just stand there!"

Imogen and the available Veloxans joined in, keeping the Reapers at bay. Here and there, new holes in our barricade appeared, but we were keeping up with their strategy and forcing them back, whack-a-Reaper style.

"It is working, keep it up!" Ja'tare shouted.

We maintained our defensive strategy, but after a minute

or so the Reapers stopped attacking, withdrawing their razor-sharp claws. They shifted audibly on the other side of the wall.

"What's going on?" Imogen asked.

"I think they're wising up," I said. "They must be altering their strategy."

Ja'tare looked behind us and shook his head. "There are still too many Veloxans on this side to abandon our post just yet."

The Reapers' heavy clawed feet thudded away from us down the hill of rubble. They didn't go far based on the grating, mewling noises they made at each other.

"They're communicating," I edged towards one of the holes the Reapers had made in our partition. "I'm going to take a look."

"Gregory, it is not safe!" Ja'tare cried.

"Don't worry, I'll be careful, promise."

I inched forward, aligning my vision with the cavity until I caught sight of the hulking, red-bodied Reapers. Six of them were assembled at the base of the mound, five lined up next to each other with one in front facing them like it was in charge. The lead Reaper shrieked at the others, and they tightened their position.

"They're lining up in some kind of pattern," I announced. "I don't know what they're doing."

The lead Reaper stomped one of its clawed feet sharply, then screeched to the others. One by one, they began to mimic their leader, pounding their feet into the ground and focusing their sickly yellow eyes on the hill.

They looked like they were getting ready for a football play. Why were they ... wait, what if they were amping up? Football players always took formation before they--

The Reapers charged forward, one collective unit of massive unholy strength.

I jolted back from my vantage point. "Everyone run, they're going to charge!"

Chaos erupted as we all scrambled. Just as I cleared the top of the heap, a huge explosion of rock and debris boomed, sending me flying. I hit the ground like a sack of potatoes, the air in my lungs snuffing out with the impact. I tried to pick myself up, but I couldn't catch enough breath. Instead I forced myself onto my back, taking in the damage.

A huge cloud of dust hung in the air, shrouding everything in a haze. Through it I could make out the forms of Veloxans scattered on the ground. Several of them staggered to their feet, while others were still down for the count. Imogen was several yards from me with cuts and a nasty gash on her forehead, but she was conscious and getting up. I couldn't see Ja'tare, but there wasn't any time to search for him. Our defenses were shattered. We had to retreat.

A resounding cry of anger from the Reapers instilled fresh fear in me. Six hulking shapes stood atop our mass of wreckage. With a gut-wrenching shriek, three of them shot down the pile, pouncing on the nearest Veloxans.

No!

Imogen pulled at me. "Gregory, get the hell up! We have to go!"

I scrambled up, using her weight as leverage. "But what about--"

"There's no time. Run, damn it!"

Imogen and I hurtled towards the enormous mountain of rubble leading to the laboratory, the screams of our dying warriors echoing behind us.

Half a dozen Veloxans shot ahead of us as we reached the bottom of the hill, Ja'tare and five others. We clawed wildly beside them, but they easily outpaced us, clearing the expanse in quick, long strides.

I pushed Imogen forward each step of the way until we

finally reached the hole in the debris that led to the gate, Ja'tare pulling us through.

They slid the hill, and I spun around for one last look. The dust had settled over the area, no longer masking the carnage that had occurred. Below, the Reapers fed on our warriors, splashes of dark nearly purple blood staining the ground in spurts. Suddenly, one of the still Veloxans jumped to his feet and sprinted to the hill, reaching the bottom. One of the Reapers took notice and catapulted towards him. It was going to be close, too close.

I held out my hand. "Hurry!"

The Veloxan doubled his pace, just feet away. As he grabbed my hand he wailed in agony, and a mist of his blood sprayed me in the face.

Terrified, I yanked my hand free, falling back, no, falling further! I rolled chaotically down the safe side of the heap, hitting shoulder, arm, knee, and everything in between before rolling out to a stop at the bottom.

My entire body throbbed with sharp stabs of intense pain. I struggled to keep my eyes open, forcing myself to focus on the ceiling above. Arms tugged at me with a fresh burst of agony as I was dragged backwards into the obsidian gate beyond. Once we were clear of the doorway, I risked a dizzying glance ahead. The first of the Reapers came barrelling down the mound straight for us.

Ja'tare lunged forward and smacked a large red button. Just before the Reaper reached us, a black metal door came slamming down.

"Gregory, do not move. You are injured," he said.

I slumped to the floor, my vision going blurry. "We didn't save them."

"We could not without risking our own lives. They made a sacrifice for the greater good. I am going to pick you up, alright? We have to get you to the medical bay."

Ja'tare picked me up and cradled me close to him, sending a surge of stabbing pinpricks through me. We entered the laboratory with a whoosh of cool air. My heart was light as the world spun into darkness.

We'd done it, we made it to the laboratory. It was time for us to go home, once and for all.

CHAPTER TWENTY-FOUR

I sat up on my small bed in the stark white infirmary and swung my legs over the edge.

Ja'tare hovered next to me and put a hand on my shoulder. "Are you sure you are well enough to move around?"

I brushed his hand off me. "For the last time Ja'tare, I'm fine."

Truthfully, I still had a headache after another excruciating round of healing nanites the medic had injected me with, but I wasn't going to tell him that. Ja'tare's overbearing concern was driving me nuts. He had insisted that the medical staff continue to run never-ending tests on me, even after my broken bones had been fully healed from my fall. If I didn't get out of here soon I was going to lose my shit.

Before Ja'tare could dote on me any further, Imogen walked up. Her injuries had mended completely, and her skin was healthy and radiant. "Well, well, well, look who's back in for the count," she said with a smile.

Ja'tare eyed me with apparent skepticism. "That is yet to be seen. He claims to be in decent shape, but I have my doubts. Gregory, if you would just let the medic run a couple more tests--"

"Stop," I grumbled. "I've had enough poking and prodding. I'm fine."

"If he says he's better, I think we should trust him on it," Imogen reasoned.

I hopped off the bed, hiding the twinge of pain in my head and stretching for a moment. "Yep, good as new. See?"

Ja'tare opened his mouth to respond when his comm device buzzed to life.

"Ja'tare, this is P'taro. How are Gregory and Imogen doing?"

"They both appear to have recovered, though I believe we should perform additional exams to be sure."

I glared at Ja'tare. I didn't need another mother. Did his overprotective attitude have to do with his broken trust? Maybe I should talk to him about this before we headed to Earth.

"I think that is going to have to do for now," P'taro said. "The council is insisting on the three of you joining them in meeting room six of the west wing. Could you head over and bring them with you?"

Ja'tare gave me another obnoxious once over, and I crossed my arms.

"I'm fine," I said through gritted teeth.

"Erm, yes, we will be right there," Ja'tare told P'taro, ending the chat.

Ja'tare, Imogen, and I left the laboratory and entered a long and empty vaulted hallway with numerous panels set into the walls. From what I forced out of the medical staff, the majority of Veloxans were taking shelter in the main hall, which explained the ghost town vibe here. But as reassuring as that was, my mind was ablaze at the sudden request from the council. P'taro made it sound important. Could something have gone wrong yet again?

I swatted my doubts away. I had to stay positive. They probably just wanted to talk about our plans for when we arrived on Earth. There was a lot to address.

We ambled down the lengthy passage for several minutes before taking a right and stopping at the third door on the left, where several Veloxan warriors were stationed. Upon our arrival they moved aside for us, the doors swooshing open.

The three of us entered the simple conference room. Six abstractly-shaped chairs were gathered around a table that resembled a giant upside down teardrop. Nehma, Kro'da, and De'jartha sat in three of the seats facing us, looking much cleaner and composed now.

I exchanged glances with Nehma and she smiled sweetly, her purple-eyes gleaming bright. Okay, maybe this really *was* good news.

She gestured towards us and we sat down. I fiddled with my fingers, waiting for them to come out with whatever they had to say.

"We are happy to hear that you are feeling better from your fall in the tunnels, and overjoyed that Imogen has decided to join us in our voyage to Earth," Nehma said.

"Thank you," I replied. "Um, I'm sorry if I'm being too blunt here, but do you know when we will be heading back to Earth?"

Kro'da eyed me with an unreadable stone-faced expression. "Actually, that is why we called you here. There have been complications since we arrived."

My shoulders slumped. More delays, I knew it. "Like what?"

"The portal generator needs more repairs than we originally thought. Our engineers are working on it at the moment, but it will take some time."

"How long?" Imogen asked.

"Too soon to tell, but we are hoping within the next few hours."

My heavy heart lifted a bit. A delayed departure, that wasn't too bad. But why did the council have frowns plastered on their faces? "Was there something else?"

"Yes," De'jartha said grimly. "We were able to get the laboratory's long-range scanners back online and we found something. Dak'kar, many of them. At least several dozen seem to be headed this way based on their trajectory from the past several hours."

I shrugged. "So? How do we know they aren't migrating?"

"We have had decades to analyze Dak'kar movement patterns," Kro'da said. "They wander, even when migrating, until they find a new mate and breeding spot. These Dak'kar are headed straight for us and have not changed course. We believe they are under the control of a hooded Dak'kar like you suggested in the way station."

I mulled over the council's words. Their theory made sense. The lesser Reapers communicated with each other. If a hooded one caught wind of a message from the ones at the way station, it would head straight here to slaughter us, influencing other Reapers along the way to build an army.

"How long do we have before they get here?" I asked.

"They are still a few hours' distance away," Kro'da said. "We are hoping that our engineers will be able to fix the generator in time, but if they cannot ..."

"Then we'll have to fight them," Imogen said.

"Correct."

I grimaced. This was bad, really bad. We'd hardly handled six Reapers in the shuttle tunnels, but *dozens*? That was something none of us were prepared for.

"We need to come up with a plan if the Dak'kar get here first," I said.

The council shot uncertain glances at each other.

"We agree," Nehma said. "But we have never faced this many Dak'kar at one time. Typically our strategy has been to strike hard before retreating. That will not work in this scenario."

"Alright, then we start with the basics and go from there," Imogen said. "How many warriors you have available, the most likely location they will strike at, things like that."

"Yeah, and from there we'll need to think on strategy," I added. "Their numbers are worrying, but if we put our heads together we may be able to find a way to isolate the hooded Dak'kar and eliminate it. Its ability to control the others would allow them to attack in a unified front. Taking that away could make the lesser Dak'kar confused, shaken. We could use that to our advantage."

"Yes," Kro'da agreed. "But how are we supposed to destroy a hooded Dak'kar? Few have ever managed that. Should we not instead focus on reducing the lesser Dak'kar's numbers?"

"You both have a point," Imogen said. "The lesser Dak'kar are a threat regardless of whether or not they are being influenced, but we can't underestimate the power the hooded one holds. From my limited interactions with them, the hooded Dak'kar won't risk its control over the others. It'll stay behind them where it's safe. So if we want to get to it, we'll have to find a way to incapacitate the others."

"And how do we do that?" I asked.

Imogen frowned. "I'm not sure. Does anyone have any ideas?"

The room went quiet as I pondered over our situation. How could we expose the Reapers' weaknesses? I focused on what we knew.

The Reapers communicated with each other. They hunted in small packs, which could be overridden with the presence of a hooded Reaper. But I was missing something, something about how they hunted. Samuel's irritating voice entered my head. *The Reapers hunt by sight and sound.*

I slapped a hand on the table in triumph, jolting everyone. "I've got it! We have to expose the Dak'kar's natural sensitivities. They hunt by sight and sound, right? So what if we create something that will overload those senses? That would disable them, giving us a chance to mow them down and go after the leader. I have an idea for a device. If you let me work with your engineers on developing it, it could be just what we need."

De'jartha's eyes narrowed. "But we only have a few hours at best!"

"I know, but this could tip the scales in our favor."

"I want to go with you," Imogen said. "I may have an idea myself."

"What about our battle strategy?" Kro'da asked.

"Ko'ta and I can be of service in that regard," Ja'tare said. "No one has better knowledge of our warriors and their capabilities, and we can visit with Gregory and Imogen when they have more details about any devices they develop to help us."

The council spoke amongst themselves before addressing us.

"Imogen and Gregory, you may go," Nehma said. "The warriors stationed outside this room will take you where the engineers are located and we will let them know you are on your way."

Imogen and I rose, and I gave a slight bow. "Thank you."

We left the meeting room in a hurry, following the guards' brisk pace.

Whatever the Veloxans were doing to fix the generator, I

hoped they would do it fast. I had no idea if my device would work, and if it didn't the blood of hundreds of Veloxans would be on my hands.

~

I LEANED over the lab table with P'taro, analyzing the quickly-drawn blueprint of a catapult Imogen had rendered. "Remind me how this is going to save us?"

Imogen narrowed her eyes at me. "If we load the catapults with pouches of poison, we can attack the lesser Dak'kar before they get close to us. The poison has worked on them time and time again, and anyone could operate it, warrior or not. Is that *okay*?"

I held my hands up in surrender. "No, no, it's great, really. Good call. We could use as many weapons against them as we can get. What do you think, P'taro?"

P'taro pushed his goggles up to perch on his horned forehead. "I like it. As long as we keep the design simple it will not take long to construct a number of these. What about your idea, Gregory? Do you have a schematic?"

I shook my head. "I'm no good with sketching, so I'll just have to explain it to you. Basically I need a device that can attack the Dak'kar's sight with an intense light to blind them. Back on Earth we have something called a strobe light. It's a device that emits a strong flash that can be harsh on the eyes."

P'taro's tilted his head. "*Strobe* light?"

"Yes." I put a finger to my lips, thinking on something I could draw reference from. "The effect I'm looking for is similar to the built-in emergency lights you have here. What we would need is a modified version that can be installed underground and triggered by motion. The light flash would have to be very intense with a fast rhythm, maybe even augmented by a high-pitched droning noise. Does that sound feasible?"

"Yes, I think I may be able to do that. I will need time to modify the hardware to adjust to your specifications."

"Hold on," Imogen interjected. "We need to test this theory out on an actual Dak'kar. Otherwise this is all a huge waste of time."

My lips pressed tight into a grimace. Imogen was right. How the hell were we gonna get access to a Reaper without getting diced into a million pieces?

"Actually, we have several Dak'kar in captivity," P'taro said. "They were trapped in some of our rooms when we first arrived. I can test the intensity and frequency of the light and audio bursts for optimal results. The other engineers will help me with this and make sure the catapults work efficiently."

A weight lifted from my shoulders. "This is really good news. Do you think it'll be enough?"

Imogen planted a hand on her forehead. "We've done all we could, Gregory. It's going to have to be."

"Um, right," P'taro agreed. "You two should rest up while you still can. I will inform the council of our developments. Much will be happening soon."

Imogen and I left the lab, wandering down the empty passage to the main hall where everyone else was located.

We'd done what we could to help ensure success if the Veloxans went to battle, and I hoped it would do some good despite my mounting worries. Plans seemed destined to fail when Reapers were involved.

Imogen stopped walking and leaned against the wall, her brows furrowed.

"Are you okay?" I asked.

"I'm just stressed," Imogen said. "This whole situation feels screwed."

"I know how you feel. Ever since I got here it's been one thing after another. I don't know how P'taro expects us to relax. We still don't even know how we're going to take out the hooded Dak'kar."

"I've been thinking about that too. Gregory, it may be up to us to stop it. The Veloxans are already stretched thin concentrating on the lesser Dak'kar. When the hooded one gets involved, they won't stand a chance."

A chill shot through me at the thought. "Yeah, I think you may be right. The hooded Dak'kar are too powerful to just throw a bunch of warriors at, but what if the Veloxans come up with something we haven't thought of?"

Imogen scoffed. "Do you really think that's possible? They've been surviving the past few decades by running and only fighting when they absolutely had to. Back in those tunnels we hardly fought off six Dak'kar. What makes you think they can handle several dozen *and* a hooded Dak'kar, even with their new tools?"

I stared at Imogen, shocked at how pessimistic she was being.

"I'm sorry," she apologized. "I shouldn't have snapped like that. I'm just scared what will happen out there. What if we lose?" Her head sagged. "I just want to go home. You reminded me what it was to be human, and now that I'm so close to having my family back, I ..."

I plodded over to her, grasping her hand and holding it in mine. "Don't worry, we'll make it through this. We've been through so much already."

Imogen stiffened. "But there's no guarantee of that. Every time we face them, we lose somebody. Who's to say it won't be you or me this time?"

I frowned. "You're right, as always. There aren't any guarantees with this battle. That's why I want you to sit this one out."

Imogen broke off from me, aghast. "What?"

"It's a miracle that I found you again, Immy. Even more that we made it this far. If something were to happen to you … I can't lose you again." My vision went blurry, but I could still see the look of discomfort on Imogen's face.

"Gregory, I can't do that. I have to fight. My warriors have been like family to me. They've taken care of me, protected me. If they go out into battle, I can't just watch from the sidelines. That's not who I am, and that's not who you are either."

I smiled weakly. Imogen wasn't the scared little girl she once was. She was strong, independent. Mom would be proud of her. I held her hand once more. "Alright, we'll fight them together, brother and sister."

Imogen squeezed my hand. "Brother and sister."

Suddenly, the emergency lights activated in the hall, bathing our surroundings in bloody red illumination. A blaring siren went off, whooping three times before starting again.

A booming voice filled the hallway, repeating a message over and over. "All uninjured report to the main laboratory hall immediately!"

Imogen and I shared a worried glance before sprinting down the hall. This was it. Either we were going home or we had a hell of a fight on our hands.

CHAPTER TWENTY-FIVE

The door to the main hall swooshed open, a cacophony of voices assaulting Imogen and I as we bolted through. We slowed down and caught our breath as we took everything in.

Vast numbers of Veloxans occupied the large passage, clustered in small groups throughout. Children and adolescents sat upon exotically colored furs away from the ruckus, while up ahead a crowd of Veloxans gathered, amassing quickly.

Imogen and I ambled closer to the throng.

"I think I see my men on the far right," Imogen said. "Let's go."

We wedged through half a dozen rows of Veloxans before joining her tall, black-clad warriors. I tried to avert my gaze, but their chiseled muscular bodies were hard not to notice and appreciate. God I missed Trent.

Imogen touched the broad shoulder of a familiar Veloxan with dark, slicked back hair and a prominent scar running down the side of his face. He looked shocked at Imogen's presence.

"What's going on?" Imogen asked. "Have you heard anything yet?"

"I, uh … I am sorry, Commander. No one has explained anything yet."

"Thank you." Imogen frowned, looking around nervously before stepping away from her troops. I followed her until she stopped and turned towards me. "His response was strange. Do you think he knows something? What if they got the portal generator up?"

I shook my head. "I don't know, Imogen. Let's wait it out and hope for the best."

I stared forward, feeling guilty. To be honest, I did think Imogen's Veloxan friend was holding something back, but I didn't want to start something. The meeting would happen any minute now and we'd find out then.

We continued to wait, the escalating whispers and outcries nearby making my stomach churn with anticipation. Something had to go right for once. We'd been through so much already. Didn't we deserve a fortuitous twist of fate?

A door at the opposite end of the long hall whirred open. Kro'da and one of the engineers emerged, approaching a small elevated platform nearby. Once atop the structure, Kro'da looked upon us with kindness in his golden eyes. The crowd went silent.

"My apologies for the delay, my brethren," Kro'da said. "We had to confirm our information before advising of any developments."

"What is going on?" a voice from the crowd demanded.

"Are we going to Earth now?" another questioned.

"My children are scared!"

Kro'da held up both his hands. "Please, let us remain calm. We are well into our repairs on the portal generator that will take us to Earth. They are going better than expected, and we should have the machine up in another couple hours. However, we have another problem to address. A band of lesser Dak'kar are approaching, led by a hooded Dak'kar. We will not have the generator fixed in time and must hold them off until the generator is operational."

My stomach flipped, and I gripped Imogen's hand tight, unable to look her in the face. Damn it, I knew this would happen. The Reapers turned everything to shit on this planet. After what we'd been through, we deserved a lot better than this. It wasn't fair, it wasn't fucking fair.

Cries of shock and outrage boomed around us.

"Are you serious?"

"How are we supposed to fight the Dak'kar?"

"There must be a way out of this. We should escape!"

Kro'da's eyes widened. "Listen, please!" he shouted above their protests.

Reluctantly, the crowd quieted.

"I understand that most of us are not warriors, but we must unite together against the Dak'kar. If we want to get to Earth to make a new way of life for ourselves, we must fight for our freedom. For too long we have hidden in the shadows of these monsters, just trying to survive. But that is not enough."

Kro'da scanned our massive group. "Earth is our chance to turn the tide against the Dak'kar, but we cannot do that if we do not make a stand now. If we truly desire to make a new home for ourselves, to foster peace and prosperity, we must do this. Who here is brave enough to look the Dak'kar in the eye and say 'today we do not back down'? Who is willing to fight for our lives and the future of our society?"

For a moment all was quiet.

Though I dreaded the battle to come, I was impressed with how Kro'da handled the situation. I hoped his speech would inspire enough support to give our plan traction. It was either that or fighting them off when they broke into the laboratory, and we all knew how that would go.

One by one, small groups of Veloxans lifted hands toward the ceiling, announcing that they would join the battle until nearly the entire crowd had their hands raised.

I looked to Immy, and she gave me a nod. We stepped forward, breaking free of the cluster of Veloxans around us. "We will also fight," we said in unison.

Upon seeing us, Kro'da mouth fell open. "Gregory, Imogen, what are you doing here? Ja'tare was supposed to…" He scanned the crowd quickly. "Ja'tare, Ko'ta, come here! "

I gaped at Kro'da. What the heck was he talking about? I glanced behind me. The crowd parted for Ja'tare and Ko'ta, who slowly made their way towards us.

"I am sorry, but we cannot allow you to fight," Kro'da said. "You have both done more than enough for us, and while we are grateful for your offer, your roles as ambassadors on Earth are too vital to our survival to risk now."

"You can't do this!" I protested. "You need our help. What about the hooded Dak'kar?"

Kro'da's brows furrowed, his lips straightened into a stern, thin line. "Do not worry yourselves with this."

Imogen stepped forward, gesturing to her Veloxans. "I *will* fight with my faction. I owe them that much."

The warrior with slicked back hair placed a hand on her shoulder and shook his head. "No, Imogen. Kro'da is right. This is our fight. We cannot allow you to intervene."

"Ja'tare, Ko'ta, please take them away," Kro'da commanded. "Make sure they are somewhere safe and comfortable."

Ja'tare and Ko'ta broke through the last layer of Veloxans behind us. Ja'tare dashed forward and grabbed ahold of Imogen, who thrashed against him.

"Let go of me!" she screamed. "You don't know what you're doing!"

Ja'tare pulled her away when Ko'ta came beside me, gripping my arm in an iron vice. "Come along, Gregory. Please, do not fight me."

I stared in disbelief at Ko'ta. Not allowing us to fight would surely make things worse for them.

When I didn't budge, Ko'ta leaned in ever so slightly. "*Trust me,*" he whispered.

I looked into his brown eyes. Something in them seemed reassuring. Was he trying to tell me something?

Reluctantly I let myself be led away from the crowd, throwing a fierce glare in Kro'da's direction. Whatever it was in my gut that told me to trust Ko'ta, I hoped I was right.

JA'TARE AND KO'TA escorted Imogen and I out of the main hall into the labyrinth of passages beyond. I allowed Ko'ta to guide me along, but Imogen flailed and yanked at Ja'tare like a wild animal.

While I felt just as betrayed as she did, I wasn't sure if I should trust the feeling or not. Something about Ko'ta's words to me made me think he and Ja'tare weren't going to stop us from aiding them in their last battle despite their orders. Still, until I saw evidence to the contrary, I didn't have much choice but to go along with whatever this was.

We continued along the winding hallway for a long while before stopping at a door like many others we'd passed. It swished open, revealing a small lounge with a pentagonal-shaped couch and a table. As soon as the door closed behind us, Ko'ta broke his hold on me and Ja'tare released Imogen. She nearly fell to the floor from her thrashing, then picked herself up and spun around, just inches from his face.

"How dare you haul me off like that! Do you have any idea how long I've been fighting for this?"

Ja'tare reached his palms out to her in a calming manner. "Imogen."

"I've lost good Veloxans. *Killed* to honor their bravery. You can't just sever my bond with my faction like that. It's not right. Do you hear me? It's not right!"

Ja'tare grabbed Immy by the shoulders. "Imogen, stop! There is no need to argue."

Imogen pushed him off, backing up with an upset yet quizzical look. "What are you talking about?"

"After the two of you left the meeting, Ko'ta and I convened with the council. They advised us to have you two watched until the battle is over."

I crossed my arms, staring at Ja'tare. "And?" I hoped he was about to say something reassuring before Imogen and I went ballistic.

"They do not know you like we do. This fight will be extremely difficult to win, especially without the two of you. We have seen how strong, intelligent, and adaptive you are in battle, and we must stop the Dak'kar."

Imogen shot Ja'tare a skeptical glance. "Get to the point already."

Ja'tare and Ko'ta looked at each other, then back to us.

"We have decided to defy the council's orders," Ko'ta said. "We want you to fight with us. We need you."

Imogen's grimace morphed into a smile, and I breathed a sigh of relief. It was good to know that they valued what we could contribute to the fight, but now my head was filled with even more questions.

"Okay, so if we do this, how do we get onto the battlefield without the council noticing?" I asked.

Ko'ta smirked. "After Ja'tare and I leave to prepare for battle, two guards will be placed in here to watch over you."

He reached into his pocket and pulled out two small vials, each with a tiny spray nozzle. "Spray this on them and they'll pass out long enough for you to escape. The hallways should be vacant since the engineers have already towed your devices outside and set them up. You will meet with P'taro in a secured room in the next hall over, the first one on the right. He will have weapons and armor for you, then once you have changed he will show you to the side exit we have secured on the east side of the building."

Imogen paced, scratching at the back of her arms. "That should work, but what about the Dak'kar? Do you have further information on them since the meeting?"

Ko'ta pulled out a tablet and punched several buttons on the screen before displaying it to us. On the screen, a large grouping of Reapers crept forward on the dreary landscape outside, headed by a single Reaper in a black cloak. My blood chilled.

"There are around fifty Dak'kar, led by a single hooded one. While we outnumber them three times over, it will not mean much since the majority of our forces are untrained, lack experience, or are simply not mentally prepared for battle."

I shook my head as my gaze lingered on the bulking masses of Reapers coming straight for us. "Jesus, there's so many of them."

Imogen frowned. "All the more reason to strategize. What plan have you and the council devised?"

Ko'ta turned the tablet over to Ja'tare, who punched in more commands. "I am glad you asked. We will need your input on the devices you created to ensure placement is ideal on the battlefield. When we return any modifications made to the council they will believe everything is going according to their plans. Here, take a look."

Ja'tare handed the tablet to Imogen and I. On the screen

was a lifelike rendering of the black-earthed field outside, with the laboratory itself on the bottom edge. Spread across the area were a collection of simple, varying shapes symbolizing troops.

Ja'tare pointed a long finger to the eastern edge of the map. "This is the direction that the Dak'kar are coming from and will almost certainly attack." He dragged his finger over to the far west side. "The triangles represent the catapult machines you helped construct, each manned by two Veloxans for ease of loading poison pouches and firing. The square symbols in front of them are our long range spear throwers, followed by our infantry, designated as circles."

I nodded along with his explanation. So far this seemed like a sound battle plan, at least on paper, plastic, whatever this gadget was made of.

Ko'ta pointed a bit ahead of where the infantry were placed where several zigzag shapes were. "P'taro installed a number of your audio-enhanced strobe lights like you suggested, each to be triggered by a motion sensor. Once the Dak'kar get close enough, the light flashes and sound will activate. While they are incapacitated, our forces will strike."

Imogen and I made slight modifications to the positioning of our devices before handing the tablet back.

"This looks pretty good," I said. "But what about the hooded Dak'kar? At any point in time it could disrupt whatever advantage we have. Do you have anything planned to counter it?"

"Yes, and what are your plans besides utilizing the tools we've prepared?" Imogen asked. "If they malfunction or are taken out, you'll have to face the Dak'kar head on."

Ja'tare frowned. "Unfortunately, we have not been able to come up with any other strategies to make the Dak'kar vulnerable, especially the hooded one."

"Then we'll do it," Imogen said. "We'll attack the hooded

Dak'kar while you fight the lessers."

Ja'tare and Ko'ta looked like someone had just killed Santa Claus.

"But how?" Ja'tare asked.

"We don't know just yet," I admitted, "but with us attacking separate from the main group we will have the advantage of surprise. That's got to count for something. If we fail to slay the beast, then you can come in and finish the job."

"I do not like this plan. It sounds extremely risky."

"Like yours doesn't?" Imogen snapped, then caught herself. "Sorry, I'm a bit stressed. Why don't you focus on the lesser Dak'kar and let us worry about our part?"

Ja'tare's shoulders sunk. "I suppose so, just be--"

"Careful? We'll try, but you know there's never any guarantees with the Dak'kar. You guys be careful too."

A dinging sound emitted from the tablet. Ko'ta studied it, then stepped beside Ja'tare and showed him the screen. "We should get going. The council wants to see us again and the guards are on their way here."

They approached the door, then turned to face us.

"Remember, use the spray on them, then meet P'taro for your weapons and armor," Ko'ta said.

"Got it," I replied.

Ko'ta left the room. Ja'tare lingered in the doorway, his green eyes emanating many conflicting emotions.

"Gregory, I … please do be careful. I do not know what I would do if anything happened to you."

Just looking at him, my eyes got watery. Ja'tare and I had been through a lot in my time on Velerius. Without him I never would've gotten this far, and I … I … I closed the distance between us and wrapped my arms around him in a tight embrace. At first he tensed up, then he put his arms around me too.

"You be careful too," I whispered. "There's so much of Earth to show you."

Ja'tare broke the embrace, exchanging a glance with me one last time. "I look forward to it."

With that, Ja'tare left the room. I turned to face Imogen, who had a brow raised.

"What was all that about?" she asked.

"Drop it, okay? I just don't want anything bad to happen to him."

As soon as the words left my mouth, I doubted myself. Was I really just concerned about him, or was there more between Ja'tare and me? We did have a special connection, even I couldn't deny that. But was it kindred spirits or something else entirely? Suddenly all his recent unusual behavior made sense. Ja'tare had developed feelings for me.

Ugh, this was insane! Ja'tare wasn't even the same species as I was, and once we got home Trent and I would be reunited. We were supposed to begin our future together. Now what would I do when I got back home? God, I was such an emotional mess.

I shook off my thoughts and cleared my throat, focusing on the task at hand. "What about our plan with the hooded Dak'kar?"

Imogen shrugged. "With its abilities, I don't think we can plan anything substantial, but I do have an idea."

"Go on."

"When they first arrive, the hooded Dak'kar's focus will be solely on the Veloxans and its minions. It won't be expecting us. Once the strobe lights are activated it'll be confused. That's the best opportunity for us to strike. We'll probably only get one good shot at it, so we'll have to choose our timing wisely. If we fail, we'll just have to hope that luck is on our side."

I clapped Imogen on the shoulder. "I think that's as good a plan as we can have given the situation. Let's do it."

With our plan cemented and nothing to do but wait for the guards, I made myself comfortable on the hexagonal couch, my mind flurrying with worries about the looming battle.

The army of Reapers was so close now. We had a shot at winning this battle, but I worried what would happen if things didn't go according to plan. I steepled my fingers together. *If there's a god out there, please let us all get through this in one piece.*

I WINCED as the last Veloxan fell to the ground with a loud thud. That was going to leave a mark. I looked at my vial, then to the two guards on the floor. "What do you think is in this? That was almost too easy."

Imogen shrugged. "Who cares? Let's get the hell outta here."

"Right."

We approached the door. It opened with a soft swooshing sound and I peered around the corner carefully. The hallway was deserted. "All clear," I whispered. "Let's go."

Imogen and I scurried into the hall, around the corner into the adjacent passage, and to our designated rendezvous room in under a minute without a hitch. As we entered, shock knotted my stomach. The room was empty.

"Um, where the heck is P'taro?" Imogen asked. "He was supposed to be here by now, right?"

"Yeah, we did exactly as Ko'ta instructed. Maybe he got held up? Let's give it a few minutes."

Seconds seemed to drag into hours as Imogen and I waited restlessly. After a small eternity voices from the hall approached our location, dangerously close. We froze, taking battle stances. If it wasn't P'taro, we'd have to go rogue.

The door wooshed open, and P'taro calmly walked in as if he wasn't a freaking month late with a large bag in his hands.

I darted over to him. "Where have you been? We've been waiting!"

"Relax, it is going to be okay. I got held up by some of the other engineers. Everyone is really nervous out there."

"Everyone's really nervous in here too," Imogen grumbled.

P'taro ignored Imogen's comment, setting the long sack down on a table with a metallic clink. "I brought your equipment as Ko'ta requested based on your preferences."

He drew out two sheathed daggers and handed them to Imogen. She pulled them out of their sheaths, revealing razor-sharp blades with serrated edges. Veloxan symbols were etched into the hilt, which glowed a reddish hue.

"All of your weapons are infused with the standard poison we use on our spears and will weaken any Dak'kar you injure. Gregory, we do not have guns on Velerius, so this will have to do. It should suit you well."

P'taro handed me a sheathed sword three times the length of Imogen's daggers. It was surprisingly light as I pulled it out of its covering. The straight blade was elegant in design and black with a maroon glow to it. I glanced at Imogen, who was transfixed with her weapons, then back to P'taro. "I don't know how to thank you."

"Well, do not thank me yet." P'taro rifled through the bag, drawing out two ribbed black bodysuits that reminded me of those old diagrams of the muscles in the human body. "You will not survive the battle without these body armor suits. They are standard among those who will be fighting and allow full movement of your body, more so than the Veloxan garb you are currently wearing. The suits are resistant to

Dak'kar strikes, but do not get arrogant. They are not inde-structible."

P'taro gave each of us a tiny oblong device, advising us to put it in our ears so we could intercept other Veloxan communications on the battlefield and speak with them if needed. Imogen and I tested the walkie-talkie ear device several times between each other until we were comfortable with how it worked.

We had just begun disrobing when a blaring alarm went off. The lighting in the room darkened to a bloody red color.

A voice boomed over the comm system and in our ears. "All troops report to the battlefield immediately. I repeat, all troops report to the battlefield."

P'taro's red eyes went wide. "Hurry, hurry! The Dak'kar will be here any minute."

Immy and I stuffed ourselves into our suits. In minutes we would be fighting our last battle on Velerius, then we'd finally be able to go back home. I was nervous, anxious, and excited all at once. When I was done changing and attaching my holster to the surreal magnetic waist of my armor, I stretched my arms and legs.

Man, this was freakin' awesome. The suit conformed to my body's shape without snagging or pulling while retaining full ease of motion. Like me, Imogen extended her arms and flexed her hands.

"These are amazing." She looked at me. "Are you good to go?"

I quickly reloaded my gun and attached my weapons to my holster. "As good as I'm gonna get."

P'taro gave us a once over, looking pleased. "Follow me, and keep up."

The door swooshed open for P'taro and he broke into a sprint down the deserted hallway. Imogen and I bolted after him, making a number of turns until we found ourselves at a dead end.

We approached the impasse. P'taro walked along its edge, fiddling with a small device in his hand. With a sharp click, a small doorway appeared in the wall.

He turned to face us. "This small passageway will lead you out the side of the laboratory and into battle. Be safe, and good luck."

I walked up to him, placing a hand on his shoulder. "Thank you, P'taro. For everything."

Imogen and I entered the tiny hallway beyond. It was a tight fit, and we had to walk sideways to avoid scraping against the wall. Thirty feet of sidestepping later, we stood at the door leading outside.

"This is it. You ready?" I asked.

Imogen bit her lip and looked down at her feet. "Yeah, I guess so. I'm just a little nervous."

"I am too." I wiped my sweat palms against my body armor. "But we can't let that get to us. We've got a score to settle."

Imogen was about to hit the door release before I grabbed her wrist. "Wait. Before we go out there, I wanted to say something. I ... I'm glad I found you again." My vision blurred, and I hugged Imogen tightly. "I love you, little sister."

She hugged me back. "I love you too, brother. I love you too."

I let go of Immy and wiped at my eyes until my sight was back to normal. "Let's give the Dak'kar a fight they'll never forget."

Imogen smiled impishly before punching the door release. It wooshed open, and I walked beside my sister into our last battle for Velerius and the first Veloxan battle for Earth.

CHAPTER TWENTY-SIX

Imogen and I stepped outside, a blast of chilly air assaulting us. The sky was a sickly green-gray color, splintered by purple lightning that flashed in a staccato daisy chain.

The black dirt field lay before us, filled with armor-suited Veloxans a hundred feet away. I couldn't see the catapults from our partially sheltered view, but could observe the spear-throwers and infantry readying themselves. Several hundred yards to the far right, a hulking mass of red approached. Cold dread pulled at my chest. The Reapers.

Imogen followed my gaze and clenched her jaw, reaching for her dagger hilt.

I gently put a hand on hers. "Remember the plan. Once the Dak'kar trigger the devices we can strike."

Imogen reluctantly took her hand off her dagger. "I don't like this. It's not fair for them to--" she stopped herself, exhaling deeply. "You're right. Let's just hope everything goes according to plan."

The Dak'kar drew steadily closer, coming to a halt a hundred yards from the Veloxans.

"Steady, steady," Ja'tare's voice crackled in my ear. "Be ready for the first assault when the flashes begin. Wait on my mark."

All was deathly still as the two opposing parties faced each other. My breathing seemed deafening in the silence.

An enormous, gut-wrenching shriek emitted from the back ranks of the Dak'kar.

The first line of lesser Dak'kar thrust forward on all fours, leaving the rest behind. They advanced swiftly and were twenty yards from the Veloxans when bright bursts of light flashed all around them, reinforced with a piercing static noise that rang in my eardrums. The Dak'kar screeched in protest, coming to a halt as they clutched at their hearing cavities and attempted to shield their eyes.

Imogen took a step forward, but I stopped her.

"Not yet. There's no opening on the hooded Dak'kar. It still has several dozen protecting it. We can't take it down like this, not without help."

Imogen grimaced but didn't move any further.

"Catapulters, now!" Ja'tare commanded through my comm device.

Large pouches of poison shot into the sky, raining down on the first line of Dak'kar like bullets. Several of them gave otherworldly screams of pain as the poison made contact and ate away at them.

"Spear throwers, go!"

A hail of spears descended upon the disabled Dak'kar, who wailed in agony as the weapons pierced their emaciated bodies.

"Keep attacking!" Ja'tare ordered.

The spear throwers prepared for another round when a strange pulse echoed, just like when I could sense the electrical interference of the Dak'kar. The earth rumbled, and I watched in horror as our flashing, screeching devices began to levitate into the air.

Imogen gasped. "What the--"

"The cloaked Dak'kar is going to destroy the traps. Damn it!"

The devices floated several more feet in the air before crumpling in on themselves, forming sharp, blade-like remnants.

"Everyone, take cover!" Ja'tare shouted.

The broken devices hurled towards the first line of Veloxan infantry.

The cries of our warriors filled the comm channel as they tried to dodge the shrapnel, but several were hit and went down.

"Flash offense is down!" Ja'tare voice boomed in my ear. "Uninjured first infantry, attack! Second infantry, escort the wounded away and reinforce the first."

Several dozen armored Veloxans charged forward with a fierce battle cry, brandishing their weapons. At the same time, the remainder of the front line of the Dak'kar had recovered from our initial assault and bolted forward to meet them, closely followed by a second wave of Dak'kar.

My body tingled as adrenaline pumped into my veins. "Immy, I see an opening. Now's our chance--"

Imogen sprang towards the center of the chaos, drawing her daggers as the opposing forces ahead neared impact.

"Immy, wait! Shit!"

Damn it, this wasn't the plan! We were supposed to attack the hooded Dak'kar together. I didn't have a choice now. I'd have to join the fray and hope we got the opportunity later.

I drew my Glock and ran after my sister as the two armies collided, Dak'kar screeches of rage and agony mirrored by the Veloxans.

Imogen shot forward, diving behind the chaotic front line of assault and disappearing from view.

With her out of reach, I had to reassess the situation. From my vantage point, the thick infantry defense was holding, but the Dak'kar were expanding out, almost as if they were ... Oh god, they were surrounding them!

I clenched my jaw. *Like hell they are.*

I neared the core of the skirmish from the outskirts, watching the Dak'kars' formation. If I targeted the ones on the edges trying to encircle the warriors where they were the thinnest, I could help turn the tide and get a few lethal shots in before they caught on. Then I could double back, contact Imogen, and regroup so we could focus on the leader.

The leftmost Reapers were noticeably spreading out, already doubling up on several Veloxans. That's where I needed to go. I bolted ahead, aiming my Glock on the unsuspecting Reapers once I was within twenty feet. *Blam! Blam! Blam!*

All at once, three Reapers before me went down, only one of them still writhing around afterwards. I ended its life without a thought. Man, this was too easy. "Ah!"

A Reaper rocketed towards me out of nowhere, slashing its long spindly claws in a wild arc. I parried its crazy strike at the last second and shot it twice as it lunged past me. I cursed, realizing I hadn't fatally injured it when it swung back around. It leered at me with yellow, enraged eyes before lunging for me again. I fired three more shots. The Reaper smashed into the blackened dirt, a black acrid ooze seeping out of its forehead and other bullet wounds.

I spun around to double back to the safe side of the battle when an impossibly heavy weight slammed into me. My gun went flying from my hands as I was sent sprawling a few feet away. I tumbled to the ground, recovering my balance in a roll, but as I rose back to my feet the Reaper was already on me again.

I drew my sword just in time to defend against its razor-sharp claws. This one was definitely faster than the last one. I guarded with my blade, but it struck again and again, stronger each time it hit. On the fifth strike, my weapon was thrust out of my hands to the dirt below and I fell back to the ground on my butt.

Fuck, fuck, fuck! It can't end like this!

The Reaper raised its hand to strike with a screech when a spear suddenly pierced through its chest. Black ooze sprayed from its wound, misting me in its life force before it thudded to the ground.

Ja'tare ran up to the fallen Reaper and yanked the spear out. He offered me his free hand and I took it.

"Thanks." I scrambled to find my sword in the dirt. My Glock was still MIA, but there wasn't any time. "Have you seen Imogen?"

"I am sorry, no. I have to go back. The infantry will not hold much longer at this rate."

Ja'tare ran off into the fray, and I activated the device lodged in my ear. "Imogen, where the hell are you?"

No answer. *Fuck!* I scouted around the fast-moving sea of Veloxans and Reapers desperately. Reaper slashing Veloxan, Veloxan spearing Reaper, just watching made my stomach -- there!

A flash of movement caught my eye, and I spotted Imogen deep within the ranks of Reapers and Veloxans fighting to the death. She ripped her wickedly sharp daggers from a dead Reaper with a spurt of black ooze, rising quickly.

We locked eyes for the briefest of moments before she and a Reaper spotted each other. They charged at each other full sprint. As the Reaper raised a claw to strike, she cartwheeled past it. Not losing her momentum, Imogen leaped onto the creature's red, scarred back, stabbing it with a vicious war cry that carried easily over to me.

The Reaper fought to stay upright, but Imogen continued to plunge her daggers into the beast with increasing rage and frequency. In seconds, it fell to the ground.

I pressed into the side of my ear device to get Imogen's attention once more, but before I said anything a large shadow flew over me, making me jump. I glanced upward, gasping when I laid eyes on the hooded Dak'kar. It levitated high in the air and was heading straight for the middle of the combat zone. I had to warn the others!

I clicked my comm gadget. "Attention everyone! The hooded Dak'kar is heading for the center of battle. I don't know how, but it's flying. Take cover!"

The hooded Dak'kar flew with supernatural speed, clearing the distance in just seconds. It dive bombed into the core of the chaos, barrelling into the ground. A massive shockwave rocked the earth, knocking my world off balance. I fell to the dirt, then struggled back up to my feet as the earth's intense rumblings died down.

The level earth of the field was now jagged and broken, large jutting formations of stone ripping out of the ground like undead corpses.

Reaper and Veloxan alike were down, trying to recover and get up, but the Reapers were quicker. Several scraped up to their clawed feet, lunging at the closest defenseless Veloxans to them.

"No!" I shouted.

That was when I saw the hooded Reaper. It stood twenty yards away in the center of the crater its descent had created. It faced me, its yellow eyes boring into mine, challenging me. I clutched my blade tightly. I was going pluck those evil fucking eyes out of its head.

I pressed the device in my ear again. "Imogen, Ja'tare, can you hear me? We have to stop the hooded Dak'kar now!"

Imogen grumbled into her device. "Ungh, how?"

"I don't know, but this has to end now before we suffer any more casualties."

The grand beast and I exchanged glances once more. It stood in place, watching me with a strange calm. The corner of its mouth pricked up the slightest degree, making my blood boil. "I'm going in."

"Gregory, no!" Imogen cried.

I charged at my nemesis, attracting the attention of a lesser Reaper. It burst forward, cutting me off from its leader and raising its claws to strike. I dodged in a quick side roll, countering its attack with a lethal thrust of my blade.

As the Reaper fell, another came at me. I hacked wildly at it to keep it at bay before several Veloxans arrived to assist me. Satisfied, I sprinted around them, picking up momentum. Now there was nothing between me and the hooded Reaper.

I tore onward as it stood in place, watching me placidly. I don't know why it didn't come at me, but I didn't care. I arched my sword high for the killing blow. I leaped ... and was sent spinning away.

I landed hard on the blackened dirt many yards away, the air collapsing from my lungs as stabs of pain coursed through my body. I gasped for breath. Fuck, I'd failed. Why had I thought it would be that easy? I took in my new surroundings.

Ja'tare and a dozen Veloxans defended themselves against six Reapers on my right, and Imogen flanked two Reapers in the opposite direction that had cornered a couple of unarmed Veloxans.

An otherworldly shriek nearby broke my concentration, sending frigid fingers down my spine. A large Reaper had located me and was bounding towards me in quick bestial strides. I struggled to get up, but searing needles of agony sent me back to the ground. *Damn it!*

As the Reaper neared, an armored Veloxan jumped in front of me, guarding me. The Reaper slammed into the Veloxan and they went tumbling. They wrestled for control, the Reaper slashing at the Veloxan's face, the Veloxan defending with his poisoned spear.

I tried to get up again, succeeding with a dizzying surge of pain. I had to help him, I had to-- The Veloxan cried out in agony. The Reaper had slashed through his armor and into his stomach with its knife-like appendages. The monster raised its claw to strike one final blow, but before it could the Veloxan thrust its spear into the Reaper's eye and through the back of its head. They collapsed together, the mix of purple and black blood oozing together.

Bile rose in my throat at the grizzly sight. I couldn't let the Veloxans die like this. We had to kill the hooded Reaper before this got any worse, but how?

I scanned the battlefield, easily locating it. The hooded Reaper stood on the outskirts of combat some twenty yards away, its wicked claws outstretched towards a group of battling Reapers and Veloxans. One by one the Veloxans clutched at their necks, dropping their weapons and gasping for breath.

As the Reapers pounced on them mercilessly all the anger and hatred I had for these murderous creatures rushed over me in a white heat. The searing warmth burned through my body, and as the emotions overwhelmed me a guttural scream of rage ripped from my lips.

I stomped towards the hooded Reaper, my fury over-riding my exhaustion. Before I could reach it, a nearby Reaper shrieked and bolted at me on all fours. I swung my sword in a wide, drunken arc, lucking out with a strike but killing my balance. As I fell, Imogen caught me in her arms. She had numerous scratches on her and several bloody gashes on her arms and legs.

Imogen helped me to my feet and began pulling me in the direction of the laboratory. "We have to retreat, Gregory."

"No!" I struggled against her grip. "We have to kill the hooded Dak'kar!" I looked around her. It was gone. "You let it get away!"

Imogen shook me. "Listen to me! We already tried and failed. If we try again, it will make easy pickings out of either of us. I'm not going to let you die here, now come on!"

Tears welled in my eyes. I'd failed to protect the Veloxans when they needed it the most. How could I forgive myself for that, and how could we just leave them and go to Earth like nothing happened? With a heavy heart, I gave in to the need for survival and dragged my feet forward.

Imogen helped guide me back towards the laboratory in quick, steady steps as the battle raged on. We'd gotten about a hundred yards when several inhuman cries of bloodlust echoed nearby, stopping us in our tracks. Surrounding us on all sides, four red-skinned Reapers eyed us hungrily, stalking forward and cornering us in.

"No," Imogen whimpered. She put her back to me as she pulled out her daggers.

I unsheathed my blade, trying to quell the despair I felt at our hopeless situation. We might be able to end one or two of them, but all four was impossible. "Immy, no matter what happens, I love you."

The Reapers lurked closer, closer ... A resounding, warbling noise suddenly filled the air, coming from the edge of the battlefield. I looked for the source of the sound. Thick columns of armored Veloxans atop bretaren surrounded the field. With a collective war cry they charged forward, the earth shaking with a deep rumble.

The Reapers around us gave grating bleats to one another before breaking away in a sprint to escape. All the other Reapers appeared to be doing the same thing. As they collectively loped away, poison spears rained from the sky.

The death cries of Reapers filled the air as Imogen pulled me down to the ground, her arms enveloping me. I closed my eyes, focusing on my little sister. *Please whatever God is out there, protect Imogen and me. Please allow us to get back home safely.*

I repeated my silent prayer over and over until the cacophony of sounds ebbed away. Slowly, I opened my eyes.

All of the remaining Reapers littered the ground, impaled in a horrid black mess of broken bodies and limbs. The Veloxan cavalry that saved us approached fast, and our surviving Veloxans began to rise out of the devastation of the battlefield. The weight on my shoulders started to lift. Was it really over? Were we safe?

I shook Imogen lightly. "Immy, open your eyes. I … I think the battle is over."

She opened her eyes, gasping at the scene unfolding around us. "Did we win? Did we really do it?"

Her eyes were watery and I hugged her, hoping to stop the tears from flowing. "I hope so. Let's get up and see what's going on."

A throbbing soreness echoed throughout my body as I got to my feet and helped Imogen up. From the carnage all around us, it looked like several dozen of our forces had survived the battle. Up ahead, Ko'ta and several warriors from Imogen's group gathered, along with a few of the bretaren-mounted Veloxans that had come to the rescue. Seeing us, they waved us over.

"Are you two okay?" Ko'ta asked.

"We're exhausted and have some injuries, but we'll survive," I said.

"You are very fortunate. Most of our people did not make it through the battle, but thanks to this neighboring tribe we were able to save some of them."

One of the mounted Veloxans made a slight bow. "It was an honor to help defeat the Dak'kar. We received a transmission from the Verus Tower of Communications and came as soon as we could."

"Thank you," I said. "You saved our lives. Ko'ta, did we confirm the kill for the hooded Dak'kar? Where's Ja'tare?"

Ko'ta smiled and clapped my shoulder. "Do not worry, Ja'tare is alive and well. He is out helping the others tend to our fallen brothers and sisters. As for the hooded Dak'kar, I cannot be sure. I did not see it myself."

My core went cold. "Please excuse me." I rushed off towards the largest mound of Reaper carcasses I could see.

"Gregory, wait!" Imogen called. She jogged up to me and blocked my path. "I said wait. What's going on?"

"Did you see the hooded Dak'kar fall?"

"Well no, but I--"

"Then we have to find the body. Until we can confirm it is dead, we're still in great danger." I shook my head. "That bastard killed so many of our people. We have to find it and burn it."

Imogen grasped my hands. "I understand completely. Let's make sure this is really over."

For what seemed like hours, Imogen and I searched among the dead littering the ground, keeping our face masks up to lessen the stench of rotting corpses. We'd inspected countless bodies and although we still hadn't found the hooded Dak'kar, a nagging part of me insisted the monster was still alive.

Imogen tugged on my arm, catching my attention. "Look, it's Ja'tare!"

Twenty meters ahead, Ja'tare and several other Veloxans

gently hauled their fallen brethren onto a flat, floating platform. Ja'tare saw us and broke away from the others towards us with a wave. "Gregory, we did it!"

I couldn't help but smile at his positivity. That was, until I saw the cloak Ja'tare had just stepped over. My heart stopped. The hooded Reaper!

"Ja'tare, look out!" I cried.

I bolted for Ja'tare as the hooded Reaper rose and wrapped its wicked claws around Ja'tare's face. Ja'tare screamed in agony as his skin lost its color where the Reaper had touched him and spread fast.

With one last burst of energy, Ja'tare drew a long knife, stabbing it behind him into the Reaper. He fell to the ground as the hooded monster wailed in pain.

I tore forward, drawing my sword as I gained momentum. I tackled the Reaper, forcing it down to the ground.

"You fuck!" I brought my blade down as hard as I could. I yanked it out, bringing it down again, again, again … I knew the Reaper was dead, but it didn't matter. It wasn't enough. It never would be. What they'd done to the Veloxans, to the humans, they deserved to die a million deaths over in retribution.

Suddenly something grabbed me, and I spun around. Imogen sprung back, holding her hands up cautiously. "Gregory, stop. The hooded Dak'kar is dead."

I stared blankly at her, uncomprehending as rage coursed through my veins.

"For Christ's sake, help Ja'tare! I'm going to get help." Imogen ran off to the Veloxans with the floating platform.

Ja'tare lay on the ground just feet away, still. Too still. I dove over and hovered above him on my knees.

The effects of the Reaper's touch were taking its toll. His tan skin was now a sickly gray color, his emerald eyes dull and fading. I was scared to touch him, but put my hands on the sides of his face anyways. "Ja'tare, stay with me. Imogen went to get help. We'll … we'll figure this out somehow."

Ja'tare smiled sweetly at me before wheezing in a coughing fit. "It is too late, you already know that." He removed my hands from his face and held them in his. "Go home to Earth with my people. Show them that Veloxans and humans can exist in peace. Fight the Dak'kar, live a good life. I … I care deeply for you, Gregory."

"I care for you too." I gripped his hands firmer.

Ja'tare's body began to twitch in spasms. I tried to keep him still, hot tears burning down my cheeks. *God, why can't I save him? He doesn't deserve to die!* The tremors escalated violently before his body went deathly still.

I pressed my forehead to his with a whimper. After a long moment, I sat back up and placed Ja'tare's hands peacefully at his sides. I closed his eyelids, then sat down on the backs of my feet.

Ja'tare was gone, and there was nothing I could do to bring him back. As much as I wanted to cave to sadness and despair, I fought the urge. Ja'tare's resilience and optimism had kept me going this long, and now I had to carry that on myself. As I looked over his body I made a vow never to forget the love and kindness he'd shown me or the sacrifices he made for his people. I would honor his memory by setting a better example for all of us. Humans and Veloxans could unite against the Reapers, but someone had to show them the way of peace. That was my responsibility now.

Crunching footsteps approached and Imogen sat down next to me. "I'm so sorry, Gregory. Ja'tare was such a brave commander. He helped bring us back together, and I'll never forget that. "

A tidal wave of emotions bunched up in my stomach, but I was all out of tears. "I can't believe he's gone. He always knew the right thing to do, always showed compassion and caring no matter how fucked up things got."

Imogen rubbed my back lightly, and a tiny shred of my pain eased. "With the Veloxans and our people together things will get better. It'll take time, but we have to have faith and support each other. I'll always be here for you."

I smiled as I looked at Immy. "Thanks."

She hesitated a moment. "The others will be here to collect Ja'tare in a moment. Take as long as you need, but I have to get to the infirmary for my wounds. They're really starting to hurt."

"Alright, I'll be in shortly."

Imogen left me alone with Ja'tare and my thoughts. I took his hand in mine. It was already colder. I brought it to my chest and closed my eyes. *May you find peace, dear friend.*

I forced myself to my feet and followed a small trail of bruised and broken Veloxans back to the laboratory. Despair, anger, and a strange empty feeling washed over me in vacillating waves.

The war with the Reapers was far from over, but we'd won this battle. Though we'd lost a lot, our sacrifices hadn't been in vain. Soon we would head back to Earth and forge a new destiny with the Veloxans, and I would do whatever it took to foster peace and exterminate the Reapers, for good.

CHAPTER TWENTY-SEVEN

I sat up on my cot in the infirmary, watching Imogen several beds down from me. After applying a strange, clear liquid on Imogen's wounds, her damaged skin had fused back together in minutes. Now a medically-trained Veloxan stood before her, asking question after question and noting her responses in his tablet. Man, this was taking forever. Was something wrong?

I got the attention of another medical assistant as they walked by. "Hi, could you tell me how my sister Imogen is doing?"

She glanced at her tablet, punching in several commands. "Though she had some deep lacerations she will be fine. There should not be any scarring."

"Thank you."

I focused my attention back on Imogen. She sat erect in her bed, answering the medic's continued queries with brief, increasingly agitated answers. She was antsy, and so was I. With the battle with the Dak'kar over, everyone was anxious to leave for Earth. We couldn't survive another fight like that and the longer we stayed here, the more risk we took.

A sudden clatter interrupted my worried thoughts.

"I told you I'm fine," Imogen grumbled. She hopped off the bed and straightened the form-fitting Veloxan garb they'd dressed her in.

The doctor scrambled to pick up the tablet Imogen must have smacked away, and she came over to my bed, indicating the exit with a tilt of her head.

"Come on, let's go."

Imogen and I stormed down the winding hallway, the hustle and bustle of the main hall getting louder as we approached.

"Hey, slow down a sec," I said.

Imogen spun around to face me.

"I can tell something is wrong. What's on your mind?"

Imogen sighed. "I … I couldn't stand being in that room any longer. I just want to go home. For years I never thought it was a possibility, and now that we're this close I don't want anything else to go wrong."

I grabbed her hand and gave it a tight squeeze. "I know how you feel. Not a day went by that I didn't think of you, and after all the setbacks since getting here I'm a little anxious too. I understand."

Imogen smiled. "Thanks."

Content, we continued on, a wall of noise assaulting us as we entered the main hall. An enormous crowd of bedraggled Veloxans filled the space, huddled in groups. A small band of surviving warriors made their way through the masses, speaking with some of them briefly. The ones they talked to cried out in grief and mourning.

I kept my gaze lowered out of respect as we crossed the hall. I had no idea what the body count was, but clearly it wasn't good. There were maybe a couple dozen of us on our feet when we left. The rest had been injured or were dead.

Everyone here had lost someone; a dad, a mom, a brother, a friend …

The faces of the people I'd lost flashed in my mind: Ja'tare, Carlos, Dad, so many others.

Going through the battle with the Reapers and seeing its devastating results had put everything in perspective. We couldn't go back to hiding in the shadows while the Reapers killed and tortured however they pleased. Survival wasn't enough anymore. We had to take the world back for ourselves, and I would help lead our people to victory. I didn't know how we were going to do it all just yet, but we finally had the support we needed and would figure things out together.

We located a small vacant fur and sat down. "Are you okay?" Imogen asked. "You seem distracted."

I grimaced. "Sorry, I just keep thinking about what will happen once we get back."

"Me too. Do you think Mom and your friend Trent are still okay?"

Despite my worries of how I left them, I smiled at Imogen reassuringly. "If anyone could survive, they would."

My response seemed to please her, and I was grateful when she took her eyes off my face. The truth was, they had to be okay. Not for Imogen or the Veloxans, but for me. I needed Mom and Trent like air. Thinking of them had gotten me through so much here on Velerius, and I didn't think I could take another loss like I did today.

Imogen and I had been resting for several minutes when the laboratory's comm channel buzzed to life. "All Veloxans, please report to the main hall for briefing."

"Well, I guess our little break is over," Imogen said. She helped me up and we meandered over to the same flat platform as last time. Veloxans crowded in around us tightly, murmuring to each other.

Within moments a scientist and the Veloxan council arrived, approaching us. The crowd erupted in shouts, cries, and curses.

"My lifemate is dead!"

"When are we going to Earth?"

"How could you let the Dak'kar do this to us?"

The scientist and council were visibly shaken by the outburst.

Nehma stepped onto the platform with an air of dignity and compassion, arms outstretched to us in a gentle, soft-hearted manner. "Everyone, please. Let us see reason."

Slowly the crowd silenced themselves.

"We deeply apologize for the events that have occurred today. All of us hurt. The pain and suffering the Dak'kar have brought upon us is unfathomable, and as much as we wish there was a way to bring back our dead, we cannot. All we can do now is honor their memory. Fighting the Dak'kar was the last thing we wanted to do, but together we have defeated them on the battlefield. For that, we owe you an enormous debt of gratitude and our lives. Change lies ahead of us on Earth, change that will test our love and devotion to one another much like today did. Let us all join together, take care of each other, and enter a new age of prosperity for Veloxans and humankind alike."

The crowd murmured to each other, but the negative energy from before had dissipated. Nehma stepped aside and the scientist, Kro'da, and De'jartha ascended the platform.

Kro'da cleared his throat. "Thank you, Nehma. We want to extend our thanks to the neighboring tribe of Veloxans that came to our aid as well as Gregory and Imogen, who risked their lives on the battlefield regardless of our objections. That being said, many brave warriors were slain in the battle, including our beloved Commander Ja'tare. May our fallen find peace."

The crowd bowed their heads in mourning.

After a long quiet moment De'jartha approached the crowd, his blue eyes sparkling. "Despite this solemn occasion, we have good news. The portal generator is fully functional and we will leave soon. Please ready yourselves to leave Velerius to our new home of Earth. It will still be dangerous, but with the guidance of Gregory and Imogen in this foreign landscape we will thrive together with the humans. Thank you."

The crowd disbanded and Imogen and I lingered about. As the masses dispersed, the council descended the platform and walked towards us. Nehma caught sight of us and smiled, motioning us to her.

"How are you both recuperating?" she asked.

"We were a little banged up, but thanks to your advanced medical technology we healed in no time," I said.

"That is good to hear. If you are ready, would you please join us in the portal generator room? There are some last details we must go over."

THE DOOR to the portal generator room swooshed open, revealing a space that looked almost identical to the one I'd arrived in. Hulking in the middle was an enormous mass of cables and coils that connected to the three metal heads of the portal generator. Behind it, several Veloxans were hard at work on an elevated platform where they tinkered with a computer console.

At the opposite end of the room was a small dead-ending hall with a faint outline of a door set in the wall. A five-foot wide walkway led up to it, outlined in red. The room was a bit dingy, but all rubble and dust had been swept aside.

The council and their scientist headed to the center of the

room. As we followed, I noted the doe-eyed look on Imogen's face. She probably hadn't been in a portal generator room since she was taken, and I could only imagine the dark memories that were swirling in her mind. I hoped she would be okay.

Kro'da gestured to the portal generator. "Our scientists have been working diligently since the engineers repaired the generator. It is now fully operational, but there is one last detail to be worked out. The coordinates of our destination."

I scratched my head. "Coordinates?"

"Yes," the scientist chimed in. "The portal generator will need geographical coordinates in order to transport us safely to Earth. The network it operates on keeps a log of coordinates used from all laboratory locations. Before the battle, Ja'tare had given us the time and place of your arrival, but we were not sure if the location you came from was where you wanted to arrive. Did you have a different destination in mind?"

Images of the library and how things had been left flashed in my mind. Had they fought off the hooded Reaper or was it a breeding ground now? There was no way of telling what we would be walking into, but we didn't really have any other choice. I'd be lying if I said I had any idea of what other coordinates to use.

"Gregory?" Imogen glanced at me, her brows drawing together.

I waved my hands. "Sorry, sorry. Yes, please use those coordinates. That's the safest location I know of, and it will be a good starting point to finding my group again."

"All right, we will use those coordinates," the scientist said. "Thank you."

He walked off, and De'jartha cocked a dark eyebrow at me. "Find them *again*?"

"Yeah, it's been over a week since I was brought here, and

there's no telling what happened since I left. We had just found the library when all hell broke loose, so I'm hoping they were able to fend off the Dak'kar and wait for my return there. But there's no guarantee of that. For safety, Imogen, myself, and the warriors should go through the portal first."

The council members looked at one another, then nodded in agreement.

"We believe that would be prudent," Kro'da said. "The generator will be ready once we enter those coordinates, so you can stay here or tie up any loose ends you may have. We will announce the departure shortly."

I was about to insist on staying put when I noticed the lack of weight on my back. "Actually, I've gotta find my knapsack." I looked at Immy. "Wanna tag along, sis?"

"Sure."

We left the generator room and re-entered the maze of hallways, moving at a brisk pace. The last thing I wanted was to stall our return to Earth.

"Where'd you leave your bag?" Imogen asked.

"Where P'taro met us before the battle, I think."

I led the way, nearly getting lost before righting myself. Finally, we arrived at our destination and the door whooshed open for us. I scanned the loungey room. Sure enough, my bag was sitting in the corner where I'd left it. I snatched up the bag and was ready to depart, but Imogen had already sat down on the awkwardly-shaped sofa.

She had a distant look on her face and seemed rattled, which was completely understandable to me. I mean, we *were* travelling between worlds here, not just taking a stroll down the street. We'd probably never see this planet again.

I plopped down next to her, messing with the strings on my knapsack. "How are you feeling about everything?"

Imogen stared down at her feet. "I don't know. Conflicted? I've spent most of my life here. Velerius has been my home. I know it's time to go back to Earth, but there's still a small part of me that's going to miss this place, Dak'kar aside." Imogen took a deep breath, then seemed to shrug off a weight that had been on her shoulders. "How do you feel? Ready to go home?"

"Yes and no. I guess I'm just scared. This whole time, I've been holding on to the hope that Mom and Trent would be okay, but what if they aren't?"

Imogen gave me a reassuring squeeze on my arm. "It's hard to know what to believe, but we've got to have faith. I think you're right. They must have survived, and I'll be there to help you find them again."

A smile stretched across my face. "Yeah, you're right. Thanks, Immy."

"Of course."

The laboratory's comm system crackled to life. "The portal generator is ready to be activated. Everyone, please report outside the generator room, combatants and humans first for safety."

I looked at Imogen. "Well, that's us. Are you ready for this?"

"Yeah, let's get going."

We headed down the interconnected hallways, and as we turned the last corner a massive crowd awaited us. Countless Veloxans gathered in an increasingly endless line for the generator room, adults chatting to one another in excitement while small children ran this way and that. Periodically, saddled bretaren stood in groups, stockpiles of supplies strapped atop them. A couple of warriors barred entry to the room's doors, and when they saw us a look of relief flashed across their faces.

"Can you believe how many of them there are?" Imogen asked. "There must be hundreds."

I shook my head. "When we were rescued on the battlefield, it didn't seem like there were that many. Guess we were wrong. Come on, it looks like they're waiting for us."

Immy and I skipped the line and were ushered inside the portal generator room along with a squadron of warriors.

Inside, the space was cramped and chaotic. Scientists and engineers ran back and forth between each other and the portal generator. Several groups of soldiers lounged in corners of the room, speaking quietly amongst themselves. I spotted the council not far from the elevated platform behind the portal generator and rushed over to them.

"We're here. What now?"

Kro'da gave me a once over. "You are ready? There will be no going back from this."

"Yes, let's do this."

Kro'da gave a signal to the scientists on the platform, and a voice boomed in the room. "Activating portal generator. Everyone stay outside the red marked lines on the floor, and avert your eyes."

A deep mechanical rumbling began, filling the room with its intensity. A surge of static accompanied it, making the hairs on my body stand on end. The brambles of coils and metal on the generator sparked electric blue , and the heads of the machine rotated, slow at first, then faster, faster--

"Gregory, close your eyes!" Imogen cried.

I closed my eyes just as a blinding light blasted through the room. Even with my eyes closed, the luminescence stung.

The portal generator continued to roar, making the ground quake with its raw power.

Gradually, the brilliant light faded until a voice spoke on the loudspeaker. "Portal generation complete. You may open your eyes. First group, approach the door and proceed to the other side."

I opened my eyes. The room was filled with a black, curling smoke that dissipated slowly. I couldn't see the door itself, but there was an outline of blue, almost ethereal light up ahead.

On reflex, I took Imogen's hand.

"You can do this, Gregory," she whispered. "I'm right here with you."

We inched forward to the red-lined boundary, joined by a squad of warriors armed to the teeth. With each step, my nerves grew more and more erratic.

This was it, we were really going home. What would we find? *Please let Mom and Trent be okay, please let Mom and Trent be okay.*

We arrived at the door. Up close, it resembled the one I'd seen appear in the library, from its burgundy color down to the scratched, peeling paneling. I separated my hand from Imogen's and wiped my sweaty palms on my pants before giving her one last glance.

"Do the honors?" she asked.

I put my hand on the knob and turned it. The door opened ...

CHAPTER TWENTY-EIGHT

*I*mogen and I stepped through the door into almost complete darkness. Faint light filtered into the large area from small windows above. I squinted as my eyes adjusted. Toppled bookcases littered the ground with massive heaps of books scattered in a million directions. Thin, broken overhead lights dangled by wire strands.

I couldn't believe it, we'd actually done it. This was the reading space I'd been in when Trent and I had been attacked.

"We're here, we're really here," I muttered.

"Where exactly is *here*?" Imogen asked. "And where is everybody?"

I fished my flashlight out of my knapsack, pointing it this way and that. My stomach dropped.

Immy was right, no one was here. If my group had killed the hooded Reaper, then this area would be in better shape or at least cleaned up. It was possible they abandoned the library for a more ideal HQ, but where would that be?

One thing at a time.

"We're in the library my group was staying at. This is the

exact spot where we were attacked by a hooded Dak'kar. You're right, something is off here. Let's wait for the others"

I turned to see the first dozen Veloxan warriors emerging from the portal and we walked over to them. "We may have potential Dak'kar. I'll need a few of you to scout things out with Imogen and I. The rest of you, secure a perimeter around this room. Protect the civilians and do not stray."

Six Veloxans followed after Imogen and I as we ventured to the far end of the room. From what I remembered, it connected to the main hall of the library where my group had stayed the first night.

A pungent, foul smell radiated, getting stronger as we progressed. We turned the corner into the main hall, and the sight before me flipped my stomach upside down.

Numerous bodies of women, children, and men covered the ground in unnatural, contorted positions. Their bodies had been disemboweled and partially eaten, bloody remnants spackling across the floor and walls.

I ran forward, inspecting the bodies with my light. None of them were Mom or Trent. As grateful as I was, a cold dread settled in my core. It had taken us five years to gather our group together. Five years of hard work, of never-ending struggle, gone.

Imogen placed a hand on my shoulder. "Gregory, this isn't your fault."

I spun around, unable to look her in the face. "The hooded Dak'kar that sent me to Velerius did this," I announced to the group. "Arm yourselves. Dak'kar could be anywhere."

"Wait, shouldn't we go back to the others?" Imogen reasoned. "The civilians are at risk now too. We have to protect them."

I bit my tongue. As much as I wanted to argue that finding survivors was a priority, we were a community now.

No matter how desperately I needed to find Mom, Trent, and the others, our well-being had to come first. "Come on everyone, let's head back."

When we came to the wrecked reading area, it was jam-packed with Veloxans of every shape and size. The portal door hadn't closed yet but less people were arriving, and to be honest I was relieved. It was starting to get loud in the space, and if Reapers were here it wouldn't be long before they came for us.

I spotted Kro'da nearby and waved him over.

"What is wrong? You seem troubled."

I spilled the beans as fast as I could, emphasizing how much danger we were still in.

"What can we do to help?" Kro'da asked.

"We have to clear the library entirely. Every entry and exit has to be barred and monitored to keep Dak'kar both out and in. Once we are secure we'll do a sweep, rooting out any lingering Dak'kar. Hopefully we'll locate some human survivors in the process. I'll need to borrow a good amount of soldiers to help, and everyone else will need to stay here in the meantime. "

"Agreed. I will make an announcement to everyone. Thank you for your sharp eye, Gregory. I do not know what we would do without it."

Kro'da explained the situation to the crowd and a couple dozen warriors joined Imogen and I. Before we split up, we gathered flashlights and other supplies from the dead amongst ourselves. I even managed to find a loaded gun among them. I felt bad about looting my former comrades, but this was vital in helping us locate what survivors there were.

I told our teams of the entries that I could recall, but I honestly had no idea how big this library really was, so a lot would be left to chance. We divided into small groups, and I advised them to stay in constant contact on their comm devices.

Imogen, five other guards, and I patrolled around to the front, face masks up to minimize the smell of decay. Several Veloxans had just secured the front entry and were working on fortifying the blockade in place.

We turned back around, passing aisles of bookshelves that my human group had used for shelter that first night. As we walked past an especially dark row of bookcases, I stopped and shone my light for a better look. The aisle stretched far, and beyond its end I could see another area.

"You guys, hold up. I think I found something."

They headed back over to me, and I showed them what I saw with my light.

"It looks like it keeps going. Let's check it out."

Together we inched down the aisle with our weapons raised.

"Do you think Trent and Mom might be down this way?" Imogen whispered.

"I don't know. We didn't fully explore the library before we were attacked, but if there are any signs of Dak'kar nearby, they can't be all that far away."

We emerged from the row into an old study area and spread out. Numerous cobweb-ridden tables and chairs dotted the space, some of them recently overturned and damaged based on the lack of dust on them.

"Something happened here," I observed.

"Gregory, over here," one of the Veloxans called.

He waved us over, pointing to the far end with his flashlight. It illuminated a wide staircase leading downward.

"Let's get a closer look," I instructed.

I took the lead, shining my light into the deep darkness. Reaper veins covered the handrails and clutched the walls. Imogen touched one hesitantly, strings of gray flem sticking to her hand. She flicked it off her and rubbed her hand on her pants.

"This is fresh," she said ominously.

"Alright everyone, we're going down. Stick together."

I quickly advised what we found over the comm channel, ordering additional Veloxans to stand by for support if needed. Our group descended, an overwhelming humidity making sweat run down into my eyes. There was no doubt about it, this was Reaper territory.

We reached the basement landing and shined our lights around, getting a dim picture of our surroundings. A circular kiosk stood to our right with rows of vein-covered bookcases on the left, many of them housing large plastic covered tomes. Up ahead was another study section of chairs and tables, some of them wrecked and shattered. Still, there was no sign of any Reapers.

"Split up into two groups and fan out," I ordered. "The Dak'kar can't be far."

Imogen, myself, and one other Veloxan trudged through the study area cautiously. Although the Reaper veins were fresh, we had no real idea of how long they'd actually been here or how many of them there were. They could've been sleeping and breeding here long before my group first arrived.

A brief scuttling sound echoed ahead to our right. I scanned with my flashlight and gun cocked, but couldn't find anything. I activated my comm device. "I don't think we're alone. Stay sharp."

We reached the end of the study area without conflict, arriving at a rusted metal door. It had deep Reaper claw marks in it, but it looked like the breakin attempt wasn't successful.

"What do you think happened here?" Imogen asked.

"Hard to say. If I had to guess, someone may have hidden

in the room beyond, but--" I tried the handle. It was locked. "Even if there is someone here, they're not going to come out willingly if there were Dak'kar here recently."

"We should at least try. Give it a knock."

I shrugged. "Couldn't hurt." I raised my hand to knock when the Veloxan accompanying us called several yards away.

"Gregory, Imogen! I think you should come see this. *Now.*"

We followed after him to the far corner of the room where an enclosure of several glass bookcases stood. Wedged in between them were two pulsating gray masses with veins clutching at the wall to keep them upright.

My stomach dropped. Reaper offspring sacs. From the look of it, they weren't quite ready to hatch, but I was no expert on the matter and that certainly hadn't meant much in the past. Any sudden noise could awaken them prematurely.

I guided Imogen and the Veloxan away a safe distance before contacting the other group with my comm device. "We've just located Dak'kar offspring sacs. Have you guys located any?"

"No, we haven't … Ah, you're right! We just spotted several of them. What do you advise?"

"Stay close to the sacs and wait for my command to destroy them. We can't risk them awakening, and that should draw out the mother and her mate. Then we can kill them too."

I rifled through my knapsack, drawing out my lighter. Fire was most effective, but I didn't want to burn down the whole library. I turned to Immy and the Veloxan. "Have either of you seen a fire extinguisher anywhere?"

They gaped at me. Oh, right, they had no idea what I was talking about. "It's a big red canister of sorts, usually set in the wall."

"I think I remember seeing something like that," Imogen said. She and the Veloxan left, returning with a dusty fire extinguisher.

"I'm going to light the sacs on fire. After they are burnt through, pull that pin right there, aim the nozzle at the base of the fire, and squeeze the trigger."

Imogen handed the Veloxan the extinguisher and drew her daggers. "Just in case you need backup."

I activated the comm channel and verified everyone was in position. "On my mark. Three. Two. One!"

I lunged forward, lighting the Reaper offspring sacs in two quick movements. They caught like dry grass in a wildfire, and I backed away a couple feet for safety. Within moments, tiny glass-shredding cries emanated from inside. I watched the sacs intently.

The one on the left was in full blaze with no further signs of movement, but something was moving around in the one on the right. Without warning, a tiny flaming Reaper about the size of a chihuahua ripped its way out of the sac, scrambling forward.

I lunged back, aiming my gun, but it was too fast. Just when it was about to jump at me, Imogen slammed her dagger down onto the unholy birthed creature with a small spray of black blood.

I took a deep, grateful breath. "Thanks."

We waited several more seconds to ensure the sacs were consumed by the flames before extinguishing them.

"Everyone okay?" I asked over the comm channel.

The rest of our party reported no injuries, and for the next minute all was deathly calm. I was almost ready to believe the Reaper mother had abandoned her babies when several sets of massively heavy footsteps thundered from above, sending small clouds of dust drifting down on us.

The booming footsteps shot behind us towards the entry to the basement.

I spoke into my comm device to the other group. "You guys, we've got company approaching the basement stairs. Get over here!"

"Yes, Gregory," a Veloxan chimed. "Regrouping now and heading your ... ah!"

"Shit! Come on, we have to help them!"

We darted stealthily down the study area, creeping between bookcase aisles for cover. We were about halfway back to the basement landing when several grating Reaper cries stopped us in our tracks. I peered through a gap in the bookshelves for a look.

Three adult Reapers loomed on the other side, their ravenous yellow eyes glowing in the dim light. One of them hovered over the still body of one of the Veloxans eating away at him, while the other two stomped forward with their backs arched.

Our three other guards were backing away towards the other end of the basement. Tiny additional figures darting about caught my attention. *Fuck, Reaper offspring!* We must've missed some sacs when we scanned around.

"We have to move now," I whispered. "Immy, we can attack from behind. Get the one eating away at our friend there." I glanced over at the frightened Veloxan next to us. "Help your brothers get away from the Dak'kar after we start the attack. Go towards that door we found."

"But there are three of them. What if they--"

"It doesn't matter. We can't let your brothers die. Let's go!"

Imogen and I jumped into action, darting out from our hiding spot behind the three Reapers. Imogen took the lead and launched herself onto the Reaper feasting on the fallen

Veloxan. It gave an ear splitting shriek and flailed around like crazy.

A second Reaper spotted me, but the third was still focused on the Veloxans. I prayed it would last.

Keeping away from Imogen's Reaper and its wild erratic spins, I drew my sword and dashed toward the second Reaper, who came charging at me like a freight train.

Just as the beast's razor claws came down at me I slid to the right, catching it by surprise. Its claws came down hard on the ground and I countered with my blade, slashing several fingers off with a sickening crunch.

The Reaper howled, flinging me backward with its huge red palm. I crashed into a nearby bookcase, books toppling on top of me. The world spun as the Reaper lunged at me again, its yellow eyes crazy with hatred.

I leaped out of the way just in time, hitting the ground hard. The Reaper catapulted into the bookcase, dazed by the impact. I jumped to my feet and raised my sword high, plunging the blade deep into its back.

The beast shook in its death throes before slumping to the floor. I yanked my sword out of its body and turned around to see the third Reaper stampeding at me just feet away. It tackled me, and I was flung to the ground like a rag doll. My sword flew feet away. The beast roared in my face and raised its claws for one final attack.

Oh god, no!

Suddenly, several bullets pierced the Reaper's chest and head. It gave a horrid cry of agony before falling backwards in a growing pool of black ooze.

I stumbled to my feet, perplexed as gunfire continued to erupt around me. What the hell? I was the only one with a gun. I turned towards the noise.

Back towards the study area, three unknown humans finished off the Reaper offspring skittering about, shooting them with expert aim and backing towards the rusted metal door.

I looked to my team. The three Veloxans seemed alright and were staring at the humans fighting the small Reapers. Imogen had killed her Reaper and was crouched beside it, her eyes widened saucers. Her gaze met mine.

"Who the hell are they?" she asked.

"I don't know. I didn't get a good look, but they saved me. Maybe they're from my group. Either way, we have to talk to them and see what their intentions are."

I helped Imogen up and we headed over to the three other Veloxans. The gun blasts stopped by the time we reached them.

"Whoever these people are, they cleared out the Dak'kar offspring," I said. "They must be on our side."

"We don't know that," Imogen insisted.

"Okay maybe not, but they could've easily taken us out and didn't. That has to count for something." I paused for a moment, thinking over our options. "We approach them in good faith. Sheath your weapons for now."

"But we'll be defenseless!"

"I understood your concern, but approaching them armed might send the wrong signal."

"Fine, but I think this is a terrible idea," Imogen grumbled.

We moved forward by the light of our flashlights. Ahead, the three humans we'd seen were at the end of the study area at the scarred metal door. They appeared to be speaking through it.

"Hello?" I called.

They spun around, one of them shining a blinding light right into my face. I shielded my eyes with my hand. "Can you lower your light, please? We mean you no harm."

The light's beam focused on the ground at my feet.

"Thank you for saving us back there," I said. "Who are you? Are you from the group that was here a little over a week ago?"

The center figure responded in an oddly familiar female voice. "Yes, how did you … wait, your voice sounds very familiar."

"Yours does too," I admitted.

"Gregory, what is going on?" Imogen whispered to me.

"I don't know … I think I know them."

The middle figure edged closer, the others staying back.

I turned back to our Veloxans. "Quick, give me an orb!" They threw me one, and I approached the figure cautiously. "Listen, I'm going to activate a light source you've probably never seen before. It will illuminate the room, but won't blind us. Is this okay?"

The figure stopped. "Yes, that's fine."

I activated the orb with a slight twist. It levitated from my hands, bathing the room in a cold, blue light.

The woman before me stood about my height in a black and red stained tank top. Layers of dirt and grime covered her, but I could still make out her dark, wavy hair and facial features. My world shook. "Oh my god. Mom?"

"Gregory? Gregory, is that really you?"

"Mom!" I ran to her and wrapped my arms around her tight as warm tears spilled down my face.

"Oh my sweet, sweet boy. Thank god you're alive." Mom gave short sobs as she held the back of my head in her hands. "I was so worried you were dead like the others, but we never found your body. I never gave up on you, not for a second."

"What the--" one of the other humans shouted in horror. "Demons!"

Oh shit, the Veloxans! I pushed away from my mother and drew my gun, aiming it at the human. I faltered for a moment as his dark skin and muscular physique registered in my brain. *Samuel.* He had a gun cocked and was aiming it at the Veloxans behind me.

"Samuel, put the gun down!" I shouted. "You don't understand. Let me explain."

"Explain demons from hell? What more is there to understand?"

I inched into the line of fire to distract him while protecting the Veloxans. "I said drop it! I won't hesitate to shoot you. We've been through way too much crap for me to deal with your bullshit right now. Lower. Your. Weapon!"

Samuel hesitated but kept his aim focused.

Mom pulled out a revolver and aimed at Sam as well, brows creased in anger. "Do as he says. There's more going on here than we can presume to know. Do it, god damn it!"

Reluctantly, Sam dropped his weapon to the floor and backed away. Obviously something had shifted in the leadership since I'd gone, but there wasn't time to mull over that right now.

I lowered my weapon and faced Mom. "There is a lot to explain, but I've been gone the past week or so. A hooded Reaper forced me through one of their doors in the library. It took me--it took me somewhere very far away where another race called the Veloxans live." I gestured to the three male Veloxans behind me. "Please don't misinterpret their appearance. They are peaceful and I owe them my life many times over. There's plenty of time to get into more details, but the most important thing is that you are safe."

Mom lowered her weapon slowly. "You're right. I'm so glad you made it back in one piece."

"It's not just me, Mom. I ... I found Imogen and brought her back with us."

Mom's eyes widened, sparkling with tears. "Imogen? I ... I don't understand."

Imogen stepped beside me, lowering her face mask with a weak smile. "Mom, it's me."

A million emotions warred on Mom's face, joy and heartache winning out. She cried out, lunged forward, and enveloped her arms around Imogen. "Oh, my sweet babies. You've come back to me. Bless you, Gregory. Bless you."

After several long moments, Imogen slowly peeled Mom off her. "We hate to speed things along like this, but there are hundreds of Veloxans waiting upstairs. Are you all that's left of the group?"

"I-Is Trent …" I struggled to find the words.

Mom wiped at her eyes. "About a dozen of us were able to escape the hooded Reaper's attack, and we hid down here in the repository. Trent is alive and well." She turned to the third human present. "Curt, tell the others to come out."

The tall, olive-skinned man headed over to the door and knocked in a complex pattern. With a grinding shriek the door opened and one by one, disheveled grimey humans entered the area.

The last one out was a tall, lanky man just an inch shorter than me. His medium length brown hair stuck out in all directions, just like I remembered. We locked eyes.

"Gregory?"

"Trent? Trent!"

We ran to each other. Trent wrapped his arms around me and lifted me off my feet. When he lowered me, his lips locked with mine. As I reveled in his embrace, a rush of over-whelming warmth washed over me. This was all really happening. Imogen, Mom, and I could be a family again. Trent and I could finally be together. Our group could start over, and this time nothing would stop us.

I broke off from Trent, addressing the others. "Let's get upstairs. We've got a lot to discuss."

CHAPTER TWENTY-NINE

opened my eyes as I nestled in the warmth of Trent's arms. I scooted into the nook under his shoulder with my arm draped across his lean, toned abs. Trent turned his head, eyes closed, and gave me a kiss on the forehead that trailed down to my lips. I accepted the kiss, his tongue sending shivers of excitement through my body.

"Good morning." He opened his blue eyes.

Heat rushed to my cheeks. God, how was he so sexy? I snuck in another kiss, then ruffled his errant hair. Trent rolled his eyes.

"Morning," I said. "What time is it?"

Trent pulled his watch off the beaten up bedside table. "Nine a.m. Still a bit early."

"No, I'd better get dressed." I got out of bed, walking over to the small pile of clothes we owned.

Trent groaned. "Come back to bed. Then we can really have a good morning."

I glanced back at Trent. He waggled his eyebrows, and a laugh burst from my lips.

"After last night? Any more and I'll be walking funny."

Trent shrugged with an impish grin. "What can I say? You bring out the beast in me."

Just looking at him was getting me excited, so I turned back around and started getting dressed. It had just been a few days since I came back to Earth with the Veloxans, and I already had a lot on my plate.

After returning to the Veloxans with the human survivors, Mom, the council, Imogen, and I took the reins of the situation. We secured the library, finding no additional Reapers, then had a series of pow-wows that went deep into the night.

We came up with a basic plan for shelter, food, and security, planning on further talks of fortification and expansion. Everyone was given a job. I had something of a supervisory role of our operations, making sure everything was working as it should be and helping out where needed. That's why I was up at nine a.m. and not romping around in the sheets with Trent, which believe me, would be happening very soon based on the past couple of days' experience.

Speaking of that handsome devil, Trent asked me to be his boyfriend the second we were alone. I said yes, can you blame me? His adorable scruffy face, those passionate kisses that made my knees weak, his hands on my-- Okay, you get the point. We were together and insanely happy.

I slapped on some undies, picked out a pair of jeans, then rifled through our clothes pile for a clean shirt, something still in short supply.

"You ready for the big gathering tonight?" Trent asked.

I grimaced and faced him. "Honestly, I'm a bit nervous."

"Aw, don't be. I'm sure you'll do just fine."

I turned back around, not wanting Trent to see the warring emotions that were probably plastered on my face.

The first big gathering of our people since arriving here

was happening tonight. Mom, the council, and I would each give a speech before we dined together.

For two days I'd pored over the preparation of my speech, but anything I came up with was too stiff or discombobulated. I'd have to wing it tonight and hope that things would be okay, but there was a lot of pressure on my shoulders. I was supposed to be brave, fearless. I had to prove that I had the potential to be a great leader, not some dumb teenager. But how could I do that when I couldn't even speak in complete sentences in front of a crowd?

Trent got out of bed with a squeak of our flimsy mattress. He wrapped his arms around me from behind, sending warm tingles all over my body.

"You'll be great, Greg, I know it."

He kissed my back and my doubts melted away. I turned around in his arms, mustering my best smile. "Yeah, you're right. I shouldn't worry so much about it."

I gave him a kiss, which evolved into a minute-long makeout session. I had to pry myself off of him to control myself. "We've gotta stop, at least for now. I need to make my rounds."

Trent gave me another devilish grin. "Meet me back here at lunch?"

"You betcha."

I finished dressing, and with one last lingering kiss I left Trent, feeling light on my feet and optimistic.

I closed our room's door behind me and headed down the second-floor residential hall. I crossed the landing to the other set of rooms where Imogen was staying. She'd be home. I knew because I'd checked her work schedule ahead of time.

Everyone was going through an adjustment period right now, but Ko'ta had told me yesterday that she was acting a bit strange. He told me she was 'melting' pretty frequently, also known as crying, so I wanted to get to the bottom of it. Imogen must be going through some major shock, so whatever was wrong, I had to do what I could to ease her troubled mind.

Imogen and Ko'ta had been assigned as heads of security. Imogen had also been offered a supervisory role like mine but she declined, saying she'd rather be where the action was. I guess you can take the girl out of the battlefield, but you can't take the battlefield out of the girl. But if that were so, why was she upset?

I knocked on Imogen's door. She opened the door looking tired. She wore an oversized t-shirt that went down to her knees and her curly brown hair was a mess. I couldn't blame her for her exhaustion. She'd been working ten-hour shifts and we still had no coffee supply, not that she really knew what that was.

"Gregory, what are you doing here?" she asked.

I shrugged. "I thought I'd stop by and say hello before making my rounds. Mind if I come in?"

"It's a pigsty, but sure." Imogen opened her door and let me in. Her room, much like mine and Trent's, was about the size of a large closet. A sleeping bag was sprawled out on the floor, and her things were shoved into the corner in a heap.

"Sit wherever you like," she said.

"Thanks." I sat next to her sleeping bag and she plopped down next to me. "So how are you settling in?"

Imogen stared down at the floor, scrubbing at the carpet with a finger. "Fine, I guess."

"Is something wrong? You know you can talk to me about anything."

Imogen grunted and rolled her eyes. "Ko'ta told you, didn't he? I told him to mind his own damned business. I guess that doesn't mean anything with him."

"Immy, I just think he's concerned. We want to make sure you're alright."

"I *am* alright. At least I thought I was … ugh, it's hard to explain."

I placed a hand on my sister's shoulder. "Can you try? I won't judge, promise."

Imogen traced spirals in the carpet for a couple moments. "I'm doing what I've always done, protecting people. Making them feel safe. I should be fine, happy, but I just feel … empty. Doing the same thing isn't enough anymore, I suppose."

"But when I offered you the supervisory role you said--"

"I don't want that."

"I'm sorry. What do you want, sis?"

"I don't know. I've never had this problem before. Free time. Time to do things, time to think about my life, about the future. I don't know what I want, but I need more than this."

I nodded along at her explanation. It made sense. Imogen had spent the past five years like we had, surviving and protecting those she cared for. Now that she didn't have to be on call twenty-four-seven, she was growing restless. She wanted more out of life, but never had the luxury of finding another purpose.

"I understand what you're going through. You're not alone in this. I think what you're saying is that you need something that's uniquely yours. For me that's always been comics and books, but It's not always something that's easy to find. Let me think on this. Maybe we can try to cycle you through other roles or hobbies and find one that makes you happy."

Imogen smiled weakly. "Okay. Thanks for listening to me. Do you mind if I get some more sleep? I'm still kind of tired."

"Yeah, that's fine. I should get going anyways."

I said my goodbyes and headed downstairs, trying to suppress the worries that ran through my head. Was Imogen really going to be okay? She really did sound torn. I made a mental note to let Mom know about this.

I went downstairs and turned left, passing a number of Veloxans and a human or two as I headed to the courtyard. I hit the push bar on the door and blinding sunlight washed over me. After squinting for a couple seconds, I placed a hand over my brow and glanced around the area.

Several dozen Veloxans and a couple humans were spread throughout the house-sized space, some digging at the wide expanse of brown dirt, others uprooting small shrubs and dead roots. The Veloxans all wore hats and clothes that covered as much skin as possible, due to their sensitivity to the harsher light of day on Earth.

One of the most ambitious projects we immediately developed in our pow-wows was to start preparations for growing our own crops. We'd failed to become anywhere near sustainable at our prior school location, but with the Veloxans' prowess in agriculture, things looked promising. We'd found a meager supply of seeds on some initial supply runs, and the Veloxans had brought supplies of their own with them.

I scanned over the workers, stopping when I saw a glint of copper-colored hair beneath a battered straw sunhat in the early morning sun. I headed over, and Nehma stopped digging in the dirt with her spade to greet me. Her purple eyes sparkled bright.

"Gregory, what a wonderful surprise," she said, removing her gardening gloves. "What can I help you with?"

Something about Nehma's sunny disposition usually made me smile, and this was no exception. "I just came by to check up and see how things were moving along."

"Of course." Nehma stood and gestured to the shaded

outer sidewalk of the courtyard. We walked across stepping stones set above the dirt leading that way. "The others and I are adjusting well, and I truly enjoy what we are doing. I have missed getting my hands dirty."

"You used to grow crops?" Nehma always had this air of regality to her that made me think she was born into a rich Veloxan family, not the other way around.

"Oh, yes. For years, my family had their own farm before the Dak'kar grew to be too much of a problem. Your mother was right in coming up with roles for everyone. It is fulfilling. We are almost done clearing this space of shrubs and roots and are beginning to till the land, but since we do not have a lot of equipment, the going is slow." Nehma stopped walking and looked me in the eye. "We could really use another pair of hands."

As much as I wanted to protest, I couldn't. Nehma's motherly charm was irresistible, and besides, helping out where I was needed was part of my job . I scrunched my long sleeves up. "All right, where should I start?"

❧

SWEAT DRIPPED down my face as the baking sun beat down on me relentlessly. Christ, how could it be this hot in September? I continued to stab at the earth, loosening it before giving it a break. I swiped at my forehead. Man, this was exhausting.

I stumbled up from the small area I'd been tilling and glanced at my watch. Shit, it was already past noon! I had to make more of my rounds and try to eat something before I died of heat stroke out here.

I thanked Nehma for letting me help her out before heading back inside, grateful for the cooler temperature. I briefly considered going back to my room to see Trent, but I could already smell myself. Not exactly sexy, and bathing was scheduled out at certain times of the day. I still had about thirty minutes before the next window opened up.

The next best thing was the cafeteria, so I booked it that way. In all honesty, our cafeteria was little more than a large break room, but hey, it was what we had for the moment. It certainly beat eating outside in the heat.

I came upon a dozen or so tables, most of them filled with dining Veloxans and one or two humans, who sat with them at a noticeable distance. Even with their translator devices, our human survivors were still a bit wary of the Veloxans, but I knew that the Veloxans' peaceful, respectful ways would bring them closer together. It was just a matter of time.

I passed through the tables into the cafeteria, returning with a can of new potatoes and a couple sticks of the last artarta. Ko'ta must've said something to the Veloxan distributing meals. I'd have to thank him the next time I saw him.

Scanning the crowded tables for somewhere to sit, I spotted Mom sitting by herself at the far outer edge. I walked over to her, set my food down, and gave her a quick hug. We did that now and probably always would after what we'd been through. I took a seat.

She waved a hand in front of her nose and laughed. "Boy, do you stink! What have you been doing?"

I grinned. "Helping Nehma out in the courtyard for the past couple hours."

"Oh, she'll whip you into shape from what I've seen."

"Yeah, she doesn't mess around. How are you, Mom?"

She stared at her lunch of sliced beets and rutabaga and grimaced. "Stressed, honestly. There's so much to think about. I just don't want to mess anything up."

I frowned. Mom had the hardest job of us all. She was the

new Sam. He'd vanished in the night after we had our first big pow-wow with the Veloxans. Eh, good riddance.

Mom was now responsible for managing the direction our community took, and there was a lot to consider. Strategy, logistics, inventory, expansion. We'd unanimously decided to be a democracy, so we'd all vote on the bigger ticket items, but making sense out of the shitstorm was still on her and that was far from easy.

I reached out and put my hand on Mom's. "I'm here for you. Why don't you tell me about it? I'm your apprentice, right? I'm sure I can handle it."

Mom smiled sweetly at me. "Alright. Well today P'taro and the other engineers brought up a number of concerns. Much of the technology they brought with them was reliant on whatever alternate source of electricity they had on their planet. Everything we currently use, including these things," she tugged at the translator device around her neck, "have only so much charge, another couple weeks or so if we use them sparingly."

"P'taro claims he should be able to adapt to whatever source of electricity we have, but that would mean getting this entire place setup and sending out more search parties besides the ones we're already sending out for food and supplies. It's … it's a lot to process."

"Wow, I had no idea things were that severe. For what it's worth, I think it's a good idea. Having electricity will get us through the approaching winter, and the Veloxans are super smart. If P'taro says he can pull it off, I believe he can. As for the increased search parties, I think that's gotta happen too. There's a lot more of us now, and there are still some primary things we could use around here. Nehma and her group in the courtyard are using some pretty primitive tools to get the crops going, and that's not counting the other stuff we might be lacking."

"I know, I know. I just don't want to lose anybody else."

I gazed into my mom's brown eyes. "It's going to be okay. Right now we have to take these risks in order to get by. All we can do is have faith in the system we created and know that everyone backs our decisions."

"Yes, you're right. Thank you son." She picked at her food some more. "How's Imogen doing?"

"I'm a little worried about her. She's having trouble adjusting. I think she needs to find something besides security work to do in her spare time, some kind of skill she can develop."

"Well, she is at that age now. I can't blame her for feeling that way, especially with what she's been through. I'll talk with her. There are other more feminine things I need to discuss with her anyways."

I cringed internally. *Yikes*. "Uh, yeah, sure," I said.

Mom giggled. "It's okay, I get it. No one wants to talk about Aunt Flo coming to town." She glanced at her watch. "You'd better get in line to bathe if you don't want to smell at dinner. I'm sure you have other things to do besides just that." She gave me a knowing look.

Oh shit, Trent!

I shot up from the table, thanking Mom as I ran off and shoved the last of the artarta down my throat. I couldn't believe I'd lost track of time. I sprinted as fast as my legs would carry me, stopping in my tracks when I saw the endless line of Veloxans and humans waiting for a bath. This dinner was so screwed.

CHAPTER THIRTY

rent and I walked hand in hand down the second floor staircase toward the cafeteria where the meeting and dinner would take place. We'd spent the entire afternoon chatting and romping around in the sheets, and we were nearly late.

I felt lighter than usual, without a care, but as we hit the landing I reminded myself that this was serious and I needed to prove myself. I could already feel my hands clamming up.

Trent leaned in closer as we made our way. "Everything okay? You're awful quiet after all the fun we had this afternoon."

"Sorry, I'm still a little nervous, that's all."

Trent gave me his heart-melting sideways grin. "It'll be fine. Remember, just be you. I'll be right there to tell everyone to fuck off if they give you any crap."

I shook my head and smiled. "Not necessary. You're right, everything will be fine."

We approached the cafeteria, the way lit by a plethora of candles. Dozens of tables had been placed together in five huge rows, each filled with Veloxans and humans. Candles sprinkled the tabletops at intervals along with partially-filled wine glasses for the adults.

As we neared, I looked for Mom, Imogen, and Ko'ta. They were supposed to be sitting with the council, where Trent and I would be as well. I spotted them at the center of the furthermost row of tables and we joined them.

"Nice of you to join us," Mom said, an eyebrow cocked. "I almost thought you'd be late."

Trent chuckled. "Nah, Ms. Martin, we wouldn't miss this for the world."

"I'm glad. Well, since everyone's here let's get this thing started."

Mom rose, tinking her glass with a fork. The assembled crowd quieted. "Thank you all for coming. As you all know, I am Patricia Martin. I have recently been appointed as one of the leaders of this fine assembly of Veloxans and humans."

She smiled as she scanned over the crowd. "I understand that there has been a lot of change in the past few days for everyone. Change is scary, if not terrifying, but we will weather this storm together. To our new neighbors the Veloxans, we are eternally grateful for the kindness, generosity, and goodwill you've shown in such a short time. Before we met you, our group had been on the run, trying to survive for five long years. Thanks to your help we now have the resources to make a real home for ourselves, human and Veloxan together. Many changes are coming, some that will be trying for all of us, but I have great faith in this community."

Mom lifted her glass. "Let us toast to the bright future ahead of us."

Along with everyone else, I raised my glass and took a sip of the dry red wine, doing my best not to make a face. Mom sat, and Nehma stood up a moment later. Her copper hair was braided in an intricate pattern and her garb was the same white regal ensemble that I first met her in. She was a vision.

"Thank you, Patricia. For those who do not know me, my name is Nehma, and I am one of the Veloxan council. I am overjoyed to be here and grateful to live alongside such kind and noble people. I haven't personally interacted with humans for very long, but ever since meeting Gregory and his sister Imogen I have greatly admired and respected their kind. These young humans entered our world and showed us that all was not lost, that we could band together and defend ourselves. That we could make a new life worth living."

She turned towards Imogen and me. "Gregory, Imogen, you gave our people a new hope and destiny, and I cannot thank you enough for your dedication and sacrifice for the greater good." She raised her glass, and we took another communal sip from our wine glasses.

Nehma sat, and additional speeches were given by De'jartha and Kro'da. To be honest I wasn't paying much attention. As the seconds dragged by, my nerves ticked towards panic. I'd be up soon. What would I say? What could I say to them after everything we'd been through?

When Kro'da finished his address, my stomach flipped. *Oh shit, it's my turn.* I stood, cleared my throat, and froze as I looked at all the faces staring at me.

Suddenly, Trent's warm hand grasped mine, and I gazed down at him. He nodded encouragingly, and my nerves thawed out. I mouthed a thank you to him and took a deep breath.

You can do this.

"I had a very long journey to Velerius and back. Many times I didn't think I would make it back here. Many times I wanted to give up." Ja'tare's face flashed in my mind, and tears blurred my vision.

I blinked them away. "But Ja'tare never gave up on me,

none of you did. Many of you may think I'm some kind of hero for making it back and bringing you here, but I only did what I felt was right. My mother, Patricia, taught me that a real man will do the right thing, regardless of how difficult that journey is. Whatever your opinion is, just know this. I think each and every one of you is a hero. Together we have survived. We are strong, and in the days to come I know that we'll thrive together as a community and take the world back. Let us not forget those we've lost along the way and honor them by forging a better world for ourselves."

Just like that, the words stopped coming, and I sat down.

Everyone started clapping, and Mom hugged me tightly. "I'm so proud of you, son." She leaned over to Imogen, giving her a hug as well. As the cheering died down, several dozen Veloxans and a couple humans approached the tables bearing steaming plates of food. They made quick work of distributing them to everyone.

"That concludes the speeches for tonight," Mom announced. "We hope the Veloxans will enjoy our traditional dish of spaghetti. Let's eat!"

I STOOD NEXT TO TRENT, halfway listening to the endless conversation Mom and the council were having. The crowd was dispersing fast, and Trent's feet shuffled ever so slightly.

Mom looked our way and gave us an amused smile. "Why don't you two get going? We can talk more tomorrow."

"Thanks Ms. Martin, for all of this," Trent said.

"Yeah, thanks Mom," I agreed.

"My pleasure. Now go. Enjoy the rest of your night."

Trent and I meandered around, finding ourselves at the door leading to the courtyard. A whoosh of cool air met us as we stepped outside. The area was deserted and dark, only the partial moon giving any semblance of light. We ambled along the outer sidewalk of the space, enjoying the breeze.

"Thanks for walking with me," I said. "The moon's beautiful tonight."

"Not as beautiful as you."

Heat rushed to my cheeks, and I shouldered Trent playfully. "So how did I do? I hope I didn't embarrass myself. I keep thinking I should've--"

Trent placed a finger on my lips. "Stop. You were wonderful. Always have been, always will be."

"Thanks."

Trent stopped walking, and I glanced back at him. He had a pained expression on his face.

"What's wrong? Are you okay?"

Trent shook his head. "I'm sorry. I know we've been enjoying ourselves since you got back, but a part of me still can't believe this is happening. The past few weeks, they've been really scary for me. When we were stuck in the basement, I thought I would never see you again."

He looked at me, his eyes glistening. Was he crying?

"I never want to feel that way again."

I closed the distance between us and held him in my arms. "Hey, hey, I'm not going anywhere. I'm right here with you. Nothing's going to happen to me."

Trent wiped at his eyes. "I'm just so happy that I'm terrified something awful is going to happen again."

"Everything's going to be okay. I know things are a little shaky right now, but we are all working together to make this place as safe as possible. We've got to give it some time, yeah?"

Trent sniffled, then smiled. "Yeah, you're right. Sorry I'm over here bawling like a baby."

I gave him a kiss then turned us around, keeping an arm

draped over his shoulder. "There's nothing to apologize for. Let's go back inside and relax for the rest of the night."

Trent and I went inside and ambled back to our room. That night, we didn't make love. Instead we enjoyed one another's company, letting our connection speak for itself. For the first time in a very long while, I was truly happy.

The Veloxans, Imogen, and I had made it back to Earth. We were making our world a better place to live in, and with Trent by my side, the world was just a little bit brighter. Now all of our futures could really begin.

*J*ournal Entry #1: September 16th, 1997

It has only been a week since I arrived back on Earth, and already so much has happened.

Our library compound is safe and sound. We've only had a few Reaper attacks on our fortifications, and in all instances we were able to kill them or fend them off. We haven't seen a hooded Reaper yet, but we know they are out there. We welcome the opportunity to show them what we've learned on Velerius.

P'taro and the engineers found enough salvageable equipment to restore some semblance of electricity to our compound. They are currently working on repairs with Trent helping them. As a backup plan, the Veloxans have started teaching us their language and vice versa. It's slow going, but a necessary step for us to understand each other better.

Mom has been working with the council diligently on supply runs and expansion ideas once we reach a certain level of sustainability. They are hopeful that in a few months we will have our own supply of crops and won't have to make as many supply runs.

Imogen is still a work in progress but since Mom spoke with her, her mood seems to have changed for the better.

Trent and I are still insanely happy. We complete each other, and I couldn't dream of navigating through this new world without him.

But most importantly, for the first time since the Reaper apocalypse, we have hope. Hope for a brighter tomorrow, for a way back to civilized living, for a future worth more than just surviving like Nehma said.

Once again, I've decided to write down my story. There are so many lessons to learn from my interactions with the Veloxans and Reapers.

Maybe you'll find all this useful, maybe you'll think it's a pitifully written scary story to keep kids away from their basements and creepy-looking doors. Regardless, I hope that someone will find this useful someday and use it to their advantage.

The war with the Reapers on Earth is far from over, and we've got a long way to go, but this time we won't run. We will fight until every last one of them is wiped off the face of our planet, until we can all live in peace and harmony.

This is my story ...

Thanks so much for taking the time to read Reaper: Aftermath. If you enjoyed reading it, why not take a moment to rate or review on Amazon or GoodReads?

I appreciate you taking the time to voice your opinion and hope you enjoy my other stories too.

Thank you for showing your support!

ABOUT THE AUTHOR

Jonathan Pongratz is a writer and author of captivating horror, fantasy, and other speculative fiction stories. When he's not writing, he's busy being a bookworm, video game junkie, and karaoke vocalist. A former resident of Dallas, he currently resides in Kansas City with his halloween cat Ajax. By day he works magic in finance, by night he creates dark and mesmerizing worlds.

You can learn more about Jonathan at JonathanPongratz.com or at the social media links below.

Tumblr: https://jonathanpongratz.tumblr.com/

Reaper: A Horror Novella

Gregory and his little sister Imogen love spending Halloween with their parents. But this year is different. If he proves he can take care of Imogen all by himself, he'll finally have the allowance he's dreamed of.

That was before the basement door opened on its own. Before the strange door appeared in the basement and Imogen was taken from him by the monster.

Now everyone in town is blaming him for her disappearance, but no one is listening to his story. Where did the door come from? What was that creature? And most of all, can he find his sister before it's too late, or will he bury his memories of her along with his parents?

***

Conscience

Rory Bennels lives in a world ruled by a business entity known as the Corporation. For years he's executed cerebral uploads for the recently deceased, but when the famed anarchist Epher Lore ends up in his lab, a series of events occur that shakes Rory's world to the core.

www.ingramcontent.com/pod-product-compliance
Lightning Source LLC
Chambersburg PA
CBHW021059110726
47900CB00007B/1942